RETRIBUTION

BRIAN WALKER DENTON

authorHOUSE®

AuthorHouse™ UK Ltd.
1663 Liberty Drive
Bloomington, IN 47403 USA
www.authorhouse.co.uk
Phone: 0800.197.4150

Published by AuthorHouse   05/20/2013

ISBN: 978-1-4817-8923-3 (sc)
ISBN: 978-1-4817-8924-0 (e)

Dedication

To my wife and best friend, Audrey, for her forbearance
during my absence while writing for hours on end.
Absence *does* make the heart grow fonder.

To all my other family and friends

To all my comrades past and present with whom I served
as a regular soldier in the Royal Army Medical Corps for
15 years and later, as a volunteer in the Territorial Army,
for a further 12 years.

.

PART 1

'OPERATION TAKEOUT'

Prologue

I f there was such a thing for such an occasion, it would have been a nice day for a funeral. The early mist had lifted, the sun was shining and the few fluffy white scattered clouds were like so many tiny balls of cotton wool dotting the western horizon. Sinn Fein MP Mark Thomas Brannigan barely noticed; he was a troubled man. There were too many unanswered questions for his liking.

Daniel Doonan the Provisional IRA chief had called Brannigan to Dublin for a reason, the cock-up at Ballykelly, but what had transpired since then had left Brannigan bewildered. Why the hell did he know nothing until ten days ago about Leo Bailey, the man who had made it possible for him to be sitting here waiting for the arrival of a funeral cortege in order take his revenge on both the IRA and the British?

Leo Bailey, the alleged British Army deserter turned Provisional IRA recruit, had turned up in the middle of the night at the safe house known as 'Danny's Bar', along with the known IRA courier Liam Casey, seeking refuge? Casey had vouched for Bailey when they both appeared dressed in filthy mud-caked clothes, soaked to the skin and in a state of near collapse after having been on the run from the RUC and the Army for several hours. Danny Monaghan, the owner of the bar and one of Brannigan's three loyal lieutenants, had no reason to disbelieve the fugitives having earlier that evening seen the news flashes on television about their escape from custody. The general public had been warned not to approach them because they were armed and dangerous.

Brannigan had been at a meeting that evening and had not seen the news about the escape of the two men from a prison van after it was said to have been involved in an accident while transporting three prisoners; Danny Monaghan had told him all about it.

The other prisoner, Eamon Flynn, another of Brannigan's lieutenants, and the RUC driver were reported to have been killed in the crash but Leo Bailey and Liam Casey, had survived and made a run for it after releasing themselves from their shackles with a key taken from an unconscious guard who they assumed to be dead but who had apparently survived albeit in a critical state.

Leo Bailey had owned up to being one of IRA Quartermaster Bernard Cluskey's newly recruited associates but after such a short acquaintance with Bailey, Brannigan was not sure. He would know the answer to that one later in the afternoon after making himself scarce following the confusion and the mayhem planned at the funeral. As Official Prison Visitor for the Sinn Fein party, he planned to visit Cluskey in the prison where he was confined. The recently arrested Provisional IRA Quartermaster for Derry was being held on a charge of gunrunning and concealment. Right, however, Brannigan had an important job to do.

From a pre-selected viewpoint half a mile away, Brannigan sat in his shining black status symbol and looked out across the shallow vale at the gently rising ground leading to the church and graveyard beyond the road from the village of Ballypatrick. Brannigan loved his car almost as much as he hated the fact that it had been manufactured in England.

The RUC constable and the British Army sergeant had given him some strange looks as the car, sporting a black pennant on one wing and an Irish tricolour on the other, rolled up at the check point where Brannigan presented his hastily acquired formal invitation to the funeral of local hero General Sir Patrick St. John Fitzpatrick MM, MD, DSO, ex Irish Guards and a veteran of two world wars.

Out of earshot, the sergeant had spoken briefly into a walkie-talkie before waving Brannigan on.

It had been Leo Bailey's bright idea that Brannigan should personally attend the funeral so that he could remotely trigger the explosive devices that had been placed under the evenly spaced whitewashed boulders lining the driveway to the church and the graveyard along which the funeral cortège would be slowly moving on foot behind the hearse.

Members of Brannigan's gang led by Leo Bailey and dressed as British Military policemen, had planted the bombs the previous day while appearing to be searching for clues to possible mayhem planned by the Real IRA or some other dissident group.

It was a brilliant plan thought up by Leo to distract Brannigan whose intension was to embarrass both the British Government and Daniel Doonan. The Provisional IRA had been on ceasefire since October the previous year. Brannigan and his gangsters were now in danger of wrecking it.

Doonan had ordered Brannigan to disband his gang and get out of the country after an unfortunate atrocity at Ballykelly or face execution by firing squad. The Provisional IRA had been blamed for the incident but had hurriedly stated publicly that they had not been involved. They hinted at the possible involvement of the breakaway Real IRA.

Brannigan had reluctantly agreed to Doonan's order to retire and disband his gang but he did not intend to go out with a whimper. He had been at a loss to know what to do to take revenge on his adversaries but Leo Bailey had come up with the perfect solution.

During the half hour that Brannigan had been waiting for the funeral to begin, a coach full of soldiers in dress uniform, highly polished ammunition boots and white gloves had arrived. The men alighted and, with heads bowed and rifles reversed, took up their positions between each of the boulders lining the 100 metre long carriageway leading up to the church and the graveyard.

Along with representatives of the media, groups of onlookers had gathered behind the guard of honour on the grassed areas on each side of the drive. A couple of satellite dishes had been set up so that TV camera crews could broadcast and record the event.

Brannigan was quite happy in the knowledge that a substantial number of innocent people, both Protestant and Catholic, would die that day as a token of his defiance against the authorities of the British Government in Whitehall and Daniel Doonan in Dublin both of whom were desperate for a lasting peace in the province.

It was close on 9 a.m. when the funeral procession turned into the driveway and began the slow drag up to the church. Brannigan got out of the car and watched through binoculars as the drive slowly filled with mourners. He took the remote control from his pocket and fitted a new PP9 battery then climbed back into the driver's seat, wound down the electric window and waited.

He was blissfully unaware of the two SAS men observing him from cover and with strict orders from their commander not to make a move until 0905 hours precisely.

At precisely 0900 hours, when the last of the mourners had entered the drive, two men dressed in combat clothing and carrying firearms, broke cover and ran from opposite directions towards the parked Jaguar as Brannigan pointed the remote control and pressed the button.

Chapter 1

Leo Bailey walked slowly away from Sunderland General Hospital and made his way to the beach at Ryhope not far from his parent's home. He sat on his usual rock and gazed out to sea as he tried to make sense of what had happened. His twin brother Peter finally caught up with him.

"I thought I might find you here, are you OK?" Peter asked looking anxious. He had stayed on at the hospital to talk to the doctor before returning to the house to find Leo missing.

"I'm having difficulty in getting my head round this," answered Leo, "why would anyone do a thing like that to a sweet inoffensive human being, what could mum have done to deserve it?"

"It most probably has something to do with Northern Ireland," said Peter, "it's been twelve years since we left there, mum and dad should never have gone back for a holiday no matter how quiet things appear to have been. The Troubles have obviously not gone away they are still smouldering beneath the surface. But why anyone should target the parents is beyond me unless they have enemies they don't know about".

The twins were on compassionate leave from the Military Academy at Sandhurst where they were nearing the end of their training.

Their parents Joe and Mary Bailey, now living in Ryhope near Sunderland, had taken a B & B holiday touring Northern Ireland where Mary had been born and raised. While they were staying at a farm near Antrim, John McCann, a long forgotten adversary of Joe's, when he lived and worked in Belfast, had learned of their presence in the province from a friend who still worked at the Belfast Marine Engineering firm. His friend had overheard a conversation between two secretaries over lunch on the next table in the staff canteen and knowing that Joe Bailey, as acting personnel officer, had once sacked McCann for stirring sectarian dissent, had passed on the information including the area in which Joe and Mary were staying. After a couple of days snooping around, McCann spotted Joe and Mary leaving a restaurant and followed them to the farm where they were staying. There he planted a bomb beneath their car in the middle of the night before skulking off back to Belfast.

Joe and his farmer host had taken a few drinks together before retiring the previous evening and Joe felt in no fit state to drive the following morning.

After packing their luggage away in the boot Joe asked Mary to do the honours and drive. She dutifully got into the driving seat but just as Joe was about to get into the passenger seat he remembered the case of Bushmills Irish whisky, bought as presents for friends and colleagues back home, which he had left in the hallway.

Leaving the passenger door open, he retraced his steps to the house. Mary opened the driver's door and made some humorous remark about his tipsy memory cells while she started the engine.

The bomb, placed beneath the floor on the driver's side, exploded throwing Mary's seat backwards and shattering both her legs below the knees. Had the bomb been inside the car with both doors closed, she would certainly have been killed instantly but the effect of the blast was reduced sufficiently by the open doors to save her life. She was, however, so badly maimed that that Joe thought she would surely die from the shock of blood loss before he could summon help. He did not attempt to move her while he applied what first aid he could in order to stem the bleeding. The driver's seat was still tilted back which probably saved her life while Joe applied pressure to the femoral arteries until an ambulance arrived.

The paramedics immediately requested a helicopter then set about stabilizing Mary and injecting her with morphine in preparation for air evacuation to emergency treatment at Belfast where her lower limbs were amputated four inches below the knee joints.

The boys were informed at Sandhurst soon after the incident had occurred and where flown immediately to Belfast. They were horrified by what had happened but at the same time relieved that both their parents had not been killed; they returned to duty the following day with an assurance from the surgeon that their mother would survive.

Mary was flown to Newcastle a week later and transferred to Sunderland General Hospital for further treatment. At Sunderland their mother, having been kept under heavy sedation for the entire journey from Belfast, was still unconscious when the brothers arrived to join their father at her bedside. She regained consciousness five hours later and smiled faintly at the three anxious faces peering down at her.

*

Twenty-five years earlier, Joseph Watson Bailey was a newly qualified marine engineer trained at Doxford in Sunderland Tyne and Wear in the days when Sunderland was part of the county of Durham. His firm had links with James Ellis & Co, marine engineers of Belfast in Northern Ireland. Joe travelled between the two companies twice a year for a two-week seminar on behalf of his firm to compare notes and exchange ideas. James Ellis, a bachelor, took a shine to Joe and treated him more like a son than a representative of the Doxford firm.

Ellis lived with Mary, his orphaned niece, whose mother had died of cancer shortly before her father, Ellis' brother and business partner, had died at sea in an accident while testing a new marine engine. When Mary and Joe showed an interest in each other, James Ellis encouraged the relationship. The fact that Mary was a Protestant and Joe a Catholic did not bother either of them.

Mary's uncle James employed both Protestants and Catholics in his firm without discrimination. Allusion to a specific religion was excluded from job applications and only ascertained after acceptance in employment for statistical purposes in case a priest or other minister was required in an emergency. And so it was that, after a one-year courtship during which the couple exchanged visits to each other on a quarterly basis, Mary and Joe were married in a Belfast registry office followed by blessing ceremonies in their respective Anglican and Roman churches.

Uncle James made Joe a non-executive junior partner in the Belfast firm as a wedding present and he and Mary bought a Victorian house in Magherafelt, then a non-sectarian area, and Eighteen months later in April 1965, the twins Peter and Leo were born; Peter was the eldest by two minutes.

The question of the faith into which the boys should be christened was settled by the toss of a coin. Joe later regretted using the double-headed penny he had made as an apprentice at Doxford. The boys were duly christened into the Catholic faith; Mary never found out about Joe's playful deception.

The twins were a generous mix of both parents. By the time they started school at the age of five they could already read and do simple arithmetic as a result of their mother's tuition. They had also inherited her infectious sense of humour.

They were both well on the way to being tall and fair like their father Joe who, at the grand old age of twenty-nine, was still very fit. He trained regularly and ran the local youth football team in Magherafelt. Given the choice, he would have become a professional footballer himself having trained with Sunderland FC Junior team from the age of fifteen but his father had insisted on his pursuing an engineering career.

Magherafelt was a quiet and peaceful town where the Protestant and Catholic communities lived in relative harmony unaffected by the troubles in Belfast and Londonderry. By the time the boys were seven years old, however, hatred between the republican and loyalist factions had started to spread with fungus-like threads into the wider community and life-long friends began to view each other with suspicion and caution.

For the first time in living memory, James Ellis & Co began to notice tension among members of staff. A young Protestant labourer named John McCann, a secret member of the Ulster Defence Association contrary to the Company's strict policy of non-sectarianism, began spouting anti Catholic rhetoric in an attempt to split the workforce. In the absence of the personnel officer on maternity leave; it fell to Joe Bailey to take McCann to task.

McCann was defiant and consumed with hatred for all Catholics. He seemed to know instinctively that Joe was Catholic and took an instant dislike to him. The feeling was mutual but Joe approached the problem professionally with an open mind.

McCann was given a verbal warning that if he continued to stir trouble among the workforce, he would be sacked. A month later, he was fired and peace returned to the shop floor. Joe Bailey, however, became a marked man in the mind of John McCann, a UDA apprentice bomb maker and a potential killer as yet untried.

Months after the incident had been forgotten, Joe began to receive threats against himself and his family. The telephone would ring late at night and a muffled voice would warn whoever answered it of the possible consequences of their mixed marriage prior to the call being abruptly terminated.

Joe did not take the threats seriously at first because it had become common in the no-go conclaves of Belfast and Derry for one side to threaten the other if a member of one religious faction consorted with a member of the opposite sex of the other side. But Magherafelt was different, people were not like that and they mixed quite freely. Mary, on the other hand, took the threats very seriously having been born in the province and having grown up with the troubles albeit from a distance until now. She worried about the effect it would have on her boys who she protected as best she could.

The twins went to a Catholic school by bus each day and played football and other games with a mix of Catholic and Protestant friends on most evenings and weekends without anything more than the odd squabble that occurred naturally among groups of children playing together. The threatening phone calls at home ceased when Joe went ex directory but they continued at his office without Mary's knowledge.

Inevitably, the creeping mycelia-like threads of contagious hatred spread to Magherafelt where the odd fight occurred in one or other of the bars in the town. It was usually started by a small gang from outside the area imported for the sole purpose of stirring up sectarian trouble. Outside one bar after another, notices went up to proclaim the sectarian status of the premises. The men of violence had introduced the wedge of separation, hatred and mistrust. The Bailey family became increasingly isolated and avoided by one-time friends from both sections of the community; life slowly became intolerable.

Just prior to the school summer holidays, some months after the twins had celebrated their eighth birthday, an incident occurred that caused the family a great deal distress. It was Mary's daily routine to meet the boys from the school bus at the T-junction at the end of the lane where they lived and to walk the quarter mile home. As she was about to leave the house one day to meet them, the telephone rang. When she answered it, the female on the other end asked her to wait while she was connected to Joe's office. She waited and waited for about five minutes then she was disconnected. She shrugged her shoulders and ran from the house to meet the boys but as she walked up the lane, she broke into a canter when she saw no sign of them. By the time she reached the junction, she was beside herself with panic. The main road was deserted in both directions but there was the tell tale aroma of diesel fumes from the recently departed school bus.

She ran back to the house and called Joe at his office to learn that he had not called her earlier, which caused her to panic even more. Joe tried to calm her as she told him what had happened and she became almost hysterical. He told her to call the police, the school, and the bus company and to try to remain calm while he drove home. The police were waiting for him on his arrival an hour and a half later after a hectic journey along congested roads out of Belfast.

Meanwhile, police had located the bus driver who confirmed that he had dropped the boys off as usual. He had seen nothing out of the ordinary as he drove off to the next village but he had wondered why Mary had not been there to meet them as she normally was.

A small search party had then been organised and sent off with a police constable in charge while a larger group awaited Joe's return home. Maps of the area were laid out and sections marked off like the spokes of a wheel in a two-mile radius around the house. The search parties were instructed to fan out along the spoke lines as they searched and to stay within sight of the group on either side. They were just about to start the search when the boys turned into the drive leading up to the house. Everyone stared in disbelief as the dishevelled pair approached grinning like Cheshire cats as they surveyed the scene before them.

Mary and Joe, with tears of sheer joy, ran forward and embraced the bemused boys. The search party cheered loudly and dispersed with sighs of relief that the twins had returned safe and sound. The police radioed their colleagues accompanying the initial searchers and reported that all was well.

All, however, was not well. The kidnapping of the twins had been organised by a member of the UDA under strict instructions from John McCann. His task was to organise a group of Protestant boys, some of whom were friends of the twins, to play a prank on them but not to harm them in any way. It was made to look like a game but the real intent was to terrorise the twins and their parents. The whole thing had been planned to perfection and the hooded participants had been rewarded with sweets and T-shirts afterwards.

McCann was now a big player in the UDA ranks and had many sources of information. One such source worked in telecommunications which made it easy for McCann to obtain the ex directory telephone number of Joe and Mary. One of his girlfriends had rung Mary at the specified time and the plot had been hatched.

When the school bus had stopped at the end of the street where the boys lived, there was no one there to meet them. They watched the bus disappear around a bend and wondered what had happened to their mother who was always there when they got off.

Having been bribed by an agent of McCann's to play truant from school and to play a trick on the twins, the dozen or so Protestant boys with stocking masks on their heads emerged from cover and grabbed them. The twins were blindfolded and led away noisily and at the double to some woods about a mile away where they were tied to a tree. The contents of their satchels were strewn about while their captors chanted offensive slogans at them for what seemed like hours but in reality lasted for only about forty minutes. Then suddenly, all was quiet as one by one their captors slipped noiselessly away. The game was over and nobody had been hurt.

The twins were shocked and trembling after their ordeal but at least they were unharmed; it took them a little while to collect their wits. Peter was the first to wriggle free of his bonds, he untied Leo's hands and feet then together they collected the contents of their satchels and wondered where they were.

Leo looked at his watch, the time was 5.35 p.m. They had learned only the week before, at the cubs, how to set a watch to find directions. He pointed the hour hand to the sun and determined that the line between the hour hand and twelve o'clock pointed due south. Remembering where the sun went down after one of those pleasant evenings in their garden, they set of eastward in the hope of reaching home. It was a bit of a gamble but Peter recognised the range of hills to the south as they emerged from the woods and decided that they were going in the right direction.

The following day, the case having been handed over to the police to investigate, Joe recounted the incident to James Ellis who was extremely disturbed by the event. His near-fatherly love for Joe and Mary extended to their boys on whom he doted like a grandfather. Before the day was done, he called Joe to his office and made him an offer that would kill two birds with one stone.

Ellis had been secretly negotiating for some time the takeover of Joe's previous employers at Doxford. A decision was imminent and if it proved positive, Joe had been earmarked to run the Sunderland branch as an executive managing director. Joe, having been sent on outside business during the negotiations, was purposely kept in the dark. It had been meant as a surprise on the occasion of his and Mary's wedding anniversary but the events of the day before had spoiled the surprise while at the same time offering a solution.

Sworn to secrecy, Joe confided only to Mary what uncle James had told him. Mary was not too happy at the prospect of being forced to move to England from the place of her birth but for the sake of the children, she finally agreed. What had been made to look like a prank would surely be the start of more sinister tactics aimed at terrorising the family and Mary was taking no chances. They sat together after the boys had gone to bed and began to plan their mysterious disappearance from Magherafelt.

The takeover of the Doxford firm was finalised the following week and Joe was obliged to accompany his Company's solicitor and one of the other directors to Sunderland for the formal signing. It was only an overnight trip but still too long away from home and family in Joe's opinion.

Nothing untoward happened, however, but the seed of terror had been planted in Joe's mind and all McCann had to do back in his Belfast retreat was to sit back and smile while the germinated seed took root. The Bailey family were marked down for revenge. It was a personal thing with McCann but he had to make it look like a sectarian conspiracy in order to fan the flames of hatred between the opposing factions.

While at Doxford, Joe was introduced to his new secretary. He remembered her from his apprentice days when she had been a junior clerical assistant; they were about the same age. He asked her to send him as much information as she could about property for sale with vacant possession within a five mile radius of the firm, preferably Victorian like their house in Magherafelt because of Mary's collection of furniture and artefacts from the period, and preferably detached with a reasonable size garden.

Just three days after arriving home, he and Mary were looking at a picture of their proposed new house. It was in the village of Ryhope about five kilometres south of Sunderland town centre. A large Victorian detached family house set in a quarter of an acre of landscaped garden, designed for a leading Victorian industrialist, at the edge of the village.

Joe immediately rang 'Miss Efficiency,' a nickname she was now stuck with, thanked her and instructed her to secure the property in his name subject to survey; he received confirmation within the hour.

Within a week, the structural survey had been completed, a solicitor had been appointed, and the contract was on his desk for signing subject to the usual search which would probably take some time. 'Miss efficiency strikes again,' he mused; he was impressed. Joe asked her to scout around for suitable rented accommodation until the house purchase was completed.

The boys were due to begin their annual school holiday in four weeks time, which fitted nicely with Joe and Mary's plans to quit Northern Ireland. They had taken the boys on adventure holidays since they were 4 years old. They had spent one holiday in Scotland, one in Wales and one in Southern Ireland. The plan this year was to take them on a walking holiday to the Lake District in England for a whole month, staying in a static caravan at a lakeside site at Keswick while the purchase of the new house was being finalised. The boys, however, were told that they were bound for the Mountains of Mourne, which excited them just the same and they lost no time in telling their friends and neighbours.

Miss efficiency had other ideas and suggested to Joe that he and Mary should leave the twins with their great uncle for a weekend while they flew to England to look at the new house and choose the décor. She would personally take care of the operation on their behalf and see to it that the job was done to their satisfaction by trusted professionals that she knew. This agreed, the grateful couple dropped the boys off at Uncle James' house by prior arrangement and set off that very weekend to attend to business. The holiday in Keswick would now last longer than two weeks during which time their furniture would be delivered and stored pending the finalisation of the house purchase.

The next step was to organise the clearance of the Magherafelt house and the removal of the contents to storage at the Doxford yard. While the twins were at school, Mary set about emptying cupboards, wardrobes and drawers and packing their contents into wooden boxes and crates that she and Joe stacked in the old coach house at the back of house out of sight of the boys. It had always been kept locked so the boys would have no idea what was going on in their absence at school.

In faraway Sunderland, 'Miss efficiency' organised a private firm consisting of a father and his three strong sons to travel in an unmarked removals van to Larne, stay the night in a hotel at the Company's expense then go on to Magherafelt the next morning, by which time the Bailey's would have begun their holiday, and to load and transport their belongings to the house in Ryhope.

The father, a trusted friend of Miss Efficiency's family, was given specific instructions should any nosey neighbour question him about the removal. He was to say that the Bailey's were moving closer to Belfast, as a consequence of recent events, so that the twins could be boarded out for the remainder of their schooling. He was to say that his instructions were to deliver the contents of the house to a warehouse at the premises of Ellis & Co., Marine Engineers, Belfast where they would be stored while the house, the location of which he had not been told, was being re-renovated while the Baileys were on holiday in

Mourne. It all seemed a plausible enough explanation but in the event, no one questioned the removal, which was carried out under the personal supervision of James Ellis.

McCann had manufactured, and delivered by courier, a timed incendiary device that he planned to have planted in the Bailey's vacant house by a newly recruited Magherafelt confederate while the family were on holiday. It was the inexperienced confederate who, on complying with his orders, discovered the removal in progress while he reconnoitred the place.

Being unable to locate his go-between he reported the occurrence directly to McCann from a call box at the specified time but too long after the event to make a difference. Not daring to take the initiative, the man had skulked away and pondered the situation before making the decision to call. The opportunity to follow the van had been missed by hours and McCann was furious that his quarry had effectively eluded him. In his rage, he threatened the unfortunate young man with pain of death, which frightened him so much that that he left home without explanation to his mystified parents and was never heard of again.

The twins had been asleep when Joe arrived at Larne the previous evening for the crossing to Stranraer. They had changed into their travelling cloths as soon as they got home from school and ate sandwiches in the car as they set off on their holiday half an hour later. The class had played games almost all that day instead of doing academic work and that, combined with the effect of the food that they had just eaten, made the boys sleepy despite their excitement and they were asleep in no time.

Unnoticed by Joe, the incoming removal van rolled off the ferry as he waited to roll on. He did not awaken the boys until they were on the boat, which he told them was to be a surprise treat. After a snack and a two and a half hour exploration of the ferry's engine room, Joe having presented his credentials to the captain, they arrived in Stranraer at 10.30 p.m. Half an hour later, they were safely installed in pre-booked B & B accommodation in Newton Stewart about twenty miles inland. The next morning they made their way to Keswick and the caravan site.

*

The Bailey family could justifiably count the next twelve years as a golden period in their lives. The acquisition of Joe's old firm at Doxford was a great success for Ellis & Co and Joe was an integral part of that success. Mary settled into an idyllic new life making many friends who could not care less about her Northern Irish roots or her religious persuasion. To them she was just Mary, one of the nicest kindest people around and fun to be with. She became a member of several groups from the Women's Institute, to Friends of this and Friends of that.

The twins had been found a place in a private school in Durham where they boarded on weekdays and spent happy weekends at home with their parents and had no trouble finding new friends. They both possessed their mother's sense of humour and shared her Northern Irish accent, which, through time, they could switch on and off to suit the occasion.

At the age of eighteen, the twins entered university and joined the Officer Training Corps. Three years later, they emerged with degrees in engineering having decided at an early age to join their father's business. But having enjoyed their time with the OTC, they decided to apply for officer training at Sandhurst with a view to taking short service commissions before settling down to business life.

Having passed out successfully and received their commissions, they had been awaiting their chosen corps, the REME, to post them when news of their mother's hospitalisation reached them resulting in them being sent on compassionate leave.

*

They walked slowly along the beach together each with their separate thoughts. Peter was the practical one and Leo the spiritual one but so close were they as twin brothers that they could almost read each other's minds.

After their mother was free of the anaesthetic hangover and was sitting up in bed with a cradle over what was left of her lower limbs, they had talked with their parents about resigning their recently awarded commissions. Mary was typically bright and communicative and philosophical about what had happened to her. Whoever had caused her horrific injuries would not have the satisfaction of dulling her spirit as far as she was concerned.

"You cannot do that, you have earned those commissions and you have your whole life ahead of you," said Mary, holding Leo's hand, "you have both worked so hard and I forbid you to throw it all away on my account. Whoever did this was trying to kill both your father and me. As far as I know, neither of us has enemies so I have to assume that it was a terrorist acting on wrong information about a couple of strangers in the area."

Joe nodded in agreement. "It would serve no purpose giving up your careers because of what has happened. We have both been very lucky when you consider what might have been. As it is, I have only lost a part of your mother, everything else including her intellect is intact and I am thankful for that." He said. "Sacrificing your careers would just cause her unhappiness so let us hear no more defeatists talk."

Outside the hospital after leaving their parents to talk, Leo asked, "where do we go from here brother? The parents don't want us to chuck the army so why not make the most of it and become fighting soldiers instead of messing about with machines, there will be plenty time for that when we join dad and the Company?"

"Fighting who?" asked Peter.

"Terrorists of course," answered Leo.

Peter stopped in his tracks and stared at his brother. "Explain," he said.

"Mother thinks that she was a victim of terrorism, right?" said Leo. "How many innocent folk become victims of these people? In Spain, Germany, the Middle East, Africa, South America, mainland England and Northern Ireland, almost every country in the world has a problem of some kind. The news is always full of stories and despite the efforts of the police and the security forces too many of these people are getting away with murder."

"And what difference could we make?" asked Peter. "We don't even know who was responsible for what happened to mum."

"I know we haven't got a cat in hell's chance of getting the actual person who planted the bomb, but at least we could help in the fight against his or her kind," said Leo, "someone has to do it and I'm game, how about you?"

They began walking again deep in thought. "You're thinking SAS aren't you?" said Peter.

"Yes," said Leo, "how did you guess?"

"Because the thought had also occurred to me," said Peter, "great minds and all that, we never fail."

"Do you think they would take us?" asked Leo.

"Why not" said Peter, "we're young and fit, we have done the infantry bit, and we are qualified marksmen all we need is a reason to apply for Selection?"

"We cannot mention mum, it would sound too much like revenge," said Leo. "I doubt if they would go for that, I think adventure in the pursuit of natural justice would be our best bet, what do you think?"

"Or the preservation of national security might be a more acceptable reason if we are asked," said Peter.

On their return to Sandhurst they requested an interview with the Commandant. They explained what had happened to their parents and requested permission to have their commissions postponed pending the results of an application for Selection to the Special Air Service. The Commandant tried to talk them out of their decision without success but he secretly admired and envied them for their motivation.

After a searching interview at the SAS HQ at Stirling Lines in Hereford, their applications for transfer to the elite regiment of the British Army were accepted subject to passing the rigorous Selection process that they would have to undergo and pass before being presented with the famous winged dagger symbol of the SAS. Their commissions with the REME were put on hold for the foreseeable future at their own request.

During the Selection period, they marched, yomped, staggered and crawled for hundreds of miles in all kinds of terrain while carrying heavy Bergen rucksacks and an assortment of weaponry. They fan-danced in the Brecon Beacons, evaded capture in desolate scrubland and forest, half drowned in swollen rivers, and resisted interrogation at the hands of pseudo enemy captors who were out to break their spirits. A year later they were presented with the coveted winged dagger badge of the SAS.

Both men were adept in the art of climbing courtesy of their father Joe and regular holidays in the Lake District. Peter chose mountaineering as his speciality while Leo opted for intelligence gathering. They served as troopers with different Squadrons for three years before being stationed together at Bessbrook in Northern Ireland.

Their Commanding Officer, Major 'Nosey' Parker, called them to his office one day after going through their files where he had discovered their Sandhurst officer training credentials. He asked them why they had not applied for a commission in the SAS. Peter explained that they believed that they would have to be RTU'd, returned to unit, after spending just three years with the SAS. Major Parker confirmed their suspicions but explained that the rule applied to officers from different regiments, having successfully gone through the Selection process, if the twins took their commissions while serving with the SAS, they would have no unit to be returned to but the SAS. The twins took their commissions accordingly and Captain Peter Bailey was given command of A Squadron while Captain Leo Bailey opted for attachment to 14 Int on covert surveillance in civvies.

Chapter 2

It was a peaceful sunny morning on the hill overlooking the wooded valley, the silence broken only by the chorus of a host of unseen birds proclaiming the dawn; an unusual prelude to what was about to go down.

Under the cover of hedgerows, three armed men in combat clothing and balaclava masks had lain in wait since before first light. At the bottom of the hill, the cottage of the recently deceased Sarah Finnigan stood in a neat little garden well back from the elbow in the bend of the minor country road. In front of the cottage, innocently parked, was a yellow VW Beetle packed with explosives.

With any luck, an Army patrol would be passing that way during the morning. There was no guarantee that they would turn up because they did not conform to a regular pattern for security reasons. Random patrolling was the name of the game but a dropped word in a loyalist pub, frequented by off-duty British Army squaddies, the previous night had alerted a certain young lady prostitute whose job it was to gather snippets of information for her pimp Sean Cunningham, one of three lieutenants in Thomas Brannigan's criminal organisation.

The narrow, pot-holed road was seldom used by other than farm traffic because of the many twists and bends. However, the Army patrolled the district at random intervals; two arms caches had been discovered in the area in the past year.

Unknown to the hooded men on the hillside, the lone figure of an ex Provisional IRA hit man, Eamon Flynn, lay concealed in the woods on the other side of the road opposite the cottage. His instructions from Thomas Brannigan were to finish off any soldiers who survived the blast from the car bomb before making himself scarce. He wore army-surplus combats and a dark green woollen hat to conceal his bright ginger hair. His freckled face was smeared with commando make-up; he blended in well with his surroundings.

The youngest of the three men on the hill overlooking the cottage was Patrick O'Riordan. He was on his first killing mission as part of an initiation and loyalty test. The dubious honour of remotely detonating the car bomb had been delegated to him and he was not very happy about it. Petty criminal though he was, he had no stomach for killing in cold blood. But he was in a catch 22 situation in that if he carried it through he would be mentally scarred for life and if he refused, he would probably end up in a ditch with his knee caps blown off.

O'Riordan cursed the day that he and his pal Liam Casey had stolen the yellow VW and allowed them selves to be inducted into first the Provisionals and then into Brannigan's criminal gang. Fuck Cunningham and the rest of the evil bastards, he wished he had never become involved with them although he had benefited financially from the armed robberies, prostitution, and the drugs dealings of the criminal gang; you couldn't have it all ways.

The pimp, Sean Cunningham, a man in his late fifties, was in charge of the operation and would make damned sure that young Patrick O'Riordan carried out his orders. Cunningham reported directly to Brannigan and was one of only four men in the gang who knew that Brannigan was their leader. If anything went wrong with the operation, it would be Cunningham's balls on the chopping block. He knew the boss from way back.

The third member of the team, Roland 'Dixie' Dixon, was the bomb maker. He had packed the VW with fertilizer and a Semtex fuse to be detonated by remote control. If the patrol did not appear, as had happened on two previous occasions, he would have to disarm the bomb and stash the car until another opportunity arose. Today, however, things looked a bit more promising.

Dixon looked a lot older than his fifty-six years. Small in stature and with a weasel-like face, he sported a shock of wiry grey hair that he kept as neat and as slick as a wig with old-fashioned brilliantine. He was not strictly a member of Brannigan's gang, he reported to the local PIRA battalion CO, Barney Meehan, who loaned him out to Cunningham on occasion for the odd bombing job. He was an expert bomb-maker but his retirement was imminent because of a serious drinking problem. Cunningham kept him well supplied with enough poteen to guarantee his cooperation. The IRA godfathers had promised Dixie sufficient financial reward to enable him to settle in the States where he could drink himself into oblivion.

Stood down since the ceasefire, Provisional IRA Derry Battalion commander Barney Meehan opened his eyes, gazed at the ceiling and yawned deeply. It was 7.30 a.m. He had overslept after lying awake for what seemed like hours after he had taken to his bed. He was a worried man who found it difficult to understand why the PIRA supreme commander, Daniel Doonan, tolerated Brannigan and his seedy criminal mob. He had told Doonan what Brannigan was planning but Doonan had said that the PIRA would simply deny any involvement.

Brannigan had been an active Provo in his youth but for some reason, he had embraced politics while serving time in the Maze prison for being a member of a terrorist organisation. He had managed to convince the authorities that he was a reformed character and they had granted him leave to pursue a political career. He represented Sinn Fein in the Bogside and Creggan areas of Londonderry and was very popular among the republican community. Since winning his seat twenty or so years earlier, he had managed to keep the tribes apart to some degree, which pleased the authorities and won him a few favours.

Barney knew of Brannigan's criminal associations but was sworn to secrecy by the Provo code and by Doonan personally for reasons of his own; he probably got a cut of the action. Knowledge could be dangerous thing.

Meehan dressed, made himself some coffee and toast, and sat reading the morning paper while he waited for a call from Cunningham to say whether the job was either on or off. The past two days had taken its toll on Meehan, it was no wonder that he could not sleep and little wonder also that, conversely, he could hardly keep his eyes open.

He had recently turned fifty years old but still had a good head of jet-black curly hair. Maybe one of his ancestors had landed with the Spaniards after the armada when some of their ships had been wrecked off the Donegal coast. He had always kept his fairly slim 5' 11" frame in a good and fit condition.

His young nephew and lodger, Liam Casey, bore the family resemblance. He could have been mistaken for Meehan's son rather than his nephew, which pleased Meehan because his wife had died, along with their second child, a boy, while giving birth twenty-five years previously. His only daughter was married to a farmer near Ballykelly on the other side of the border. He tried to protect Liam from the seamier side of IRA involvement by employing him as a courier.

Just after 8.30 a.m., Dixie Dixon touched Cunningham's arm and pointed to the bend in the road to their left. The first of the soldiers appeared, looking around him with caution and pointing his weapon in his line of sight. The others followed at intervals of several metres, scanning their surroundings in a similar fashion. The two men bringing up the rear turned and walked backwards alternately. As they neared the parked VW, they automatically kept their distance on the opposite side of the road.

Cunningham gripped O'Riordan's shoulder and gestured him to get ready to blow the car. O'Riordan was just about to flick the switch when he heard the sound of an approaching vehicle and hesitated. Both Dixie Dixon who suffered with tinnitus, and Cunningham, whose hearing was not as keen as that of the younger O'Riordan, could not yet hear the vehicle that was approaching from the right and heading towards the army patrol.

Everything seemed to happen at once. Unusually, on the little used narrow country road, a bus had been diverted from the main road through Ballykelly because of a bomb scare outside a high street bank. It rounded the bend in the narrow road too fast sending the soldiers diving for cover. O'Riordan appeared to hesitate. Cunningham grabbed the remote control and pushed him to one side. He pressed the button on the remote at the exact moment that the bus came opposite the VW.

The massive explosion, combined with the tilt of the bus on the camber of the bend in the road, hurled it across the road smashing it sideways into the trees shattering the windows and instantly killing the driver, seven of the school children on board and badly injuring another ten. The children were aged between five and seven years. One of the soldiers was killed instantly and two of the others sustained serious injuries.

An eerie silence descended on the scene. The birdsong ceased and the smell of explosives hung in the air as the dust and debris settled. The cottage was totally demolished and where the VW had stood, there was nothing left but a crater.

Three of the unfortunate children who died, two of them twin sisters, had been catapulted through the shattered windows when the bus was hurled against the trees. They landed in a grotesque heap near to where Eamon Flynn lay concealed. Hardened terrorist killer though he was, the horrific sight of the small lifeless bodies made him shudder; they were innocent children. He made off into the woods seeking his own survival forgetting about the soldiers who were carrying out what first aid they could and comforting the dazed and frightened surviving children, some of whom were crying for their mothers, while the platoon commander radioed for back-up and medical assistance.

Patrick O'Riordan got slowly to his feet and gazed down on the scene below while absently rubbing his sore cheekbone where Cunningham had caught him a glancing blow when he grabbed the remote. Cunningham's mouth opened and closed but nothing would come out. He looked at the remote control in his hand and cast it away from him as though it was a poisonous snake. Shielding his face, he shook his head in disbelief as he cowered away from O'Riordan who had turned to face him with fists clenched and a look of hatred in his eyes. Cunningham turned on his heals and ran.

Dixie was on his knees praying to his God who, he had been led to understand, forgave all in the Holy struggle; Dixon had been well brainwashed. O'Riordan took him by the arm and half dragged him away, picking up the remote as he went.

Barney Meehan paced the floor of his living room willing the phone to ring with the news that the mission had either been completed or abandoned. The deadline had been 10 a.m. and it was now almost 11 a.m. He had been against the whole operation from the beginning and had told Doonan so but he had been shouted down. Brannigan's contributions to the PIRA coffers gave him far more clout than Meehan thought he deserved. He hated the arrogant bastard.

He switched on the television for the 11 o'clock news bulletin and caught an urgent news flash. The wreck of the school bus with the barely recognisable name of **'St. Mary's Convent Infants School'** on the battered side, showed on the screen. The Newsreader was reporting:

"The bus driver had apparently taken a detour on a seldom used country road around the town because of a bomb scare outside the bank in Ballykelly where the traffic was held up by the RUC. The children were due to travel to Belfast this morning to spend the day at the Zoo. The side of the bus took the full blast of the car bomb, apparently meant for an army patrol in the vicinity at the time, killing the driver and seven of the seventeen children instantly. One soldier was also killed and two others were seriously injured. It was thought to be the work of the Provisional IRA but a hurried denial was received almost immediately after the news was released. The spokesman blamed the atrocity on a dissident Republican group calling themselves The Real IRA who had broken away after the Provisional IRA cease-fire had been announced before Christmas last year."

The news proper began but Meehan was not listening. He was dumb struck by what had happened. His twin granddaughters went to St. Mary's and they surely would have been on the bus. They had been so excited about the trip to the zoo when he had seen them in church the previous Sunday. He began to panic as he picked up the phone to call his daughter. Meehan lived forty-three miles away in Buncrana, just over the border into Donegal.

There was no reply from his daughter's house and Meehan feared the worst. He dropped the phone and let out a wail of anguish. Alone in the house, he began to shout and blaspheme.

"Fuck you Brannigan, you won't get away with this. I'll take you down you evil bastard." He picked up a cushion and hammered his fist into it. "Bastard, bastard, bastard, I'll get you if it's the last thing I do." He flung the cushion into a corner and fell to the floor crying and banging his fists like a child having a tantrum.

SAS Major, Cedric 'Nosey' Parker, was called to the phone in response to a coded message from a high ranking member of the Provo's via the RUC station in Ballykelly. The man, Barney Meehan, had important information to impart but he would only speak face to face with a senior member of the security forces. A map was studied, a rendezvous arranged and the information passed on to Meehan.

Two SAS Sergeants, George Davidson and Mal Spencer of A squadron, both ex Royal Marines and veterans of the Falklands war, were already in position when Meehan's car reached the rendezvous. Using the natural cover, Spencer crawled, slid, and rolled his way to within fifty metres of the other side of the vehicle. He and Davidson were in whisper contact by radio.

Meehan waited in his car for half an hour in the lay-by on the quiet country road while the two SAS soldiers scanned the area for a possible ambush. They had split up in order to approach the car from different directions. Mal Spencer inched his way forward and at the pre-arranged moment he crouched beside the driver's door of the car and tapped gently on the window taking Meehan completely by surprise. He pointed with his Heckler and Koch sub machine gun, opened the door, and motioned Meehan to place his hands on top of his head. He then instructed Meehan to move over to the passenger seat, which he did without hesitation. The Sergeant frisked him thoroughly then started the engine. The rear offside door opened and George Davidson dived into the back seat. He blindfolded Meehan as the car sped off to the SAS HQ at Bessbrook.

Barney Meehan was low down on the wanted list of known terrorists from years back when he had been an active IRA Player. Nothing had been heard of him since he had joined the Provisional IRA and had become the CO of the Derry battalion but now here he was offering to tell all he knew about the Ballykelly bombing and the perpetrators, Brannigan and his criminal gang; the Provo's would be off the hook.

After Eamon Flynn left the scene of the car bomb blast, he made his way to the hideout where he lived a life of solitude in an old touring caravan parked behind a high stone wall in the corner of a pinewood near Ballyshannon on the Donegal side of the border on the property of an IRA friendly farmer. Flynn visited Danny's bar on the other side of the border once a week to take a drink and receive his instructions from Brannigan either in person or via Danny Monaghan.

Flynn was still shaken by the events at Ballykelly and wondered how Brannigan would take his disobedience of orders and desertion from the scene. There was no way that the chief would understand how he felt when he saw those poor bloody kids lying in the undergrowth like discarded rag dolls. The picture refused to leave his mind and, hard man though he was, he had cried uncontrollably for an hour after he had returned to his caravan. He decided to give it a few more days to allow the heat to die down before he went to Danny's Bar.

*

Flynn and Brannigan had met in the Bogside twenty-nine years earlier when Flynn was just a ten-year old boy. He was the youngest of eight children in a family ruled by a drunken brute of a father. His mother died when Flynn was only nine years old and he was left traumatised. Her reassuring presence held the family together but after she died, one by one the older children drifted away from home to escape the abject poverty and their father's tyranny.

Eamon Flynn became a tearaway who hated the world for what life had done to him. His drunken father found him difficult to control and one night he lost his temper and beat the boy so badly that he could hardly stand. Flynn spent a week away from school because of his injuries and, even at his tender age, he silently vowed to take his revenge.

One day at school his class was being lectured about the dangers of drinking from bottles without proper labels. A pupil had drunk from a lemonade bottle which contained bleach borrowed by his mother from a neighbour. The child had survived but was seriously ill; the seed of an idea was sown in Flynn's mind.

A few weeks later, when all the fuss had died down, Flynn broke into a shed in the garden of the local council parks department and half filled a pop bottle with weed killer. He watered it down until the colour resembled that of whisky, poured it into an empty whisky bottle then he waited another two weeks before placing it in the corner of a high shelf in a kitchen cupboard for his father to discover; he did not have to wait long.

The old man returned home one night a little worse for booze. He was in a foul mood because he had run out of money before he had drunk his fill. He rummaged around the house until he spied the half-hidden whisky bottle and retrieved it with the aid of a stool. Flopping down in his filth-stained armchair, he took a long hard swig.

The verdict was death by misadventure and a grateful community was glad to see the end of a violent and hated man.

Mark Brannigan was then a local Sinn Fein councillor who had taken an interest in the Flynn family. Young Eamon had been left an orphan and none of his family wanted anything to do with him because he was never out of trouble. Brannigan saw himself in the boy because he had been brought up in a similar environment but had pulled himself up by his bootstraps.

He managed to find an orphanage to look after Flynn and visited the boy once a week after school on Wednesday evenings. He privately educated Flynn in Irish history and gradually alienated him towards the British who Brannigan believed were the root cause of all the conflict in Northern Ireland. Once a month, he took the boy to his home for a weekend and became like a second father to him. Flynn took a great liking to his benefactor and would do almost anything for him.

*

Prior to Brannigan's Ballykelly operation, SAS Captain Peter Bailey, as commander of A Squadron, was carrying out a four man surveillance operation accompanied by veteran Sergeant Alec Shiells and two troopers. They had been in position for almost ten days observing the home and the movements of a character named Bernard Cluskey the stood-down Derry Provisional IRA battalion quartermaster suspected of covert activity in defiance of the cease-fire.

Another suspect Player, whose day job was rubbish collecting, had been taken into custody for questioning. He had been identified by a witness after the attempted murder of an off-duty RUC officer in a restaurant where the officer had been enjoying an anniversary dinner with his wife. The inexperienced assassin had panicked and ran off when his first shot had missed the officer who had drawn a weapon in response.

An observant spinster-lady diner had recognised the masked young man as the person who emptied her dustbin every week. He bore a distinctive round white patch about two inches in diameter on the right side of his close-cropped black hair. He had stupidly failed to conceal it and the lady informed the police.

On checking the man's employment details, the police discovered that he had given Bernard Cluskey's name as a reference for the job with the local Council. The Council knew Cluskey as an honest insurance broker who worked from home and visited clients in their own homes and places of business. It had been a good cover until now because it had given him unlimited freedom of movement. However, when Cluskey learned that the young refuse collector had been arrested, he decided to take no chances. He informed Doonan in Dublin about the probability of his cover being blown, and was advised to plan his retirement and disappearance from his home.

The four-man troop watched Cluskey's house from separate observation posts at the front, sides and rear of the isolated ranch style bungalow. Among the several visitors who came and went, they recognised two of them as previously wanted Provo Players. They had turned up together one evening in a pick-up truck containing what appeared to be empty dustbins. Cluskey came out to meet them and handed them a map which they studied as he pointed and gestured.

Peter's SAS troop of four had two mobile back-up troops at their disposal with which they were in radio contact. The troops used different vehicles every day to tail Cluskey's few visitors back to their destinations. Peter supplied the registration numbers of the visitors' cars and the direction in which they travelled. The back-ups, in unmarked vehicles, followed and reported to the SAS HQ at Bessbrook where flags were stuck in a wall map. The security forces were gradually unravelling Cluskey's command structure known only to a select few of the Provisional IRA hierarchy.

When the two men in the pick-up truck left Cluskey's place, they were discreetly followed to what turned out to be an arms cache. They were not intercepted at the time but were allowed to transfer the contents of the cache to the dustbins prior to carting them off to a new location. They made several trips during the night until the dump was empty then they sealed it. Had the captive refuse collector, while in custody, disclosed the original location of the dump to the security forces, they would find nothing.

Peter's twin, Capt Leo Bailey, was working undercover in the Shankhill Road area of Belfast. A group of Loyalist gunmen had been causing problems in Republican enclaves since the Christmas cease-fire had been announced by the PIRA. They were hoping for a Catholic backlash but the Sinn Fein politicians were being successful in keeping a tight lid on things in the face of provocation by Loyalist gunmen encouraged by a prominent Unionist politician with the dubious title of Reverend.

Now a leading member of the Ulster Defence Association, veteran John McCann, was thought to be the main coordinator of the sporadic raids into the Republican areas by Loyalist gangs bent on the desecration of Catholic churches as well as the destruction of Catholic homes and businesses. Up to three car loads of thugs would appear from nowhere and create as much mayhem as possible in around ten minutes then disappear as fast as they came. No one knew where the gang would strike next.

Leo Bailey posed as a social worker and drove a maroon Ford Escort with 'Belfast Social Services Dept.' printed in yellow on both sides of the car. The vehicle itself was a passport into most areas as people from both sides of the religious and political divide needed the services of a social worker from time to time.

Leo was six feet tall and sported a designer beard and an unruly mop of mousy blonde hair. A loose fitting tweed jacket, baggy brown corduroy trousers and desert boots, completed the picture of the type of person he was trying to portray. He had resurrected his Northern Ireland accent which had lain dormant since childhood and now passed off easily as the 'fella' from Magherafelt.

He was having little success in tailing the suspect John McCann who seemed to prefer public transport to a car for moving about the province. Leo felt that the Ford Escort stuck out like a gouty toe as he followed behind buses and taxis. McCann always got off in a busy shopping area and then disappeared into the crowd making it difficult for Leo to park up then follow.

Leo was about to change his disguise and tactics when he got an unexpected break. One day, McCann took the same bus that he had taken on one other occasion and Leo took a guess at its destination. He went ahead and parked the Escort in a public car park and waited near the bus stop where he thought McCann would get off. He had guessed right, McCann got off and glanced furtively about him before hurrying off through the crowd.

Leo followed him at a safe distance to a bar in the city centre. McCann was in a corner talking to another man who Leo recognised from a list of known Loyalist villains. When the two men left and went their separate ways, Leo followed the other man to the same public car park were he had left the Escort. When the man drove off, Leo followed him to his destination and noted the address

A couple of days later the man was again followed by an undercover SAS team of four in a high performance banger. He picked up three passengers at different Loyalist estates and met up en-route with two other vehicles that rendezvoused at a pub car park on the outskirts of Belfast. Twelve men went into the pub and sat drinking in three separate groups until the light outside began to fade.

The SAS team watched the men pile into their cars and drive off one behind the other. The team followed at a discreet distance and radioed ahead for backup.

The three suspect cars drove into a Republican estate where one stopped outside a church while the other two sped off towards the nearby shopping precinct. At the church, the driver stayed in the car while one man, armed with a handgun, knelt and waited for resistance. The two men in the back seats leapt out and opened the boot of the car and produced a crate of petrol bombs that they were about to ignite when the SAS troop, who had dismounted and taken cover, shouted the warning,

"Armed police, drop your weapons."

The terrorist with the pistol raised his weapon and fired blindly towards the warning voice. He died instantly in a hail of SAS bullets. The two petrol bombers dropped their bottles and dived into the car and sped away. Another hail of bullets took out the two front tyres and the car swerved into a lamppost bursting into flames. The two men in the back seats managed to dive out but the trapped driver perished in the blaze.

Two of the hooded SAS men ran forward and pinned the terrorists to the road with their heavy boots and ordered them to put their hands behind their heads until the RUC arrived to cart them off.

The two other terrorist teams realized that the game was up and tried to make a run for it but the backup team was on them. They tried to shoot it out but ran into a roadblock where they were forced to stop and surrender without further bloodshed. McCann's marauders were no more but McCann was not with them; he was too crafty for that.

By the time Leo and his masked undercover team carried out a dawn raid on McCann's lodgings, he had packed up and left just after midnight without so much as a good-bye to the landlady. He had however, paid in advance and still had a week to go. Leo was disappointed but at least they had captured his bullyboys. He wondered where McCann would turn up next.

Major Parker listened patiently and with interest as Barney Meehan reeled off everything he knew about Brannigan and his known associates. He went even further by naming upper echelons of the Provisional IRA. Most of them were already known to MI6 and to the SAS but enjoyed a temporary armistice during the current cease-fire

Seven and a half hours and three pots of coffee later, Major Parker stopped the tape recorder and had Meehan taken away for a meal and a shower before having him bedded down in an unlocked cell for the night. He called the duty Controller and instructed him to recall the twin officers from their respective duties.

Under cover of darkness, one of Brannigan's Lieutenants Sean Cunningham slipped in through the back entrance to Danny's Bar. Brannigan had left earlier in the day after discussing with his best friend and senior Lieutenant, Danny Monaghan, the implications of what had happened at Ballykelly.

Cunningham was worried, he had to tell Brannigan his version of events before O'Riordan got to him but Danny told him that O'Riordan had already been and gone after telling his side of the story. The two Lieutenants swapped condolences, not for the bus driver and the tiny victims, but for the perpetrators of the atrocity. Cunningham set off for his home in Lislap to await the inevitable call from Brannigan.

The house was Cunningham's favourite retreat of four that he owned and maintained. The madams he employed to run his string of brothels lived in the other three, one in Liverpool, one in Glasgow and one in Dublin. He had carefully chosen each of the three women after the idea of pimping had first occurred to him.

*

Sean Cunningham was the son of an Anglican Vicar of the Church of Ireland who had Roman sympathies. Instead of having young Sean confirmed in the Anglican faith at an early age, he had allowed him to make up his own mind at the age of sixteen. Sean chose Catholicism because most of his friends in the local youth rugby team were RC. He suffered for his decision at the hands of his fellow pupils at the Anglican school and got his first insight into sectarianism. He decided not to stay on for further education and left school the same year.

Jobs were not easy to come by for sixteen year olds who had dipped out of school. It had always been his intention to go on to university and do something with his life but here he was with no direction whatsoever. In an effort to earn a living while he waited for an opportunity to arise, he took a job as a door-to-door salesman peddling cleaning materials and utensils. It was a commission only job, which meant that he would have to work long and hard to earn a decent living. To his great surprise, he discovered that he had a flare for selling. At the age of eighteen, he became an area supervisor and by the time he was twenty-one, he was a regional manager and earning more money than his father.

He had a winning way with people and an appreciation of the money he earned from supplying their needs. He spent very little and invested a lot until he had accumulated a small fortune.

While on his first holiday abroad in Ibiza, he met and fell in love with Molly O'Hare from Dublin. She was on the second week of her holiday and he had just arrived. Neither had ever bothered much with the opposite sex although he was tall and handsome with an athletic figure, deep blue eyes, and a mop of black wavy hair. Molly was about six inches shorter with a trim, lithe figure, hazel eyes and naturally curly auburn hair. Something inside them had told them that they were meant for each other. They struck up an easy friendship that developed into a deep and tender love.

They were married within three months and Sean bought the house in Lislap. They went back to Ibiza for their honeymoon and experienced sexual intimacy for the first time in their lives. It was a fumbling, sensitive, and exhilarating experience for them both which resulted in Molly becoming pregnant. They were extremely happy and looking forward to the birth until something went drastically wrong. The pregnancy had triggered a dormant hereditary blood condition that manifested itself after six months. Molly miscarried and lost her life along with that of the baby.

Sean Cunningham was devastated and lost control of him self for months afterwards. He began to drink to excess and suffered fits of depression. It all came to an end one day when he crashed his car into a tree on a country road not far from his home. He was unhurt because he had had the good sense to wear his seat belt but he was so drunk when the police discovered him, that he was jailed for three months. It was while he was in jail that he met Brannigan who was by then studying law while serving time for being a member of a terrorist organisation. The two of them became friends and promised to stay in touch after their release.

After his discharge, Sean began to pick up the pieces of his life and returned to direct selling. The double-glazing market was just beginning to take off and he decided to apply for a job with a leading Company on the mainland. After his initial training, he worked harder than anyone in his team. He cold-canvassed for four days a week from 9 a.m. until 2 p.m. and booked appointments for the evenings and weekends. He averaged sales of 1 in 4 in his first few months then, having quickly got the hang of it, his presentation to sales ratio went up to 1 in 1.5. Within six months, he was an Area Manager with half a dozen salesmen who earned him 3% overriding commission on their sales as well as his own. Within a further six months, he was a Regional Manager earning another 3% from six area managers and forty men as well as full commission from his own sales. He was like a money magnet; it just kept rolling in without much effort. He banked with the Manchester branch of a Dublin bank and when he finally came to the notice of the Inland Revenue, he transferred his account to the main bank in Dublin and returned to Lislap without leaving a forwarding address.

It took a year of widowhood for his libido to return. He was in a bar one night when a beautiful girl approached him and asked him for a light. He told her he didn't smoke and asked her if she would like a drink. One thing led to another and they ended up in bed together in his rented flat.

He was surprised to learn that she was only eighteen years old and had been on the game since she was fifteen. The sex had cost him a hundred pounds, which did not bother him, but when she told him how much her pimp took, he was incensed. He asked her if she would like to go into business with him and, after listening to his proposition, she agreed and became the youngest madam in the business.

He bought his first high-class brothel in Liverpool and the rest followed. His Madam's recruited girls from the age of sixteen upward and he vetted them over a period of six weeks during which they shared his bed alone. From them, he learned several lovemaking techniques, gleaned mostly from the Karma Sutra rather than from experience, which he told them their clients would appreciate. He preached strict hygiene and insisted that they use condoms on every occasion. He also insisted that they dress well and present themselves in such a way as to distinguish them from common whores and streetwalkers. They loved Cunningham as did most people who came into contact with him.

It was after he opened the Dublin brothel that he came into direct contact with the Provisional IRA. The brothel had been operating for about six months when he received a message via the Madam that a Mr. Daniel Doonan wished to meet him at a bar called Murphy's. A refusal to do so would not be to his advantage, and would threaten the future of the Dublin enterprise.

Sean took the threat seriously and met with the infamous Doonan after first contacting Brannigan who he had not seen since they were in jail together. Brannigan had seriously advised him to see Doonan and to agree to his demands. He suggested that Cunningham might like to take a ride over to Danny's Bar near Derry the following weekend to discuss a proposition. Sean agreed and as a result of that meeting the three of them, Brannigan, Monaghan and Cunningham, formed a lifelong criminal partnership and Cunningham became a member of the Provisional IRA, albeit reluctantly; if you can't beat 'em . . . .

Other enterprises involving Brannigan and company followed and their criminal empire grew steadily. Bank robberies however, were the exclusive domain of Brannigan, Monaghan and Cunnigham in collaboration with one Alfredo Ricocco, alias Freddy Ricco, a third generation Irish Italian. He was an excellent get-away man, having been a grand prix driver before having to retire as a result of a bad accident. He was paid 10% of each haul but, for his own good, he was not allowed to know the identity of his hooded passengers. Brannigan would ring him at his Fiat garage just hours before a job then turn up in his workshop with his two partners fully armed and masked-up ready for the job then disappear until the next job. What you don't know, you can't tell.

*

Patrick O'Riordan had arrived at Danny's bar before Cunningham and had told Monahan about the cock-up at Ballykelly. He stayed for a while drowning his sorrows with a pint of porter or two before setting off on his motorbike for his home where he hoped his courier pal Liam would be waiting to share his burden of guilt and remorse.

Liam wasn't there, so he set off for Buncrana and the house of Liam's uncle Barney with whom Liam lodged. The place was deserted when he got there, he sensed that there was something wrong and went back to Danny's bar where he was given a room for the night.

'Dixie' Dixon had shut himself away in the shed of his allotment garden and got out a bottle of poteen then proceeded to assassinate a few more of his ever decreasing brain cells and to harden his liver a little more. If only Maureen had still been alive, he would not be in this state. But she had died of cancer five years before and he was now beyond hope. He drank himself into a stupor and pissed himself where he sat in the tattered old deckchair in the garden shed.

Only four people knew Brannigan's Jaguar car phone number, Danny Monaghan, Sean Cunningham, Barney Meehan, and Daniel Doonan, the Dublin PIRA supremo. Brannigan was on his way to Meehan's house when he noticed the red light flashing on the phone in the holder attached to the dashboard. He stopped the car and picked up the handset expecting to hear one of his Lieutenants on the other end of the line but it was Daniel Doonan.

"I've seen the news about Ballykelly Brannigan, what the feck are your men playing at? Never mind, just get your feckin' arse down here now and meet me at Murphy's in four hours. Don't answer, just feckin' do it or you're feckin' dead meat."

The phone went down and Brannigan was left white-faced and shaking. He felt like running and hiding somewhere but he knew instinctively that he could never hide from the Boys. He forgot about Meehan and set off for Dublin in the hope that he could make it in time for the meeting. The Jag was up to it but he would be taking a chance with the law. Shit, shit, shit.

Chapter 3

I t was 1 a.m. The last light had been switched off in Bernard Cluskey's house just before 11 p.m. and Peter had got his head down after extricating himself from the cramped, sweaty OP, to roll off into the undergrowth for a much-needed dump. It was the only thing he hated about surveillance but at least, with no dogs around to sniff out the body waste, he did not need to save it in a plastic bag out here in the woods, a shallow grave and a handful of leaves would do the trick.

There was not a cloud in sight and no street lamp pollution to spoil the view of the night sky. The stars twinkled brightly through the breaks in the trees and the bright shining planets were clearly visible with the aid of army binoculars.

Cluskey's house, bordered on three sides by woodland, was under close observation by the four man SAS surveillance team each in a separate concealed observation post consisting of a shallow dugout excavated under cover of darkness some nights before and covered by a pegged-down groundsheet concealed under a blanket of leaves and twigs.

Trooper Jock Shand, a 5'4" ex-paramedic from Shetlend and as tough as a Shetland pony, was within sight of Peter's hide at one side of the house and that of Sergeant Alec Shiells' at the other. Jock had been on watch for two hours from his position beneath a clump of gorse on the opposite side of the road to the front of the house which was set well back from the road and fronted by a neat lawn with a half circle of driveway running from separate entrance and exit gates. The fourth member of the team, Mal Spencer, had been recalled by Parker to pick up the informer Meehan the day before.

After seeking relief in the woods Peter had taken a brief kip while Jock was on watch. Now wide awake and very much alert, Peter, in response to a whispered radio message in his ear piece, heard by Jock and Geordie, acknowledged then slipped away to rendezvous with one of the two back-up teams half a mile away.

There was an urgent message for him there from Major Parker ordering him to report to HQ. He relayed the message on to Geordie and Jock leaving the two of them to keep watch before setting off to rendezvous with one of the two-man back-up vehicles.

Peter's twin Leo was in a deep sleep in the Belfast safe house used by the SAS when his mobile rang and he was also ordered to report to HQ.

At 3 a.m., the lights went on in Cluskey's house as a vehicle approached from the east. It turned into the drive and the horn tooted twice. Geordie Shiells could not see the front door from where he lay. He bleeped Jock and asked him what was happening. Jock told him that the vehicle was a taxi and that Cluskey was loading several pieces of luggage into the boot. It looked as though he was doing a runner.

Geordie alerted the second back-up team who in turn informed the RUC and the chase was on. Cluskey did not get far and offered no resistance when the taxi was stopped at a roadblock. He was taken into custody and in response to a message to Geordie confirming the fact the remaining back-up vehicle picked up him and Jock and returned them to HQ.

After a welcome shower and a few hours in a comfortable bed, followed by a cooked breakfast and a change of clothes, the twin officers presented themselves before a very tired Major Parker. He had spent the night listening to Meehan's confessional tape and dictating notes to his WRAC secretary Corporal Sandra Smethurst who looked completely exhausted. She was told to fall-out when the two officers reported and went gratefully to her billet where she fell into bed fully clothed. She knew nothing more for several hours.

Major Parker briefed the twin officers on the Ballykelly incident and the subsequent surrender of Meehan who had turned informer. He handed them each a file that he and his secretary had prepared during the night. All the players that Meehan had named were listed. Some of the names had an asterisk beside them. At the foot of the last page, next to the asterisk, was the word 'TAKEOUT', the code for summary execution, the twins looked at each other and nodded.

"The RUC are not aware of Meehan's whereabouts gentlemen and I want it kept that way for the time being. If the politicians get hold of this, our hands will be completely tied; understood?" asked the Major.

"Understood," said both officers together.

"Right, now you will have to excuse me gentlemen because I am completely fucked after forty eight hours without sleep. Take the files away with you and study them, then see me back here in four hours time with a plan of action, OK?"

The men stood as the CO made to leave the room but he stopped and turned with a hand in the air as if remembering something important.

"Peter."

"Cedric?"

"You should know that our Mr. Cluskey tried to make a run for it soon after you were recalled. According to tickets found in his possession he was all ready for a flight to America. Your Sergeant alerted the other back-up team who followed his taxi, they alerted the RUC who set up a roadblock and arrested him. Give the lads a pat on the back when you see them, they should have RTU'd by now and be tucked up in their pits. See you later." He shuffled off with a tired wave of his hand.

The SAS HQ was located in a huge hanger at a helicopter station run jointly by the Army Air Corps and the RAF. The RAF Regiment guarded the perimeter and was responsible for station security. Residential caravans inside the hanger provided comfortable accommodation for the SAS troopers. Each of the caravans slept a team of four and was plumbed for water, sanitation, and electricity. Cylinders of propane gas were provided for cooking. Each team catered for itself including the Major and his admin, signals, and intelligence staff. Portacabins provided office and briefing-room accommodation, while shipping containers contained the armoury. It was a cosy place to get back to after the privations of surveillance duty under the cover of hedges and muddy ditches in all kinds of weather conditions.

The twins shared a caravan all to themselves as the only two commissioned officers in the HQ apart from Major Parker. They spent most of their time with their individual close-knit teams. This was the first time since they had been posted to Northern Ireland that they were given the opportunity to work together on the same job. They had been accustomed to taking orders from their respective section commanders who were usually sergeants with more service and experience than they themselves in various theatres of operation, rank was unimportant.

Their brief from the Major was to formulate a plan for 'taking out' the perpetrators of the Ballykelly atrocity. They had the names of the Players from Meehan plus the name of the man who had sanctioned the operation but was denying all knowledge and placing the ball firmly in Brannigan's court as the leader of a dissident gang. That man was Daniel Doonan, the top man in the Provisional IRA. But he was based in Dublin and untouchable.

*

No one in the security forces, and especially the SAS, was in any doubt about why they were actively serving in an integral part of the United Kingdom. The sad history of the province spoke for itself. Prior to service in Northern Ireland, all units were briefed on the reasons for being sent there.

In October 1968, when the twins were only two and a half years old, clashes between police and crowds in Londonderry marked the start of violent and long-term disturbances in Northern Ireland.

In January 1969, the Peoples Democracy march from Belfast to Londonderry was broken up by the RUC. This was the start of escalating unrest in the province, centring on political parades.

In April the same year, Belfast post offices and the main bus station were attacked and firebombed.

In May, James Chichester-Clark became Prime Minister of Northern Ireland. A three-day street battle after the Apprentice Boys March in Londonderry on the 12th August prompted the handover of policing and security in Northern Ireland to the British Army.

In October, the Hunt committee, in their report on Northern Ireland, recommended the disarming of the police and the disbandment of the 'B Specials'.

On the 22nd December, Bernadette Devlin MP was sentenced to six months imprisonment for incitement to riot in Belfast.

There were further violent disturbances in Belfast and Londonderry in June the following year and in August the Army fired rubber bullets for the first time.

Internment was introduced in 1971 for those suspected of being members of or giving assistance to the IRA. In February, Troop reinforcements were sent to Belfast after further violence. More Troops were sent in March, bringing the total to 9,700. Chichester-Clark resigned as Prime Minister of Northern Ireland and was succeeded by Brian Faulkner. Internment without trial began on 9th August and the following month, Prime Ministers Heath, Lynch and Faulkner met at Chequers for discussions about the province.

On 30th January 1972, 13 protest marchers, in a demonstration by unarmed Catholics, were killed by British troops in Londonderry. The following month, an IRA bomb in Aldershot, killed five cleaning ladies, a gardener and a Catholic priest.

*

Although they were Catholic as was their father, the twins had no sympathy with the Republican cause. They might have felt differently had the cause been essentially political but the fact that terror from both sides of the argument had been used as a weapon, and that criminals from both sides had also climbed aboard the band wagon to fuel the problem, was anathema to both of them. Leo, the theologian of the two, had tried desperately to make head or tail of the situation, especially after one side or the other had singled out their parents for punishment.

When he was at university, Leo had taken an interest in theology and had read quite a lot about other religions and beliefs in an attempt to try to understand people better. After one lecture by a Sri Lankan doctor named Sivananthan, he began to look at people in a different light.

The good doctor, a small bright-eyed young Tamil in his early thirties, smart, well spoken and a Fellow of the Royal College of Physicians, had given a lecture entitled 'The Sanctity of Human Life'.

He had begun with the process of human conception without going into too much detail about the sex act, which he had asked his audience to accept as a matter of fact. It was the miracle of conception that he was trying to put across. He went on to explain that while the human female is born with around 4000 eggs stored in her body, a male ejaculated something like 40,000,000 sperms during the performance of the sex act over a lifetime. Only one of those sperms would penetrate and fertilize a female egg under normal circumstances. Countless millions of sperms would therefore be discarded one way another during the lifetime of a single person. It followed that the chances of being born at all were several millions to one. It further followed, in Sivananthon's opinion, that every single person who made it to the egg, conception, and eventual birth, was a VIP in his or her own right and should be respected as such. They had fought and won the hardest battle they would ever experience in an entire lifetime and no one had the right to deprive them of that life; God said 'Thou shalt not kill.'

After the lecture, Sivananthan was given a standing ovation and was surrounded by students for over an hour and bombarded with questions. Leo was impressed at the time and still held the belief that everyone who had made it to the egg was a VIP.

Peter, however, accepted life as it was. He was something of a fatalist who took life as it came. The acceptance of that fate was a matter for the individual as far as he was concerned and influencing the outcome was fate in itself. The one thing they had in common, however, was the belief that unlawful killing was wrong. Terrorists and criminal psychopaths were trained killers by their own volition, soldiers and armed policemen were there to protect the public from terrorists, schizophrenic psychopaths and murderers.

"Terrorists are everywhere." Leo had said. "The Provisional Irish Republican Army, The Ulster Defence Association, The Red Brigades of Italy and Japan, The Basques in Spain, The Klu Klux Klan in America, Black September, FALN, Hamas, al Qaida, the Tamil Tigers, you name it, they do not discriminate. They all kill innocent men, women and children as well as servicemen, policemen, and judges. And the SAS along with Special Forces in most countries are the only active service personnel employed against them. The armed forces of most democratic countries are there to back-up the police and to help them to uphold the law. The poor sods usually end up themselves as targets for terrorist snipers." Each of the twins respected the other's views and opinions without rancour.

*

"OK Peter, what have you got for me?" asked Major Parker when the twins reported.

"We put the names of the people earmarked for 'Takeout' into a hat and drew lots. I drew Brannigan, Flynn, and Cunningham, and Leo has drawn the other three but we can't understand why Liam Casey is not on the list."

"He's Meehan's nephew," said the Major "and he is only a courier. Meehan assures me that the man has never been involved in anything worse than the theft of the VW which was used for the Ballykelly bomb but it was actually stolen by one Patrick O' Riordan."

"I've got O'Riordan down for 'Takeout', along with a Roland Dixon who apparently made the car bomb and a Daniel Monaghan who owns a pub once used as a safe-house for Provisional IRA members but currently for Brannigan's HQ. Wasn't O'Riordan the one who detonated the bomb?" Leo asked

"According to Meehan, it was supposed to be his initiation test," said the Major.

"What do you want us to do with Casey?" asked Leo.

"Find him and bring him in, I'm sure we'll be able to pin something on him." said Parker. "What is your plan of action gentlemen?"

Peter went over to a map of the province on the wall of the office and pointed out two places marked with a cross.

"This is the village of Ballyshiel," said Peter, pointing to a group of black dots, one of which had a cross attached. "And here is the church. This little dot some distance from the village on the right hand side of the road, going towards the border, is the pub called Danny's Bar. Although he assures us that he has never been there, Meehan is sure that it is a safe house for Brannigan and his gang because Cunningham goes there regularly to meet with some of the other members. But there is also a farm about ten miles from Ballyshiel where Meehan has been before and which he believes is another safe house.

He also believes that Cunningham keeps a store of military equipment there including arms, ammo, and explosives. He's not absolutely sure but he knows for certain that the IRA bomb maker Roland Dixon gets his stuff from there when he's not supplied by the Provo's through Cluskey the Quartermaster, i.e. when he is on loan to Brannigan. And, as coincidence would have it, when Cluskey's associates moved the arms cache from the woods near his house the other evening, they relocated about three miles from Ballyshiel which is half a mile on this side of the border according to the back-up team that tailed them. I've organised my section to go over there after dark and set up an LUP (laying up position) to keep an eye on the place in case the Provisionals attempt another move."

"OK so far," said Parker, "then what?"

"While it is still light, I'll hitch a ride on a Lynx with the Air Corps and over fly the area and take a few pictures today. I'd like to look for somewhere to lay-up for a couple of days to watch Danny's bar to see who comes and goes." said Peter. "And while I'm about it I'll over fly and photograph the area around the farm."

"Sounds fine," said the Major, then, turning to Leo. "What's your plan Leo?"

"Well Cedric, as you know, Meehan lives just over the border near Buncrana and O'Riordan lives not too far away from him." Leo pointed out the locations on the map. "I took the liberty of sending two of my section out-of-bounds to see if there was any sign of either Casey or O'Riordan or both; they are pals after all."

"Anything so far?" asked the Colonel.

"They got into position about two hours ago while you were still sleeping but we've heard nothing since the initial report. The places look deserted apparently," answered Leo.

"Next move?" asked the CO.

"While Peter recces the pub and the farm, we have decided that I should try to find Casey. If he has done a runner, the most likely place he would go would be to Belfast. He has a sister there apparently, Meehan told us, and they used to be quite close. I still have the use of the 'Social Services' car which I used on the last job and it is fairly well known around town along with my ugly mug." said Leo. "I'll keep in touch with my big brother by mobile phone, with your permission, but we will use normal coms with our sections."

"And what about the three players you've drawn for 'Takeout', don't they take priority?" asked Parker.

"Peter and I felt that they would be keeping their heads down for a couple of days till things cool off, then make for one of the safe-houses. So while Peter's section is watching them, I intend to make myself useful until Peter shouts for help then my section and I will join him."

"Fair one." said Parker. "Keep me posted and break a leg."

Parker knew from their files that the twins had both been into amateur dramatics while at university. The two young officers raised their eyebrows and smiled.

Brannigan had little to smile about. He had just got back from Dublin after his meeting with Doonan. The *bastard* had ordered him to 'Feck off out of the country and take your feckin geriatric feckin crew with you.'

Well fuck the Provisional IRA, they did not tell Brannigan what to do, he would show them. He phoned Danny Monaghan and ordered him to round up Cunningham and meet him at the farm. He tried to phone Meehan but there was still no reply, funny, he was almost always there. He had tried all evening without success and began to wonder.

He rang Danny Monaghan again and informed him of his unease. Danny told him about O'Riordan's attempt to contact Meehan and Casey after the Ballykelly incident also without success. He then told him about a tall blonde stranger in the bar downing his third pint of Guinness. The instinctively suspicious Brannigan's eyes narrowed, there was something wrong somewhere, Danny's Bar hosted mostly locals and farmers.

He told Danny he would be there by noon the next day and ordered him to contact Eamon Flynn and direct him to be there when he arrived; he would get to the bottom of this and heads would begin to roll if satisfactory explanations were not forthcoming.

Chapter 4

The light was fading when Peter pulled into the small car park behind Danny's Bar. He dismounted the 1000cc Gold Wing motorcycle with the huge side panniers and propped it on its rest. He went through the back door and into the bar as though it was his local haunt. There were no more than a dozen people in the room. They all turned and stared at him as if they had never before seen anyone wearing a black leather bike-suit, calf-length biking boots and a black crash helmet from beneath which, hung shoulder length blonde hair. The wig was Peter's idea.

"Good evening," he said, in his best Magherafelt accent, to Danny who he recognised immediately although he looked much older than the man in the photograph on the 'wanted list' from years back. He still had a shock of strong blonde hair which was just beginning to turn grey at the temples. Despite being a little on the paunchy side, Monaghan still looked quite fit for his fifty-five years of age.

"What can I get you?" asked Danny, ever suspicious of strangers.

"A pint of Guinness please and have you got anything to eat, I'm bloody starving. I've been on the road for hours," said Peter removing his gloves and his helmet and shaking-out his natural-looking wig.

"We don't do meals," said Danny, pulling the pint, "just snacks, there's a couple of 'Dooley's Delicious Pork Pies' fresh in this morning, there's pickled eggs, and there's crisps." He put the drink on the bar in front of Peter.

"I'll take both of the pies," said Peter, "and a packet of bacon flavoured crisps if you've got them, how much is that?

"Two fifty six to you. Are you from these parts, I don't think I've seen you around here before?" inquired Danny handing Peter the change from a fiver.

"Magherafelt originally," said Peter taking a long swig from the glass, "Jesus, that's beautiful, you obviously keep a good cellar." He finished the Guinness in one more swig and handed Danny the glass. "I'll have another one of those please but I promise to drink it more slowly next time." He began cutting into one of the pies and reached for the mustard on a tray at the end of the bar.

"I'm a welder in a Belfast yard nowadays, hot smelly boring bloody job but it pays well. Got a decent bike out of it though, gets me about, love touring and camping around, never been this way before though, lovely countryside. How far are we from Donegal?" He was deliberately talking loudly with his mouth full trying to appear casual. The assembled patrons of Danny's bar listened intently and muttered among themselves.

Patrick O'Riordan, who was sitting by himself in a corner, got up and went outside to look at the Gold Wing. It was gorgeous, Christ wouldn't he just love one of those;

he'd piss off to pastures new if he had one. He went back inside.

"Beautiful bike," he said with his thumb up to Peter as he passed and went back to his seat.

'That was O'Riordan,' thought Peter, 'I could take the pair of them out right now and save Leo the bother but we would probably lose the others, best wait.'

"Best thing I ever bought," he shouted back to O'Riordan, "would you like a drink?"

Danny shot O'Riordan a glance and he got the message.

"No thanks, I'm just on my way, maybe some other time." He got up and walked out.

Liam Casey's sister's house was in one of the nicer suburbs of Belfast city on a wide street lined with beech trees on both sides. It was the kind of street where you might find professional people, doctors, dentists, teachers, solicitors or retired business people living next door to each other.

Leo had learned from Meehan that his niece was called Siobhan and that her last known address was in Belfast. He wondered what Miss Casey did for a living to afford to live in an area like this. He drove past the house and glanced up at the windows. The curtains were drawn but it was only 7 p.m. and still daylight. It was a fair bet that someone in there had something to hide.

As he drove slowly past, the front door opened and a young woman came out and locked the door behind her. Leo parked between two trees and watched through the offside wing mirror as she walked towards him. He pretended to look at something on a clipboard that he pulled from under the seat as she passed but she did not even appear to notice him. He got out and locked the car then followed her at a discreet distance.

Just around the next corner, she went into the local Catholic Church and Leo followed. Inside the church she put money into the candle-box and took a candle, lit it and placed it with the others. She knelt and prayed while Leo himself took a candle and followed her. He lit and placed the candle and knelt about a metre to her right and studied her out of the corner of his eye.

She was quite beautiful with jet-black curly hair that shone in the candlelight. Her skin was pale and wonderfully smooth. She reminded him of his mother when she was younger, and a strange new sensation went through him as he gazed at her.

She flinched as though a charge of electricity had just shot through her body. She turned and looked directly into Leo's eyes. They held each other's gaze for what seemed like an eternity and slowly she began to smile at him. She was more than just beautiful, she was . . . . , he could not think of a suitable adjective. He smiled back at her.

"I'm sorry," he said, "I didn't mean to stare at you.

She blushed, looked at the floor for a few seconds, before looking up again with a hand across her mouth to hide a smile. The priest, who was watching them from a distance, cleared his throat to let them know he was there. They stood up and walked to the door still staring at each other until they got outside. Leo held out his hand and said,

"Hello, I'm Leo, how do you do."

She hesitated for a moment then took the outstretched hand and shook it firmly and smiled. He was quite good looking she thought.

"I'm Siobhan and I'm fine thank you," she said, "do you live around here?"

"No, I've got digs in town but I got up late and missed mass this morning. I was working in the area when I saw the church. I thought I would light a candle for the poor sod I've been to visit today. He's recovering from a drug-overdose, I'm a social worker," he lied easily. "I take it you live in the area?"

"Just around the corner actually, I don't normally talk to strangers. But when I saw you in church just then, I had the strangest feeling that we had met somewhere before," she said. "I'm sorry, I was mistaken I must be getting back." She turned to go.

"That would explain the flinch then, was it like an electric shock?" asked Leo.

She swung round. "How did you . . . . ?"

"Because I felt it too," he said, interrupting her. He left her standing there with her mouth open and went back to his car. He waved to her as he drove past and she involuntarily waved back but stopped her hand in mid-wave.

It was around 7.30 a.m. the following morning when Leo parked on a piece of open ground at the top of the road where Siobhan lived. Half an hour later, she came out of the house and set off down the street. Leo followed at a distance and watched her while she boarded a bus. He noted the number and destination then went back to his car and gave chase. He had no problem catching up as the bus halted at stop after stop until it came to a row of shops on the other side of town. Siobhan got off and walked about two hundred yards to the supermarket where she worked.

God but she was beautiful, he knew instinctively that he fancied her but he did not know how to handle it. It was a sensation he had never felt before with any of the casual girl friends he had known. He wondered if he should hand over the job of taking in Liam Casey to another colleague but thought better of it, he'd drawn the name from the hat and there was a duty to be carried out. He thought about Peter and his theory on fate, 'if it happens it happens and if it doesn't, it isn't meant to'. They had laughed when Peter had said, "as the Irishman said to the chiropodist, 'me fate is in your hands.'

Brannigan was in a quandary, what the hell had happened to Meehan and Casey. Why had they disappeared? Had they done a runner, had they been lifted, where the fuck were they? He searched his mind for an answer and suddenly remembered a snippet of information. Casey was a pal of O'Riordan's from way back when they were kids in Belfast. Cunningham had mentioned something about a sister but Brannigan had only been half listening to the boring old fart at the time because Cunningham had a habit of rambling on when people were trying to think. Maybe Liam Casey had done a runner and was hiding at his sister's place. But where did she live? O'Riordan might know.

Brannigan phoned Danny and asked him to extract the information from O'Riordan as surreptitiously as he could; Danny was good at the cock-and-bull stuff. After a few free beers and an innocent question or two O'Riordan would unwittingly tell all. Danny had the address within the hour.

Brannigan never ventured into Belfast if he could avoid it. He had made an enemy of the local crime boss there when they were both young bloods in the IRA in the days before the Provisionals.

*

Forty years earlier, at the age of eighteen and newly initiated into the Derry Brigade of the IRA, Brannigan had been sent to Belfast to carry out an undercover assassination as an initiation test of loyalty. The intended victim was a taxi driver with a reputation for talking too much. He had a habit of chatting to all of his fares about religion and politics and boasted that he knew most of the Players in both the Loyalist and Republican camps. It was his misfortune one day to harangue a senior Player from Derry who was visiting his opposite number in Belfast and whose name the taxi driver had mentioned. When the Derry man reported the fact to his colleague, it was decided that the 'gob shite' must be silenced. The Derry man offered the services of his new recruit, Mark Thomas Brannigan, for the job so as not to compromise the Belfast Brigade

Brannigan was duly dispatched to Belfast with instructions and a photograph of a co-apprentice Belfast Brigade contact. They met as arranged in the Central Station bar and became instant buddies; the contact was Daniel Monaghan, known to his friends as Danny. That night, they toured the Catholic bars where Danny introduced Brannigan as his long lost cousin from Derry.

The following day, they went to the station taxi rank where Danny pointed out the target. That night, they planned how they would go about luring the man to his death then went on the town to celebrate without a hint of conscience.

Brannigan was at the station when his victim turned up for work the next morning. He went straight to the man and asked him if he could get him to Larne in time for the 11 a.m. ferry to Stranraer in Scotland. The taxi driver said that it would take about two hours but the cost of going all that way by taxi could be prohibitive. Brannigan produced a huge wad of notes and he told the taxi driver that it was not a big problem he just had to get him there in a hurry. The man's eyes lit up at the sight of the wad and told Brannigan to get in and hold on to his seat.

The driver talked incessantly as he weaved in and out of the early morning traffic and headed towards the coast road. The J type Vauxhall cruised along at 80 mph after they eventually hit the open road which was not very busy.

Brannigan was bored to tears listening to the driver's ramblings and wished to hell the job was finished. At length, he tapped the man on the shoulder and told him that he thought that a car had been following them all the way from Belfast. The man looked in his rear view mirror and saw the Morris Minor that matched his speed. He slowed to 40 mph and the Morris Minor slowed down to the same speed. He got up to 70 mph and the other car did the same. After two more miles of alternating his speed, the driver told Brannigan that he was worried and asked him what he thought he should do. Brannigan suggested that he stop at the next lay-by and if the other car did the same, it was a fair bet that he was being tailed. That worried the driver even more.

"What would you suggest if he does follow me into the lay-by?" the man had asked.

"Just sit tight and see if the driver gets out of the car." Brannigan had suggested.

"And if he does?" the man had asked in a worried tone.

"Wait until he gets up to the taxi, then hit the accelerator and put your foot down." Brannigan had answered.

When they reached the next lay-by, the taxi driver pulled in and waited. The Morris Minor stopped about six meters behind but the driver did not get out. Brannigan pressed the Luger pistol into the back of the driver's seat and squeezed the trigger. The man shot forward onto the steering wheel and died instantly with a bullet through the heart that left a gaping exit hole in his chest. Brannigan caught him by the collar and propped his head against the door pillar as though he was taking a rest. He coolly joined his new friend in the Morris Minor and together they returned to Belfast. Brannigan was now a blooded IRA killer having passed his initiation test.

He stayed on in Belfast and gradually gained a name for himself. But he was regarded as an outsider and made a few enemies among some who were jealous of his popularity with the IRA godfathers. One of them eventually shopped him to the authorities as an active member of the IRA. He was duly tried and jailed for the offence.

Danny Monaghan found out the name of the informant and, suitably hooded to conceal his identity, he shot the man dead in front of his wife and four children.

*

Nowadays, when Brannigan did go to Belfast, it was usually for a Sinn Fein political meeting and he did not hang about for too long afterwards. At one such meeting, he had befriended a member of the opposition, a UDA man called McCann. They were on opposite sides of the political fence but on the same side of the law, the wrong side. Brannigan had heard of McCann's reputation as a criminal and looked upon him as a kind of soul brother who exploited the troubles for his own ends. He put in a call to a go-between in Belfast and left a message for McCann to call him on a phone box number at a specific time. He was on his way to the farm the next morning to meet Danny Monaghan and Sean Cunningham, when he stopped at the nominated lonely phone box. McCann called on time and Brannigan asked him if he would do him a couple of favours for old time's sake. McCann readily agreed.

Peter had spent part of the previous evening briefing two of his troopers, Mal Spencer and George Davidson, posing as policemen in RUC uniform. They had mocked-up one of the army Land Rovers to look like an RUC vehicle by painting it grey. The men were on standby under a camouflage net off the main road behind a spinney about a mile from Danny's Bar in case Peter needed them in a hurry.

After briefing the two pseudo RUC men, Peter sneaked up on Geordie and Jock in the LUP that they had set up the night before within sight of the recently moved PIRA arms cache. He was within a few feet of where they lay concealed and could just about hear their conversation by cupping his right ear in his hand. Geordie was whispering.

"I'm just a bit worried about our lass, the bairn is almost due and she keeps writing to ask if I'm getting any leave. Women just don't understand do they? I mean you can't just piss off on leave at a minutes notice because your wife's having her first bairn, not when you're in a job like this."

"It depends what your priorities are pal, I'm no' married m'sel but if I was, my wife and kid would come before anything. But maybe that's why you're a Sergeant and I'm still a bloody Trooper."

"Have you done any promotion courses yet Jock?"

"I did a Corporals course while I was in 2 Para but I was called for Selection before the results came through, so I don't know how I did."

Peter made a mental note to contact the Para Records Office.

"Bang, you're dead," he said as he approached them from behind.

Geordie feigned surprise and called him a 'sneaky Makam bastard' and Peter pretended to be hurt. They had a giggle and he left them to return to his pup tent in the field opposite Danny's bar.

Danny Monaghan had returned from the farm by the time Peter turned up at the pub for a couple of jars and a snack at lunchtime.

There was a highly polished black Jaguar car in the pub car park when Peter parked his bike. He hadn't a clue about who owned it and he did not recognise the smartly dressed Sinn Fein MP, Mark Thomas Brannigan, sitting in the corner of the room where O'Riordan had sat the night before.

Peter was on his second pint when the door opened and a man with a freckled face and bright ginger hair strolled up to the bar. He turned and nodded to the smartly dressed man who raised his glass in recognition.

"Givvus a pint of Guinness Danny," said Flynn, looking at Peter with narrowed eyes as he spoke. Peter just smiled at Flynn and raised his glass at him while Danny pulled the man a pint. Peter had his hand in his pocket and his finger on the coms button, which he pressed three times. The Guinness was taking it's time in coming as Flynn waited and continued to eye-up Peter with an unwavering and unnerving stare. Peter went to take a drink from his glass when a figure dashed into the bar from outside and warned.

"There's an RUC Land Rover coming fast up the road."

Peter grabbed his crash helmet and made for the back door at the run. He jumped on the Gold Wing and started the engine as Flynn burst through the doorway behind him and looked around like a scared rabbit.

"Get on," shouted Peter.

Flynn hesitated for a split second then made up his mind. He dived on behind Peter who let out the clutch and shot out of the car park and up the road towards the border. Shots rang out behind them as the Land Rover gave chase but the bike was too fast, streaking up the road at almost 100 mph.

Flynn clung on for dear life and tried to keep his head out of the wind that stung his eyes and pulled at his red hair. Two miles up the road Peter pulled off onto a track and made for the site of the arms cache. When he stopped, Flynn was off the bike first, pulling a gun from the waistband of his trousers and confronting Peter.

In the observation post, Geordie Shiells froze as he realised that Peter was between him and Flynn. He dare not move in case Flynn fired, he could only hope that Peter would move to one side or that Flynn was just being over cautious. Neither of them moved position as Peter half raised his hands in a gesture of submission.

"You have a nice way of showing your gratitude," he said to Flynn. "Why the hell did you follow me out and whose bloody side are you on anyway?"

"Shut your fuckin' mouth, I'll ask the questions," said Flynn. "Now who the fuck are you and why did you run out like that?" he demanded. "It had better be good or you're fuckin' dead."

"The names Pete Bailey and I was at Danny's waiting for a contact."

"What kind of contact, who sent you" asked Flynn, his gun pointing at Peter's forehead?

Peter took a chance. "Does the name Cluskey mean anything to you?"

Flynn lowered the weapon and said, "The Quartermaster, he sent you?"

Geordie relaxed.

"Yes," said Peter. "Someone was supposed to meet me at Danny's bar yesterday. I was told it was a safe house, but I'm not so sure now. Was it you I was supposed to meet? I'm sorry I don't know your name."

"Never mind me, why did you run?"

"I'm wanted, why did you run?

"I don't like the fuckin' RUC that's why. I thought they were onto me."

"Why, what have you done?"

"That's for me to know. What are you doing up here near the border?"

"I have some stuff to hand over but Cluskey wouldn't give me a name, he was ever the cautious one. He said his contact would get in touch with me at Danny's."

"What's to hand over?"

"It's over here, it was moved recently from near Cluskey's place after one of his team was taken into custody," said Peter deliberately turning his back on Flynn and walking towards the arms cache that had been exposed by Geordie and Jock.

Flynn moved forward stood with his back to Peter, now confident that they were both on the same side, and stared down into the hole.

"So that's why Brannigan was at Danny's," said Flynn, thinking out loud.

'So that's who the well dressed gentleman was' thought Peter, and the picture of a much younger Brannigan flashed through his mind. Out loud he said, "Thanks Flynn."

Flynn froze in the realisation that he had not told Peter his name. The thought sped through his brain and exited via the frontal lobe with the help on a 9mm bullet from Geordie's Browning. Flynn pitched headlong onto the plastic sheet covering the arms cache in the pit; his body twitched a couple of times before lying still and lifeless. Peter crossed himself and holstered the weapon he had half drawn from his leather jacket.

"Poor psycho bastard," he whispered, "one down six to go".

"F'kin'ell Makam, that was close, I was shiters, I thought you were going to cop it there," said Geordie as he and Jock ran forward from the OP.

"Thanks Geordie," said Peter. "Did you do the business on that lot?" he asked, pointing to the pit.

"To the letter boss, we gave the rifle barrels a little squeeze. If anybody tries to use them, they'll blow their friggin' heads off. The ammo's been contaminated with acid and the fertilizer has been neutralised. All we have to do is cover the cache and leave Flynn as a nasty surprise, OK?"

"Brilliant," said Peter. "Well done lads, see you back at the hanger."

Back at Danny's Bar, Brannigan could not fathom what was going down, he saw Peter move first when the RUC Land Rover arrived and he saw Flynn follow him out the back. The last thing he saw was the Land Rover speeding off in pursuit of the faster Gold Wing with Flynn on the pillion his red hair flowing in the slip stream. Could he and the biker possibly have known each other; who the hell was the stranger anyway?

He told Danny to get hold of Sean Cunningham and Dixie Dixon and to meet him at the farm the following morning He then made himself scarce before the Land Rover returned. It drove past Danny's bar half an hour later carrying two extra passengers along with their kit.

Leo had parked the Ford Escort in a public car park before going in search of breakfast. He'd wandered around the shops killing time until lunchtime found him along the street from the supermarket where Siobhan worked. He saw her come out and glance up and down the road before walking to a ladies clothing shop further along the street. She emerged fifteen minutes later carrying her purchases and went into a cafe' further along.

He waited a few minutes before following her inside. She was sitting half way along the wall opposite the counter at a table for two with her back to the door. He ordered coffee and a light snack and made his way to where she sat. Approaching her from behind, he said, "Excuse me is that anyone's seat?"

He feigned surprise as she turned and answered in the negative then he gasped in recognition. "Good God, it's you from the church last night! What are you doing at this side of town?"

"I work at the supermarket just along the road, what are you doing here?" she asked, with an equal look of surprise.

"I have a couple of druggies to see in the area," he lied, "It's a never ending battle. Do you mind if I join you?"

"Be my guest, I'll have to be going shortly anyway, I only have an hour for lunch and I've spent half of it shopping. I normally have lunch in the staff room otherwise we would not have met again," she said, looking at her watch.

"That would have been a pity," he said, "It really is nice to see you again. It must be kismet."

"What's that when it's at home?" She asked.

"Arabic for destiny," he answered, smiling.

She blushed again. He was very nice and she was enjoying the attention. She did not bother much with men or rather men didn't bother much with her. They stared a lot but did not make advances. But then again, she rarely went out at night, she preferred to sit and read and keep her own company. She didn't like going alone to pubs or clubs, it was not her scene and most of her work friends lived too far away from her side of town.

"Would you think I was forward if I asked you out to dinner tonight?" he asked. "I would really like to get to know you better."

"Yes, I would think you were forward, I've never been asked to dinner before." She answered.

"That is unbelievable, would you accept?" he persisted.

She felt a little thrill. "Where did you have in mind?" she asked.

"Do you like Chinese food?" he asked. "I know a good Chinese restaurant in the city I've eaten there on quite a few occasions."

"Do you take all your girlfriends there?" she asked, feeling a little apprehensive about what he might answer.

"I don't have any girlfriends," he said truthfully.

She got up to leave and walked towards the door without giving him an answer. He stood up and watched her go then she stopped and turned.

"What time?" she asked.

His heart rate quickened with a touch of excitement. "I'll pick you up at 8 p.m. what number is your house?" he asked, knowing full well.

"Twenty eight," she said then she was gone.

She almost floated back to the supermarket and spent the afternoon in a dream state; she had a smile for every customer. Mother of mercy she was in love, oh God she was in love. At tea break, she told her friends about the meeting with the handsome social worker and about the dinner date.

Leo finished his lunch then returned to Bessbrook; Peter and his section returned shortly afterwards. He told Leo about his encounter with Flynn and how Geordie Shiells had taken him out. He told him about seeing Brannigan, O'Riordan and Monaghan, about his intention to stakeout the farm with the troop and, hopefully round up the whole gang in one operation.

Leo told him about his date with Liam Casey's sister but neglected to tell him his feelings for her. He did not wish to be taken off the assignment until he had completed his mission to bring Casey in despite the difficult situation.

On the night of their date, Leo parked his car on open ground at the top of the street where Siobhan lived. All the spaces between the beech trees lining her street were already filled with the residents' cars.

He didn't take much notice of the man on the trials bike that pulled away from opposite Siobhan's house. But the naturally observant man had recognised Leo's car, he had seen it on several occasions prior to his gang being ambushed by the SAS and now, unfortunately, he had seen Leo. McCann sped off to report to Brannigan.

Leo rang Sid Morrell's taxi firm on his mobile.

Chapter 5

Leo knocked at the door of number 28 at precisely 8 p.m. Seconds later, the door opened and Siobhan stood framed in the entrance. She had taken the trouble to dress for the occasion and she looked stunning in a high-necked Chinese-style blue dress. Leo took a pace back and almost stumbled off the step with surprise and delight. She went to grab him and ended up in his arms as he steadied himself. Their eyes met for a moment and he had to stifle the urge to kiss her. Instead, he held her at arms length and looked her up and down.

"Wow," he said, "you look absolutely terrific did you buy the dress especially for the occasion?"

"No," she said, "it was my mother's, she bought in the sixties when they were all the rage and kept it, I can't bear to part with it." The taxi arrived and took them to the Blue Dragon in Victoria Square.

McCann managed to contact Brannigan by 8.30 p.m. He told him about the red Escort and about the driver who he now suspected of being an undercover member of either MI6 or possibly special branch. He told him about the ambush of his men on the republican estate and how he had seen the Escort on several occasions prior to the ambush and had put two and two together. Brannigan thanked him for the information and told him to stand down while he took care of the situation. McCann did not protest, he told Brannigan he would do as he was asked but he already had other ideas.

Leo and Siobhan talked throughout the meal with the ease of two people who had known each other all their lives. Fleeting moments of unease drifted in and out of Leo's mind as he realised that he was hopelessly falling in love with the sister of an enemy of the people. He'd been out with girls before but this was different and he felt it difficult to come to terms with his feelings. It passed through his mind to come clean and tell her why he was there but he suppressed the notion.

"Do you still live with your parents?" he asked casually.

She lowered her head and the happiness that had shone in her face a moment before, turned into a look of sadness.

"They were both killed in a car accident some years ago," she half whispered. "There's only my brother Liam and I now but he went to live with an uncle in Buncrana."

Leo gave a silent sigh of relief at the thought that her brother might not be staying with her.

"Oh God, I am sorry," he said. "Shall I change the subject?"

"No it's OK, it was a long time ago and I'm over it now but my brother has never recovered properly from the trauma."

Leo seized the moment, gently taking hold of her hand.

"In what way?" he asked, genuinely concerned.

"Up until the time when my parents were killed, he had always been a well behaved kid. He was fourteen years old at the time, four years younger than me. I was due to go to university but I had to forego the opportunity to look after him. As the eldest, I inherited the house and some money held for us both in trust that I've left untouched although I can access it if I want to now that I'm past twenty one." She paused for a drink then carried on. "Liam got in with a wrong crowd of kids and was constantly in and out of trouble until he was eighteen years old when, about four years ago, my uncle Barney offered to take him off my hands."

"And I take it you have not seen him since," said Leo, "what does he do for a living?"

She paused for a moment before answering. "Whatever he does, he won't tell me, he turned up out of the blue a couple of days ago and asked if he could stay for a while. I'm worried about him I think he's running away from something because he told me not to tell anyone where he was."

"Why are you telling me?" asked Leo

"Because I trust you," said Siobahn

Leo flinched with a feeling of guilt but continued.

"To do what?" he asked

"Talk to him, find out what's wrong. It's your job isn't it? You are an experienced social worker and I can't handle it," she said, tightening her grip on his hand.

"Would he see me?" asked Leo

"Wait a minute," she said, getting up to go to the phone.

Leo watched her as she went to the reception desk and asked for permission to make a call. She spoke quietly into the mouthpiece for ten minutes or so, turning now and again to look at him as she spoke, then she returned to the table.

"He says he'll talk to you, he was reluctant at first and accused me of betrayal but I convinced him of the confidential nature of your job and he agreed to see you. I think he needs to get something off his chest before he bursts." She took his hand and looked at him pleadingly.

Leo felt like a complete fraud but at least he was getting closer to Liam Casey. God he hated himself right now. He wondered how it would all end and if she would ever forgive his deception. He paid the bill, called Sid Morrell and waited.

Liam Casey put down the phone and wondered if he had done the right thing by agreeing to see a complete stranger. Siobhan had assured him that the man was a trained counsellor and could be relied upon. He trusted his sister, and he was trapped. He wanted to be free of his uncle Barney and the bloody Provisional IRA. He wanted to lead an ordinary life. After all, he had done nothing really terrible, but then, there was the car.

On the day of the Ballykelly bombing, he had been waiting for O'Riordan to return home. He'd stayed with him the night before and put away a few cans of Dutch courage prior to his friend's initiation test. He'd watched the 11 a.m. news on television and realised to his horror that his two second cousins would have been on the school bus. He'd rushed off to comfort his uncle Barney but as he neared the house, he saw him drive away. He followed at a distance along lonely winding lanes that led to an unmanned border crossing and watched him park just across the border and wait. He was tempted to approach on his motorbike but held back near some bushes, sensing that something was not quite right. His uncle was acting out of character; he never went near the border if he could help it. He saw the armed and hooded men emerge from cover, get into the car, and drive off with his uncle. Were they IRA or security forces? Liam could not tell. It looked as though the meeting had been prearranged and that Meehan had possibly turned informer. Dismissing the idea as ludicrous, Liam returned to Buncrana and packed a few personal possessions into a rucksack then set off for Belfast and his sister's house, she'd always protected him. As he drove, he wondered if O'Riordan had managed to get away, there would be serious repercussions as a result of the Ballykelly bombing.

Roland 'Dixie' Dixon's mind was in a state of turmoil as he waited for Siobhan and the red Escort driver to arrive back to the parked car. At the top of the street, on the piece of open ground, Dixie's white van was parked about a hundred metres from Leo's vehicle.

Brannigan had managed to get hold of Dixon after McCann had called. It had taken Dixie just half an hour to knock-up a car bomb and to attach a strong magnet with which to fix it beneath the Escort. He had been instructed by Brannigan to trigger it by remote control to make sure that the suspect M16 agent was permanently removed from the game.

By the time he had arrived in Belfast and found the street where Siobhan lived, and where the red Escort was parked, it was dark enough for him to slip across the open ground and attach the bomb. He returned to his van and sipped poteen as he waited for the unfortunate intended victim to return. He had been warned to keep off the 'mountain tea' when he was working but how would Brannigan know if he'd disobeyed and taken a wee drop? 'Fuck Brannigan, Doonan was his real boss' he thought. Twenty minutes and half a bottle of poteen later he was sound asleep on a grubby mattress in the back of the van.

McCann had also made up his mind to do something about the Escort and the suspected undercover man who had been the undoing of his hit team. Was he SAS, MI6 or special branch he wondered? Never mind, he'd be dead whatever he was, McCann would make sure of that and Brannigan would thank him for it, he would owe him a favour or two.

He set about making a highly complicated device he called a 'pendulum bomb'. After a few mishaps in the past when some of his victims had escaped with serious injuries instead of being blown to pieces, he had devised a new kind of bomb that would fit under the driving seat instead of beneath the car. When the bomb was secured, all he had to do was remove a retaining pin and the pendulum would be free to swing when the car was driven off, activating the detonator.

It was gone 11.30 p.m. when the taxi pulled up at Siobhan's house. The place was in darkness and the heavy curtains in the living room had been drawn for two days. Siobhan switched on the light to reveal an unshaven and dishevelled Liam Casey slumped in an armchair beside the fireplace. He looked thin and pale through lack of sleep, huge bags hung under his eyes. His shoulders were rounded as he hunched forward; he looked twenty years older than his twenty-two years.

Leo recognised him immediately as the man he had been sent to arrest but for the sake of Siobhan, he would hear the man out and decide accordingly what action to take. He went over and held out his hand in implied friendship but Liam just stared at him with dark sad eyes.

Leo drew up a chair and sat directly opposite him. He put a hand on his shoulder and squeezed gently as he said, "Come on my friend, I'd like to help you if I can but you have to tell me what's worrying you, is it drugs?" he asked, knowing the real answer.

Liam continued to stare at the stranger then suddenly gave way to a cry of bottled-up anguish followed by a flood of tears. Siobhan ran forward and cradled her brother's head in her arms and looked tearfully at Leo with pleading eyes.

Leo swallowed a lump in his throat and turned away from them wondering what to do next. Shit! He was going soft but composed himself immediately and looked around for the location of the kitchen and a temporary escape.

"A brew might help," he said, "if you will show me where the kitchen is then maybe we can sit down and talk this thing out, whatever it is." Siobhan pointed him in the direction of the kitchen while she continued to cradle her brother.

Leo took his time making a pot of tea while he thought about how to proceed. It would be easy just to arrest the guy now and take him in but there was something niggling about the man. He seemed to be a bit too timid to be seriously tied up with a bunch of killers and gangsters. And of course, there was also his new love to think about, he felt he owed it to her to hear what her brother had to say; some hard arsed SAS soldier he had turned out to be. He shrugged his shoulders in resignation and carried the tray of tea into the living room. Liam had stopped his weeping and looked more in control. Siobhan played mother while Liam began his story.

*

He was just 14 years old, four years younger than Siobhan, when their parents had been tragically killed in a car accident. Their only living relatives were a widowed uncle in Buncrana and a cousin in Ballykelly who was married to a farmer. Their uncle, Barney Meehan, and their mother had fallen out about something when Barney last visited the family when Siobhan was only 5 years old and Liam was just a baby. They never found out what the argument was about, their mother would not have her brother's name mentioned in the house. Whatever it was about, Barney Meehan never visited his sister again.

It was several weeks after the tragic accident that Meehan wrote and conveyed his condolences and saying how sorry he was that he had missed the funeral. He also said that if there was anything they ever needed, he would try to help in any way he could.

Siobhan's university education was put on hold while she set about looking after them both. She took a job in a supermarket across town and settled down to a kind of single-parent existence. They had the security of the house, their parent's nest egg, the accident insurance, and substantial compensation from the insurance company of the drunken driver who had ploughed head-on into their parent's car. They were left reasonably comfortable although none of the money in trust could be touched until Siobhan was 21 years old.

Liam however, was badly traumatised by the loss of their parents and began to play up. He was forever in trouble at school and afterwards in the evenings that he spent with a gang of unsavoury youths. Patrick O'Riordan, an older boy, was the ringleader and the only son of aged parents who had great difficulty in controlling him. He was a budding criminal and a bad influence on Liam who followed him around like a little pup.

Siobhan put up with all the bad behaviour for two years until Liam left school and looked for a job despite the fact that he was given the chance to stay on for further education. Jobs came and went on an almost monthly basis because of his increasingly unsocial behaviour. Eventually, he was caught in possession of stolen goods after the gang broke into a wholesale electrical business premises.

O'Riordan and the other members of the gang had managed to evade capture. Liam was sent to a young offenders detention centre for three months. He was now a hero in the eyes of the others because he had refused to grass on them.

Siobhan, now 21 years old, continued with her job at the supermarket. She became increasingly concerned for Liam's future as a potential gangster. She decided to write and ask her Uncle Barney's advice, although she did not know him at all.

Uncle Barney replied immediately and expressed concern for Liam and said he would be pleased to take him under his wing. He also wrote to Liam and invited him to visit for a holiday in order to get to know the boy before fully committing himself.

Liam was excited at the prospect of the visit; he had never been across the border. He wrote and accepted Meehan's invitation and asked if he could bring his best friend with him for company. Uncle Barney had said 'yes' and two weeks later, Liam Casey and Patrick O'Riordan turned up on his doorstep.

Barney took to the boys immediately. They were young and handsome and brimming with energy. Liam reminded Barney of himself at that age. They were boisterous and boastful, but most of all, potential PIRA recruits. The lads being petty criminals appeared to be more of an asset than a liability to the Provo's, it made them more malleable.

They spent the next two weeks sightseeing in both the north and the south. Barney educated them as they went along. He recounted the history of the country from as far back as the Celtic kingdom, the potato famines of the 19th century, the absentee landlords, the deaths of a million starving people and the exodus of a million others, and the events that led right up to the present tribal warfare. The boys were impressed by his knowledge of the past 300 years and beyond.

He preached to them about the futility of petty crime when there were better ways of making money. The boys listened and promised to mend their ways if Barney would be prepared to guide them. He told them that if they ever felt like quitting Belfast, they could stay with him and he would try to find them work.

They returned to Belfast with a different outlook on life and took jobs together as packers in a factory. After six months of regular pay packets, they had not put a foot wrong and Siobhan heaved a sigh of relief. She wrote to her uncle and thanked him for his trouble, telling him that he had worked wonders in just a couple of weeks.

Sometime later, Patrick O'Riordan's mother died after a stroke. A week after that, his father died of a broken heart. O'Riordan was left with a furnished terraced house and no money so far as he knew. He had fleeced his parents of everything he could since he was a small boy and they had spoiled him with their giving. However, he did find little stashes of cash around the house and there were insurance policies that amounted to more than the burial fees.

His uncle, who had been named as executor of the will, took Patrick to one side after the funeral and produced a savings account in his name. To his surprise, his parents had deposited thousands of pounds on his behalf since he had been born. He felt a touch of remorse for the way he had repaid them, but it was only a touch.

Now that he was alone in the world, O'Riordan suggested to Liam that they should quit Belfast and take up his Uncle Barney's offer to find them a job in the south. Liam talked it over with Siobhan and suggested that now he was 18 years old, he was capable of looking after himself with Uncle Barney's help and she would now be free to go to university. Siobhan had mixed feelings about him leaving home for good but she felt it would be selfish of her to hold him back. At least he would be under the influence of Uncle Barney who would hopefully keep him out of trouble. She kissed him and wished him luck.

Liam wrote to his uncle with all the news and asked him if his offer still stood. Barney wrote back and said he would be delighted to see them both again and that he was sure that he could find work for them.

The boys gave two weeks notice at the factory and began to prepare for a new and exciting life in the south away from the turmoil of Belfast. O'Riordan asked his uncle to arrange for the disposal of the house and contents keeping the proceeds from the contents for his trouble; his uncle agreed.

Patrick and Liam had not, however, completely reformed. In order to get to Buncrana, they intended to steal a car rather than use public transport that had been painfully slow the last time they'd used it to go there. Patrick had set his sights on a nice little yellow VW Beetle some time ago. It belonged to a rival suitor of a girl he'd fancied but the bodybuilding boyfriend had threatened to cut his dick off and stuff down his throat if he did not back off. Beneath the tough-guy veneer, O'Riordan was a bit of a whimp like most of his kind. Stealing the bloke's beloved car was the best he could think of for taking revenge.

He and Liam had enjoyed stealing cars and joy riding during their early teens until they were almost killed by an army patrol one night. They had refused to stop when confronted and narrowly missed one of the soldiers who dived out of the way as they sped past. The other soldiers opened fire but by some miracle, they had escaped injury apart from a few scratches from flying glass when the rear window was shot out. It was the last time they ever stole a car but they had not forgotten how to do it.

O'Riordan knew the gym where the bodybuilder worked-out for three nights every week. Behind the building was an unlit staff and customer car park. Having made their farewells to Siobhan and their mates, the boys took a taxi to within a few hundred yards of the premises. They were dressed in tracksuits and trainers and carried their luggage in sports bags. No one took any notice as they turned off the busy street and into the car park behind the gym.

O'Riordan was in the car in seconds and had it hot-wired in quick time. He pulled away slowly and eased into the traffic heading for Strabane and the border. Barney had shown them a couple of farm track crossing points that avoided contact with the police and the military.

Barney Meehan was pleased to see them both and greeted them with hugs and handshakes. He had been a lonely man since his Nancy had died but he hadn't realised how much until the boys' last visit. He could not have been more pleased to see them.

Although it was after midnight when they arrived, Barney insisted on knocking up a huge meal. They chatted over cans of beer until 3 a.m. when Barney said casually. "Nice little car Patrick, have you just bought it?"

O'Riordan smiled and bragged, "I stole it just before we left." He was grinning from ear to ear.

Barney's attitude suddenly changed as he stood up, knocking back his chair as he did so. "You did what?" he shouted.

"I stole it," repeated O'Riordan. The grin now replaced with a sheepish look.

"Jesus feckin' Christ," said Barney, calming down almost as quickly as he had exploded. "I guessed you were a couple of feckin' hotheads but I didn't think you were feckin' stupid with it. The last thing I need is a feckin' stolen car outside my feckin' door. What the feck am I going to do with you?" He was now smiling and shaking his head. He picked up the phone and dialled.

Liam wondered who he could be phoning this time of morning. He looked at O'Riordan who seemed to guess what he was thinking; he just shrugged.

"Dixie?" said Barney to the voice on the other end of the phone. "I'm pleased you're still awake, how much of the mountain tea have you drunk?"

The answer must have been reassuring.

"Right, I want you to get hold of Sean Cunningham as soon as you can and get yourselves over here. I have a hot motor to get rid of, have you still got that empty shed on you allotment?" He paused for the answer, "good, can you stick it in there until a job comes up? I'll contact you-know-who and let him know." He put down the phone without as much as a 'thank you' and 'good night'.

When they awoke the following morning, the car was gone. From that moment, the boys belonged to the Provisional IRA.

*

"How are you involved with the Provos?" Leo asked Liam.

"Uncle Barney made me a courier, travelling between cells with written messages and small packages that would not be safe in the post. I've acted as a lookout on a few occasions but apart from that, Uncle Barney has kept me away from the rough stuff."

"What about your pal O'Riordan?" asked Leo.

"After we had finished our training in the south, he bought a cottage, not far from Uncle Barney, with the money from the sale of his parents' house. He was put to work for the fella named Sean Cunningham who had taken away the car. Patrick doesn't tell me much but I don't think what he does is legal, he's always been that way but apart from that, he's harmless. I couldn't believe that he would blow up a bus full of school kids it just isn't like him. He didn't want to go on the job anyway but they forced him into it."

"Was that the Ballykelly thing on the news the other day?" asked Leo.

"Yes, but I was not involved." Assured Liam

"Why are you on the run then?" asked Leo

He looked at Leo long and hard before he answered. "I simply want out," he said. "Sooner or later they are going to ask me to kill somebody and I couldn't do that. Neither could Patrick but they must have forced him."

He began to cry again. "I couldn't live with a thing like that hanging over me and I feel sure that, wherever he is, if he killed those people, Patrick is feeling suicidal."

"Siobhan took her brother in her arms and cried with him. She obviously had not had the faintest idea about what Liam was going through.

McCann had spent four hours assembling his bomb. He put the detonator in his breast pocket and the bomb into a rucksack. Rather than take his motorbike out on the streets at this time of morning and risk being stopped by the security forces, he took a series of buses laid on for shift workers. They were a safe and secure form of transport that he had used many times before. By 3 a.m., he had managed to get within half a mile of the open ground where Leo's car was parked.

Dixie's body clock began to tick again after the effects of the poteen had worn off and he was dying for a pee. He slipped out of the van and pissed into the bushes behind it. It was 3.15 a.m.; the Escort was still there thank God. He thought he had better try to stay awake in case the driver of the car decided to return. There would be hell to pay from Brannigan if he missed him. He reached for the bottle of poteen then thought better of it.

McCann made a tactical approach towards the parked Escort with the yellow lettering along the sides. The only other vehicles in sight were a long-distance lorry parked at the far end of the open ground and Dixie's white van parked facing the rear of the Escort about a hundred metres away.

Assuming a crouch position, McCann approached the car and broke into it with practiced ease keeping his head well down below the window. He slowly opened the door hoping that there was no alarm fitted and slid into the passenger seat. He removed the bomb from the rucksack, fitted the pendulum-retaining pin then the fuse and gently placed the bomb under the driver's seat. He raised his head a fraction to see if there was anybody about before pulling out the pendulum retainer. It was at this point that Dixie saw the slight movement. God, the driver had sneaked into the bloody car and he had almost missed him. He pointed the remote and flicked the switch.

Both Dixie's and McCann's bombs went off almost simultaneously blowing McCann to pieces and sending fragments of the Escort in all directions. The lock from the boot lid shot out and hurtled like a bullet towards the white van. It took out the windscreen and embedded itself neatly in the forehead between Dixie Dixon's eyes, catapulting him into the back of the vehicle.

At the sound of the massive explosion, Leo ran to the bay window and pulled the curtain aside. Lights were coming on in the houses along the street and people were rushing out to see where the noise had come from. He guessed rightly that it was his car that had been targeted; it was only a matter of time. He told Siobhan and Liam to pack as much as they needed and get ready to move on his say so. He showed authority and they did not argue.

Half way up the street, he stopped in his tracks. He could see a crater where his car had been. Returning to the house, he rang Sid Morrell on the special security number and got him out of bed. He told Sid what had happened and asked him to come personally to collect Siobhan, Liam and himself from the Catholic Church down the street and around the corner from where he had dropped them after the dinner. They left the house by the back entrance, went through the garden and down an ally without being seen. Sid was at the church within ten minutes and fifteen minutes later, they were in the safe house that Leo had used when he was tailing McCann and his gang.

Sid Morrell was an ex SAS sergeant who had retired from 23 battalion SAS Territorial Army Unit in Northumberland in 1992 after seeing service in Northern Ireland, Belize, and the Gulf as a medic. In civilian life, he was a mental nurse just along the road in the town of Prudhoe were he worked at the Geriatric Unit of the hospital not far from the village of Riding Mill in Northumberland where he lived with his widowed mother. He had joined the TA when it was known as the Territorial Army and Volunteer Reserve, in the 1970's. The Association was known as TAVRA.

Sid had spent most of his time-off doing fitness training in the Cheviot Hills where he was obliged, at least once a year, to trudge over forty kilometres in two days in shit order, carrying a fifty pound Bergen as well as an automatic weapon in order to stay in the SAS. He would sometimes get lucky on the odd weekend and wander into the tented TA Field Hospital of 201 Northern General Hospital doing weekend training out of Fenham Barracks in Newcastle. He knew some of the medics and could scrounge a bite and a hot drink before trudging on; scrounging was not against the rules.

He had met and married the lovely Bridie Byrne from Coleraine after working under cover in Northern Ireland. Being a talented folk singer and guitarist, he had used his talent to spy around the pubs and clubs in the province for two weeks every year which constituted his annual camp. He never came under suspicion when the venues were raided and wanted terrorists were arrested.

He grew to love the country and decided to return there when he left the army. TAVRACABS was his idea for the name of his taxi company that provided a secure form of civilian transport for special-forces personnel on covert duty in the province as well as for ordinary civilians. All of his drivers were hand picked loyalists from the various TA units in the area.

Chapter 6

Brinnigan's farmhouse was two miles south of Ballyshiel and a mile from the border with Donegal. From his observation post, set up over night on a boulder-strewn island covered with gorse bushes in the middle of a sloping fallow field, spotted earlier during his aerial reconnaissance, Peter could see the farm buildings clearly. The place looked quite deserted with no vehicles in the outbuildings except for a rusting and battered old tractor. There were no animals in the fields or in the farmyard; in fact there was no sign of life at all. Barney Meehan had said that he had met Thomas Brannigan and Eamon Flynn there on a couple of occasions to plan jobs that were more criminal activity than Provisional IRA business. Meehan had never liked Brannigan but was under orders from Doonan to cooperate fully with him.

Peter, acting as head-shed for this mission, and his troop had taken up their positions in the dead of night. Geordie Shiells, Mal Spencer and Jock Shand were concealed in a small copse on a rise overlooking the other side of the farm. They had sufficient water and compo rations to last them for a couple of days and, in addition to normal coms, Peter had a mobile phone for direct communication with Cedric Parker at the hanger and with Leo presumably in Belfast. It was a pity that it had begun to rain just after Peter and his team had got into position, there was nothing quite like a pissing-wet LUP or OP but by the time dawn broke, the rain had stopped and the clouds were drifting away to the east.

Caretakers Mary and John Kennerley lay naked on the bed staring up at the ceiling while enjoying a smoke. They delighted in being alone together at the farm; it gave them the opportunity to indulge in their favourite pastime, unbridled and uninterrupted sexual intercourse. They were members of Cunningham's cell within Brannigan's gang specialising in the theft of handbags, wallets and anything else that might contain credit cards or cash. Cunningham believed that they were the best husband and wife team in the business.

Their real names were Mary and Kevin Bradley. Kevin was a British Army deserter and both he and his wife were originally from Liverpool. They had met while he was a serving soldier and she was in the WRAC attached to the Royal Army Logistics Corps as a clerk. She had become pregnant and was forced to leave the services. He did the proper thing and married her but she lost the baby.

Sean Cunningham had recruited them some years before when they had gone to Northern Ireland for the funeral of a Catholic relative killed in a shoot-out with an Army patrol. The victim had been a PIRA activist as well as a member of Cunningham's gang. Until that point, Kevin Bradley had considered himself to be a true Englishman.

Cunningham had taken him to one side after the funeral and sales-talked him into desertion from the army and into a lucrative business with him. Mary had been a pushover with the promise of all the trimmings of wealth when Cunningham had also spoken with her afterwards.

What Kevin Bradley did not know however, was that his dead relative had been a spy in Cunningham's camp. He was one of Daniel Doonan's Intelligence Officers and a plant that had kept Doonan informed about the Brannigan gang's criminal activities. It was essential that the PIRA Godfathers could distinguish between what was being perpetrated in their name, and what was criminal activity for personal gain.

Daniel Doonan was incognito at the funeral to pay his respects to his man Frankie Bradley. Other Players at the funeral that recognised him knew better than to approach him direct. If he needed to speak to anyone, it would be on his terms. To those who knew him, his code name was simply 'Dan' if he ever approached them.

He saw Cunningham speaking to the young couple at the reception. The woman was very attractive and stood out among the other females. His curiosity got the better of him, and uncharacteristically, he edged over to the trio.

"Hello there Sean, I haven't seen you in a donkey's age, how are you?"

Cunningham swung round in surprise.

"Oh! Hello Dan, it's nice to see you again after all this time, wasn't it a funeral then?"

"No, it was that wedding in Castlebar when Eamon Devlin married that great big girl from Mulrany, you know, the one with the cruel nick name, what was it now, oh yes, 'The whale of Clew Bay'."

Cunningham and the Bradleys fell about laughing to the disgust of some of the older mourners.

"And who are these fine looking young people Sean, don't I get an introduction?"

"I'm sorry Dan, this is Kevin Bradley, Frankie's cousin, and this is his wife Mary. They are from Liverpool and it's their first time in the Emerald Isle. Kevin's dad went over the water thirty-five years ago to work in the Liverpool docks and never returned, even for a holiday. Kevin here is in the British Army but he is seriously thinking of buying himself out and coming into business with me."

"Kevin and Mary, meet my old friend Dan."

Doonan turned to Kevin and shook hands.

"How do you do young man, and is it that easy to get out of the British Army Kevin?"

"It's no problem, all I have to do is give six months notice, and I'm out."

"What do you think of the old Country now that you are here?"

"We both think it's lovely, dad talked about it quite a lot but we never got that holiday he promised us year after year. He would have been here today but he's in a terrible bad way with his kidneys. He's on dialysis twice a week, and just can't travel at all now. He doesn't touch a drop of the hard stuff these days."

"That's a shame, I never met your father but I knew his brother, Frankie's father, God rest his soul, they were a fine Catholic family. Are you a church man yourself?"

Bradley looked at his wife and took her hand and kissed it.

"Mary and I were married in a Registry Office the church holds no attraction for us. Weddings and funerals are the only time we attend. I even used to scive off church parade in the army. The Padres tried everything to get me to go but it isn't compulsory nowadays thank God, whoops!"

They laughed again and the mourners scowled.

The Bradley's had two weeks leave and the funeral had taken up the first weekend. Doonan invited them to look him up at Murphy's bar in O'Connell Street in Dublin if they managed to get down the country that far. He could be found there most days between noon and 2 p.m., it was his office; they all laughed again, the mourners scowled again. Doonan wished them all 'good luck' and left the reception.

The meeting in Dublin took place the following weekend. The Bradley's were duly inducted into the Provisional IRA and tasked with the ongoing espionage within Sean Cunningham's organisation, without his knowledge of course, carried out previously by Frankie Bradley deceased. There was a lot more on offer from Doonan than there was from Cunningham but with a foot in both camps, the opportunity could not be sniffed at.

Cunningham loaned them a van in which they travelled back to their married quarters at Catterick Camp in North Yorkshire before their leave was over. They spent two days packing their belongings and moonlighted in the dead of night; why wait six months when there was a fortune waiting to be made right there and then?

They started work for Cunningham almost immediately and were given the farm as a temporary refuge with the job of caretakers.

They only worked at thieving on Saturdays when they would prey on unsuspecting shoppers in the crowded streets of Belfast or one of the smaller towns like Coleraine and Magherafelt. By the afternoon of the same day, they would be over the border and spending like there was no tomorrow before discarding the stolen bags, purses and credit cards. They banked what cash they managed to steal, in their own names, and were paid by Cunningham for what they managed to purchase by credit card to bring back over the border. Cunningham laundered the merchandise through a chain of Army Surplus and gift shops.

The Bradley's got up and dressed at 8 a.m. and began to prepare breakfast for four expected visitors, Sean Cunningham, Danny Monaghan, Dixie Dixon and a surprise fourth person.

It was around 9 a.m. when a Land Rover pulled up at the farm. Two men got out, Cunningham and Monaghan, but for some reason, Dixon had not turned up at Danny's Bar as arranged. Brannigan would not be happy with the little poteen plonker.

Cunningham knocked on the front door of the building and to Peter's surprise the door was opened by a pretty young woman; he had thought that the place was deserted. The party went inside then, around five minutes later, Brannigan arrived in his sleek black Jaguar and joined them.

When Leo, Siobhan and Liam Casey arrived at the Belfast safe house, Leo excused himself and went to his bedroom and phoned HQ. He asked the duty controller to wake Major Parker. When the Major came on the line, Leo told him everything that had happened and promised to report back within a couple of hours after working out his next move.

He had no idea who could have been responsible for trying to take him out. Perhaps he had been spotted by a PIRA man looking for Liam or by a UDA man who had recognised his car. Either way, he had been lucky to escape. Someone must have scored a home goal while planting the device which had gone off with a very loud bang; it must have been a whopper.

Liam was sleeping fitfully on the sofa and Siobhan was tucked up in Leo's bed while he lay wide awake in a sleeping bag on the living room floor trying to figure out his next move. The thread of an idea began to form in his head. He got up and dressed then went out in search of something for breakfast; he had guests to feed.

The guests were still asleep when he returned to the house. He put the food in the kitchen, locked himself in the bathroom and rang the Major to tell him his idea. Cedric Parker told him he was 'a bloody nut case' but he would see what he could do. Parker then phoned Ulster TV and asked for an urgent appointment with the top man. They met within the hour.

As Leo set about making the breakfast, he smiled to himself as he remembered his time at university when he and Peter had taken an interest in amateur dramatics. They had only done it for kicks but it had turned out to be one of the fun times of their lives as they hammed it up on stage in the many shows in which they performed. The drama training had come in handy on several occasions and both he and Peter were masters of dialect and deception.

He was laughing silently to himself when a polite cough sounded behind him. The egg he was cracking at the time splashed onto the floor as he turned in surprise to see Siobhan framed in the doorway. She looked as beautiful as ever even though she wore his pyjamas with the legs and the sleeves rolled up. They both looked at the egg-splattered floor and fell into fits of laughter most of which was tension release after the traumatic events of the night before. She composed herself as he cleaned up the mess.

"Good morning," she said, "did you manage to get some sleep?"

"Not a lot, how about you?"

"I can hardly remember my head touching the pillow. What do you think last night's shenanigans were all about?"

"I'm not sure," he lied. "I think one of Liam's associates might have been watching the house and figured out that he had contacted my department with a view to grassing on the Provisional IRA. After all, he was a courier for them and he would know some important Players in the organisation."

"What about the explosion?" she persisted.

"I think someone was planting a bomb when it went off prematurely, it has happened more than once in the past. Maybe they thought I would be taking Liam in for questioning or something like that and meant to kill us both."

Siobhan shuddered at the thought. Leo didn't think he was coming across too well and wondered if he should just come clean and say who he was. Instead, he turned his back to her and carried on cooking.

A sleepy Liam appeared behind Siobhan, rubbing his eyes and stroking his unshaven face.

"What's all the noise about," he asked, pecking his sister on the cheek.

"Leo cracked a good yoke," she said, and laughed at her own pun.

"She egged me on," said Leo.

"Lay off it," said Liam, "my brain is scrambled with all this chicken shit." He smiled for the first time since they had met.

"You feeling better?" asked Leo.

"Much thanks, what's to eat? I've had nothing inside me for almost three bloody days." he said, obviously on the mend.

"Bacon, eggs, mushrooms, tomatoes, and as much toast as you can eat, orange juice, tea, coffee, whichever you prefer; be my guest."

After breakfast, the refreshed trio talked about the next move. Leo suggested to Liam that he give himself up to the authorities and throw himself on the mercy of the courts. Liam blanched at the idea pointing out that the PIRA had no time for informers and would hound him to the ends of the earth.

"You could be spirited away and given a new identity," said Leo, "they would never find you."

"And spend the rest of my life looking over my shoulder? No thanks. I'd have to have plastic surgery and maybe have a limb cut off to succeed," said Liam. "And even then, there's no guarantee that they would not find me. Do you know how many sleepers they have in the field for Christ's sake? They are everywhere, I wouldn't stand a chance."

"Your chances would be much better than they are now," said Leo

"He's right," said Siobhan, "it would be better than being on the run all your life."

"I would always be on the run; I know them they never give up," said Liam, "They would find me wherever I go."

Leo looked at his watch it was mid-morning. He turned to Siobhan and said. "You can't go back home just yet they will probably have someone watching the place."

"What shall I do?" she asked.

"Ring the supermarket and tell them you are sick," he suggested. "Then I will take you to some colleagues of mine, I've already alerted them in anticipation of Liam's cooperation. Don't worry, I won't let any harm come to him if I can prevent it." She believed him.

Brannigan thanked the Kennerley's for the breakfast and told them to leave him alone with Monaghan and Cunningham to discuss business; they obediently retreated to the kitchen to wash-up.

Brannigan produced a newspaper with a full account of the Ballykelly atrocity. No names had been named so he felt confident that no one had talked, but he still could not be absolutely sure. The PIRA had blamed the whole incident on a dissident group calling themselves the Real IRA stating that the PIRA had no idea who they were.

Brannigan turned to another page where he had ringed a second story and passed it to the others to read. He then told them about his meeting with Doonan in Dublin and how he had been ordered to retire and to take his 'feckin' geriatric lieutenants' with him or else.

"I assume you told him to go and fuck himself?" said Monaghan.

"If I had, we probably wouldn't be having this meeting right now Danny, you of all people should know what the bastards are like. When they shout 'shit', you jump on the shovel or you get buried with the shit."

"What are we going to do now?" asked Cunningham.

"That article I've just shown you has given me an idea but it goes no further than this room for the moment OK? I want you to call in all of our people for a meeting here at the farm. When we have them here I will tell them who I really am and announce our retirement. But we won't be going out with a whimper, I want to leave the bastards with something to remember us by, both the PIRA and the bloody British."

"Have you thought out your next move then?" asked Monaghan.

"Not quite, but by the time our people get here, I'll have a better idea of what I am going to do. Just make sure that they are all here by 9 a.m. the day after tomorrow that will give your sleepers time to make it from the mainland Sean."

Cunningham nodded his acceptance and Monaghan wondered what his wily old friend had in mind.

Brannigan went off somewhere with the newspaper and when he returned, he called Mary and John Kennerley from the kitchen and instructed then to be ready to accompany him at 6 p.m. He would give them instructions over dinner about a party he was planning towards the end of the week when he would introduce himself to the other members of the gang and reward them all for the service they had given over the years. He asked them if they would kindly prepare the catering, and told them that a van would be made available for the shopping the following day. He handed them £500 in cash and with that, he left.

The SAS team watched him drive away followed shortly afterwards by Monaghan and Cunningham.

Leo phoned Sid Morrell at TAVRACABS, and asked him to come personally to collect him and Siobhan. When they were in the taxi, Leo explained to her that he was connected to the security forces and that he was going to try, with Liam's help, to infiltrate the enemy camp and bring some very nasty people to justice.

Siobhan was stunned. "You've just used me to get to my brother haven't you?" she said, recoiling into the corner of the cab. "But I thought you . . . ."

"I'm afraid so." said Leo, "I'm not really who you think I am. I'm sorry, I should have handed the case over to someone else when I realised that I had fallen in love with you."

She appeared not to have heard his last statement.

"What are you going to do with Liam?" she asked. "Will you take him in and have him arrested and jailed?"

"If he agrees to help me to get at the others, I'll do all that I can to get him off the hook. If everything he told me last night was true, he should have little to fear."

"And what have you got planned for me?" she asked, with more than a hint of sarcasm.

"I won't ask you now, I wouldn't dare, but when this is all over, assuming that we reach a successful conclusion, I plan to ask you to marry me."

"Marry me!" she exclaimed. She turned away and stared out of the window. She knew she loved him but she could not declare it under these circumstances. He had used her to get to the brother she loved, her only brother.

Cedric Parker met them at the SAS HQ. Siobhan was then taken to a small two-seater RAF trainer that flew her to RAF Leeming in Yorkshire where Joe Bailey met her and took her to his home in Ryhope near Sunderland to meet the lady with the false lower limbs.

At 6 p.m. precisely, Brannigan called for the Kennerley's and took them out to dinner.

Peter waited until the light was just beginning to fade, then contacted Geordie and told him to cover him while he tactically made his way across the field to the hedge. He found a wildlife opening through the blackthorn, and used its cover to make his way down to the farm. Once there he looked for signs of life, feeling instinctively that the place was deserted but he wasn't taking any chances.

He made his way to the rear of the building, where he was now observed darting between the farm buildings by Geordie and the others in the team. He looked around for a possible open window but found none. There was however a small window with a mesh screen that he guessed was part of an old walk-in pantry. He took out his knife and gently prised the mesh from were he guessed the window catch would be. He had guessed right and made just enough of a gap to get at the catch with the blade of his knife and push it upwards. After a couple of slips, he found a solid bit and pushed again, the catch gave at last and he opened the widow. It was a tight squeeze through the small aperture but he made it, and, making absolutely sure that he was alone, he tapped the mesh back into place and locked the window.

The spacious farmhouse was sparsely furnished and had an eerie feel about it; there was no welcoming spirit about the place. Peter could see no evidence of the bomb-making equipment, guns, or ammunition that Meehan believed to be stored there. He began to wonder where the stuff could be hidden if it existed at all.

There was nothing in the kitchen except for an old fashioned cooking range, a huge heavy pine table, four ancient wooden chairs and a tallboy with some bits and pieces of crockery on it. Peter studied the place for a while before turning his attention to the uncarpeted stone floor. There was a faint half circle on the stone slabs coming from the left hand side of the tallboy. He went over to it and gently pulled it from behind. It opened easily on a single castor and well-oiled hinges attached to the wall behind revealing a doorway and steps to a cellar. He made his way down, found a switch and turned on the light. Bingo! There were guns, grenades and mortar bombs, boxes of ammunition and enough fertilizer and Semtex to demolish a village. He micro-photographed everything then made his way back up the steps then pushed the tallboy back in place before taking a look at the six large bedrooms upstairs.

Five of them were completely empty but the other one had only a double bed, a small untidy dressing table, an overflowing wardrobe, and a chair with a pile of used clothing on it. Looking up, Peter noticed that there were dirty finger marks around a hatch-cover leading into the attic; he wondered how to get in there. He found a set of steps in the airing cupboard on the landing and with them, gained entry into the dark void above. He had a small torch that he shone around the floor and walls but, apart from an old rolled carpet, there was nothing there.

As he switched of his torch and prepared to climb down, he noticed a chink of light on the far wall. He switched on the torch again and shone it on the spot but could see nothing. He switched off the torch and allowed his eyes to become accustomed to the gloom, the chink of light appeared brighter. He climbed back into the attic and made his way across the beams towards the light source, noticing as he progressed, that there was no dust where he put his feet. When he reached the wall, he found that it was false and covered with stone-effect wallpaper. He searched and found a doorknob and let himself into a brightly lit attic room.

It was a bomb factory. The benches were littered with all manner of electrical bits and pieces, timers, primers, various types of detonator, containers of all shapes and sizes and numerous books and charts in both English and foreign languages one of which was Arabic. Peter knew that the Libyans were suspected of supplying arms to the IRA. Under the bench, Peter found a box of what looked like remote controls and timing devices, one of which was a sophisticated Russian Seconda piece with resettable date and time dials. He helped himself to it and others for evidence. Again, he photographed the contents of the room and, just as he was about to leave, he noticed a newspaper in a litterbin with a photograph of the battered Ballykelly school bus on the front page below the headline;

DISSIDENT IRA GROUP SLAUGHTERS INNOCENT CHILDREN.

There was a brief article about the bloody event but over the page was another story that had been circled in red ink. It announced the death of General Sir Gerald Fitzpatrick at the age of 91 years and went on to say that his body was to be brought back from London where he had died while staying with friends, and that he was to be buried with full military honours in the village churchyard near his home in Ballypatrick the following Friday.

The newspaper was just days old, which meant that the funeral had not yet taken place. The event would give the terrorists an ideal opportunity to strike again. Peter

left everything as he had found it and made his way back
to the basement where he put together a surprise package
with one of the Russian remote controlled detonators. He
secured it beneath a bench and made his way back to the
LUP where he phoned his report to Parker at Bessbrook.

Leo and Cedric Parker watched the video prepared by
the BBC along the lines of Leo's suggestions. The pictures
were from rejected old footage that had not been seen by
the general public. There were clips that had been edited
out of previous news stories that were about two years old.

The picture showed an armoured minibus, used for
transporting prisoners, lying on its side, in a country lane,
with one rear door lying on the ground and the other
hanging on one hinge. Two armed RUC officers were
standing guard with their backs to the camera.

The commentator was reporting.

*"The bus, carrying three prisoners, two guards and
a driver, was on its way from a police station in Limavady
to a detention centre in Belfast when the incident occurred.
One of the guards and one of the prisoners were pronounced
dead at the scene and the driver is still unconscious and in
a serious but stable condition in hospital. The other guard is
recovering well. The other two prisoners escaped with guns
and ammunition. They are named as Leo Bailey, a British
Army deserter who has been wanted for over a year, and
Liam Casey, a suspected Provisional IRA member, who may
have been involved in the incident at Ballykelly four days ago
when seven of seventeen children aboard a bus, the driver and
a soldier were killed by a car bomb planted by a dissident
IRA terrorist group. The prisoner who died, was a known
Provisional IRA terrorist named Eamon Flynn who had been
wanted for questioning for some time by the authorities. It is*

not known whether or not the escape was executed with the help of a third party, the conscious guard is still too weak to be questioned. The escaped prisoners may be on foot and are armed and dangerous. Members of the public are warned not approach them."

Photographs of Liam supplied by Meehan and a younger version of Leo, with close British Army style cropped hair, obtained from his military file were shown on the screen.

"Brilliant." said Leo. "It all looks very convincing we can only hope that Brannigan swallows the bait. Can you arrange to have it shown as a news flash every hour on the hour during this evening while I get back to Casey and talk him into the plan?"

"I still think you are taking a big risk Leo, why don't you just bring him in then join Peter and take the rest of them out at the farm and at Danny's Bar?" said the Major.

"From the intelligence we have so far," said Leo, "Peter and I both believe that there are several more people involved with Brannigan and we would like the opportunity to bag the lot of them, or as many as possible, as well as the big guns."

"OK, I'll give you two more days maximum to come up with something concrete then it's 'Takeout' time."

Leo returned to the safe house where Liam had caught up on some sleep. He was on his way to the bathroom to clean himself up when Leo arrived.

"Don't wash and shave yet for Christ's sake," said Leo, "I need you in shit order for the next few hours at least."

Liam looked at him in surprise. "Why, what's happening?"

"Sit down and listen and I'll tell you but first of all I have to apologise for deceiving you, but it was for Siobhan's sake. The less she knows the less she'll worry OK? I want you to help me to infiltrate a criminal organisation. What does the name Brannigan mean to you?"

"You mean the Sinn Fein guy? I've heard Uncle Barney mention him on occasion, he hates him but apart from that, nothing, why?"

Leo went on to tell Liam everything he knew about Brannigan, Cunningham, Monaghan, Dixon, O'Riordan, and Cluskey, and about Danny's bar and the farm.

Liam listened impassively. He was quiet for a while then he stood up and walked across the room. He turned and looked at Leo and said. "Would I be right in thinking that you are not who you say you are"?

"Right," said Leo, "but I can't tell you more than that, I'm going to have to ask you to trust me."

"You deceiving bastard, why in fuck's name should I trust you?"

He thrust his head forward and clenched his fists but made no move towards Leo who just sat there.

"Because you are still alive mate, and I intend to keep it that way. I was sent to take you in for your part in the Ballykelly bombing but that was before I heard your side of the story. And now, for Siobhan's sake, I have to try and get you off the hook."

"You used my sister to get at me didn't you? You slimy bastard, and we both trusted you."

He turned away again and beat his fist into the palm of his hand. Leo tensed for a possible fight.

"I'm sorry about that Liam, but I didn't expect to fall in love with her."

"You are in love with my sister!" exclaimed Liam, turning round to face Leo.

"I fully intend to ask her to marry me when this is all over," he said calmly. "Assuming of course that you decide to help me get Brannigan and that we both get out in one piece and, most importantly," he said, going down on one knee with hands in the prayer position. "You'll take me for your brother-in-law."

Despite himself, Liam began to laugh, very quietly at first, then louder and louder and then, more hysterically.

He turned and faced Leo again. "I don't believe this, first you come to take me in, and then you ask me for my sister's hand in marriage!"

He slumped into an armchair and laughed uncontrollably. He calmed down eventually and looked into the smiling face of Leo.

"You're bloody serious aren't you?"

"Yes," replied Leo, "I fell in love with her the moment I saw her. She is the most beautiful creature I have ever seen, I'm afraid I had no control over it. I should have dipped out of this job right there and then but the thought of never seeing her again was just too much to bear."

"Jesus Christ," said Liam. "My life just lumbers from one fucking crisis to another. Just when I thought you had offered me a lifeline with all your fine talk of a new identity and a change of country, you ask me to help you to infiltrate Brannigan's mob. What makes you think we can do it and more importantly, why would you want to; why don't you just shoot the bastard and get it over with?"

"I have my reasons," said Leo, thinking about his mother's false limbs and of what Cedric Parker had said along the same lines. "I want the whole gang in one go if it is at all possible and the only way we can do it, is to get in amongst them. But I need your help."

"How do you plan to do it?" asked Liam.

"Turn on the television while I make a brew," said Leo as he headed for the kitchen.

It was 5.55 p.m. and a quiz program was just coming to an end. At 6 p.m. the news began with the video of the 'great escape'. Liam watched and listened in amazement as the story unfolded and the pictures flashed across the screen. It was unbelievable, it was pure fiction he knew, but he also knew that Brannigan and his cronies would swallow it hook line and sinker.

"How did you manage it?" he asked Leo as he brought in two mugs of tea.

"I'll tell you some time, what do you think, do you reckon Brannigan and company will go for it?"

"I would if I was him."

"Shall we do it?"

"Why not, all we have to lose is our lives."

Leo outlined the plan and Liam listened with interest. He could not help but admire Leo's organisational ability and despite everything, he liked the bloody man.

"You are a devious bastard, do you know that? What's in this for me when it's all over, assuming we make it out of the lion's den?"

"Freedom Liam, freedom from the IRA and freedom from the law, it's a promise. You could change your name and choose a new location where the likes of O'Riordan would be out of your hair. But somehow, I don't think anyone could lead you by the nose again after what you have been through since your parents died."

"Except you, you devious bastard," he said, smiling at his future brother-in-law.

Leo called Major Parker and told him that the plan was a goer. Parker wished him luck and told him to keep his stupid head down.

When Peter reported in after his search of the farm, Cedric briefed him on Leo's plan. He listened with interest but made no comment.

Brannigan returned to the farm with his passengers and left at around midnight for Danny's Bar. Peter contacted Geordie Shiells, Mal Spencer and Jock Shand and told them that he did not expect any further movement at the farm and to get their heads down for the rest of the night. His men spent the next half hour taking turns peering through binoculars at the nude figures of the Kennerleys chasing each other around the bedroom. Peter could see nothing from his OP.

Chapter 7

It was well after midnight when Brannigan arrived at Danny's Bar. Monaghan told him about the television news flashes that had been shown every hour on the hour all the previous evening while he was out wining and dining the Kennerleys. Monaghan had recorded the 9 o'clock news and together, they studied the video.

They were saddened by Flynn's reported death but at least he had not talked otherwise the place would have been crawling with police and the army. Brannigan decided to stay the night and turned in after they had both had a farewell drink to their confederate.

O'Riordan had retired earlier after a few pints of porter. He had also seen the news flashes and was relieved to know that Liam had escaped along with the young man who he recognised as the one who owned the Gold Wing bike albeit with shorter hair.

Sean Cunningham had also been in touch about the television news flash. He reported that he had managed to contact all of his people and had ordered them to report at the farm. He asked Danny, if he saw Brannigan first, to pass on his condolences about Flynn.

Leo had thought it best to wait until late before setting off for Danny's Bar, which he and Liam had decided was the best place from which to infiltrate Brannigan's set-up. He rang Sid Morrell to ask him how long it would take to get to within a couple of miles of the place. Sid said it would take about three hours by taxi and that would be pushing it. Leo got him to take them to Bessbrook instead where he arranged for a chopper to drop them in open country.

After what seemed like five miles of yomping instead of the actual two and a half they arrived covered in mud and drenched to the skin outside Danny's Bar. They looked like two men on the run which was the idea. They rang the bell and banged on the front door until a window above them opened.

"What the fuck are you banging for at this time of fucking night?" shouted Danny. "Who in fuck's name is it?"

"Leo Bailey and Liam Casey." whispered Leo as loud as he could.

There was a pause then Danny whispered back. "Hang on I'll be right down."

He let the two bedraggled men in and ushered them to the bar and put on the light.

"You look a right mess the pair of you, where's all your fucking hair gone?" he asked Leo.

"The RUC cut it off the bastards." Leo answered, massaging his close-cropped scalp.

"And you'll be Barney Meehan's nephew I take it?" said Monaghan turning to Liam. "Do you know where your uncle is?"

"I think he is custody," said Liam. "They were waiting for me when I arrived at his house from Patrick O'Riordan's place where I'd spent the night before the Ballykelly job. Have you any idea what happened to Patrick, did he get caught?"

"He's upstairs sleeping off the drink. We saw the news of your escape on the television last night but nobody expected you to turn up here."

"I was told by Bernard Cluskey that this was a safe house," said Leo. "Some fucking safe house after the last time I was here." 'God almighty,' he thought, 'I'm using foul language and beginning to sound like a squaddie. Ah well, it is only an act, carry on.' He continued. "I heard on the drums at the police station that he had been caught trying to leave the country just hours after sending me over here to meet someone. He didn't say who would meet me he just said that he would tell whoever it was that I was coming and what I looked like and my contact would make himself known. Bernard has always been a furtive bastard. He told me that I was to show that person where the arms cache had been moved to from near his place but nobody here seemed to be interested, I was beginning to wonder if I had been sent to the right place when Flynn turned up and then all hell broke loose."

"It's becoming more like a fucking halfway house never mind a safe house," said Danny looking over Leo's shoulder at the doorway.

Leo pulled his gun and swung round to come face to face with Brannigan who was also pointing a gun.

"Shit man, you spooked me," said Leo, lowering his weapon. "You must be the famous Brannigan that Flynn told me about. I've seen you in here once before on that day when we made a run for it. I take it that you were the one I had to meet?"

"What happened to Flynn?" asked Brannigan, not lowering his gun. His unflinching gaze met an equally unflinching stare from Leo.

"We ran into a trap," said Leo, remembering the cover story that he and Peter had concocted, "the Garda were waiting for us at the border. I tried to go across country but they took out my tyres. They arrested us both and handed us over to the RUC who were in hot pursuit, it looked very much like it was a set-up, as if they knew we were here."

"That bastard Cluskey must have opened his mouth," said Brannigan, "I never trusted the swine. He was always trying to play the big man. I wondered why the RUC had turned up so quickly out of the blue."

Brannigan finally lowered his gun. "Give the boys a drink Danny and see if you can find them some dry clothes and a bite to eat."

He turned to Liam. "You must be Barney Meehan's nephew Liam Casey, do you know were he is right now?"

"I told Danny just now, I think the army or the RUC have got him. They were waiting for me when I got home to his place."

"Did you know Bernard Cluskey?" asked Brannigan.

"I delivered a few messages to him but I didn't know him well, why?" replied Liam.

"Someone has obviously been running off at the mouth," said Brannigan," and it can only be him. How did you meet Pete here?"

Liam swung round to Leo "I thought you said your name was Leo?"

"I used an alias," smiled Leo. Danny nodded knowingly as he poured them both a double Bushmills.

"So what's the story, how did you both escape and how did Flynn die?" asked Brannigan.

"Will I tell it or will you?" Liam asked Leo. He was beginning to enjoy this game of charades.

"I'll tell it," said Leo. He felt confident that his plan was working and he felt pleasantly surprised and slightly relieved that Liam had fallen so easily into the game. There was no more sign of fear in the man; remarkable.

"Let's get comfortable first," said Brannigan. "Get out of those wet clothes and have something to eat, then we'll settle down somewhere. Is the upstairs sitting room OK Danny?"

"Fine," said Danny. "I'll go and light the fire and bring up some grub."

He produced some dry clothes then showed Leo and Liam into a room with twin beds and a washbasin He told them they could bed down there for the night and left them to change.

Liam was just about to start talking when Leo put his finger to his lips and motioned him not to speak. He pointed to the wall then to his ear and mouthed, 'walls have ears.' Then, out loud, "Jesus I'm fucked after that trek, I'll be pleased to hit the sack tonight, or should I say this morning. It was a pity that Flynn didn't make it with us, I was just getting to know and like him back there in that nick."

"I saw them bring you both in," said Liam, catching on to the game. "You didn't look too buddy-buddy then, what did they do with your leathers?"

"They told me to strip off then they cut off all my fucking hair the bastards. Then they gave me these stupid rags to wear. Those leathers cost me a fortune."

They finished dressing and went to the upstairs sitting room to tell Brannigan and Monaghan their well-rehearsed tale. It was 4.30 a.m. and dawn was beginning to break.

"Flynn and I were taken to the police station in Limavady after we were captured," began Leo. "We found out that Cluskey was being held there but they wouldn't let us see him. They forced us to strip off and they took our clothes away for forensic tests, or so they said, and then they chopped off all my hair. We were questioned separately for over three hours but neither of us said a word. They would not allow us to have legal representation at Limavady but said that they would be moving us to a detention centre in Belfast where we could call a lawyer."

He paused for a drink and a bite of the cold sausage that Danny had provided.

"They decided to move us yesterday morning and that's when I first met Liam here. He'd been there a couple of days or so."

He looked at Liam for confirmation.

"Three days actually," said Liam.

Leo continued. "There were two guards in the van, Flynn was handcuffed to one of them and I was handcuffed to the other, Liam was handcuffed to an upright."

Liam nodded his confirmation as Leo spoke and a serious looking Monaghan nodded in understanding. A stern looking Brannigan also nodded and Leo felt like laughing at the lot of them as he spun his well rehearsed tale. They reminded him of those bobbing plastic storks that dipped their heads into a glass of water. He was enjoying every minute of it.

"All of a sudden," said Leo, raising his voice for maximum effect, "that crazy bastard Flynn lunged at his guard and tried to grab his gun but the guard, who was cuffed to me, was too quick. He drew his weapon and aimed it at Flynn but I pushed him and the shot went wide and hit the driver. His second shot took Flynn through the head as the van began to swerve all over the place. It eventually ran off the road and turned onto its side."

He paused again for effect and watched the faces of Brannigan and Monaghan while he took another swig of whisky and bit into his sausage. Brannigan looked insensible but there was the hint of a tear in Monaghan's eye. He must have been a good friend of Flynn.

"The two guards were out for the count and I got a bump on the head but I was still conscious. Liam was OK, he'd held on to the upright and saved himself, he didn't get so much as a scratch."

Liam nodded agreement and took up the tale while Leo finished his sausage.

"I took the keys for the handcuffs from the guard's belt and freed us both. I then handcuffed the two unconscious guards together. Flynn was obviously dead and we thought the driver was too but we didn't bother to check, we just wanted to get the fuck out of there. We got as far away as we could before we stopped for a breather and to decide where to go from there. Leo suggested that we come here and you know the rest."

He was quite proud of himself for having finished the factious tale. Leo gave him a look and a nod of approval.

It was 5.30 a.m. when they eventually got into their beds.

Geordie Shiells, Mal Spencer, and Jock Shand had slept fitfully after a night of rain and drizzle. Damp clothing in a pissing wet LUP was all part of the job but they didn't have to like it. Jock had awoken first and was scanning the Kennerleys' bedroom window for signs of movement but there was none.

"Fucking pervert," said Geordie yawning and trying without success to stretch. There was little room for manoeuvre in the shallow grave of a dugout.

"Bollocks, I'm just checking to see if anybody's up," said an indignant Jock.

"Up where?"

"Don't be filthy."

Geordie's radio beeped once. He responded, "Delta two."

"Delta one, did you sleep OK."

"Not too bad, how about you?"

"OK, anything to report?"

"You missed the strip show last night."

"That all?"

"Jock and Mal made a bell tent."

"Dirty sods, one out."

It was 5.30 a.m. Peter smiled to himself and shook his head as he opened a tin of compo baked beans and sausage and ate them cold from the can.

The Kennerleys' were stirring; they had a long day ahead of them. Members of the gang would be turning up in dribs and drabs on Cunningham's orders. They had found out only the day before that Brannigan was their real boss and not Sean Cunningham as they had always believed.

Something was going down but Brannigan had not told them much over the excellent dinner apart from the fact that there would be a gathering and an important announcement over the next couple of days. He had given them a wad of money to go shopping for enough food to cater for around twenty-five people for two to three days. Mary told Brannigan that she was up to the catering but the farm was short of cooking and eating utensils. He gave her another two hundred pounds and told her to take care of it; disposable stuff would suffice for the time that they expected to be there.

Peter watched through binoculars as the Kennerley's came out of the farmhouse and locked the door behind them. They were presentably dressed for what looked like a day out. They went to one of the outbuildings, which Peter had thought was empty, and opened it to reveal a couple of long-wheel-base Land Rovers then drove off in one of them.

Leo and Liam surfaced at 9.30 a.m. when a smiling Patrick O'Riordan appeared with a mug of tea for each of them.

He called cheerily, "Wake up you two there's some breakfast downstairs when you're ready."

Liam dived out of bed and shook O'Riordans hand and hugged him like a long lost brother. "Are you alright Patrick, I thought the buggers had got you?"

"I'm fine Liam and pleased as hell to see you safe and sound." He looked down at Leo and smiled. "Nice to see you again too Pete, what happened to that beautiful machine of yours?"

"The real name's Leo," he said, sitting up in the bed and holding out his hand. Patrick took it and shook it firmly. "I'm afraid the bloody Garda have it, I don't suppose I shall ever see that again. Pity, I loved that machine."

The talk of 'Nice to see you again', of 'Flynn', of 'bikes', of 'hair cuts', and other odd bits of conversation had Liam puzzled, these people seemed to know Leo quite well but he had said nothing. He would quiz Leo later.

They did their ablutions, dressed then joined O'Riordan in the bar where the breakfast had been laid. Brannigan was up and away to his office early but had promised to be back by ten to take them to the farm. Danny Monaghan was busy in the cellar when the three of them sat down to eat.

"What the hell happened at Ballykelly Pat?" asked Liam, trying to keep his voice low.

"It was bloody tragic," said O'Riordan, his face was serious and sad looking. "It was the fault of that stupid old shite Cunningham, the deaf bastard." He looked around to make sure that Monaghan was out of earshot then proceeded to give them his account of what had happened.

When he finished, Liam gripped his arm and said, "I knew you couldn't have been responsible, I told you didn't I Leo?"

"Leave it," whispered Leo as Monaghan's footsteps could be heard on the cellar steps.

Siobhan Casey had never before been out of Northern Ireland and could not believe the difference in the countryside and the people when she got to England. She loved the Bailey's home in Ryhope; it was Victorian like her own home in Belfast. She wondered if and when she would ever see it again.

It was the most wonderful thing too that in England, Catholics and Protestants lived side by side in perfect harmony and even intermarried. There were even coloured people like the Indian surgeon and his GP wife who lived just along the road and who went freely about their business. And there was the Bangladeshi shopkeeper in the village store. There were no enclaves with barricades and no pavements with painted Union colours or Irish tricolours to show the demarcation lines of the tribes. The only rivalry was between the red and white Sunderland FC 'Makam' fans and the black and white Newcastle FC known as the 'Toon Army,' it was marvellous.

She was an instant hit with Mary and Joe. Mary in particular was pleased to have someone who spoke the same dialect as they chatted incessantly. Joe left them to it and was happy for Mary who had recovered well from her injuries over the years and pottered around competently on her false lower limbs. He could not help but notice how much Siobhan looked like her when he and Mary had first met. He could well understand his son's feelings for the young lady who had already expressed her feelings to them for Leo. Joe also loved the idea of having a daughter.

The Kennerleys' chose Strabane for their shopping spree. They put in a call to Dublin and left the phone number of a cafe' with a private kiosk that they used on occasion.

Doonan rang them at the appointed time. They were surprised to know that he already knew about Brannigan; another clandestine person. He asked them to keep him informed about what was going down at the farm but they told him it would be difficult without any form of outside communication at the premises except for Brannigan's car phone which was out of the question. They promised to contact Dublin as and when an opportunity arose.

Four of his men in two cars had arrived at the farm when Sean Cunningham drove up. The five of them stood around talking and laughing while they waited for someone to come and let them into the farmhouse. Brannigan duly arrived in his Jaguar, which was fully laden with passengers. Monaghan got out of the front passenger seat and Leo, Liam, and O'Riordan alighted from the back seat.

Peter smiled when he saw Leo through his binoculars. He'd had a haircut, was clean-shaven and looked reasonably smart. He had obviously been successful in fooling Brannigan and the others. All the same, he could still be in danger.

Peter studied the faces of the rest of the men there, he recognised O'Riordan from the pub and Cunningham from the wanted list and of course he knew Danny Monaghan. The other four, however, were complete strangers.

Brannigan produced a key and they all went inside. The Kennerley's arrived later with the cooking utensils, the catering supplies, boxes of disposable plates, plastic eating utensils and long packages of plastic cups. Peter kept radio silence until the prescribed hour; roll on midnight.

During the day, several more vehicles arrived containing more gang members. The sound of recorded ceilidh music coming from somewhere within the farmhouse began to drift upwards towards Peter's LUP. The reunion party seemed to have begun early.

Brannigan suddenly appeared from the farmhouse with Kennerley and went to the boot of the Jaguar from which they extracted a large screen television set and a video recorder.

At midnight, Peter called the Controller at Bessbrook and told him he was coming in with his troop. Two minutes later he contacted Geordie and gave him the order to RTU. They rendezvoused with their support vehicle a mile from the farm and vacated the area.

Back at the HQ, Peter stood the men down and reported to Cedric Parker.

"I think Brannigan is planning something to coincide with the General's funeral," said Peter after briefing Parker about his break-in at the farmhouse and what he had discovered there.

"You could be right, I can't think of any other reason why he should call in his gang of cut-throats, pimps, and pushers. How did Leo look when you saw him?"

"Pretty cool and pretty well-in with Brannigan, it was all smiles and lots of handshakes all round. I hope the bugger knows what he's doing. What reporting arrangements have you agreed?"

"He's got his secure mobile for use when the opportunity arises and if he gets into trouble or needs to call in the cavalry, the 'star' button has been programmed to send Morse. In addition to that, now that he has successfully infiltrated the enemy camp, I'll get the Squadron into position around the place. Both he and Liam Casey are well armed with plenty spare clips concealed in a body belt in case they have to shoot their way out, but after that, they are on their own. What do you propose to do now Peter."

"I'll take the Squadron and do a recce of the area around Ballypatrick just in case we are right about Brannigan planning something. We'll select places to set up OP's around the area and I'll leave a couple of people to monitor movement in and out of the place. According to the map, it is a one-horse village with a single through road and a few forest tracks leading nowhere in particular.

He produced an ordnance survey map of the area and used a pen to indicate the various points of interest. "As you can see, there is only one way in and out of the place which makes road blocks easier but I suppose the RUC will be taking care of that. Do you think we should contact them at this stage?"

"Only to tell them that we know about the funeral and to offer our services with regard to covert observation," said Parker. "Remember, there is a cease-fire and we don't want to jeopardise that by showing a high profile. That is another reason why I would prefer to have these people taken out quietly and without fuss like Flynn was."

"Fair enough," said Peter, resuming his tour of the map. "This is Ballypatrick Hall and the estate which lies at one end of the village to the east, and this is the church where the funeral will take place at the other end. In between, is the village that looks as though most of the buildings are scattered about apart from what looks like a small cluster in the centre, probably the village shop and Post Office, that kind of thing. It's about a mile from the Hall to the church as the crow flies but taking the drives and the estate roads into account, the distance could be nearer one and three quarters of a mile. I would expect the funeral procession to be mostly on foot if the organisers stick to Irish tradition. That would mean a walk of at least half an hour at funeral pace.

The whole place is like an island in a sea of forest to the south, and open farmland to the north. The contours show that the forest slopes gently upwards from the valley floor and the church appears to be built on the top of a mound. It's a snipers paradise and it would appear that Brannigan has around twenty people at his disposal. It would be better to recce it on the ground to get the feel and the lie of the place"

"Right, go and get some sleep, you look like you could do with a decent night's kip. I'll see you in the morning."

"Good night Cedric."

Cunningham's pimps, pushers, and bank robbers were still arriving until well after midnight. Some were from the mainland and managed Cunningham's chain of Army Surplus stores and gift shops used as a front for their criminal activities. The gang members doubled as sleepers for the Provisional IRA and provided temporary work and accommodation for active-service players, bombers and assassins, now on standby, who were sent to the mainland from time to time. Leo and Liam were introduced around as the heroes of the hour and the video describing their 'great escape' was shown to each new batch of arrivals.

Brannigan had given them a grand tour of the farm earlier in the evening and it had turned out to be a revelation. What appeared to be a bunch of derelict outbuildings, were actually storage areas for a huge variety of military equipment. One building contained folding tables and chairs, 'Z' beds and sleeping bags, as well as blankets, sheets and pillows. They were neatly packed in protective plastic bags stacked on pallets and protected with more polythene sheeting. Leo was suitably impressed with the logistics.

Another building contained a variety of uniforms from DPM and denim fatigues, to No.1 and No. 2 dress uniforms. There were forage caps, berets in khaki, green, red, and black and a variety of Regimental and Corps cap badges. There were four Land Rovers in total and even a four-ton truck. Leo wondered how the vehicles could have been driven there under the noses of the security forces.

Everything had been purchased legitimately at Military Surplus Auctions, at Woolwich Arsenal and other W.D. sales venues, by Cunningham who had been well known in the business for many years. It was easy to ship supplies across to Northern Ireland so long as the paperwork was in order.

Brannigan showed them the arsenal in the cellar along with the fertilizer, TNT and the Semtex. He explained that the PIRA hierarchy knew nothing of his private cache unless Meehan or Dixon had said something to Doonan; they were not members of his gang. Dixon, when he was on loan, was the only one who had access to the explosives but always under the supervision of either Monaghan or Cunningham. It was unlikely that he would talk in case the poteen supply dried up.

He then took them to the attic and showed them the bomb factory before they all went downstairs and joined the party. Leo's mind was working overtime.

Siobhan lay awake for some time wondering what Leo and her brother were doing. Why had neither of them been in touch, what really was Leo's job? His parents had told her that he was a Captain in the army but she knew him to be something different. She now suspected that he was an undercover member of the security forces and that his parents were not aware of the fact. Should she say something? She thought not.

Mary had shown her a picture of him with an identical twin brother, he had not mentioned a twin, but then she barely knew him despite the fact that she had fallen desperately in love with him when their eyes had met that day in the church. Yet he knew all about her and Liam. She now realised that their second meeting had not been an accident, he had been after her brother all along. But why had he not just arrested him and dragged him off to face the law? She would find out one day.

She knew without a doubt, her feminine intuition had told her, that he loved her. There was more than mere lust in those eyes of his; a woman knew these things instinctively even though she had had little or no experience of men. She fell asleep wondering.

Brannigan, Monaghan and Cunningham left the party together at 1 a.m. to return to Danny's Bar and more comfortable surroundings. Leo, Liam, and Patrick sought out 'Z' beds and sleeping bags from the bedding store and found an empty bedroom to crash-out in. They had taken a good drink but the past couple of days had caught up with them. Leo and Liam fell asleep almost as soon as their heads touched down while O'Riordan rambled on happily to himself in drunken slumber.

Geordie Shiells sat on his bed deep in thought after reading the letter he had received from his wife Kitty. She was expecting their first child any time and he felt that he should have been at home with her.

They had been trying for four years without success to start a family and had almost given up hope when he had learned the good news a month after their return from holiday in Rhoda on the Greek island of Corfu. He'd run around like a kid on a new bike, telling all his mates and anybody on the base that only knew him by sight. Peter and the rest of the Squadron had celebrated with him and then tucked him into bed after a few drinks. But Kitty was now getting near her time, which gave him more to worry about than the current operation.

He had met Kitty in a bar in Plymouth on the night he had celebrated the presentation of his green beret, having successfully passed the Commando course. He had transferred from 58 Medium Regiment Royal Artillery.

Kitty was the youngest of four daughters and two sons of the Quartermaster of 59 Commando who was nearing the end of his service after 35 years in the Army. Geordie and Kitty were married the following year, shortly after her father's retirement, and lived in married quarters in the town.

Life was great for a couple of years but there was no sign of pregnancy. Geordie became restless after his best mate had applied for and had been accepted for Selection into the SAS. He and the childless Kitty were drifting apart and he thought that maybe 'absence would make the heart grow fonder' as they say, if he followed his mate's example and spent some time away from her.

He had persuaded Kitty to move to Newcastle after they had spent a spell of leave with his parents in Byker. Her own parents were not too far away in the border town of Coldstream. Her father had transferred from the Coldstream Guards into 59 Commando as a young Sergeant before Kitty was born but had now rejoined his regiment.

Geordie bought a house on the Chapel House Estate in the West Denton area of Newcastle and Kitty moved in alone while he was doing his Selection bit in Hereford, the Brecon Beacons, and other places.

Jock wandered over to him with a couple of cans of beer in his hands and a worried look on his face.

"What's up mate? You're looking fair serious, has something happened at home?"

"It's our lass Jock, the bairn's due any time and I'm stuck here. I wanted to see our first one born at least. We've waited long enough. I should be there and I can't ask for leave until this lot's over. Somebody has to look after Makam or the stupid sod'll get him self killed, although he is good at the Squadron Commander bit, it's almost as bad as having a bairn to look after."

"You worry too much, that's your trouble. Makam's a good bloke, he can look after himself, and anyway, you don't think Mal and me would let anything happen to him do you? Christ, you're not his keeper Geordie even though he's a mate. His brother is more of a fucking nut case from what I hear, the stupid bastard's supposed to have infiltrated that gang we've been watching at yonder farm. The two of them should be sent for psychiatric assessment at the Army Mental Hospital at Netley."

"Thanks for the beer and the advice Jock, now piss off and leave me to my self-pity."

Jock made himself scarce and went in search of Peter.

Chapter 8

The RUC had already done a sweep of the area around Ballypatrick when Peter paid a courtesy visit to the area Chief Inspector, Jeff McArdle. They went over the security arrangements together. Vehicle checkpoints had been planned for the approaches to both ends of the village. The one to the west would be about half a mile from the church and the one to the east would be a similar distance from the entrance to the Ballypatrick Hall and Estate. A reasonably level fallow field situated between the Hall and the village had been set aside for parking. The SAS would be watching the outlying forest and farm tracks while keeping a low profile. One Armoured Personnel Carrier with a Sergeant and six men from the 4th/7th Dragoons would be deployed to cruise up and down between check points to discourage any Republican activity.

Peter told the Inspector that intelligence reports had suggested that there might be an attempt by a dissident terrorist group to disrupt the funeral proceedings in order to end the cease-fire. He complemented McArdle on his security arrangements and informed him that there would be a covert SAS presence in the area just in case. The Inspector thanked him for the information.

Sean Cunningham returned to the farm after breakfast to be followed later by Brannigan and Monaghan. He gathered everybody into one room and told them that there would be an important announcement from Brannigan when he arrived. He informed them all that Brannigan had been the brains behind their criminal organisation since his release from prison many years before. Some of the Provisional IRA members among the assembled criminals that had done time in prison remembered the visit they had received from Brannigan as the official prison visitor on behalf of Sinn Fein. They also remembered the follow-up visits by pseudo 'fathers' Cunningham and Monaghan who had recruited them into the gang.

It was a revelation to Leo and Liam who had wondered what Brannigan would be announcing. They didn't have long to wait. He arrived about ten minutes after Cunningham had finished his little speech. The room was abuzz with chatter about what Cunningham had said. Silence fell as Brannigan and Monaghan walked into the room.

"Good morning everybody," began Brannigan, "and thank you all for making the effort to get here and for saving Sean the trouble of kicking your mangy arses." They all laughed.

"I have brought you all together to thank you for your support for the Provisional IRA in general, and for this organisation in particular. I can assure you that our enterprises have been very successful over the years and before you leave here, there will be a substantial cash reward for each of you. However, the most important reason for my being here today is to announce that Sean, Danny, and I will be retiring shortly and heading for pastures new. You will all be given the opportunity to carry on as you are if you wish and some of you will be given the opportunity to lead. I have already received leadership nominations from Sean and Danny and at our retirement party on Friday evening you will all be given the chance to vote for the chosen few. There is, however, the little matter of the current cease-fire to consider. If it lasts, and who knows, they have never lasted too long, the Provisional IRA as an active force will probably become part of history. But that could be to your advantage because a percentage of the profit from our enterprises has been paid into their war chest since we first began operations. That may no longer be necessary if the cease-fire continues indefinitely which means bigger profits for you to share."

He took a handkerchief and blew his nose loudly before continuing.

"I also have some sad news to impart. Another of our old IRA friends, Roland 'Dixie' Dixon who was loosely connected to this group and due to retire along with us, was killed the night before last in Belfast. He had been sent over there to take care of a suspect enemy agent who, we believe, was watching Liam Casey's sister's house but it would appear that we were given wrong information. Liam was already in custody and the police and army would have known that so why would they be watching the place?"

Liam stiffened, and Leo's finger found the 'star' button on the mobile in his pocket. They waited to hear what was coming next.

"We now believe that the misinformation came from a UDA contact in Belfast who seems to have been suffering an attack of paranoia. It was because of his information that we sent Dixie to take care of the agent who we now believe to have been the boyfriend of Liam Casey's sister Siobhan and not an agent at all. The UDA man appears to have done a runner.

Leo and Liam relaxed.

Brannigan turned to Liam and said. "I'm afraid I might have bad news for you too Liam. We had someone checkout your sister's house but there was no one there. They went to the supermarket where she worked but she had not reported for work. Her colleagues mentioned something about her having had a date with a social worker on the night that Dixie's bomb went off. There was nothing left of the car, or whoever was in it, the authorities are still collecting body fragments. Dixie must have used a little too much stuff because pieces of shrapnel from the car appear to have penetrated his van and killed him outright, I'm sorry."

Liam held his head in his hands and Leo went over to him and cradled him on his shoulder. He began to laugh and cry at the same time with a mixture of relief and hysteria and everybody crowded round to pat his back and offer their sympathy and support.

Patrick O'Riordan cried real tears in the belief that everything had happened as Brannigan had said. Although Siobhan had given him a bad time on occasion for leading her brother astray, he still thought she was a nice person. He only wished that he had been blessed with a sister to care for him as much as Siobhan had cared for Liam. The gathering was adjourned for coffee and condolences.

On his return to the hanger, Peter rounded up his Troop and briefed them on the situation. He told them about his discoveries in the farmhouse, the ringed article in the newspaper, and of his suspicion that something might be going down at the General's funeral. During his recce, he had selected half a dozen possible OP's and marked them on the map. He told Geordie Shiells to allocate the OP's and to get the entire Squadron together to check weapons and communications equipment.

The funeral was to take place in three days time but he wanted his section rested and in position at least two days before. He told Geordie to stand the men down until further notice and gave him a couple of crates of beer to share between them and then to pack an overnight bag and report back within half an hour dressed in civvies for a special assignment.

Geordie had wanted to ask for leave while the team was stood down but Peter had thrown him with the new orders. Half an hour later, dressed as instructed, he presented himself before Peter who handed him a sealed envelope and told him to accompany him to the runway where the two-seater trainer that had taken Siobhan Casey to England was waiting and ready to go.

"Open the sealed orders when you are under way, this is probably the most important surveillance job of your life and I don't want any cock-ups, understood?"

"Sir," said Geordie sarcastically, in a mock American accent and saluted, turning about smartly and boarding the plane.

Five minutes into the flight, he opened the sealed orders and read.

HAVE A GOOD LEAVE GEORDIE
AND I HOPE THE BAIRN IS WHAT YOU
BOTH WANT.

MAKAM

Big brave, hard-man SAS soldier Sergeant Geordie Shiells broke down in tears. "You lovely bastards," he whispered to himself.

Three dissident Provo players calling them selves 'The Real IRA,' met in a bar in Letterkenny to discuss the mayhem they had planned for the funeral of General Fitzpatrick. They were not in agreement with the Provisional IRA cease-fire and had resolved to disrupt it at the first opportunity. The funeral, they had decided, would give them the ideal opportunity.

One of the men, Michael McCaffrey, had been tasked with stealing an 'Ulster Water' company van from across the border and secreting it somewhere until the day before the funeral; he had been successful. The compound from which he stole the van had not been very secure and if there had been a night watchman, he had not been in evidence. The van was hidden by the thief in the garage of a sympathetic relative who could be relied upon to keep his mouth shut.

A recce of the area had revealed several small culverts that carried drainage water from the wooded hillside, at intervals along the road to the north of Ballypatrick to a stream that ran through the village on the south side of the road. Declan O'Leary, another member of the group and an explosives expert, had prepared several pipe bombs to slip into the culverts the day before the funeral, when he thought that security would be low, to be detonated by remote control. The third member, Denis Boyle, would be the driver. He knew the secret location of an arms cache from where he had stolen the materials required to manufacture the bombs along with three Russian-made machine pistols and a quantity of ammunition. They drank a toast to their success in bringing about the end of the cease-fire.

During the short break in the meeting with his gang, Brannigan took Liam Casey to one side and told him that the taking of his sister's life would be avenged. He showed him and Leo the article about the death of the old General Fitzpatrick and said that he had been planning an incident at the funeral as a going away present to the British. He neglected to mention the embarrassment he intended for the top Provisional IRA echelons, he owed them a headache, especially that ungrateful bastard Doonan; but the untimely death of the bomb-maker Dixie Dixon, had scuppered his plans.

Leo found it difficult to understand Brannigan's thinking. How could any sane person contemplate the murder of innocents at a funeral? He decided that the man must be a psychopath with little or no feelings and no sense of wrongdoing. Any doubts he had harboured about his own motivation for joining the SAS were dispelled once and for all. His devious mind began scheming while he sat through the second half of Brannigan's meeting.

He had learned a little about bomb disposal on a course he had attended while at Sandhurst. It was really a Royal Engineers' thing but his interest in electronics had prompted him to apply for the course. Having learned how to dismantle a variety of explosive devices, including some commonly used by terrorist organisations, he had a pretty good idea of how to actually put the things together.

When the meeting eventually ended and everyone had wandered off for refreshments, Leo asked Brannigan to show him a map of the area where the General's funeral was to take place.

"Why would you want to know that?" asked Brannigan.

"I might be in a position to help you bring about an incident." Leo replied,

"I need a bomber, not a gun runner," said Brannigan.

"I know how to make bombs," said Leo.

"Where did you learn that? Cluskey was no bomb maker, as far as I know, Dixie Dixon did all the manufacturing for this area, and he was the only expert I was aware of," said Brannigan, his eyes narrowing with suspicion.

"Czechoslovakia actually," answered Leo smiling, "Bernard Cluskey, as quartermaster, sent me there to organise a shipment of Semtex and Kalashnikov rifles amongst other things. The Czechs taught me quite a lot," he lied.

"Forget it for now," said Brannigan. "Have something to eat and drink and then you can give me a demonstration later. He went off to consult with Monaghan and Cunningham.

Peter took one of the gunned-up bangers from the car pool and drove to a viewpoint from where he could take another look at the farm. From the shelter of a copse, he observed lots of activity with small groups of people walking around and talking, or just sitting eating and drinking outside in the sunshine. The farmyard and the area outside the farm buildings, was littered with shining newish cars collectively worth hundreds of thousands of pounds. 'Crime did pay' he thought, 'but only for a limited period of time.'

He was pleased that he had planted an explosive device when he had paid his visit to their little bomb factory. He could have had the lot of them right here and now if he chose but Leo was inside the farm somewhere. Maybe he should initially have brought the Squadron along and forced a shoot-out. But then, he could not possibly have known that Brannigan would be organising a meeting of almost his entire criminal gang.

While everyone was preoccupied eating, drinking and generally enjoying the reunion, Leo and Liam took off to the bomb factory in the attic where Leo put together a device. It took him just under half an hour to manufacture the bomb which consisted of fertilizer in a flat plastic container with a Semtex fuse and an electronic primer.

They sought out Brannigan who was still in conspiratorial conversation with his two Lieutenants. Leo showed them the device he had made and asked them to accompany him outside. He left them all behind a fence and, carrying the device, tramped across the field to the gorse-bush covered island where Peter had made his OP a couple of days before.

There was a huge boulder among others in the middle of the island that was probably the reason for the island's existence. Ducking out of sight, he took out his mobile phone and called Peter who was still at the viewpoint and had watched Leo walk across the field.

"Leo! For Christ's sake what's happening over there, are you all right?"

"Never better bro, listen, there's something going down at a funeral for some old General next Friday. I have managed to infiltrate this den of iniquity and there is a lot to report but it is difficult to find an opportunity."

"We're already onto it," said Peter," I broke into the farm when Brannigan went off the other night with those two people who are presumably looking after the place. I saw the article ringed in a newspaper and guessed the rest. I'm busy preparing a little reception party. Look out brother, there's someone walking over the field towards you," warned Peter.

"How do you know that, where the hell are you?" asked Leo.

"There is some high ground about five hundred metres about 10 o'clock from where you are, I'm in a copse. I saw you arrive at the farm yesterday. Look out, he's almost on you," he said in final warning.

Leo peeped over the boulder; it was Liam.

"It's OK, it's Liam Casey, he's on our side, stand by and I'll get back to you," said Leo as he pocketed the mobile and circled the boulder as if looking for something.

"What's up Leo, do you need any help?" asked Liam.

"Yes, this boulder is ideal for what I have in mind but I'll need to get beneath it. Can you nip back to the farm and see if you can dig up a large crowbar or something to lever the thing up? I'll start scooping out a hole behind it," said Leo

Liam returned to the fence and asked Cunningham if he had such a thing as a large crowbar. They went off together to look for one. Meanwhile, Leo rang Peter who filled him in on the details of his recce and the RUC security arrangements for the funeral.

"Who is providing the APC?" asked Leo

"The 4th/7th Dragoons from Omagh I believe, why?" asked Peter.

"Arrange for my Troop to replace the crew, I might need them, can you do that?"

"I don't think it will be a problem, I'll get Nosey to arrange it with their Colonel. Look out, Casey's on his way back to your position. Ring me if you need me, I won't compromise you by calling you, good luck."

Peter was about to ring off when Leo said. "Just one more thing before you go Peter, try to keep the Ballypatrick area clear for the next twenty four hours, I'm going to suggest a recce of the village to Brannigan, if it is all clear, he will be led into a false sense of security."

"Wilco," said Peter.

The crowbar was big and heavy and Liam was out of breath when he reached Leo. Together, using a smaller boulder as a fulcrum, they levered the huge boulder up enough for Leo to slide the bomb beneath it.

Returning to the fence, Leo handed the remote to Brannigan and asked him to flick the switch. There was a huge explosion as the boulder was blown to pieces.

"What do you think?" asked Leo.

"You've convinced me young man," said Brannigan, patting Leo on the back, and then, looking up he said reverently. "Rest in peace Dixie, enjoy your retirement."

Peter returned to Bessbrook and briefed Major Parker.

A deeply depressed Barney Meehan looked almost comatose as he sat slumped in an armchair in his cell. Cedric Parker handed him a newspaper reporting the funeral of the school children and the bus driver killed in the Ballykelly bombing. It was scheduled for the same day as the General's funeral but at 3 o'clock in the afternoon. St Mary's convent had provided a plot for the mass grave and local monks were busy carving a huge headstone bearing all seven names of the dead children. Barney merely glanced at it and handed it back, he was too distressed to comment.

"I couldn't face it even if I was free to do so, I feel as though I have personally caused their deaths." He said.

"If it is any consolation at all, I can tell you that the person suspected of making the bomb that killed them, a chap called Dixon, is dead."

"How did you find him?"

"We didn't, a bomb meant for one of my men went off while the bomber was planting it in our man's car. Bomb experts suspect that there were two bombs by the force of the explosion. One planted earlier must have been detonated by remote control setting off a second device. Dixon's van was riddled with shrapnel killing him instantly. He couldn't have suffered but the bastard deserved to. It was what we call an own-goal."

"Where did it happen?" asked Meehan.

"Just up the road from where your niece lives in Belfast. God knows what he was doing there," Parker lied.

"I guess Brannigan probably knows you're onto him then," said Meehan.

"I can assure you he does not. It will probably be the last thing he knows," replied Parker.

The Major left Meehan with his self-pitying guilt and remorse.

"What are the chances of taking a look at the area around Ballypatrick?" Leo asked Brannigan.

"The place will probably be crawling with security people, why?" asked Brannigan.

"You're looking to cause an incident at the funeral aren't you? And I might be able to help. When is the funeral exactly?" asked Leo.

"At around 9 a.m. on Friday according to the paper," answered Brannigan.

"That's two days away there shouldn't be much going on in the way of security until the day before what with the cease-fire and that. Can you get an official invite to the funeral do you think?" asked Leo.

"What would I want at the funeral of a fucking Protestant General for Christ's sake?" asked Brannigan.

"Goodwill, I should think for starters and the executioner's hand on the trigger at the end," answered Leo.

"What bloody trigger, what do you have in mind?" enquired Brannigan.

"I've been mulling over an idea in my mind but I need to have a look at the area before I do anything else, how far is it?" asked Leo.

"About ten miles from here, twenty minutes at the most," said Brannigan.

"How about if I act as your chauffeur and you sit in the back of the Jag looking important? If we get stopped, you can always say that you are checking the location while you wait for your invite to arrive," suggested Leo.

Brannigan thought for a moment. He looked at his watch, it was only 6 p.m. and they could be back by 7.30. Although he was a Sinn Fein politician, he had always tried to keep a low profile outside his constituency of the Bogside. However, he wasn't going to be around after Friday so why not go along with what Leo had suggested. He was desperate to do something spectacular before he bowed out of politics and Northern Ireland. He agreed to go along with Leo who went in search of a suitable hat to give the impression that he was a chauffeur.

Brannigan called Cunnigham over and between them they transferred a large metal box from the boot of the Jaguar to the boot of the BMW. Leo made a point of examining the Jag in anticipation of a check by any of the security forces that they might encounter. While Brannigan and Cunningham were preoccupied loading the chest into the boot of the BMW, he attached a small device between the springs and the spongy cushion beneath the driver's seat of the Jaguar.

Peter did as Leo had requested and asked the RUC Inspector to order his men to keep a low profile for the next twenty-four hours. He then deployed his men to the OP's he had selected earlier and instructed Sergeant Mick Rutherford to select four men and take the borrowed APC to show some sort of security presence. They had been in position barely ten minutes when a slow moving black Jaguar approached the village from the west.

The APC was straddling the road as Leo approached. From the cover of the vehicle, soldiers on each side pointed their weapons at the Jag while Sergeant Rutherford, wearing the cap badge of the 4th/7th Dragoons, came forward and challenged the chauffeur.

"Step out of the vehicle if you please Sir, along with your passenger, put your hands on your head and face the bonnet of the car."

He made no sign that he recognised Leo who obediently got out and opened the back door for Brannigan and motioned him to follow suit. They stood at the front of the vehicle while Sergeant Mal Spencer searched them for weapons and two of his men rummaged through the car and the boot. Leo was pleased he had made sure that the car was empty before they left.

Mick Rutherford ignored the gun concealed in Leo's shoulder holster, and the slim mobile phone in his inside jacket pocket. The package attached to the underside of the driver's seat, went unnoticed.

"Are you resident here Sir?" asked Mick Rutherford.

"No," replied Brannigan.

"May I ask the purpose of your visit?" asked Mick.

"Mr. Brannigan has an invitation to the funeral of General Fitzpatrick on Friday. We are just checking the location of the church and Ballypatrick Hall," said Leo, answering for Brannigan.

"Very well Sir, you'll find the church on your left about half a mile down the road, and the Hall is also on your left about half a mile further on from the village centre." And turning to the APC driver, he said, "move the can Corporal and let the gentlemen through."

"Yes Sarge."

Leo ventured a wink at Rutherford as he drove through but the Sergeant kept a straight face and did not acknowledge.

Just before they reached the church, Leo noticed a track leading off to the right heading up towards a line of trees. He turned into the lane and made his way towards them. Just before the entrance to the forest, there was a viewpoint with a picnic table on the left hand side of the road looking out over the valley and the church about half a mile distant. He put a cross on the map and retraced his tracks back to the main road and the church.

He stopped at the entrance to the church drive that sloped gently upwards to a bend that turned to the left and headed towards a pair of huge iron gates that led into the churchyard and the church beyond. The wide drive was lined with white painted boulders about two metres apart and weighing somewhere in the region of four hundredweight's each at a guess. Behind the boulders, newly cut lawns stretched east and west to the boundary fences.

Leo drove on through the village, which was fairly spread out with detached houses in half to one-acre plots with established gardens and foliage. The village centre was set back on the south side of the road and consisted of a small cluster of shops and a cafe, a village hall, and a post office.

Beyond the village lay the Ballypatrick Estate with the ancient Hall and several acres of land. Just before the entrance to the estate, a track ran off to the right. Leo had marked it with a cross while studying the map back at the farm. The track looked unused and Leo turned into it to investigate the dot of a building shown on the map. It was as he had suspected, the building was a derelict farmhouse.

Their progress was monitored by members of absentee Geordie's Delta Two Zero Troop from their respective OP's and relayed to Peter by radio. Brannigan was blissfully unaware that he was being watched.

It was 7.15 p.m. when they got back to the farm. On the way back, Leo stopped the car and Brannigan joined him in the front. He went over the map with him and briefly outlined his plan for the mayhem that Brannigan was bent on causing. Brannigan was impressed, he told Leo to work out the finer points of his plan and to brief him the following morning when he returned from his office. In the meantime, he would get his secretary to organise the invite to the funeral and also try to find out where Cluskey was being held so that he could pay him a visit as the Official Sinn Fein prison visitor. Alarm bells began to ring in Leo's head.

"Give Cluskey my regards when you see him." he said, as calmly as he could.

Brannigan looked for signs of anxiety in Leo's face but found none. He was reassured. Leo, however, was not. If Brannigan managed to get to see Cluskey before the funeral, the game would be up and he and Liam would be well in the shit. He went to look for Liam while Brannigan went in search of his two cronies.

Leo decided to adopt a wait-and-see policy and said nothing to Liam. They went to look for a place to sleep but all the bedrooms were littered with camp beds from Cunningham's equipment store where there was now ample space. Someone had commandeered their beds from the night before as the room filled up with new arrivals.

Leo sought out Cunningham and told him that he and Liam would bed-down in the store and take turns in playing night watchman. Cunningham had not given security a thought in light of the current cease-fire and the relative lack of troop movement around the province. Brannigan and Monaghan, having overheard the conversation, thought it a good idea to post a guard, just in case. They left shortly afterwards, Monaghan to his bar, Brannigan to the Bogside, and Cunningham to Lislap.

After a bite of supper and a couple of beers, Leo and Liam made up their beds and Liam got his head down for the next four hours before he did his stint of guard duty. Leo laid out the ordnance survey map and began to put together his plan for the following day prior to the funeral the day after. When he was sure that Liam was asleep, he sent a Morse-code message to Peter and asked him to stand-by for a call around midnight.

Siobhan lay awake in the semi-darkness and stared at the ceiling. She and Mary Bailey had become firm friends in the very short space of time they had known each other and she felt as if she had known her all her life. They had talked all day while Mary pottered around the house dusting, arranging flowers and preparing food. They stopped at intervals to drink tea or coffee on the terrace at the rear of the house.

Siobhan told Mary all about herself and Liam, and the events that had led up to her meeting with Leo. Mary told Siobhan about her life in Northern Ireland before and after she and Joe had married, about the problems they'd had in the sixties and seventies before deciding to quit the province and move to England. She told her about the twins and their achievements before joining the Army but confessed that she did not know what they were doing in Northern Ireland. As far as she was concerned, according to their letters, they were just carrying out their normal military duties. She was surprised to learn that Leo was mixed up in some kind of clandestine operation. She would write and ask him at the British Forces Post Office number he had given her for contact. She had no idea where he was actually stationed; it was not like it had been when the boys were in Germany and the UK. It was strange however, that both Peter and Leo had the same BFPO number but, as far as she knew, they did not work together.

At 1225 a.m., Leo went outside and walked around in a show of carrying out his guard duty. The lights in the farm were all out on the ground floor but two of the bedrooms were still lit up. He walked along the farm track until he was well out of earshot and rang Peter.

"What's happening Leo?" asked his brother.

"Nothing much at the moment the big boys have all gone home and left me to baby-sit."

"When will they be back?"

"Some time tomorrow I expect. I've been out with Brannigan today looking over his proposed killing ground. The man is a raging psycho. I had no idea how big his operation was until today."

"Right, do you want me to initiate 'Takeout'? We could be there within the hour."

"No, I'm working on an idea. If we move too soon, there is a chance that one or more of them will get away. We need to net them all in one operation if possible. Nosey won't mind as long as the politicians are kept out of his hair. It should all be over by the weekend." Said Leo

"What should I tell him?" asked Peter.

"Tell him we have a bigger prize than we first thought, there are twenty four gang members here as well as myself and Liam. They have all been Players in their time and most of them are still PIRA card carriers. There is also a network of safe houses on the mainland that I want to find out more about. Cunningham is a braggart as well as a professional criminal and any intelligence I can glean from him will be helpful to Special Branch and MI6, said Leo."

"OK," said Peter, "I'll brief Nosey on what you've told me. Ring me again tomorrow at the same time if you can and I'll give you his reaction. In the meantime, keep your bloody head down."

"Just one thing more before you go Peter, Brannigan is going to contact the authorities in the morning with a view to visiting Cluskey in the nick. Apparently, he is an Official Prison Visitor on behalf of his Party. Ask Nosey if he can organise it with whoever for an appointment for him around Friday lunch time," asked Leo.

"Why on Friday lunchtime?" enquired Peter.

"Because he has a more pressing engagement with a higher authority in the morning, I'll say no more than that, sleep well brother," said Leo, smiling to himself.

With special permission, the RAF trainer touched down at Newcastle Airport where a taxi was waiting to take Geordie Sheills the few short miles to his home. His mother and Kitty's mother were both there and were all pleasantly surprised to see him.

Kitty cried with delight and immediately went into labour with the excitement of it all after being a week late. The ambulance didn't make it to the house in time for the birth but Geordie's mother was a retired nurse and, with the help of Kitty's mother, Peter Leo Shiells emerged into the world with a healthy wail while Geordie looked on in wonder. "Thanks Makam mate," he whispered to himself.

The next morning, at 4 a.m., he kissed his Kitty and his new son good-bye and set off with his father for Stranraer where he would take the noon ferry to Larne from where he would rejoin his unit. He'd promised Kitty that he would apply for leave as soon as he got back. He neglected to mention the ten-day pass in his possession.

Chapter 9

Leo woke Liam at 4 a.m. with a mug of tea and a bacon sandwich then got into his own sleeping bag for a couple of hours. Liam shook him at 6.30 a.m., and while everyone else was still sleeping, Leo went to the attic and selected a basket full of primers and timers and carried them to the cellar. By 7.30 a.m., when he heard noises in the kitchen above, he had manufactured sufficient dummy charges to place beneath each of the boulders he had counted along the drive leading to the churchyard where the General's funeral was to take place. All that was missing were the Semtex fuses but, what looked like small green-insulated trailing aerial wires, protruded from each flat-pack to give the impression that the bombs were real. No one would be any the wiser; none of the others knew the first thing about making bombs.

He emerged from the cellar startling Mary Kennerley who had begun cooking breakfast for the hungry guests. She eyed him admiringly and smiled. It had not escaped Leo's notice that she made eyes and smiled at most of the men.

She was a very good-looking woman, despite the dowdy loose-fitting dress and the flat shoes with caked-on farmyard dirt. She was quite slim in the right places and stood about 5'3". He thought she would probably look even better in a different environment. Her face was a pale rose pink and framed in a shock of unruly dark brown curly hair. God how he wished he could be with Siobhan.

He returned her smile, more out of politeness than anything else, as he helped himself to bacon, eggs and beans on a disposable plate, two thick slices of bread and butter, and a mug of coffee before returning to the barn; Liam was still asleep.

It was Leo's assumption that Brannigan would go along with his plans to disrupt the funeral. He had thought out a strategy that he was sure Brannigan would agree to but he would also need the cooperation of the remainder of the gang. If he could obtain their cooperation without Brannigan ordering it all would be well and good. He would have to use all of his persuasive powers, he knew, and the time to do it was right now before Brannigan and the others returned to the farm. He woke Liam and sent him to round everyone up and to bring them all to the storeroom before they could have any breakfast.

There was some grumbling and some serious looks from a few of the older members of the gang as they shuffled into the barn. Leo lost no time in explaining the reason for the meeting. He needed six volunteers between the ages of 25 and 35 years to pose as British soldiers.

He explained to them what Brannigan had in mind about embarrassing the authorities before taking off for the States and that he had been asked to organise and plan the operation. The Brits were going to get a very bloody nose as a result and there could be extensive loss of life among the Loyalists attending the funeral. It was expected however, that a few misguided peace-seeking republican people could also be in attendance but they could take their chances, they were regarded as traitors.

There was more muttering among the group but no one ventured an objection. It seemed to him incredible that none of them objected to the wanton killing of innocent people, not even O'Riordan, he was a bloody coward.

There would also be the risk of some of them being caught or killed if the operation went wrong. Were there any misgivings about his taking the lead? No? . . . . Good. "Have a good breakfast; it's going to be a long day."

Brendon Roscoe, a 45 year old car thief and coach builder from Leeds and too old to take part in the operation, was tasked with mocking-up two of the long-wheelbase Land Rovers to look like Military Police vehicles. He set about the task with relish and the help of two of the older members of the gang.

The six men who volunteered for the Ballypatrick operation were all seasoned Provisional IRA veterans with jail sentences behind them and no love for the British. They joined Leo, Liam and O'Riordan to be kitted out with DPM combat suits, boots and red berets with Royal Military Police badges.

John Kennerley nee Bradley was the only one who looked remotely like a soldier having been one, the rest looked like recruits on their first day in the army although they had all been to the IRA training camps albeit for just a few weeks.

Leo told Kennerley to put three stripes on his arm and make sure that the others looked a bit more like real squaddies before Brannigan arrived. There was something about Leo's manner that made Kennerley obey him without question. He reminded him of the young officers he had known in the British Army but put it down to the fact that Leo was probably a natural leader.

Shortly before 11 a.m. Brannigan and Monaghan arrived together in the Jag followed by Cunningham in his BMW coupe just as Roscoe and his team were putting the finishing touches to the Land Rovers.

"What's going on here?" inquired Brannigan, looking over the vehicles.

"Instructions from Leo Mr. Brannigan, he wanted them as soon as possible, I thought you knew," said Roscoe.

"You've done a good job there Brendon, where is Leo?" asked Brannigan.

"He's inside briefing the team," answered Roscoe.

'Briefing what team?' thought Brannigan as he went inside followed by Monaghan and Cunningham.

Leo was in one of the downstairs rooms lecturing to the volunteers who were sat in a half circle in front of him. Behind him, on the wall, he had drawn a huge plan of the Ballypatrick area as he remembered it from his recce with Brannigan. He pretended not to notice as the three men slipped quietly into the room and stood listening to his instruction.

"We expect a heavy RUC presence tomorrow, which is the day of the funeral, so it is important that we move quickly today. I had planned to put the charges in these culverts along the road from the Hall here," he said, pointing with a broom handle to the Hall and the X's he had drawn along the road to represent the culverts. "However, the road leading up to the church is lined with small whitewashed boulders each weighing around four hundredweight's. They will be ideal for what I have in mind, it would be like exploding mines so to speak and it occurred to me that the fragments of stone would cause heavy casualties if the boulders were blown-up simultaneously just when most of the funeral cortege is in the drive," explained Leo.

The men mumbled their approval, nodding and smiling to each other.

'Bloody nut-cases', thought Leo, and carried on.

"There are sure to be more people in that area than there would be lining the road from the Hall. The only problem is laying the charges in sight of the enemy and that's where the Military Police uniforms come in. What we have to do is to pretend to search for explosives while we are actually laying them. We will start with the culverts and leave them empty as we progress towards the church drive. Anyone covertly observing us should be convinced that we are genuine Military Policemen and I must say that you look better now than you did earlier this morning thanks to John here," he said, pointing to Kennerley who just smiled and nodded. "Are there any questions?"

"What happens if you are challenged?" was the question from Brannigan.

"Oh hello Mr. Brannigan, I didn't see you come in," said Leo. Everybody turned to look at him and his two henchmen.

Leo answered. "We'll be well armed and mobile but not looking for a fight. There is that army patrol we saw yesterday but I shouldn't think they will give us any trouble, the boys here look pretty professional don't you think? And British squaddies have a natural respect for the Military Police which is why I chose the disguise."

"Good thinking, but what about the detonation of the charges on the day?" asked Brannigan.

"If you managed to get your invite to the funeral, you can do the honours, if you didn't, you can watch the action here on television with the rest of the boys and Liam and I will do the honours. Either way, we will stay behind in the area after the charges are laid and provide a back-up if your remote control unit fails," said Leo, grinning from ear to ear.

"What remote control," asked Brannigan?

"This one Mr Brannigan," said Leo holding out the remote as he crossed the room. "If you park where we agreed yesterday, you will be in a good position to detonate the charges beneath the boulders when most or all of the funeral procession is in the drive. But for Christ's sake don't put the new batteries into it until you are ready to blow the charges just in case you accidentally touch something you shouldn't," warned Leo.

Brannigan took the remote and the sealed pack of new batteries. He examined them before slipping them into his pocket.

"I picked up the invitation on the way here," he said, "it wasn't too difficult to get hold of. I also got the go ahead to see Cluskey in the cooler on Friday afternoon," he added, watching for some kind of reaction from Leo. "We'll discuss the timing over lunch."

Leo did not flinch. "We have no time for lunch I'm afraid," he said, "I've organised Mary to pack a couple of insulated boxes with food and drink to give the operation more authenticity for the sake of any observers. One of the food containers has the charges in it. We will eat when we get to the church drive before laying the charges. We don't want to be seen to be in too much of a hurry. I've written down a few suggestions for you for tomorrow morning. It's up to you whether or not you agree to them but I will be looking out for you," said Leo.

He handed Brannigan an envelope. Monaghan and Cunningham stared at him expecting him to bring Leo down a peg or two but he just stood there and said nothing. Leo took his silence to mean that his plans had been approved.

"OK men, mount up," said Leo, and his pseudo MPs followed him outside; he wore the insignia of a Lieutenant.

Liam carried an SMG while the remainder were armed with 9 mm Browning pistols in standard British Army issue holsters. Kennerley played the role of section Sergeant, and each of the others wore Corporals' stripes just like regular Military Policemen after having finished basic training; Leo knew his stuff. He climbed into the leading vehicle with Liam driving and O'Riordan with one other in the back. Kennerley commanded the other Landrover, which was driven by Kevin Brady, a 28-year old drug baron from Dublin. They set off at 12noon precisely.

Peter and his section minus Geordie Shiells had manned their respective OP's before dawn. Inspector McArdle had agreed to keep his men out of sight in the area until further notice while the SAS Troop, disguised as 4th/7th Dragoons led by Sergeant Mick Rutherford patrolled the main road in the APC.

Michael McCaffrey of the Real IRA team collected the stolen 'Ulster Water' van from his relative and set off to pick-up O'Leary and Boyle. The pipe bombs and the weapons had been wrapped in polythene and hidden in a fire ditch in the pinewoods just outside Ballypatrick. They were concealed with bracken and twigs. It had been Boyle's idea to stash the stuff prior to the funeral in case they were stopped en-route while carrying it. As it was, there were no roadblocks and no army patrols to worry them. They felt very confident.

The two pseudo Military Police Land Rovers approached the APC, which was blocking the road into Ballypatrick, Leo ordered Liam to stop well short of it. He dismounted and strode purposefully over to Mick Rutherford and returned the Sergeant's salute. They were well out of earshot of the others but the Land Rovers' ticking-over engines guaranteed that their conversation could not be heard.

"What's the plan boss?" asked Mick Rutherford looking past Leo towards the two Land Rovers.

Leo produced the ordnance survey map from his pocket and set it on the ground. He made a show of pointing out various locations on the map as he gave Mick his instructions.

Back in the Land Rovers Kennerley and the rest of the gang relaxed in the belief that Leo was pulling the wool over the eyes of the enemy. When he had finished, Leo returned to the lead vehicle while the APC was being reversed off the road to let them through. The Sergeant saluted as they drove past and Leo touched the rim of his beret in response. Mick Rutherford spoke into the mike attached to his helmet.

"Bravo two to Delta two zero."

"Delta two zero."

"Bravo one and alien force now inside operations area."

"Roger out."

The two Land Rovers pulled into the drive leading to the church and turned onto the grassed area behind the whitewashed boulders before coming to a halt. Liam and O'Riordan unloaded the food containers while Leo took the others on a stroll around the drive to inspect the boulders at close quarters. It would be an easy job to place the dummy flat-pack charges while the area looked deserted.

He made a quick change of plan, and while Liam and O'Riordan went about making a brew, Leo formed the rest of the men into three groups of two. One man levered the boulder while the other placed the charge beneath. The job was completed within an hour after which they rested over a lunch of beef sandwiches and hot tea.

Back at the farm, Cunningham was carrying out another inspection. He had long fancied Mary Kennerley and her husband's absence playing soldiers with Leo and the others provided him with the opportunity he had been waiting for.

The evening before at Danny's Bar, he Brannigan and Monaghan had got their heads together to discuss their replacements when they retired. Monaghan had suggested O'Riordan as his replacement; Brannigan had suggested Leo, subject to Cluskey's report, for his replacement as leader of the gang and Cunningham had come up with John and Mary Kennerley to replace him. He regarded them as professional criminals who could be trusted to take on his string of shops and other enterprises. They could have the use of the house in Lislap as well as the apartments at the brothels on the mainland that would all come under their control.

He had taken the trouble to commit the complex business details, complete with all essential data, to the hard drive on his computer. Access to it, however, was complicated by a series of passwords that had to be entered in strict sequence, the sequence had to be learned and memorised. There were three backup four-set floppy disc copies, one set to take with him to America, one set in a bank vault in Dublin and one set for Mary Kennerley if she was willing to play the game he had planned. She knew something about computers from her clerical training in the WRAC but her husband had not yet awoken to their potential.

Leo and his bogus policemen had been gone for about twenty minutes when Cunningham made his move. Mary was alone in the kitchen tidying away the cooking utensils while the remaining gang members were busy eating.

"Could I have a word with you Mary?"

"Depends what it's about," she said smiling up at him. He was quite tall to her and still fairly attractive for his years.

"I have decided to nominate you and John to take over my end of the business from tomorrow, subject of course to the others agreeing, although I don't think there will be much opposition if the nomination comes from me. What do you think? Could John handle it with your help or would you rather I pick on someone else?"

"I'm quite sure he could fill your shoes Sean although he'll never be the man that you are." She gave him a sly wink and he sensed a 'come on'. He now knew women's ways very well and he also knew instinctively when they were available.

"I'd like to take you to Lislap to show you the house where you will be living between your travels on business and also to give you the keys. We can be there within an hour and a half whenever you are ready. It won't take more than an hour to show you the ropes, it's all on the computer for you to study in your own time but you will need the access passwords. There is no paperwork involved at all for security reasons but there is a set of backup discs hidden away in case your memory fails you."

"What about this place, who will Mr. Brannigan put in here?"

"If the cease-fire lasts, there'll be no more need for safe-houses and ammunition dumps. He'll probably just leave the place empty and see what happens. One of the Bogside boys can pop over from time to time to keep an eye on things. I'll get the car and pick you up in ten minutes, is that enough time for you to get ready?"

"Time enough, I'll just slip into something comfortable for the journey." She winked again and hurried off to change.

The bathroom facilities at the farm were not of the best and were currently under a strain with so many people staying there. Mary had done her best to keep it clean and respectable but she thought that most men were not too fussy when it came to personal hygiene.

She had a quick strip-wash and changed into clean underwear, jeans and a thin sweater that showed her firm breasts to best advantage. She didn't bother with a bra and her nipples stood out as good as any professional model. She hid them from the lecherous eyes of some of the gang members, behind a silk scarf, until she got into Cunningham's sports car with its roof retracted. She removed the scarf as they set off and Cunningham had difficulty keeping his eyes on the road.

While his men were eating, Leo set off to inspect their work. They had done a good job. There was no sign that the boulders had been moved and the trailing green dummy aerials, attached to the flat-packs, blended perfectly with the surrounding grass.

He was half way round when Patrick O'Riordan caught up with him.

"Can I have a private word Leo?"

"What's on your mind?"

"I want out."

"Why?"

"I don't want to be part of anything to do with this killing, it is mindless murder and I can't handle it, just let me disappear, I'll keep quiet, I promise."

"I'm sorry Patrick but you're in it up to your neck now. If you try to bow out, Brannigan will blow you away. It would be better for you if you waited until he and the others have gone then we can talk again. It looks like I'll be taking over operations after tomorrow and I wouldn't want anyone with me that I couldn't trust. Can you wait that long or will I shoot you right here?"

"Jesus Christ Leo, you can't be serious, I thought we were pals, you me and Liam."

"Leave it until after the funeral tomorrow and I'll talk it over with Liam. In the meantime try to stay calm. I have an important job for you around 8.45 a.m. tomorrow. You will miss the mayhem on television when the bombs go off but I don't suppose that will worry you too much; will it?" asked Leo.

"I couldn't watch it in any case, what do you want me to do?" answered O'Riordan still looking worried.

"All you have to do is raise a flag, nothing too difficult," answered Leo.

Cunningham could not resist it, he pulled into a lay-by set back behind a long row of high shrubs and stopped the car. Without hesitation, he reached out and pulled Mary towards him and kissed her full on the mouth. She did not resist or feign coyness, her tongue was in his mouth and her arms went round him in a passionate embrace. He held her there for almost a minute then slowly reached under her sweater for her breasts. He freed them and began to suck the nipples one by one as she squirmed in ecstasy. He would have taken her there and then if a lorry had not entered the lay-by behind them. She pulled down her sweater and they sped off towards Lislap and the house just five more miles away.

Geordie Shiells leaned on the rail of the Stranraer/ Larne ferry and watched impatiently as the coast of Northern Ireland began to appear in the distance. He could and should have stayed at home with Kitty and the bairn, he knew, but his sense of duty to his mates was just that little bit too strong for him to handle.

He wondered if he should see a psychiatrist when 'Operation Takeout' was over. It was unnatural for a husband and father to put what he perceived to be his SAS duty before his family. But then, his mates were almost like family as far as he was concerned. They were in danger; Kitty and baby Peter Leo were not. And anyway, he had to make sure that the baby's Godfather, Makam, (wait till the bugger finds out), was fit for duty. He smiled and muttered to himself, 'bollocks to the psychiatrist.'

Leo gathered his men around him and told them the next move. They set off in their vehicles towards the Hall beyond the village centre. When they got to the track leading up through the woods to the derelict farm, they stopped and set up a road block across the entrance.

Leo left Kennerley in charge with one of the men while he deployed each of the others at intervals on either side of the track where they were to lie concealed in the undergrowth. He left Patrick O'Riordan at the top of the track while he and Liam made their way to the clearing in front of the farmhouse.

Leo fired Liam's machine gun into the air until the magazine was empty and waited for some kind of response. Ten minutes later, the APC minus two of Mick Rutherford's team, who were left at their previous location, pulled up at the road block.

"What's up mate?" asked Rutherford as he ran towards Kennerley.

"There's a bunch of players up the track there, they tried to ambush us as we were passing but we saw them in time and fired on them. The Lieutenant's gone in after them up there somewhere and the rest of the men are covering on each side of the track."

"Stupid bastards, military policemen aren't combat soldiers. I'll take my men and give him a hand. Look after the can for us will you?"

Fanning out his men on each side of the track, Mick disappeared into the trees to make a tactical approach towards the farm. The pseudo policemen concealed in the hedgerows saw nothing more of the bogus Dragoons who seemed to melt away.

Mick Rutherford was the first into the clearing but kept his head down as he made the distinctive call of a fox which all of his mates were familiar with. Leo stood and looked about him before putting his hand on top of his head as a sign for Rutherford to approach. Mick was beside him in seconds.

"What now boss?" he queried.

"Signal your men to join us then take your time from me. Try to make it look good," said Leo.

Rutherford stood up and signalled his men to fall-in on him. When they were all assembled, O'Riordan and the rest of the pseudo RMP's rushed into the clearing and surrounded the SAS men, pointing their weapons.

"You and your men surrender your weapons," Leo ordered Rutherford, "and get out of that kit now, hurry."

"What the fuck . . . ." began Mick but shut up when Leo pointed his Browning at him.

"Just do it," demanded Leo or you cop it where you stand OK?

There was a little hesitation but no resistance from Rutherford's platoon as they piled their weapons and their uniforms on the ground.

"Sergeant," Leo called to Kennerley.

"Sir"

"Get your men to collect this kit and get back to the APC with it, and you two Corporals," to O'Riordan and Liam, "get this bloody lot into the farm building and wait for my orders," he said pointing to Rutherford and his men.

When Kennerley and the others had gone, Leo went into the farm building and told O'Riordan to report to Kennerley at the APC. As he disappeared down the track, Leo told Mick and his men to get their heads down in the corner of one of the derelict rooms and to stay still. He and Liam went into another room and began to fire the SMG into the air. As they retreated from the building, still firing, Kennerley and O'Riordan came sprinting back up the track towards them.

"What the fuck's going on?" shouted Kennerley

"Stay back," ordered Leo, as he lobbed a grenade into the building and then another.

"Get back to the vehicles quickly." he ordered, and ran ahead of the two dumb-struck criminals who followed dragging their feet as they tried to look behind them in sheer disbelief.

Back at the roadblock, Leo told Kennerley to take his men back to the farm in one of the Land Rovers and report to Brannigan while he and Liam took-over the APC and the patrol duty. The remaining Land Rover would be hidden and used as a getaway vehicle after the funeral. Kennerley obeyed without question while Patrick O'Riordan was in shock after what he thought he had just witnessed. He wondered how much longer he had to live.

Peter Bailey heard the shooting and the noise of the grenades. He contacted Jock Shand at his OP and told him to investigate the shooting and report back. Jock made his way to where the sound of the shooting had come from and came upon the clearing near the farm. As he radioed back to Peter, a Land Rover raced up the track and stopped in front of the farm building. Leo jumped out and called to Mick Rutherford who emerged from the farmhouse with his men. Jock laughed to himself when he saw them all standing in their shreddies and socks.

"Are you all OK?" asked Leo.

"Yes boss, where's the rest of the baddies?" asked Rutherford.

"Gone back to the safe house," answered Leo, "except for one of them and he's with me. He's down on the road with the APC."

"What do we do now Leo?" asked Rutherford.

"Get dressed for starters your kit is in the Rover here with your weapons. You can report to Peter when you retrieve your coms."

Jock emerged from cover and approached Leo and the others.

"I'm in touch with Peter now Leo, do you want a word?" asked Jock.

Leo swung round to face Jock.

"Thanks Jock, where the hell did you come from?"

"Makam, sorry, I mean Peter sent me to investigate the shooting, what's happening?" asked Jock.

"It's already happened and it is all over you can tell 'Makam'. I'll report to him later by mobile phone tell him," answered Leo.

He turned to Mick Rutherford.

"Get the men back to the HQ for some scran and a brew and a couple of hours head-down then report to Peter for deployment around 2000 hrs. OK Mick? Pick up your coms from the APC on your way past and say nothing to the driver. He's on our side but as far as he is concerned, you are still just a bunch of cavalry crap hats."

"WILCO boss. OK men, mount up we're off for a brew and a kip. We'll pick up the other two on the way. Cheers fellas don't do anything I wouldn't do," called Mick as they ran down the track.

"Piss off you lucky bastards." shouted Jock, smiling after them.

They were barely through the door of the Lislap house when Cunningham grabbed Mary and pressed her to him and kissed her. She still felt a little grubby after so long at the farm with its inadequate facilities.

"Can we take a shower or a bath first?" she asked, gently pushing him away from her. "Come and show me where everything is."

He showed her the downstairs first with its three spacious reception rooms and the huge well equipped kitchen. The living room faced south with a 16' set of four patio doors leading onto a sizeable tiled patio surrounded by a low decorative wall with small statues of cherubs at intervals around it. Two moulded concrete wolves stood on guard at the top of three steps leading down to a beautifully kept garden.

Mary could not believe that all this would be hers and John's when Cunningham retired to America. She took his hand and led him to the stairs. There were four double bedrooms, two of which were richly furnished and had en-suite facilities. A separate room contained a Jacuzzi, sauna, steam-room and a shower, as well as a bath that was set into the floor and was large enough to accommodate two people in comfort.

"It's beautiful Sean, how could you give up all this and go off to America?"

"Because my dear, there's nothing left for me in Ireland since my wife died all those years ago. I vowed then that I would never marry again and I've kept that promise. It would hurt me to stay here with only memories. I need a complete change of scene. You and John are welcome to all of this you have worked hard for it, now let's get undressed and hit the Jacuzzi."

She giggled as she quickly stripped while he turned on the water and the bubbles.

Geordie Shiells could not believe his luck. He was walking towards the bus station when a TAVRACABS taxi pulled into the ferry terminal and set down its passengers, probably squaddies in civvies on R & R. He recognised the driver immediately; it was Sandy Blewitt.

Blewitt was an ex SAS soldier who had settled in Belfast after being invalided out of the army. He had seen service in Belize, the Falklands, Africa and the Middle East but despite being a little too old he had volunteered himself as an instructor in the Kuwaiti Special Services unit set up with the help of the SAS to fight Sadam Hussein's Iraqi insurgents. One of his Kuwaiti trainees had almost killed him when the gun he was cleaning went off accidentally. The man had not cleared the breach properly and had shot Blewitt at point blank range. The bullet narrowly missed his heart and punctured his left lung before shattering part of a rib. One of his colleagues, an ex army medic, saved his life with a sock which he pushed into the exit hole while he held a crisp packet over the entry hole, to stop the wound from sucking, until the ambulance arrived.

On his return to the UK, Blewitt's old friend Sid Morrell had heard through the SAS grape vine about his plight and invited him to join his team in Northern Ireland. Having no other ties, Sandy had accepted Sid's offer and quit his council flat in York.

"Hi Sandy," said Geordie as he opened the front passenger door and threw his bag into the back seat. "How are you doing mate."

"What the fuck!" exclaimed Blewitt in surprise as his hand went down to the concealed weapon at the side of his seat. "Christ Geordie, where the fuck did you come from? You scared the shit out of me you daft bastard. How are you doing mate I haven't seen you since the Gulf?" They shook hands.

"I'm all right Sandy mate but I'm in a tearing hurry. Can you get me to Bessbrook in quick time? Makam and the boys are about to take out some Players and I'd hate to miss the party. I'll tell you about it on the way."

"You know I can't take you all the way mate but I can take you as far as Omagh then you're on your own OK? Fasten your seat belt."

Cunningham hadn't smoked a cigarette in years but the love making with Mary had been so good that he could not resist it. She had an insatiable appetite for sex and a gift for arousing him. He took her three times in the space of the hour that they had spent together between the Jacuzzi, the bedroom, and the power-shower. Not bad far a man just short of his sixtieth birthday, he thought. All he wanted to do now was to get his head down and rest but he had to get back to the farm before Kennerley returned and found his wife missing, they had already been gone for two and a half hours.

Mary could not have cared less. What Cunningham didn't know was that she told her husband everything. He was a mental voyeur and knew all about her extramarital escapades that turned him on when she recounted the action with as much exaggeration as she could conjure. He never got jealous like most men would because he knew she would never leave him for someone else. Her particular weakness supported his particular need.

O'Riordan and John Kennerley were with Brannigan and Monaghan when Cunningham and Mary returned. They had reported with much excitement the entire successful operation that had culminated in the assumed deliberate slaughter of the unsuspecting cavalrymen and the clean getaway without casualties on their part.

Brannigan was impressed but expressed some misgivings about the killing of the troopers. It was not that he cared for their lives but any other security forces in the area could have been alerted.

"We didn't see any other army or police presence," said O'Riordan." In fact, we didn't even see any civilians; the whole place seemed deserted. The farm was pretty isolated and the only reaction to Leo's firing off a magazine was the APC full of soldiers turning up. I think they were the only ones there otherwise we might have been in trouble."

"I don't understand it," said Brannigan shaking his head in disbelief. "Cease-fire or no cease-fire, it's not like the security forces to drop their guard and put only one troop of soldiers in what could be a sensitive area over the next twenty four hours."

"They were on a twenty four hour shift according to Leo and were not due to be relieved until noon tomorrow after the funeral is all over. The Sergeant told him that the RUC were taking over the patrols at midnight tonight so that they could stand down and get some kip. But they had orders to stay in the area until they were relieved by another army patrol. It will all be over by the time they find the bodies and we should all be long gone by then," said Kennerley.

"But there will be no troop for the RUC to take over from at midnight will there?" said Brannigan. "They're all dead."

"Leo still has the APC and Liam is with him, and as far as the RUC is concerned, Leo is going to tell them that his men are sleeping in the back of the vehicle while he and Liam are on stag. I tried to point this out to him before we left him but the clever bastard had all the answers as usual," said Kennerley.

"Clever bastard indeed," said Brannigan. "He may turn out to be a bit too clever for his own good, OK, get those uniforms off and get all the gear put away. Get one of the boys to watch the television in case there is any news of the killings and tell him to report direct to me if there is anything I need to know. Well done all of you, I'll have some good news for you both tomorrow when this is all over. Danny and Sean will be staying here tonight and I'm off to the funeral in the morning. See what food you have in store John and try to rustle up a party for the boys tonight, there's plenty booze left."

Brannigan was just about to leave when Sean Cunningham walked in.

"Ah Sean," he said. "This afternoon's operation was a complete success, Danny here will tell you all about it, I have to be off now and organise the last of my packing. I'll see you all tomorrow afternoon after I've been to see Cluskey then we'll do the share-out and the job allocations. How did your afternoon go Sean?"

"I've shown Mary the house and given her the passwords. I think her and John will make a good team as always. She has a fine brain that girl, John's a lucky man." His loins twitched at the memory of their encounter and he flushed just enough for Brannigan to notice. A faint knowing smile crossed his lips as he shook Cunningham's hand and bade them all farewell.

Mary was already busy in the kitchen when Kennerley walked in. He looked her up and down; she looked more beautiful than he could remember. She ran over to him and kissed him on the lips.

"How did your day go?" he asked.

"I'll tell you when we are in bed." She said, teasingly. "You won't believe our luck. How did your day go?"

182

"I'll tell you when I get back from putting the gear away. I'll give you a hand afterwards, there's to be a party tonight to celebrate the success of today's mission."

They were five miles out of Omagh and catching up on old times. Geordie had told Sandy about 'Operation Takeout' and the present state of play as far as he knew it. Sandy had gleaned a little information from Sid Morrell via Leo Bailey but nothing went beyond the two ex SAS men. It seemed that whenever old mates in the forces got together, they gloried in taking the piss out of each other. The better the friendship was, the worse the piss-take.

"I wish I could be in on the finale," said Sandy

Geordie retorted, "You're too fucking old mate."

"Cheeky bastard, you fucking Geordies are all the same. It's a good job I love you, you cheeky bastard, or I'd put you off right here."

"No but seriously mate, I wish you were still serving. Some of the cissies who are getting through Selection these days are just about up to standard. You should see some of the rubbish that applies. I blame fucking Andy McNab and Chris Ryan for most of it. Their books are brilliant but they're encouraging gung-ho misfits who want to be fucking heroes to apply." It was not strictly true but Geordie said it anyway.

"Families change mate, it's not like it was when I first applied, most of my mates were just quiet blokes who had a thing against fucking psychos who hung their hats on the hat pegs of terrorist organisations to justify their actions. We were looking for that bastard Flynn ten or eleven years ago when one of our informants pointed a finger at him after the Brighton bombing when Maggie nearly copped it. He disappeared from the scene for ages afterwards but they got Magee. I'm pleased it was you who got that bastard Flynn, what the fuck was Makam doing?"

"He was reaching for his Browning when I fired, I couldn't take a chance on Flynn turning round, and he was armed and desperate."

"What did Makam Say?"

"He crossed himself and muttered something, I was too far away to hear; did you know he's a Roman candle?"

"I didn't, did you know I was?" asked Sandy.

"F'kin'ell! Makes you think doesn't it?" said Geordie.

They reached the barracks in Omagh and Sandy dropped Geordie outside the gates after getting him to sign a chit for the ride.

"Tell Sid I'll be sending you both an invite to the Christening. We'll get mortal and swap a few yarns," said Geordie.

"As long as we drink Guinness and not that fucking sludge you call Newcastle Brown Ale, it does my fucking head in. Have you got room for us?"

"My aunt has an eight birth caravan just up the road on a farm in Westerhope. She stays there when they come up from the south but she'll be staying with her sister for that weekend."

"Great, I'll look forward to that. Look after yourself and keep your head down, so long Geordie," said Sandy as he drove off waving.

"Tarrah mate and gan canny," Geordie shouted after him.

With Sandy gone, Geordie approached the guard at the barrier. He showed his ID and asked to see the duty Officer.

Captain George Hunter of the 4th/7th Dragoons introduced himself and inquired of Geordie's business. Geordie told him what he thought he needed to know and asked for transport to Bessbrook.

"You're lucky Sergeant, our Sergeant Walters of 'F' Troop is just about to take a patrol to Ballypatrick to pick-up an APC that we loaned your lot, then they'll carry on patrolling the area. I'll get him to drop you on the way."

"Thank you Sir, it's much appreciated," said a relieved Geordie.

The white van marked 'Ulster Water Emergency Services', moved slowly along the road having entered Ballypatrick unchallenged from the east. Denis Boyle was driving, stopping at intervals while the other two men made a show of inspecting the culverts one by one.

The pipe bombs were concealed inside short lengths of plastic water pipe on a rack inside the van. As the van moved from culvert to culvert, a windbreak was placed around each entrance. The men had what looked like flu brushes which one man pushed into the culvert at one end while the other man made a show of watching it appear at the other end. The end of the brush however, did not appear; it was being used as a ramrod in order to push the bombs into the centre of each culvert after they were passed out through the rear door of the van by Boyle.

They had almost finished the job when Boyle saw Leo's APC approaching from the opposite direction. He alerted the other two and pulled over to the side of the road and parked.

Leo told Liam to stop the APC and to don a bulletproof vest before they made an approach. The van looked innocent enough but Leo was taking no chances. They moved slowly forward to within fifty metres of the van. Leo told Liam to cover him while he went to investigate. Liam climbed out of the APC and lay on the road with his weapon at the ready.

As Leo walked towards the van, McCaffrey and O'Leary ignored him and tried to look casual as they emerged from the rear of the van carrying the wind-break, which they placed at the end of the nearby culvert then returned to the open rear doors; they did not appear to notice Leo. Boyle, with his door slightly ajar, appeared to be reading a newspaper while the other two, whose feet could be seen beneath the rear doors, were doing something out of sight at the back of the van.

Leo was about ten metres away from the vehicle when three shots rang out in quick succession. He hit the ground in quick time and waited to feel pain but none came. He aimed his SMG at the target but nothing moved for a few seconds then the driver's door swung open and Boyle pitched sideways into the road followed by the clatter of a machine pistol as it bounced on the tarmac. There was a neat hole in his forehead and another in the laminated windscreen on the driver's side of the vehicle.

The two men at the rear of the vehicle were slumped on the road where pools of blood were already beginning to form where they lay quite still. Two Armalite rifles lay beside their bodies.

"Stay down," commanded a voice from somewhere as three hooded men appeared from the woods, in the crouch position, pointing their weapons at the bodies on the road.

Having confirmed that the men were dead, the SAS soldiers removed their hoods to reveal Peter Bailey, Mick Rutherford and Jock Shand. They had their backs to Liam as they pulled Leo to his feet and patted him warmly on the back like a long lost mate.

Liam walked over to the group, and just as he reached them, Peter turned to face him.

"Jesus Christ!" Exclaimed Liam, as he looked from one twin to the other.

"Peter, this is Liam Casey. Liam, this is my twin brother Peter and this is our Sergeant Mick Rutherford, and this chunky little ex-para is the mighty Jock Shand. Nice shooting Jock, right between the peepers. Say hello and then we'll have a brew."

"Shit, I might have guessed it," said Liam, "you are all special forces."

"Don't knock it Liam, if you hadn't been reasonably clean, you might well have been one of those poor bastards over there." said Leo pointing to the three dead Players.

An RUC Land Rover approached the group and the Inspector who had cooperated with Peter the day before climbed out. The two men shook hands and went off together to inspect the dead terrorists and to organise their removal from the scene. The whole bomb-laying operation had been observed by both the SAS and the RUC but the latter had left the dirty work to the professionals.

Inspector McArdle identified the dead men from his list of known villains. The scene was photographed in detail and the players, in body bags, were loaded into the stolen van and driven away by one of the policemen.

The bomb squad were called to take care of the pipe bombs which were timed to detonate at 8.45 a.m. the next day. Even though they were simply made and easy to dismantle, they contained sufficient explosive to cause a significant amount of death and destruction.

The sentry was surprised to see Geordie in the front passenger seat of the APC as it arrived at the Bessbrook HQ of the SAS.

"Hello mate, I thought you were chilling out in Geordie land, what are you doing back in this hole?" asked the sentry.

"Our lass had the bairn last night just after I got there so there was no reason for me to stay, all the women are around her, and she'll be abed for the next couple of days so I thought I'd get back and see the job finished."

"I think you'd better go and report to Nosey, he's duty controller tonight. The word is that three players shit-out about an hour ago. Don't know any of the details, the boss'll probably fill you in after he's bollocked you for coming back early. The Hats will have to wait here with the APC, OK Sergeant?" he said turning to the NCO in charge of the patrol.

"OK mate, no prob. Get your arse back as soon as you can Geordie, we'll park over there and brew up."

Geordie was back at the APC in full kit within twenty minutes after suffering a mouthful of firm but friendly abuse from Major Parker.

The sentry was chatting with Sergeant Walters and his troop of cavalrymen and was handing back the empty mug as Geordie got near. He sniffed the air a few times and asked. "Can you smell roast arse mates?"

The lads fell about laughing and Geordie had the grace to blush as he gave his mate a friendly cuff before climbing into the APC.

"Watch your back Geordie mate." He shouted as the APC sped off.

Chapter 10

The Kennerleys' intelligence report had upset Daniel Doonan more than he would admit. If that bastard Brannigan thought he could get away with embarrassing the Provisionals, he had another think coming. It was all right to stuff the British but not his own kind. He had always been an arrogant, uncooperative shit and a law unto himself. If it hadn't been for his financial contribution to the Cause, he'd have been wearing a concrete suit at the bottom of Lough Neagh years ago. As it was he'd gained so much clout with Sinn Fein that a blind eye had been turned in his favour. It was now time for action and the initiative was Doonan's as PIRA Commander-In-Chief; Sinn Fein could get stuffed.

He called the CO of the Tyrone Brigade and ordered him to report to his Billy Thompson, the code name they applied to a public phone box that they used for secure communication, and to wait for his call. Each of Doonan's CO's used a phone box close to their homes for security reasons.

Fifteen minutes later Doonan rang the CO again and ordered him to mobilise and fully arm the best ten men he could find from his and the surrounding stood-down units and to meet him at midnight at the Dungannon safe house.

"Are we about to break the cease-fire Dan?" The CO sounded worried.

"No Ned, just a few traitorous feckin necks, I'll tell you all about it when I see you."

Peter and the RUC Inspector decided between them that the time was now right for the RUC to take over the security of the area. There was a long night ahead and the recent threat from an unexpected source had been successfully eliminated. They both felt that there should not be another incursion by anyone else before the funeral.

The RUC set up their roadblocks while Peter organised each OP to alternate and stand watch for four hours on and four hours off. When he was satisfied that everything was in order, he joined Leo and Liam in the APC.

"Well Leo, what's the plan?" asked Peter.

"Liam and I are staying here tonight, Brannigan has got an invitation to the funeral tomorrow but what he doesn't know is that Liam and I will be waiting to take him out when he finds that the charges we laid are duff."

"Could Jock and I please have that honour Leo?" said a voice from outside the APC.

They all looked up in surprise. Geordie Shiells was peering in at them through the open back door. Peter could not believe it.

"Geordie, for Christ's sake man, what the bloody hell are you doing back here?"

"Kitty's had the bairn, it was born not long after I landed, it was a boy and I watched him being born which was all I really wanted. There was no reason for me to stay there with all the attention she is getting from the rest of the family so I decided to come straight back."

"There are still nine days on your pass and when this lot is over tomorrow, you're on your bike OK?"

"Right boss, now can Jock and I have Brannigan for brekkies tomorrow?"

"Ask Leo, Brannigan is his business now, his and Liam's."

"Who's Liam?"

Leo pointed out Liam.

"Liam, Geordie Shiells, Geordie, Liam Casey."

Geordie did not offer his hand.

"I thought he was one of them," he said.

"They tried hard to get him to be but he failed selection, he wasn't cut out for the job, now he's one of us and, with a bit of luck, you might just get an invite to my marriage to his sister; assuming of course that she'll have me."

"F'kin'ell, when did all this happen?" asked Geordie

"Never mind now Geordie, I'll fill you in at the exercise debrief. Why do want Brannigan?" queried Leo.

"Mainly because of them bairns at Ballykelly, and the squaddie who was killed, I knew the lad, he was from the Fusiliers, we went to school together, I didn't even know he was in the province until I saw his name in the paper back home, I feel I owe him one. I'm going to see his mam and dad when I get back but I won't tell them that I got the bastard responsible for his death, come on Leo do a mate a favour."

Leo was considering Geordie's request when the head of Sergeant Walters appeared over Geordie's shoulder. "Can we have our can back please Mr.?"

"Oh Vic, this is my boss, and this is his brother, and that's Liam, he isn't one of us," said Geordie, pointing everyone out.

"Pleased to meet you all, I'm Vic Walters 4th/7th, what would you like me and my men to do?"

Peter and Leo shook hands with the Sergeant and Liam raised his hand in greeting. He felt like the misfit he was but he also felt more secure with these people than he did with the Provisionals. Peter took the initiative.

"As of now, Security is in the hands of the RUC, you'll find an Inspector McArdle at the school house in the village. I suggest you report to him and take it from there. Do you really need to take this vehicle right now or can we use it to kip in for the night?"

"If it's all the same with you sir you can get your heads down now then after I've seen the Inspector we will relieve you at whatever time you say."

"Brilliant, how about 0200hours?" asked Peter

"Kein problem mein Kapitan, schlaff gutt," answered Walters.

"Vielen dank Kamarad," replied Peter.

Sergeant Walters and his men went off to report to the Inspector. Geordie persisted. "About Brannigan boss, do Jock and I get the honour?"

Leo looked at Peter who nodded his agreement. Leo looked into Geordie's pleading eyes and in his best Tyneside accent, he mimicked

"Gan canny bonny lad an' divvent let the bugger see yeh. But seriously Alec, don't hit him until 0905 hours on the dot and that's an order. Synchronise your watch with mine, it is now 1817 hours precisely," said Leo

"Thank you very much Leo, where will I find Trooper Shand?" asked Geordie.

"Corporal Shand if you don't mind, Para Records confirmed that he had passed his promotion course, it's a pity they couldn't be bothered to send the results on," said Leo.

Peter showed Geordie where Jock's OP was on the map and asked him if he would like to contact him by radio.

Geordie grinned. "No thanks, I'll sneak up on the little turd and scare the shite out of him. Where should I be in the morning Leo to get a crack at Brannigan, back at the farm?"

"Not necessary, he'll be here at between 0800 and 0830 hours if he follows my instructions."

Leo showed Geordie on the map where Brannigan could be located.

"This is where he'll be parked so if you and Jock set up an OP tonight just inside the tree line here, you will only be about thirty metres away from him. Wait until precisely 0905 hours before you take him out as I said before, it is important because he will be distracted at that point wondering why his remote control hasn't worked," said Leo.

It was 1830 hours and Leo felt a sudden urge to phone home to speak to his parents and to Siobhan. She would be worried about her brother and, with a bit of luck, she might even be worried about him. He discussed the possibility with Peter who had no objections provided the current operation was not discussed.

Geordie went off to find Jock Shand and Peter remained with the APC while Leo and Liam drove to the village where they found a payphone by the village green.

"Hi mum, it's me Leo, how's everything, is Siobhan settling in OK?"

"Leo! How lovely, where are you?"

"I was just doing a bit of paperwork in the Mess when I thought I would give you and dad a ring to see how you were."

"We're fine darling, and your Siobhan is a lovely girl. She's settled in with us quite well, she seems almost like one of the family."

"I intend to make her one of the family if she'll have me mum but don't tell her I said so, I want to ask her to her face when I get home."

"Oh how wonderful, and when will that be pray?"

"Some time next week I hope, I have a small project to finish first and then I hope to be free," he said truthfully.

"How is Peter?" asked mum.

"He was fine the last time I spoke to him, we might manage a spot of leave together, one of our mates has recently become a father and he has asked us both to be God fathers," said Leo.

"And where will that be pray?" asked his mother.

"In Newcastle mum, he's a real Geordie, you know, one of those animals in black and white shirts but we've decided to humour him," said Leo laughing.

"Oh you lot and your stupid football, would you like to speak with Siobhan?"

"Yes please mum, I'll say good-bye to you for now, give dad my love."

"I'll tell him you rang, he's still at his office, he works far too hard, here's Siobhan, bye-bye darling." The sound of a kiss embraced Leo's eardrum.

Leo thought his heart would burst in anticipation as the phone was handed over.

"Hello Leo, how are you and how is my little brother?" asked Siobahn.

"I'm fine thanks and Liam is well. Have you forgiven me yet or are you still sore?" he asked.

"I could forgive you almost anything now that I've met your ma and da, they're such lovely people and they have made me most welcome. Talking with your ma is like being back at home again in Northern Ireland, I love her," said Siobahn.

"And how do you feel about me?" Leo asked.

She hesitated for some seconds before replying.

"I miss you, that is all I will say, is Liam there with you?" she replied.

"He surely is, I love you and I can't wait to see you again, hang on."

He called Liam and handed him the phone.

The Kennerleys' were in a state of excitement about their future prospects. Cunningham had shaken hands with John and wished him every success. John had asked him to elucidate but he had simply smiled and said, "Mary will tell you."

They had gone to their room when they had finished washing up and tidying the kitchen after the evening meal. Mary told John everything that had occurred between leaving for Lislap and returning to the farm, including the sexual interlude. They now wondered whether it had been wise to tell Doonan about the planned mayhem at the funeral. They would just have to wait and see what transpired and take it from there. At least, the Provisional IRA would still benefit from the proceeds of crime under their leadership. They had no idea at that moment that Doonan was heading for Dungannon and a meeting with a team of handpicked Players.

Brannigan scanned the evening paper; there was no mention of any soldiers having been murdered near Ballypatrick. Leo had covered his tracks well apparently and his choice of killing them inside the deserted and derelict farmhouse had been a wise one. There was nothing on the television or the radio except regular reminders that the deceased Colonel's funeral was taking place and that the media would be covering the entire event. By the time the soldiers' bodies were found, Brannigan thought, he would be long gone and the IRA would be left to pick up the pieces, another shock for Doonan; nobody fucks with Brannigan.

Geordie Shiells made his tactical approach towards Jock Shand's OP with a view to taking him by surprise. He dodged from cover to cover until he was within fifty metres of the map reference he had been given by Peter. He scanned the ground for a telltale mound of bracken and twigs and located the site about thirty metres ahead.

Cradling his SMG in front of him, he lay flat on the ground and elbowed his way to within a metre of the OP. He reached for a long thin branch and began poking the mound expecting a head to come up and challenge him. Instead, the sound of a weapon being cocked sounded behind him.

"Lie perfectly still and push your weapon away from you," the voice whispered.

Geordie obeyed.

"Now sit up face the front and put your hands on your head."

Geordie obeyed.

"Now turn round and tell me you still love me you stupid big Geordie git."

"Fuckin'ell Jock, I was supposed to scare the shit out of you, not the other way round. Congrats on the promotion son, you deserve it, is this your OP?" asked Geordie pointing at the small mound.

"No, that's a dummy, mine's over here, and I've been watching you for the past half hour. You need to sharpen up a bit mate. How's Kitty, has she had the kid?" asked Jock.

"Yeh, it was a boy," said Geordie looking pleased with himself.

"What the fuck are you doing back here so soon? I thought you had ten days R & R," enquired Jock.

"Don't you start Jock, Nosey's already given me shit and so has Makam. The good news is that Leo has given us the job of taking out that bastard Brannigan in the morning." He went on to explain about the dead Fusilier. "We'll set up another OP tonight near where Brannigan will be parked between 0800 and 0830hrs in the morning because we have to go in together and shoot the bastard at 0905 hours on the dot," said Geordie with relish.

"OK pal, you must be knackered after all that travelling, do you want to get your head down first?" asked Jock.

"Not a bad idea mate, oh by the way I got a lift with Sandy Blewitt from Larne to Omagh do you remember him?"

"Only by reputation, he was a bit before my time, doesn't he work for Sid Morrell now?" asked Jock.

"That's him, I've invited him to the bairn's Christening, you'll get a chance to meet him there," said Geordie.

"Och, thanks for the invite, you don't need to send a card now, that appeals to my Scottish principals, now get your head down and by the way, it's good to see you."

Patrick O'Riordan was still apprehensive about his future. He felt like taking off and putting so much distance between himself and his associates that they would never find him. He knew of course that it was impossible to escape from the IRA, even though hostilities had ceased temporarily. What was going down now would surely start the whole thing off again and lead to more senseless killing but that was exactly what Brannigan wanted. He should be shot if only Patrick had the stomach for it.

Danny Monaghan had taken Patrick to one side and hinted that there would be good news for him after Brannigan got back from the funeral and did the share out of cash from their numerous bank robberies. There was over a million punt in Irish currency alone and almost as much in sterling from the Bank of Ulster and others. He also hinted at O'Riordan taking over the Bar at Ballyshiel, which would cease to be a safe house if the IRA cease-fire continued indefinitely. Monaghan had painted a rosy picture of the future but O'Riordan still had doubts. The only consolation he had was the thought that Leo Bailey might be taking over the leadership of the gang. Despite what they had done that morning to those wretched soldiers, there was still a chance that Leo would allow him to cut his ties with the gang once the others had gone their way. He sat alone in a corner of the bedding store and consumed can after can of Guinness.

Colm Neary, the Tyrone Brigade CO, had been successful in contacting six of his elite band of Players. He had been obliged to send notes to six others in the neighbouring counties in the hope of recruiting the remaining four. By 9 p.m., they were all converging on the safe house in Dungannon. They would not know the reason for their mobilisation until Doonan arrived. That much had been made clear to Neary.

Doonan had borrowed a car from a friend and sympathiser who owned a car-hire business, if anything went wrong it would be reported stolen. He knew that if he and his men were caught and arrested by the Northern Ireland authorities they would be treated with leniency considering their mission to prevent an atrocity by Brannigan and his gang in the name of the Provisional IRA. He could, if he wished, just give the information to the police and let them take care of it but grassing was anathema under any circumstances in the ranks of the IRA, he needed to discipline Brannigan and his criminal band as an example to others with similar ideas.

He crossed the unmanned border at Newry and headed for Dungannon via Armagh. He was making good time and should be at the safe house well before midnight. As he drove, he thought about how best he and his eleven men, including the Tyrone CO, should go about taking out Brannigan and his cronies. Kennerley had given him the location of the farm and the number of people staying there. Doonan would be outnumbered and outgunned by two to one but the element of surprise was his to take full advantage of. In any case, there was no way that he and his men could hit the place before 3 a.m. at the very earliest according to his reckoning. By that time, everyone should be sleeping unless there was a sentry or maybe two. A certain amount of stealth would be called for in the operation, it could prove fatal to try to rush it, the less casualties the better. Brannigan, Cunningham and Monaghan were expendable but perhaps some of the others could be persuaded to come back to the fold. Those who put up a fight would have to take their chances. The act of summary execution of the leaders in front of their followers could play a vital part in their persuasion.

Siobhan decided to turn in early after a relaxing bath. She hadn't told Leo that she loved him when he had phoned and she felt that she really should have. Her brother Liam had sounded somehow different. He had seemed more confident and sure of himself. He had not told her what he was doing in the company of Leo; he said he would save it until he saw her again. He said he had met Peter and that he and Leo were like mirror images of each other. He thanked her for having introduced him to Leo and told her that she should never again worry about him going straight. Once this job was finished, if they all survived, he had plans for their future then he rang off.

What did he mean by 'survived?' she wondered whether or not they were in some kind of danger? Suddenly the sleepiness subsided and apprehension took over.

Neary and his men were at the safe house when Doonan arrived shortly after 11 p.m. They looked like a squad of commandos ready for action. They wore a mixture of old khaki green combat jackets and modern DPM smocks and trousers. Some wore low-ankle Doc Martins while some wore US Army calf-length boots. The only IRA standard uniform bits of kit they wore were rolled up woollen Balaclava hats with slits for the mouth and eyes. Their weapons were a mixture of Armalite rifles, Russian machine pistols and automatic handguns. They looked like a formidable fighting force; Doonan congratulated Neary on his choice of men.

Neary introduced Doonan simply as 'Dan from Dublin'. Doonan shook hands with each of the men in turn and thanked them for turning out at such short notice. He proceeded to tell them why they had been called up and why it was important to the Provisional IRA that the cease-fire should be maintained. If anyone was to break it, it would be the Provisional's and not the likes of Brannigan and his lot.

The men agreed with him, they had all been sickened by what had happened at Ballykelly and a couple of them had relatives among the tiny victims. It would be a pleasure to take out Brannigan and company.

Doonan produced a map and showed them the location of the farm. They would travel in three separate cars at fifteen minute intervals and rendezvous at a cross roads half a mile from the farmhouse. From there, they would form two columns and advance tactically on foot sticking as close as possible to the field-side of the hedgerows until they came within sight of the farm.

Doonan had brought a thermal imager with which to detect possible sentries. If there were any, two men would go forward and silently take care of them. The accent was on surprise.

According to Kennerley, there were six possible rooms in the house where people could be sleeping. It would be most important to gain silent entry and disperse in pairs to each room. Anyone who produced a weapon should be shot on the spot and the others rounded up and herded into one area.

A kangaroo court would be set up and Brannigan, Cunningham and Monaghan would be charged with treason before being executed summarily in front of their men. Clemency would be offered to those of the gang who renewed their vows of allegiance to the IRA.

There was general consensus and, after light refreshments, the group set off at 1.15 a.m. on the forty or so mile journey.

Sergeant Walters woke Peter, Leo and Liam at 2 a.m. as arranged and evicted them from the APC. It was early May and the weather was reasonably warm but the sky was overcast. Peter was pleased because the cloud cover would delay the dawn while he and his Squadron got into position around the farm.

There were six OP's, each of which was manned by two men, one asleep and one awake. They had been numbered accordingly and on Peter's signal of three double bleeps, each OP responded in turn with one bleep from number one, two bleeps from number two, and so on until all of the OP's were accounted for.

The three men in Leo's Troop, Mick Rutherford, George Davidson and Dave Affleck, would accompany Peter to the farm. One of Sergeant Walters' troopers would then transport them to within a mile of the farm from where they would advance into position before daybreak. Peter's men, consisting of Geordie Shiells, Jock Shand, and Mal Spencer, would follow on with Leo and Liam when the funeral was safely under way.

Geordie and Jock were in position overlooking the viewpoint where Brannigan was expected to park. Leo and Liam were taking turns at dozing in the Land Rover left behind by Kennerley and the pseudo RMP. From where the vehicle was parked, Leo had an uninterrupted view across the divide to the viewpoint that was about a quarter of a mile distant. Through binoculars, before darkness had fallen, he had been unable to make out where Geordie and Jock had set up their OP. He was satisfied that if he couldn't see it through well-trained eyes, the likelihood was that Brannigan would not see it either.

It was 2.45 a.m. when the last of Doonan's marauders reached the rendezvous. He split them into two groups and told them to wait for five minutes before following him and a scout. They would go forward with the thermal imager and check to see if a guard had been posted. If there were sentries, they would take care of them commando-style.

There were no sentries and the farmhouse was in complete darkness. So confident were the occupants, that no one had even bothered to lock the front door, or was it the fact that they had drunk too much at the party?

The kitchen door was also unlocked and only two people were found sleeping soundly in one of the reception rooms, Cunningham and Monaghan. They were swiftly and silently bound and gagged before the remainder of the gang were rudely awakened and herded into the large ground floor living room.

They stood around in various states of undress, rubbing their eyes and scratching their chilled bare flesh, wondering what the hell was going on. Masked raiders pointing guns surrounded them. They could have been forgiven for believing they were members of the SAS.

Doonan went forward and singled out the Kennerleys before taking them at gunpoint into the kitchen where he removed his mask.

"God, Mr. Dan! Where did you come from?" asked John Kennerley.

"Dublin, where do you think, where's Brannigan?"

"He won't be here until after the funeral, I believe he's blowing the remote charges we planted yesterday."

"He's doing what, for feck's sake, how is he getting there?"

"He has an official invitation to get him through security and the RUC check-point. According to the map Leo Bailey showed us, he should be about a quarter of a mile away to the south of the church. There is a turn-off from the main road to a picnic area somewhere on the right where Brannigan will be parked."

"Who's Leo Bailey?" asked Doonan.

"He's a new boy, one of Bernard Cluskey's secret little army apparently. He and a courier, Liam Casey, made a miraculous escape from the RUC the day that Eamon Flynn bought it. It was Leo who planned everything at Ballypatrick, he should be returning not long after Brannigan during the confusion in the aftermath."

"Right, we'll wait for this Leo Bailey whoever he is and Liam Casey and give them a nasty surprise when they get here. In the meantime, I will have to try to stop Brannigan somehow. You two get dressed and get the hell out of here and contact me in Dublin when all this is over. Take Cunningham's car, he won't need it again. Good luck and thanks for keeping me informed."

They hurried off to pack their meagre belongings then decided they would not need them anymore. They were suddenly very rich after all.

O'Riordan awoke with a jolt when he heard Cunningham's BMW burst into life and pull away into the darkness. He shook himself and looked at his luminous watch; it was 3.30 a.m. Where in God's name he wondered could Cunningham be going at this time of morning; what the hell. He snuggled down again on the camp bed and went back to sleep. The Irish Tricolour flag was beneath his head as a pillow; Leo had given him explicit instructions for hoisting it at dawn on the flagpole at the entrance to the farm.

Doonan went back to the living room and ordered his men to tie the hands and feet of their prisoners. He told Neary that the court would have to wait until Brannigan, Bailey and Casey were taken care of. He had an idea where he might find Brannigan but they would have to hurry and get into position before dawn. He must be prevented from blowing the charges or there would be dire consequences for the cease-fire. The place was only ten miles away; it would not take them too long to get there.

Neary left his senior Player in charge and instructed him to use his initiative if anyone gave trouble then he and Doonan set off to find Brannigan. They took Doonan's hire car and hid it about a mile from Ballypatrick.

They were not far from the RUC checkpoint when they saw the lights of a vehicle coming towards them. They took cover in some bushes at the side of the road until the APC containing Peter and his section sped past en route to the farm.

Using the thermal imager, Doonan detected the body heat of two soldiers concealed in the undergrowth within a hundred metres of each side of the checkpoint. Using the cover of darkness, they skirted the obstacles and by-passed them.

He and Neary trekked on until they came to the turn-off leading to where Brannigan would leave the main road and head towards the viewpoint. They waited in cover until daylight. Doonan was pleased to stop and rest, he was no longer as fit at the age of forty five as he had been in the days of active service.

Chapter 11

Brendan Roscoe, the coachbuilder, was desperate for a piss as were most of the other prisoners. They had been tied up for what seemed like an eternity and the masked men refused to speak to them or answer any of their questions. The captives naturally wanted to know who their captors were and why they were being held, why they had been tied up and what was going to happen to them when the other two got back from where they had gone. But none of Neary's men would respond to them.

Cunningham thought he had recognised the voice of the leader earlier on, but he could not be sure. It had been a long time since he had seen Doonan.

"Are you Daniel Doonan's men?" He asked the man who had been left in charge.

"Be quiet or else," the man warned.

"Look, most of these people have an urgent need to piss and whatever, couldn't you just take them outside or to the bathroom one by one. What harm would it do?"

The man in-charge went over to two of the others and consulted with them. He returned to Cunningham and viciously kicked him in the ribs.

"Right, you will be taken to the bathroom one by one but no funny business or you won't be coming back, is that clear?"

Cunningham felt as though some of his ribs had been broken as he lay there in great pain.

Roscoe was the first one to struggle to his feet after being untied and was led away. It took almost an hour to relieve all of the captives of their suffering

When it came to Cunningham's turn, he tried again to find out the identity of the raiding party. He received a hefty blow on the side of his head from one of the minders for his trouble. The one who had spoken earlier was definitely from the north but their leader was most certainly from the south.

He guessed that it might be Doonan, it had to be him. But how in hell could Doonan have found out about what Brannigan was up to? Could there possibly be a mole in the gang? And where the bloody hell was O'Riordan and the Kennerley's? 'Oh Jesus Christ no, not one of them', he thought. He was in great distress as he and Monaghan were led off to the toilet.

The driver of the APC dropped off Peter and his men about half a mile from the farm. They made their way to the copse from where Peter had observed Leo's explosives demonstration.

He scanned the farm and the outbuildings through his binoculars and noticed that there were lights on in a couple of the ground floor rooms but there no movement outside. Dawn had broken and it was beginning to get lighter although the sky was overcast. He told his Squadron that they would advance on the farm at 0900 hours and arrest the occupants.

"Why 0900 hours, why not now while most of them are sleeping?" asked Mick Rutherford.

"Because Mick my lad, at 0900 hours precisely, they will be huddled around a television set eagerly awaiting the outcome of yesterday morning's bomb-laying. The last thing they will expect is a visit from this lot and who knows, they might have a line to Brannigan's car phone."

Peter tried to picture the device secreted beneath the bench in the cellar of the farm. He wondered if he had been right to attach the explosive charges. A picture of his mother with her false limbs, and the battered side of the school bus in which seven children had died, flashed through his mind. But could he also kill in cold blood?

There had been many atrocities perpetrated by terrorists over the years but only a handful of the murderers had ever been brought to justice. As a result, several who had been captured red handed were handed over to a dedicated SAS team that escorted them to pre-selected secret sites where they were summarily executed and buried. It had been a favourite tactic of the IRA in the past when dealing with captive soldiers and they did not like the taste of their own medicine. Maybe God might forgive Peter for faking an IRA own goal, but could he forgive himself? After all, some bombers in the past had accidentally blown themselves to pieces and everybody had applauded their passing, why not now? He decided to wait and see.

"How would you like a nice cuppa Liam?" asked Leo as they sat in the Land rover.

"I'd love one if we had the makings, but everything was left in the APC, why?" asked Liam.

"Well, I don't expect Brannigan for a couple of hours yet, so what do you say we nip over to the RUC Command Post and scrounge a brew?" asked Leo.

"You're the boss, lead the way," said Leo. They set off in the Land Rover for the village and the schoolhouse.

The RUC checkpoint shift had just changed and the in-coming policemen were lined up at the tea urn. Leo waived to the Inspector as he and Liam joined the queue.

The Inspector, Jeff McArdle, was leafing through an album of wanted people when Leo joined him. McArdle explained that his men were trained to look out for wanted Players and criminals who might try to use the occasion to create an incident especially at roadblocks set up for events such as the funeral. The pictures of the three dead Real IRA men killed the evening before had been ringed and crossed.

Leo recognised pictures of most of the gang back at the farm who had been wanted in the past. The album showed pictures in a separate section in the back of the book of soldiers who had disappeared without trace for one reason or another. Kennerley's picture was among them under the name of Corporal Kevin Bradley, Army Logistics Corps. As far as the authorities were concerned he had disappeared while on leave to attend a family funeral in the province.

"I know him," said Leo, "that's Kennerley, he's one of Cunningham's men. He and his wife are caretakers at the farm Brannigan uses as a safe house and equipment dump. Brannigan also has a cache of arms and a bomb factory there. I think our Corporal Bradley is earmarked for Cunningham's position when he retires. Some hope."

Leo pointed out the picture to the Inspector.

"Peter should be at the farm by now with his section ready to take the place at the appointed hour. I will be joining him after the funeral, we will hand-over Kennerley, I mean Bradley, to you and your men afterwards and you can do the honours," said Leo.

Doonan and Neary watched Leo's Land Rover as it travelled to the village then return half an hour later to the cover of a hedgerow situated between the church and the road along which Brannigan would be entering the village. It was now 7.30 a.m. and fully light although the sky was still clouded. It looked to be clearing from the west and at least it was dry apart for the morning dew that had seeped into their clothing as they crawled through the undergrowth.

Three busloads of soldiers went past the place where Dooanan and Neary lay concealed and cars were already arriving in a slow trickle. A huge vehicle marked 'Ulster Television' with a satellite dish on its roof went past and made its way towards the grassed area below the church.

Doonan wondered if they could stop Brannigan before he had a chance to blow the charges. He had no idea where the man could be at that moment, all they could do was to wait until they had sight of the distinctive Jaguar then act accordingly.

The current cease-fire had to be protected at all costs because the Prince of Wales was due in Dublin for an official visit the following week and Doonan had a surprise reception all lined up for the occasion. Doonan had assisted in the assassination of the Prince's grandfather, his grandson Nicholas and their boatman in August 1979. Although he had not planted the actual bomb, he had been a lookout for several days leading up to the incident at Mullaghmore. He had been a lot younger and fitter in those days.

Leo was surprised at the number of people arriving for General Fitzpatrick's funeral. There were far more than he had expected but a lot of it could be down to the freedom of movement enjoyed in the province since the Christmas cease-fire had been announced. People were slowly gaining in confidence and venturing out.

It was late spring and there had been a noticeable increase in traffic, particularly at weekends, in the province. A fair crowd was forming on the grassed area at either side of the drive leading up from the road to the church as well as along the route from the village. He thought of what could have been if he and Liam had not managed to infiltrate the gang. It was too horrible to contemplate but Brannigan would have gloried in it had he planned it all instead of Leo.

At 8.41 a.m., the earpiece on Leo's coms beeped.

"Bravo one."

He listened to the brief message from the policeman at the roadblock.

"Roger out."

Brannigan had arrived at last. Leo kept his binoculars focused on the road approaching the track where Brannigan was expected to turn off. Everything was going according to plan. Brannigan turned onto the track as instructed and slowly made his way to the viewpoint parking area.

Leo failed to notice the bobbing heads of Doonan and Neary as they emerged from the bushes where they had been hiding. They immediately went down on their bellies and began to crawl slowly through the long grass in the direction of the retreating Jaguar.

O'Riordan glanced at his watch and shot out of bed, either the bloody alarm had not gone off or he had not heard it. He should have raised the Tricolour at dawn in accordance with Leo's instructions. He slung the flag over his shoulder and wandered outside the barn and proceeded to relieve his bladder. Mick Rutherford observed the movement and touched Peter's arm and pointed. When O'Riordan had finished his pee, he made his way to the entrance of the farm drive about a hundred metres from the house.

There was a flagpole that had not been in use for more than ten years since the staunch Presbyterian farming family had been forced out of their home by Republican thugs.

The union flag had previously flown proudly from the pole every day until the family had moved out. Now O'Riordan discovered that the rope attached to the pulley wheel was probably too rotten and flimsy to support a flag. He dare not try to attach the Tricolour for fear the rope snapped. He draped the flag over the fence and returned to the barn to hunt out a piece of new rope.

It was 8.45 a.m., and the television set in the farmhouse had been switched on for the funeral. The prisoners sat in a half circle in front of the set while their captors stood behind them.

Peter left his section in the copse while he and Mick Rutherford moved tactically towards the farmhouse. When they were within metres of the buildings, Peter told Mick to take cover and keep an eye out for O'Riordan.

Crouching low in one of shallow overgrown ditches on each side of the drive, Peter crept forward to the living room window. With his back to the wall and using a small mirror, he slowly moved it into position so that he could just see into the room. One of Doonan's men had his back to the window and was engrossed in the scene before him. Everyone else in the room was watching the television screen.

Peter pocketed the mirror and peeped over the sill into the room. There were hooded and masked men with guns standing behind Brannigan's men who were kneeling on the floor with their hands tied behind their backs. He wondered what was going down. As far as he was aware, there were no other troops in the area.

He made his way round to the back of the building to the half open kitchen door and waited. Two of Doonan's men entered the kitchen and put their weapons on the table, removed their masks and lit up cigarettes. Peter peaked through the crack between the door and the stanchion. One man had his back to the door but Peter could clearly see the face of the other man. He recognised him as a wanted Player but wondered what he was doing there with a bunch of armed confederates.

"The job's done," said the man facing him. "They are both dead."

"Did they squeal like pigs?" asked his companion.

"I didn't remove the gags, I just stuck them from behind; they didn't know a thing.

"Doonan will be happy at that then," said the other.

'Doonan!' Thought Peter, 'what the hell was going on?'

O'Riordan found his rope and returned to the flagpole where he attached one end of the new rope to the frayed end of the old rope and carefully pulled it upwards towards the pulley wheel. He was completely oblivious to what was going on around him when Mick Rutherford tapped him on the shoulder. O'Riordan yanked the rope in surprise. It snapped and the whole lot crashed down around him and Mick entangling them both.

"What the hell!" exclaimed O'Riordan trying to untangle him self.

At precisely 8.59 a.m., Leo spotted two hooded figures, one on each side of the car, approaching the Jaguar at the run with their weapons aimed at Brannigan.

"Jesus Christ Geordie, you bloody idiots, I said 0905 hours," he cried out in alarm; he knew he could not be heard from that distance. As he watched in horror, he saw the puff of the explosion followed by the dull and distant thud as the bomb beneath Brannigan's car seat detonated. The two hooded figures were hurled upwards and backwards away from the vehicle that burst into flames.

From their OP, Geordie and Jock had watched as Brannigan pointed the remote out of the driver's side window of the car. The two hooded men seemed to appear from nowhere as the bomb exploded. They watched them fly into the air with the force of the blast, and lie smouldering and still on the ground at each side of the wrecked and blazing car.

Peter looked at his watch, it would be all over for Brannigan by now, or maybe it was Brannigan who would be all over, he mused. All he needed to do now was to order his men to remain at a safe distance, remove the seal on the remote control device concealed in his smock, flick the switch, and send the whole of Brannigan's gang to Hades where they belonged. The gang them selves would be credited with the expensive home goal and he and his men would be hailed as heroes. Unfortunately, it was not so easy to take out between thirty and forty men in cold blood. It would be murder and he was not sure he could do it and live with his conscience. He had been trained to kill but he was not a trained killer, there was a difference. There was also the matter of the armed and masked minders. They were obviously IRA but what were they doing at the farm?

A shot rang out from an upstairs window at the front of the house. O'Riordan's body slumped across Mick Rutherford as he tried to extricate himself from the entangled rope. Mick lay still and waited for a second shot to end his life but it did not come.

Peter made himself scarce and raced for the safety of the copse. Mick saw him rounding the corner of the farmhouse. He threw the badly wounded O'Riordan off him and began to give covering fire towards the house, retreating as he did so. Shots rang out from the copse as the SAS Squadron gave covering fire to their fleeing colleagues.

The army Land Rover, the APC and the RUC Land Rover all arrived at the same time at the scene of Brannigan's demise. The vehicle was burning fiercely and the two hooded and smouldering figures of Doonan and Neary were moaning as they regained consciousness. Leo ran over to them one by one and pulled off their smouldering hoods to discover that they were not who he thought they were. He heaved a great sigh of relief when the welcome Geordie voice shouted out behind him.

"Who the fuckin 'ell are they? They're not ours."

The Inspector joined Leo and positively identified Doonan and Neary as two known IRA Players. But why were they after Brannigan and who was responsible for the car bomb?

Leo turned and faced away from the recovering Daniel Doonan, shrugged his shoulders and said, "It could have been anybody," he said, "Brannigan must have made a few enemies in his time. I can imagine him having been an embarrassment to his masters. They don't like their people stepping out of line any more than we do."

Leo handed over security to McArdle and called in the remainder of the Delta Two Zero Troop. They piled into the Land Rover and set off for the farm at speed.

As they approached the copse, they heard the sound of the firefight and stopped well short of the entrance. A bloody Patrick O'Riordan had regained consciousness and was busy trying to extricate himself from the tangled rope he had attempted to attach to the pulley. The IRA sniper's bullet had grazed his scalp and knocked him out momentarily.

Leo deployed his section and told them to cover him while he and Liam donned Kevlar vests and went to rescue O'Riordan. He couldn't let the poor sod die out there; he wondered why.

Peter ordered his men to give covering fire as he watched Leo and Liam race towards O'Riordan who was still lying face down but obviously not dead. The two men left their weapons at the side of the track before taking an arm each and grabbing O'Riordan by the waistband of his trousers and running with him. As Peter watched the rescue through his binoculars, he saw both Leo and Liam suddenly pitch forward. He felt a searing pain in his back and realised instinctively that his twin had been shot; the three bodies lay motionless. The firing from the house, that had been intense for the past half hour, intensified more as Doonan's men sorted them selves out. Brannigan's men had begged to be cut loose to join them in the firefight; there was enough stored arms and ammunition to sustain a long siege.

Cunningham and Monaghan were lying upstairs with their throats cut on the orders of Doonan to the man he had left in charge. The other members of the gang were not so important. They were cut free of their bonds and allowed to arm themselves.

Roscoe hurried to the cellar followed by the others who grabbed what weapons and ammo they could find before dashing back to man the windows facing the SAS positions. Roscoe stayed in the cellar and smashed the blackened glass of the only window that could be seen about a foot above ground. He pointed a Thompson machine gun towards the copse where Peter's men were dug in and pinned them down.

As the firing intensified further and his men were in danger, Peter made his decision. He crawled away from the copse and through the long grass to the boulder—strewn island in middle of the field where he had set up his previous OP. From there, he could clearly see the cellar window. He pointed the remote control and pressed the button. The strong infra-red signal bounced around the cellar until it made wireless contact with the detonator on the bomb that Peter had placed under the bench. There followed a dull thud as the device went off triggering a chain reaction.

The resultant explosion was enormous as the entire arsenal of ammunition and explosives stored in the cellar went up. A second explosion followed almost immediately as the bomb factory in the attic detonated. When the dust settled, the farmhouse was no more. There was a huge crater where it had been and the outbuildings had also suffered extensive damage. The criminals' expensive cars were flattened and covered with debris. Bodies lay around in grotesque poses, some up too fifty metres from the centre of the blast. Peter felt sick but at least there were no casualties in the Squadron apart from Leo.

He sprinted to where Leo, Liam and Patrick lay moaning. Geordie Shiells and Jock were already on the scene removing the heavily dented Kevlar armour from Leo and Liam. They had both been shot from behind but the armour had withstood the shock. O'Riordan had survived the volley because he was being carried face down and all he had was a violent headache from the previous graze on his scalp. Leo had sustained a flesh wound on his left arm onto which Geordie was applying a field dressing. Liam was fine apart from some painful bruising on his back.

The Kennerleys' were nowhere to be seen and Cunningham's car was gone. Leo, with his arm in a sling, questioned the bandaged O'Riordan who, having slept in an outbuilding, had not even seen or heard the arrival of Doonan and his men. He did however, remember having been awoken by a car starting up in the middle of the night but he had gone straight back to sleep. And, thinking about it, he also remembered having overheard Cunningham telling Brannigan about his trip to Lislap with Mary Kennerley when he and John Kennerley had reported back to Brannigan after planting the charges along the church drive. There had also been some speculation about who would be taking over the running of things when the big three retired. Kennerley's name had been mentioned as a possible replacement for Cunningham but it had all been conjecture.

"Do you still want out Patrick?" asked Leo

"Even more so now but how could that be possible?" asked O'Riordan

"You are every kind of rogue Patrick O'Riordan but you're not a killer, both Liam and I know that. I'm going to give you a chance to turn Queen's evidence against this lot," said Leo.

"What's in it for me?" asked Patrick.

"New start, new name, new country, America, Australia, Canada, anywhere you like really, what do you say?" asked Leo.

"And if I refuse?" asked Patrick.

"If you were a dog, you'd get six months in a tripe shop with a muzzle on but, with your human criminal record, you'll probably get at least ten years. No one will ever believe that you didn't detonate the bomb that killed those poor bloody kids at Ballykelly. Flynn, Dixon, and Cunningham are no longer here to take the rap and dear old Mr Brannigan switched himself off this morning. So what's it going to be Patrick?" asked Leo.

"I don't have much choice do I? I'll do it," said Patrick.

The helicopters ordered by Peter arrived and transported the SAS men and the two civilians back to the Bessbrook HQ leaving the scene of destruction and carnage to be discovered by others.

At the exercise debrief, Cedric Parker did not ask for and Peter did not volunteer an explanation for the demolition of the farm. It was assumed that either a stray bullet had sparked off the explosion or the IRA had scored an own goal. In any case, the only people who knew of the SAS presence on the scene were the SAS themselves, Liam Casey, Patrick O'Riordan and the RUC inspector. No names meant no pack drill.

The floor of the living room in the Lislap house was littered with strewn bank notes discovered in the chest in the boot of Cunningham's BMW. The Kennerleys' were lounging in the Jacuzzi drinking champagne and celebrating their luck when the bathroom door flew open and two armed Military Policemen walked in.

"Corporal Kevin Bradley, you are under arrest for desertion, get out of there and get dressed. You stay where you are Mrs. Bradley, there's a policewoman to see you concerning a robbery or two."

Epilogue

The destruction of Brannigan's farm base was assumed to have been a tragic accident in the absence of any evidence to the contrary. The SAS had gathered up their spent cartridges with the aid of a metal detector before departing the scene.

The discovery of the backup database disc complete with passwords amongst Mary Bradley's personal affects produced all the evidence required by the police to put any remaining mainland members of Brannigan's gang away for a variety of offences.

The safe houses, shops and brothels on the mainland were raided and closed down and the sleepers who had not been required to attend the farm were arrested. They were all treated as common criminals and denied the status of political prisoners as members of the IRA.

The mystery surrounding the planting of the bomb in Brannigan's car was never solved. Various theories were bandied about from in-fighting and jealousy within the ranks of Sinn Fein/IRA and disenchanted members of Brannigan's own gang. One thing for sure was that whoever was responsible had done the world a great favour.

Daniel Doonan and Colm Neary spent several weeks recovering in hospital after plastic surgery. They were released without charge when it transpired that Doonan in order to save the cease-fire was trying to prevent the atrocity planned by Brannigan.

In the absence of hospitalized Doonan from his office at Murphy's bar, the visit of the Prince of Wales went off without incident. Doonan eventually stood down as Commander-in-chief of the Provisional IRA.

Patrick O'Riordan was not required to give Queens Evidence but his widely published refusal to do so, earned him his deliverance from the clutches of the IRA. He was simply released without charge due to lack of evidence. He sold up and set off on a ship to America in search of a new life.

Replaced by A Squadron, D Squadron SAS were posted back to Hereford from where they went on R & R for two weeks.

Geordie invited every one of them, plus Sandy Blewitt and Sid Morrell, to the Christening of baby Peter Leo Shiells. To everybody's amusement, the child wore a black and white striped Christening gown. The Bailey twins were both Godfathers.

Peter and Leo decided to retire from active service and to join their father in the family marine engineering business. They felt that their mother had been avenged after forensic and DNA tests on recovered fragments of flesh and body parts around the site of the car bomb intended for Leo in Belfast revealed that the bomber was none other than John McCann. Joe put two and two together and had come up with an answer to the mysterious attempt on the lives of him and Mary.

The twins felt that there was no longer a future for them in the SAS but they remained in reserve on the Rapid Response Team.

Leo and Siobhan were married within two months and Peter stood as best man. Liam Casey returned to his parents' Belfast house on the offer of a job from Martin Ellis. He took a day-release course in engineering at the University of Belfast and discovered to his amazement that he was quite bright.

PART 2

'OPERATION WIPEOUT'

Prologue

D aniel Doonan was completely baffled and seriously depressed; the IRA Godfathers had disowned him since he stood down as C in C of the Provisional IRA just two years previously. Unwelcome changes had occurred during that time, Northern Ireland was in danger of being unanimously voted out of the Union by the people of England, Scotland and Wales in a referendum. The divided people of the province had been denied the right to vote because of their intransigence. Doonan felt he had to resume command of a resurrected IRA; his comeback had not been welcome.

Apart from a handful of his senior Players, including Leo Bailey, Barney Meehan and his nephew Liam Casey and few other people in outlying areas, almost his entire command had been wiped out and the bodies of his assassinated CO's had disappeared without trace, probably buried in secret graves. It was an old IRA tactic against the British security forces that had caused so much distress to the families of those and other people they had murdered in the past. The tables had been turned and the medicine tasted foul.

The relatives of Doonan's lost army were clambering for his blood and he was now on the run. Murphy's Bar, Doonan's old Dublin HQ and his Brother Bryan's pub, had been wrecked and burned to the ground by the four sons of his vanished Tyrone CO and close friend Colm Neary. Doonan had barely escaped with his own life but who was behind it all? He could not think. Most of the British Army and the dreaded SAS were long gone from the province.

The Loyalist paramilitaries and criminal gangs had suffered a similar fate to their Republican enemies. Doonan did not think that the police had the wit, the will, or even the resources to carry out such a clandestine operation, and the planned new Northern Ireland Army was still in the womb. Could it possibly be the Godfathers of the old IRA in league with the Irish Army Special Forces? Or maybe the so-called Real IRA was behind it. Who were these faceless people who had struck terror into the hearts of the opposing terrorist tribes? Were they British or Irish or both? Doonan had to find out who was behind it and mete out a little punishment of his own.

He had managed to get a message to Martin McCaffrey the Sinn Fein MP at Stormont and elder brother of Michael McCaffrey killed by the SAS at Ballypatrick. They had been good friends once when Martin McCaffrey was younger and a member of a Derry Brigade ASU (Active Service Unit) until Bloody Sunday 30 July 1972, the day that thirteen innocent civilians had allegedly been killed by members of the Parachute Regiment during a peace rally.

Martin McCaffrey had been so sickened by the event that he had given up the gun for the ballot box and had turned to politics for a solution to the troubles.

They met in country pub just outside Letterkenny. Doonan was unshaven and his clothes were crumpled and scruffy. McCaffrey was clean and smart by comparison and smelled of aftershave although he sported a beard. He handed over a small suitcase to Doonan who disappeared into the men's toilet for a wash and shave and a change of clothing while McCaffrey ordered a meal and drinks for them both. When Doonan emerged he looked clean smart and refreshed. He felt like a new man after three days on the run; the men talked as they ate.

"You've changed a lot since I last saw you Dan," said McCaffrey, "what happened to your face?"

"Plastic surgery," said Doonan, "I had a run in with your Sinn Fein colleague, Mark Brannigan in '95. You must have heard about what happened to him. One of the boys and me was going to teach him a lesson when I found out what he was up to but his car was blown up just as we got to him. The bomb had been planted by one of his top men who confessed to me recently. It turned out to be Brannigan who shopped the Derry Quartermaster, Bernard Cluskey, to the RUC. Did Sinn Fein know about Brannigan's criminal activities?"

"He would not have represented us in the Bogside if we had known; it was one of the best kept secrets in the world. He had three very loyal lieutenants who reported directly to him and they ran everything between them on his orders as far as we can gather. Did you know about him?" asked McCaffrey.

"I did, and so did Barney Meehan and Dixie Dixon, but I gave them the order to keep their mouths shut because Brannigan funded us for his own protection. A mole in his gang kept me well informed of the gang's activities." answered Doonan.

"What can I do for you now Dan, why did you ask me to come and meet you?" asked McCaffrey, changing the subject.

"You must have seen the papers and the television reports Martin, both the Loyalists and our selves have been badly hit by an unknown third force. I can't imagine it being the police or the British Army. I want to find out who and what these people are before they wipe us out completely. You must have some idea at Stormont about who they are," said Doonan.

"We don't know who they are. Only the British SAS are capable of that kind of operation but as far as we know, they left Northern Ireland before the gradual withdrawal of the British Army apart from a possible token rear guard. We know where they operated from but all of those locations are now deserted and are already showing signs of neglect," said McCaffrey. "But one thing we do know is that the present Defence Minister was the CO of the last SAS contingent to leave the Province and is now an advocate, maybe even the architect, of the current policy towards Northern Ireland. We believe that the recent referendum on the exclusion of the province from the Union was one of his bright ideas so I would not be surprised if he had something to do with your current trouble.

"What's his name?" asked Doonan.

"Parker, Cedric Parker, the Defence Minister, his last tour of military duty was in the province with the SAS I believe and I've heard he has since been nominated for a knighthood in the New Years Honours List. He is the only person I can think of who would have the knowhow to mount such an operation but there's no evidence," said McCaffrey. "I've never met the man but I have seen his picture in the papers and I've seen and heard him speak on television."

"Could you get me a picture of him and tell me where I can find him," asked Doonan.

"Why, what have you in mind?" McCaffrey asked.

"I'd like to meet him and confront him," answered Doonan.

"You'd never get anywhere near him, the security at Whitehall is too tight, particularly now. You just can't knock on his office door and ask to speak to him, his home will be a fortress I suspect, or at least until after the province joins the EEC," said McCaffrey.

"I'm not that stupid Martin, if it was as easy as that, there would be a lot more dead Brit politicians. I need a photograph, an appointment, a pass, and an identity tag. I don't need a shooter," said Doonan.

"You surely don't expect me to go along with that do you Dan?" said McCaffrey. "I gave up the guns and the bombs a long time ago, don't ask me to get involved in anything violent because I will refuse."

"You don't have to do anything more than get me a blank House of Commons ID tag and I'll go it alone from there. I know what I'm doing and you will not be involved in any way, neither by word nor deed," said Doonan.

"Government ID blanks are accountable documents Dan, not easy to come by but I'll try if that's all you want, where will I send it if I get my hands on one?" McCaffrey asked.

"Lend me your pen and give me some paper and I'll give you an address in London. I have an old sleeper there who I can visit with for a while. I can't stay here any more, the feckin' bastards have even got my own people looking for me," said Doonan.

He wrote down the address of the sleeper and handed it to McCaffrey who looked at the name and address.

"Mother of God, is he still around? I thought he would have been dead by now, he must be past seventy," said McCaffrey.

"Seventy eight and the old sod still believes he is serving but we haven't asked anything of him in twenty odd years, we just like him to feel wanted. I've told him that I am going to visit him to stand him down officially and take him out for a couple of drinks. I intend to stay with him for a while until things have cooled down here," said Doonan.

"I'll do my best Dan if you don't hear anything after a fortnight you'll know I have been unsuccessful." McCaffrey got up to leave and pressed two hundred pounds in twenties into Doonan's left hand as he shook the other. "You'll need that to tide you over Dan. I'll pay for the refreshments on the way out. Good luck with Major Nosey bloody Parker."

Chapter 12

S ir Anthony Warbacker, the British Prime Minister, arose early to take advantage of the glorious sunrise in the garden of the Irish Taoiseach's country residence. The British newspapers had been delivered by courier from Dublin airport, where they had arrived on the 3 a.m. flight and had been left in the back porch of the house by one of the perimeter guards.

Sir Anthony and his family were guests of the Irish Premier and due back in London in two days time. It had been a seven-day working holiday during which both heads of government had discussed the worsening crisis in Northern Ireland. The fragile peace initiative set up in 1996 seemed doomed to final failure due to one set-back after another.

The Official IRA and the Provisional IRA had sued for peace. Their members had been ordered to lay down their arms and to pursue their aims by political means as opposed to ongoing but fruitless armed struggle.

The so-called Real IRA flatly refused to give in to pressure from the two other factions nor was it thought would the criminal fraternities, both loyalist and republican, that had benefitted hugely from the Troubles for many years. The loyalist paramilitary organisations had made no response whatsoever to the call to disarm.

First the republicans would conjure an excuse for stirring up trouble to which the loyalists would then respond in kind. Dispute would be followed by disturbances causing the loss of innocent life and several thousands of pounds worth of structural damage to both communities leaving the British tax-payer to pick up the bill.

Escalation was inevitable as the hate mongers in both camps stirred a malevolent broth of discontent and fed it to their less than innocent youth. Criminal elements on both sides fanned the flames for their own selfish ends.

Politics and religion had been the root causes of the past Troubles but they were no longer the main factors. Greed for possession and lust for power had crept into the equation as the criminals who benefited from the conflict saw their livelihood at risk if a peace deal succeeded. Peace committees faded into oblivion under intimidation from the ever-growing forces of evil.

It seemed never ending and answers were not forthcoming from the think tanks of both Britain and Eire. UK taxpayers were picking up the bill at an average rate of £750 per head of population per annum in one form of tax or another and the cost was continually escalating.

Demolished main-route border posts were being hurriedly reconstructed and troops were being rushed into the province once again to assist the civil police force. The old RUC was gone as an organisation and the force that replaced it was a domesticated tiger by comparison. Policemen and soldiers alike were once again being caught in the crossfire. Businesses were moving out of the province at an alarming rate driving up the unemployment figures and increasing the financial burden even further.

The headline in the Daily Mail the previous day had read:

'Sir Anthony Warbacker in deep despair'

The article went on to tell of his business-cum-holiday trip to Dublin and to report on the lack of progress in the talks. It told harrowing stories about the recent atrocities, and the hopelessness of the situation.

Columnists and other commentators offered the usual armchair-expert solutions and opposition party members showed little sympathy for Sir Anthony and his beleaguered ministers, in fact they revelled in the discomfort of the PM and his colleagues as always. The opposition, no matter whom, always knew better than the government of the day how to handle difficult situations but rarely came up with answers and so it had ever been; no one had any real solutions to offer.

Shelley Warbacker and the children would be joining Sir Anthony and the Taoiseach's family later for an alfresco breakfast in the warm sunshine forecast for the morning.

Declan O'Hara, a hardened killer and a member of the Real IRA, had travelled south from Belfast in the dead of night. He had crossed the recently closed border at one of the network of secret crossing points that were used only occasionally so as not to leave tell tale trails. Once inside the Republic, he had been met and taken by car to within two miles of the target area.

The going had been quite easy but he had yet to gain entry to the Taoiseach's country estate which he expected to be heavily guarded. He was armed with a lightweight high velocity rifle and silencer that folded and tucked neatly into a sheath at the side of his rucksack. A small pocket infrared telescope, capable of being used as a night sight, and a 250ml. bottle of water, were the only other things he carried apart from a couple of bars of chocolate. He always travelled light.

Veteran SAS Sergeants Mick Rutherford and Alec Shiells had been assigned to the close-quarter protection of Sir Anthony and his family during their stay in the Republic. They wore civilian clothing and posed as gardening staff on the estate. One of them was never far from the Prime Minister and the other stayed fairly close to the PM's wife when she was outside the house.

They were ably assisted by a couple of men from the Special Forces of the Irish Army and the four of them got on very well together considering, but then, the Irish Army were not the RIRA nor did they have much sympathy with terrorists.

It always amazed Alec Shiells how British soldiers got on so well with foreign soldiers when their countries were at peace. Soldiering created a kind of worldwide brotherhood that Alec found hard to fathom. He especially liked the Germans with whom he had been on NATO exercise on a number of occasions. Unlike many of his colleagues, he had taken the time and the trouble to learn to speak the language, which helped considerably. The only problem he had was getting them to understand his Geordie sense of humour which always seemed to go over their heads.

With the aid of his night sight, O'Hara had managed to place all six soldiers of the perimeter guard that patrolled at regular intervals within about a mile radius of the house. He timed their round and, under the cover of darkness, slipped easily between two of them without alerting their dogs.

He made his way to within 200 metres of the house and selected a vantage point beneath a dense patch of rhododendron in line with the side of the building from where he could observe movement from both the front and the rear entrances.

He was totally unaware of the well-concealed Irish Special Forces trooper 100 metres forward of him and slightly to his left in the shrubbery. It was while he was jostling for position that he broke the infrared beam just in front of him and set the bleeper going in the SAS minders' duty room.

Mick Rutherford was well away in dreamland but Geordie was still on watch. He shot off the bed where he had been reading and switched off the bleeper as he peered at the relevant CCTV monitor. The camera, set on night-vision, slowly arced automatically between the two sensors where the break in the infrared beam had occurred. Geordie knew from the location of the indicator that it could not be one of his Irish colleagues who was well forward of the detectors ringing the estate between the perimeter fence and the house. He switched off the automatic heat seeking mechanism and slowly scanned the area manually for the slightest movement. Patience was rewarded as O'Hara wriggled and shuffled himself into a comfortable firing position.

Geordie zoomed in on the movement but, with the aid of the night sight, could only just make out a pair of eyes behind a balaclava mask. His Irish colleagues would not be wearing masks, their faces would be cammed up and so it obviously was not one of them. The remainder of the man's body was concealed beneath the rhododendron; Geordie grudgingly admired the intruder's professionalism.

It would be light soon and he would be able to get a better look at whoever the intruder was. There was nothing the man could do from where he lay until someone in the household went outside. Geordie could have alerted his Irish colleagues taking a chance on losing the intruder. He decided not to bother the others; he would quietly take care of this bugger himself.

He kept watch on the man until it was almost daybreak then realigned the CCTV camera before waking Mick Rutherford and telling him to stand by while he went to do his ablutions; a little porky pie.

Not being too good at that time of day, Mick merely grunted and began his morning series of stretches before reluctantly climbing out of his beloved pit, it had always been the worst time of his day and he wondered how the Hell he had ever managed to get through Selection for the SAS. He'd slept in what he was wearing except for his boots. He pulled them on, donned his regulation Kevlar vest, and made it to the kitchen just minutes before the PM. He was making a brew when Sir Anthony appeared in the doorway.

"Good morning Sir, would you like a cuppa?"

"Thanks Sergeant, would you mind bringing it outside when it's ready, I'm going to enjoy the sunrise while I catch up on the news. We will all be taking breakfast in the garden later this morning I believe."

"No problem Sir, but do you think it's a good idea to sit out in the open?"

If the PM was a worried man, he showed no indication. Apart from his hair, which had gone white in the past six months, he still looked quite a bit younger than his years. He was tall and slim with no hint of a stoop and his face had that Peter Pan quality which had distinguished him from successive contenders for office in the past three elections.

"I'll take my chances Sergeant, I'm surrounded by a good team, no sugar for me thanks."

Mick spoke into his collar microphone, "Mike to all stations, stand by, stand by, UK Sunray exiting back door to patio area, eyes peeled, over."

The recipients replied in sequence. "WILCO, out." The concealed guard forward of O'Hara acknowledged with two clicks of his collar mike.

Geordie had slipped from the house through a ground floor window out of sight of the intruder. He concealed himself beneath another clump of rhododendron and got a bead on O'Hara through the telescopic sight on his rifle. He was adjusting the viewfinder when Mick Rutherford gave the 'stand-by'.

"F'kin'ell," whispered Geordie under his breath, he'd fucked up, he should have told Mick and the others about the intruder; he was losing it

"Sierra to Mike urgent, recall Sunray pronto suspect bandit 200 metres, go go go."

Mick dropped the empty cup he had just picked up from the bench and dashed outside as the PM was about to sit down with the first newspaper. Mick was between Warbacker and O'Hara when O'Hara fired. The force of the bullet, hitting him between the shoulders, catapulted Mick into the PM. They both hit the ground with a crash of garden furniture that scattered in all directions.

"Stay down and don't move Sir," gasped Mick as he lay breathless on top of the PM shielding him from further bullets. The crash of the low velocity missile into his bulletproof vest had felt like a hammer blow but the Kevlar armour had held. O'Hara raised his gun for a second shot when suddenly the lights went out.

Mick and the PM had not heard the sound of the first shot from O'Hara's silenced weapon but they heard a second shot that obviously had not come their way.

"Sierra to Mike, enemy down, get Sunray back inside pronto."

In accordance with standing operating procedures, the remainder of the household were lying flat on the floor when Mick and Sir Anthony dashed into the house at the crouch. Mick ordered the PM to join his wife and children as they lay in the hallway. He returned to the kitchen door and took up a position just inside.

"Mike to Sierra, sitrep, over."

"All clear, out"

Geordie called the guardroom and requested a sweep of the estate in case O'Hara had not been alone though he felt sure that he would have been; assassins rarely worked in groups.

Mick called in his two Irish colleagues and bade them stay with the families, until the security sweep was complete, while he and Geordie went to take a closer look at O'Hara.

The would-be assassin was laying face down still clutching his weapon as though he had fallen asleep on the job. There was a circular patch of blood and brain tissue on the man's balaclava mask at the base of the scull where Geordie's 9mm round had exited having entered in the centre of the man's forehead.

"Nice clean shot Geordie mate, not much mess, let's see who the bastard is."

Geordie turned the body over and removed the balaclava.

"F'kin'ell it's Declan O'Hara, I thought he'd copped his lot years ago. He must be in his late fifties or early sixties by now, do you remember him? He was one of Brannigan's UK sleepers that were netted in '95"

"Got him, I thought they'd all got life."

"Bloody amnesty, I guess it was part of the deal with the Provisional IRA to continue the cease fire. O'Hara must have gone over to the Real IRA, some people don't know when to let go. It's rumoured that he was one of those murdering bastards behind the Omagh bomb but had been taken-out by the PIRA for his trouble. Just goes to show you shouldn't listen to rumours. The only good thing he ever did was to confess to firing at the Para's on Bloody Sunday. The lads always said they'd been fired on first. I think O'Hara only confessed in order to embarrass Sinn Fein even though two of their lot had been involved in the Londonderry march when they were active Players. Never mind, this bastard's a real sleeper now, come on mate let's call in the sanitation squad."

Chapter 13

News of the attempted assassination was kept secret for security reasons and O'Hara's body was disposed of without fuss. Anyone showing an unusual interest in his whereabouts would hopefully lead MI6 to the Real IRA cell that planned the mission.

The only people who knew what had occurred were the two PM's and their respective families, Geordie Shiells, Mick Rutherford, and the two Irish Special Forces troopers. The perimeter guards were too far away to have heard the gunshots but even if they had, there was a small practice range on the estate that was used regularly by both the Guarda and the military when they were on duty during state visits; there were no questions asked.

Sir Anthony Warbacker and his family were badly shaken by the assassination attempt, as was their host. Shelley implored her husband to resign and get out of politics altogether. After all, he had given his party and his country many years of loyal service including six-years as Prime Minister which had taken its toll on the pair of them both physically and mentally.

A general election was due in six months time anyway so why not resign now and bring it forward? The Chancellor, Gordon Green, was just waiting for his chance to take over the leadership of the party and people would surely understand the PM's wanting to stand down if they knew what had happened.

But they did not know and they would not be told. He would have to plead physical illness brought on by mental stress then the public would surely accept. However, Warbacker knew better, people would call him a wimp or even worse but he couldn't care less what they thought. He loved his country but he loved his family more and was not prepared to die on the whim of some psycho assassin from a terrorist organisation.

Warbacker had been seen by the civilised world as the ultimate peace broker much to the chagrin of the opposition who felt that he should have been at home settling petty industrial disputes instead of trying to prevent conflict and bring about peace between warring factions around the world. The mentality of some of his press and political critics was questionable.

International terrorists were ever on the move while attempts were being made to locate and starve them of funds to finance their malevolent activities. But The Troubles in Northern Ireland seemed to be going on forever at the expense of the British taxpayer and Warbacker had had more than enough. He would approach the recently crowned King who had acceded to the throne the previous year on the abdication of his mother, and offer his resignation; perhaps His Majesty would surely understand. Bypassing his private secretary, Warbacker phoned the palace direct and arranged an appointment.

Ex SAS Major Cedric 'Nosey' Parker had turned down a promotion to Colonel and retired from active service at the end of December 1995 at the age of thirty-nine after a successful Army career.

The Bailey twins, both now Majors had been called back into service around the same time because of the escalating violence in Northern Ireland.

After his retirement from the SAS, Parker had gone into politics and joined the Liberal Democrats. Within two months, he had been nominated to stand for a constituency that had lost its MP due to cancer. Parker was duly elected and in a Lib Dem Party reshuffle he was offered the job of shadow Defence Spokesman.

His involvement as a young Welsh Guards officer in the Falklands conflict in 1982, his secondment to G Squadron of the SAS as Commander in 1985, his covert activities in Iraq in 1991, his intimate knowledge of the Northern Ireland situation after a successful tour of duty culminating in the rejected offer of a senior command, made him an ideal candidate for the job. Paddy Ashurst had strongly endorsed the party leader's decision to appoint Parker to the post of Defence Spokesman.

For his own part, at the end of 1994 and the beginning of 1995, Parker had not been happy about the prospect of elected Sinn Fein politicians being allowed to use the office facilities at Westminster, at a prohibitive cost per annum for each office paid from the public purse, when they positively refused to sit in the House of Commons or swear allegiance to the British crown. There was some unfairness about the situation but this was what peace with the Provisional IRA was going to cost. The alternative was ongoing conflict with that organisation which had ceased hostilities in August 1994, turned to politics, reportedly in association with Sinn Fein although it was never confirmed, and had repeatedly promised to put its weapons beyond use.

However, other Republican terror groups who were actively recruiting and carrying on where the PIRA had left off had filled the vacuum. Many of the old PIRA arms dumps had been relocated and appropriated by the other dissident Republican groups.

There were several defections of ex PIRA members to criminal organisations or to dissident rebel factions and the war went on. Efforts by the old guard of the IRA and Sinn Fein to curb the growing power of the defectors and dissidents resulted in a bloody internal feud and several assassinations took place.

Lots of senior Players on both sides got their comeuppance during the process to the delight of the security forces and the police who had experienced past difficulties in bringing these same people to justice.

Loyalist paramilitaries had also increased their activities as a direct result and random sectarian killings were once again on the increase. One by one the Loyalist factions were abandoning the peace process and responding to renewed Republican activity while exacerbating their own internal conflicts.

The current escalating violence began in the Ardoyne in the autumn of 1995 when Loyalist residents tried to prevent Catholic children from walking through their estate to the RC primary school in North Belfast. The frightened children had to be escorted by their parents who ran a gauntlet of verbal and physical abuse from supposed fellow Christians albeit Anglican and Presbyterian.

Loyalist paramilitary activists lurking in the background incited Protestant youths to hatred and mayhem; the order of the day.

A peace march by thousands of people in December 1995 did nothing to douse the fires of hatred. Violence in the Ardoyne and other small pockets escalated out of control with the burning of vehicles and property. Petrol bombs were used against the hard-pressed police and security forces trying to intervene but could only respond with plastic bullets and tear gas. Satan was gathering his forces once more in a final attempt at wrecking the peace process.

The tactics of the warring rebel factions had caught the imagination of Cedric Parker at the time and had given him the seed of an idea that began to germinate in his furtive mind during his service in Northern Ireland. But there was nothing he could do about it until after his retirement from the SAS. The seed had now taken root, however, and his mind would no longer accept the shelving of the concept. He had to expand it and get it down on paper. It was Parker's contention that those known terrorists and criminals that violated the human rights of their innocent victims, should have their human rights denied and be shot on sight. The Liberal Democrats might disagree but few, apart from a handful ex service personnel, had experienced the violence that Parker had experienced during his years of active service.

Chapter 14

Cedric Parker's plan was quite simple when, as a newly nominated opposition Spokesman for Defence, he had suggested to the Party leader, Charlie Kinnear, "simply terrorise the terrorists, give them a taste of their own medicine."

"How do you propose to do that?" asked Kinnear.

"Set one side against the other, then go in and wipe out the survivors," Parker had said. "Allow the hatred they have for each other to consume them completely. After all is said and done, they would rather die than live in peace together, so why not help them along with it and grant them their death wish? We should have done that in Iraq in '92 and let the Sunnis and the Shiites fight it out between them instead of interfering."

"Sounds fine so far but a little over simplistic don't you think. How do you suggest we go about isolating the trouble makers and furthermore, if and when we eliminate the survivors, would we not be as guilty as they are of the crime of murder?" Kinnear offered.

Cedric Parker, having given the entire plan a great deal of soul-searching thought, answered. "Expel the province from the UK, declare Northern Ireland a Republic, take the Union Flag away from them and withdraw Stirling. Force them into total self government and self reliance. As far as eliminating the survivors of any resultant civil or gang warfare is concerned, I would consider it a public duty to destroy the remnant criminal element. They have been responsible for the death of thousands of innocents over the years in Northern Ireland, on the mainland and even at our military bases in Germany."

"Expelling them from the Union would require an act of parliament and royal assent, providing, of course, that the general public went along with the idea and that would necessitate a referendum. And as you say, it could also lead to civil war in the province."

"Exactly Charlie and that is how we could isolate and identify those antagonists from both tribes who are motivated mainly by blind-hatred and the criminals that feed off that hatred. Especially the criminals, the extortionists that prey on their own business people who secure contracts in the camp of the opposite side then are forced to pay for the protection of their workers.

"And what about the majority of peace-loving people who live outside the troubled areas, what do we offer them?" Kinnear had asked.

"Those who want to remain British, both Protestant and Catholic, offer them resettlement in the UK, in England, Scotland or Wales. I feel sure that we could bring Eire on board and get them also to offer sanctuary along the same lines. After all, it would be in that country's long-term interests. A peaceful northern and southern republic, both members of the common market with a possible euro economy, would eventually form an amalgam through a catalyst called peace. Those who preferred to stay and become part of a Northern Ireland Republic would have to take their chances."

"Resettling hoards of people could cost millions." remarked Kinnear.

"Pulling the plug on the province would save billions, you must know what it is costing the state right now and if the situation were allowed to carry on, we would eventually become a bankrupt nation which I believe is the aim of our enemies worldwide. I'm quite sure that a referendum outlining my proposals would produce positive results. People are always telling the government to get the troops out and pull the plug."

"A referendum in Northern Ireland in the seventies indicated an overwhelming desire of the people to remain British, what makes you think it would be any different now?" asked Kinnear.

"Well Charlie, if my memory serves me right, only the people of the province were asked to make the choice at that time. And I don't have to remind you that the majority are Protestants. The result was a forgone conclusion. If the rest of the UK had been given the opportunity to vote, and it is they that were footing the bills, I'm sure that things would have been different. The people of Northern Ireland have had sufficient opportunity to live in peace with each other since the peace initiative of 1994 as well as on previous initiatives. They have blown the chance again and again as far as I am concerned. They have consistently allowed their situation to deteriorate. They could quite easily have taken out the activists who are forever resurrecting the Troubles for their own selfish ends but they appear to have a death wish that won't go away. Parents allow their children to be indoctrinated and to be drawn into the blood feud, as they themselves were when they were children. It's a vicious circle that has to be broken if there is ever going to be peace in that place," said Parker.

"You could be right about the last referendum Cedric," said Kinnear." I was just a kid at the time but I remember my parents being quite incensed at not being given the chance to vote."

"So was I," said Parker. "As a boy, all I knew about Ireland in general was that it was full of funny folk that people told jokes about but now it has gone beyond a joke and something positive has to be done."

"OK," said Kinnear, "assuming the province eventually becomes a republic and civil war does result, who would be responsible for taking out the warring factions? A newly constituted Northern Ireland government would initially be in too much turmoil to cope. Reorganised NI regiments, the police, financial and other services would take ages to get their act together. In the meantime, I can imagine the warring factions having a field day and who could stop them?"

"An outside voluntary third force could," answered Parker.

"You mean mercenaries don't you Cedric, and where would this third force of volunteers come from?" asked Kinnear.

"The SAS, SBS, MI5, MI6, ex RUC Special Branch and anti-terrorist personnel," explained Parker. "My personal database contains over a thousand names of people who I would trust with my life. Some are still on active service while several others have served in the province within the past twenty years or so. Some are a bit long in the tooth now I admit but they are still fit and active. There are also those among them who have a special interest in the province and there are others with a few personal scores to settle with past and present Players. They were too law abiding to act summarily when the odd occasion arose while they were serving. For what I have in mind, I only need around a hundred active volunteers with a further hundred in reserve for what would essentially be a very covert SAS style hit-and-run operation."

"Would a UK government be compromised in any way? Would any of your 'third force' be identified as British mercenaries if they were captured?" asked Kinnear.

"Everyone would be a nameless and faceless volunteer acting ostensibly on behalf of the opposite side to whichever side captured him or her, if and only if, God forbid, any one of them ever fell into enemy hands," explained Parker. "The likelihood is remote, however, as would be any face-to-face enemy contact. I envisage sniper rather than close-quarter confrontation."

"What happens to your volunteers when it's all over?" asked Kinnear.

"Serving volunteers would simply return to duty while civilians would resume their normal lives," said Parker with a shrug of satisfaction.

"I like it," said Charlie Kinnear with a smile, "I think it could work if we could just get the Monarch and the government to go along with the expelling of the province. But before any of that, we would first have to win the election. The polls look very encouraging but they have been wrong in the past. In the meantime, get everything down on an encrypted disc and keep it under wraps as a contingency.

Bloody well done Cedric and very well thought out. I think you will go places if we win the election."

"You mean 'when we win the election Charlie surely, positive thinking eh?"

"We're getting there," said Kinnear smiling broadly and shaking hands with Parker before leaving.

The recently recalled SAS officers, Peter and Leo Bailey, were shown into Cedric Parker's office. He rose to greet them with genuine comradely affection.

"Peter, Leo, it is so good to see you again, how long have you been back in harness?"

"Three months now," said Peter, shaking Cedric by the hand. Leo nodded and shook hands.

"Congratulations Cedric on your new post, it's nice to see a round peg in a round hole for a change, did Paddy Ashurst have anything to do with this?" asked Peter.

"His endorsement helped me I must admit. We met a couple of times when he was serving and I was just out of Sandhurst but we were not what you might call close friends, until now that is. I've had a couple of secret sessions with him and the party leader. He's quite a good listener and also good for sound advice even though he is now retired from confrontational affairs of state. It's a pity he didn't get into number ten before he went out of politics, things might have been different now. But never mind, he's still available and always ready to help with advice when needed." Parker pressed a button on his desk and a secretary appeared at the office door.

"May we have a large pot of coffee please Sandra my dear, you do remember these two old reprobates don't you?"

"Very well sir." And to Peter and Leo, "how are you both gentlemen, I haven't seen you since Northern Ireland."

"Good God!" Leo exclaimed. "You were Nosey's, whoops sorry, I mean Cedric's scribe were you not?"

"Best ever," said Parker. "She is still army but has been seconded to my department at my request for as long as it takes. It isn't very often that you get three wise monkeys rolled into one female Homo sapiens; now then Sandra, how about that coffee?"

A flushed, but smiling, secretary retreated with a mock salute.

"We will get down to business as soon as the coffee is served gentlemen. In the meantime, tell me what has been happening since I last saw you.

There had been an extensive inquiry into the events leading up to the demise of the 10 stood-down Provisional IRA members that had volunteered, at the request of Daniel Doonan, to take out Sinn Fein politician Mark Thomas Brannigan and his criminal gang on the day of the retired Colonel's funeral at Ballypatrick in the early summer of 1995.

There was no forensic evidence to indicate why the arms and ammunition dump in the cellar of Brannigan's farm cum safe house had been blown up with such devastating results. The only two survivors had been Daniel Doonan and his Tyrone CO, Colm Neary, both of who, in an attempt to save the IRA ceasefire, had been badly burned and injured attempting to assassinate Brannigan just as he was blew himself and his car to pieces.

The inquiry concluded that the arms dump had been either hit by a stray round or that the explosion had been the result of an accident by one of the Players inside the house. No blame had been attached to the pinned down SAS Squadron involved in the fire fight because there were no other witnesses.

Patrick O'Riordan, the only member of Brannigans gang not to have been in the farmhouse at the time of the explosion, had disappeared after being acquitted for lack of evidence of active involvement in Brannigan's gang and for having volunteered to turn Queen's evidence. His pal Liam Casey was now the brother-in-law of Leo Bailey and employed in the family marine engineering business.

"How is Siobhan, does she like living in England?" asked Parker.

"She loves it; she has made lots of friends. She gave birth to twin boys in March this year, twins run in our family on my father's side. The north east is awash with them," said Leo.

"Are you in married-quarters?"

"No, we bought my parents old Victorian house near Sunderland, it is ideal for a family. Uncle Martin retired from the Belfast branch of his marine engineering business eighteen months ago and dad has taken over there. Siobhan's brother Liam is a junior partner and is living in his parent's old town house."

"And what about you Peter, any sign of wedding bells yet?" asked Parker.

"No fear, I haven't even got a girl friend. I can't find anyone remotely like Siobhan or my mother. They have made me too choosy I'm afraid but I can wait, there's plenty time," said Peter.

The coffee arrived and the men got down to business. There was no need to swear the security-vetted twins to secrecy. Parker outlined his plans in detail and they both listened with interest until he had finished.

"What do you need from us Cedric?" asked Peter.

"I would like you both to jointly head the operation and recruit the necessary volunteers. Organise the logistics, everything from safe houses, to communications, transport, movements, arms and ammunition, emergency rations, you know the sort of thing you've done it all before. I want contingency plans in place before we announce the fate of the province."

"When do you expect it to happen? Leo asked.

"If and after we win the coming election and the Country gives its approval to dump the province as the result of a referendum, and if and when the King exercises his prerogative to authorise the government to proceed. That should give you around three months to get organised and if the referendum does result in the amputation of the province as I expect, you should move in then as sleepers until the whatsit hits the proverbial which should not be too long after that. The UK government would then give the people of the 'New Republic' a further three months, for those who wish it, to resettle outside the province. I've done a survey of councils throughout the country and the result of property audits has indicated thousands of empty council houses and flats. The government would fund the renovation of these properties that would be offered to migrants from the province. Those who decide to stay in the province will have to accept a provisional government, set up a new police force and other essential services, reorganise a military force with volunteers from the existing NI regiments, convert their Stirling assets into

Euros or create a new currency and get some kind of social security system in place.

It is a radical solution gentlemen but it can be done. It needs to be done. I already have advisors drawing up guidelines to pass on to the existing Assembly in Stormont as soon as the referendum results are known. I'll give you a week to talk it over between you. Don't feel bad about saying no, there are others I could call upon but you are my first choice. At least we know and trust each other."

The three solemn men shook hands and the meeting was at an end. Cedric Parker was now a busy minister in waiting.

Notices went up the following day at the HQs of the SAS at Hereford and the SBS at Plymouth.

. . . .

NOTICE TO ALL RANKS
COVERT OPERATION 'WIPEOUT'
VOLUNTEER DETAIL & BRIEFING
OPS ROOM 0900 HRS THURSDAY 10TH INSTANT

. . . .

Leo Bailey conducted interviews at Hereford and Peter at Plymouth. Among the applicants at Hereford nearing retirement, were veteran Captains George Davidson, Eddie Graham, Denis Cross and Dave Affleck. Warrant Officers Mal Spencer, Alec (Geordie) Shiells and Mick Rutherford, Staff Sergeants Sammy MaGuine and Bart Mumford, Sergeants Jimmy Frazer, Alan Barclay, Jock Shand, and Andy Pickering, Corporals Wally Norley, Bernard McLean, Stan Sheavills, Frank Stanton, Malcolm Gadsby and twenty-one Troopers. A similar number volunteered at Plymouth.

Everyone selected and still serving would be temporarily discharged from the Army for the duration of the tour with the promise of automatic RTD (return to duty) on completion.

Leo had also been busy in Belfast recruiting old friends. Sid Morrell, who ran the taxi firm, had been first choice on Leo's list of possible candidates. He was a Northumbrian married to a local Belfast girl and all of his drivers were either serving or ex Territorial Army men from the province. He already had a ready-made team of trusted people and had indicated that he could muster at least a further dozen.

Apart from his partner Sandy Blewett's half dozen or so close Brit orientated Catholic friends his drivers in the Derry branch were Protestants but had no affiliations with Loyalist organisations. The rival Catholic-owned cab company drivers drove black cabs and most had affiliations with Republican organisations but the two firms coexisted peacefully enough. God only knew how long that would last after the results of the referendum were known.

Infiltrating the Protestant camp would not be difficult once the referendum was announced; the Loyalist paramilitaries would also be looking for volunteers. Catholic volunteers needed to infiltrate the Republican paramilitary groups would be the most difficult to recruit. Sandy Blewitt, the Derry branch taxi manager, was a Catholic but his Yorkshire provincial accent was all wrong. However, he could still be useful to Parker's mercenaries as a sniper and he might even know a couple of pro-British Republicans who would be willing play mole.

It was during that early recruiting period, while he had been driving through the city, that Leo Bailey had spotted a familiar figure waiting to cross the road at a Zebra crossing.

'Jesus Christ,' he'd thought, 'Patrick O'Riordan! What in Heaven's name is he doing back here and, good God, he's wearing a priest's dog-collar?'

He had tooted his horn and wound down the window. O'Riordan had looked at him with some surprise and then recognition had dawned. Leo had gestured to him to get into the car.

Chapter 15

The King sympathised with Sir Anthony's decision to resign after hearing his reasons and gave him his royal blessing. After all, he had always been at risk himself along with the rest of the Royal family but they were in no position to resign. There were many other prospective prime ministers amongst the MPs but nobody could replace a Royal except another Royal, or maybe a post-revolutionary president, which was not a likely prospect.

Warbacker's resignation caught the opposition on the wrong foot. They were not yet properly prepared for an election. The Conservative leadership had changed in 1993 but nothing else had. The new leader spent more time slagging off the opposition than trying to win the hearts and minds of the electorate by offering them clear-cut policies designed to cure the country's ills. He used school-boyish diatribe on the floor of the House of Commons backed by sleazy innuendo from some of the

Tory press. A senior colleague who set about reuniting the party soon replaced the leader with some success.

Differing views of the party members on the important issues of the European Common Market and the Euro currency, adopted by eleven of the EU nations, still persisted and divided the party, which was in a state of disarray.

The left of the Conservative party wanted to move with the times while the right wanted to stand apart from the rest of the world and retain traditional values shared by a minority of land-owning gentry, their narrow minded serf-like followers, well-healed old maids, xenophobes, and people with nationalistic leanings.

Some of the older electorate felt a kind of nostalgia for Stirling while others, who lived from week to week on low pay and inadequate state pensions, people with little or no savings, could not give a damn what currency they were paid in so long as they could live, as opposed to exist, on the income. The Conservatives were well out off touch with the majority of the electorate.

Sir Anthony Warbacker's resignation also forced Labour into what turned out to be a destructive and unnecessary leadership contest.

Most people, at first, were behind the main contender, Gordon Green, because he had been one of the best chancellors the Country had ever known. But the party as a whole had misjudged the mood of the rural communities.

Charlie Kinnear and most of his Lib Dem colleagues were mostly in support of the people and their grievances thereby winning an increasing number of hearts and minds.

The main threat to Labour came from the far left of the party who opposed Green and championed their own candidate, Arthur Blemish, who wanted to bring back the old days of nationalisation, sky-high taxes for the rich, trades union controlled industry, total equality for anarchistic minority groups, cash handouts for the work-shy something-for-nothing brigade, illegal migrants, homosexuals, drug addicts, single teenage mums and crank organisations.

It was a bitter and bloody contest which the chancellor eventually won but at the expense of a hitherto untarnished personal reputation. The Socialists were no longer the champions of the poor, there were still too many including the increasing army of pensioners who found it difficult to survive on the state pittance after 45 to 50 years of contributing to fluctuating Taxes and ever increasing National Insurance.

The Tories were no longer the champions of the rich and greedy, there were now too few of them to make any significant impact. Most of their fortunes were hidden in offshore accounts in order to avoid paying UK taxes.

The well off well-educated hard working and talented so-called middle classes now shared most of the country's wealth. They were the people who fuelled the property market with supply and demand. They were the travellers who took their holiday money abroad and exchanged it for Euros and got used to the new currency of their European neighbours.

They were the British Europeans who did business with their French, German, Italian, and Spanish European neighbours in Euros and in their own languages.

When Britain would eventually decide to adopt the Euro, it would not be a problem for the Euro Brits. They were the people who stood to lose most if either the Socialists or the Conservatives got back into power with a majority vote. They knew that if either one of the old adversaries was elected, it would be the workaholic high earners who would continue to carry the bulk of the tax burden of the country and foot most of the bill for the ongoing struggle in Northern Ireland, a conflict for which the majority of UK citizens, both Catholic and Protestant, had no more stomach. It had lasted too long and there seemed to be no end to the brutality and no point to the killing other than the sheer hatred of one tribe for the other or for criminal gain.

Both the Socialists and the Conservatives had promised to throw more money and more troops at the problem but the Liberal Democrats had promised to end the conflict once and for all if they were elected. They would not, however, be drawn on the subject of how the seemingly impossible task could be achieved. Only two people knew the answer to that question but the talks between Charlie Kinnear and his newly appointed Defence Spokesman, Cedric Parker, were a closely guarded secret now shared with the Bailey twins. Kinnear had approved Parker's plan but did not confide it to his deputy Alan Bleach who, being a committed Christian, may not have readily approved of such radical action.

Despite promises by the Conservatives to improve the National Health Service, to raise education standards, increase state pensions by 30%, increase public service pay above inflation for teachers, police, firemen, doctors and nurses while at the same time cutting taxes, a bemused electorate relegated them to second place in one opinion poll after another prior to the elections. They had heard it all before, not too long ago.

The deceitful dinosaurs were dying on their feet. In the 80's under the then Prime Minister Marjory Thrasher, they had tamed the Trades Unions. Then gradually, through under investment, they had devastated the coal industry, allowed it to run down and then sold off the nation's state owned wealth in rail, gas, electricity, water, steel, the Post Office, and public transport at knock-down prices to their 'business friends and speculators.' They in turn had rewarded their customers with higher prices, poor service, and reaped high profits for shareholders in the process.

A pride of fat-cat multimillionaires was created, including many government ministers moonlighting on Boards of Directors. The Tories had even tried to privatise the ailing NHS by the back door but were voted out of office before they could do any more damage.

But now, they had the temerity to blame the present Government for the state of those industries and services. However, the British electorate never forgets nor does it allow any political party to veer too far to the left or to the right. It was called democracy.

The Liberal Democrats had spent years improving their prospects right across the country quietly winning seat after seat in by-elections. They had literally sneaked up on the opposition parties from behind and put themselves into a commanding position ready for the sprint to the finishing line.

Their charismatic, no nonsense leader, Charlie Kinnear had quietly coached his team into a formidable political force. With the help of his deputy, Alan Bleach, he had purposely targeted the very people he knew were responsible for the wealth of the nation, who Labour often referred to as Middle England, and who had most to lose if either of the other parties got back into power. Kinnear had listened to them and he had learned.

Despite the past pleadings of the Liberal Democrats, none of the other parties would ever entertain proportional representation. They paid lip service only but it was to their own eventual detriment. It looked like the Lib Dem's would not only be first past the post, but would also command a record majority of seats in the House.

Charlie Kinnear had offered the electorate a stark but simple choice based on past experience. Choose the Conservatives who basically advocate a dog-eat-dog society in which the strong profit from the weakness of others. Or re-elect a Labour government that would look after everybody's interests whether they liked it or not, and impose so many strangulating dictatorial rules and regulations on people that they wouldn't be able to fart in a public place without a permit.

The Lib Dem manifesto offered better primary and secondary school education and university places funded jointly by government and industry, further general education in combination with technical training for high school academic failures, and secure apprenticeships for those who elected to go straight into industry from school.

They promised a better health service subsidised by the national lottery, the tobacco companies, the breweries and distillers, all of whom contributed to, and profited from, the illnesses caused by the addictions that plagued society and filled hospital beds. And by the medical equipment and pharmaceutical companies who reaped huge profits from the treatment of those illnesses.

A study into free nursing care for the elderly was also being undertaken but final conclusions had not yet been reached. It was envisaged that retired senior nursing staff would be offered employment in running state care homes in return for free accommodation and a reasonable tax-free stipend. A proposal to reintroduce National Service, both military and civil, for sixteen to eighteen year olds not in full time employment or education would be considered if the Lib Dems were elected. The result would be an unlimited turnover of young care staff.

It was proposed to abolish child allowance which would be replaced by a living wage, based on the number of children in a family, paid directly to mothers who elected to stay at home and bring up their offspring in a secure family environment instead of being forced to go out to work to earn sufficient extra money thus depriving eligible single school-leavers of employment.

Career women with children would be assumed not to be dependant upon child allowance but would instead enjoy a tax allowance for each child in full time education.

The net result would be higher employment for school leavers and graduates, a healthier nation, a more secure home life for thousands of parental-care-deprived children, and therefore less crime and vandalism on the streets.

Parents of children below the age of sixteen, who were convicted of crime, would be prosecuted. Persistent juvenile offenders would be removed from the family unit and placed in a special junior regiment staffed by specially trained youth leaders recruited from the three services.

The reintroduction of National Service would also be seriously considered as a means of instilling a sense of discipline and responsibility into the youth of the country. Both males and females would be given the choice of serving either in the armed forces, the police, the fire service, the teaching profession, the ambulance service, or the hospital services from the school leaving age of sixteen unless they were either in secure jobs or full time education. University graduates and undergraduates would be exempt but would be expected to serve some voluntary time with charitable institutions or the OTC.

The Labour party had proposed that every person above the age of employment would be issued with a new Euro/Brit smart identity card containing a National Insurance number, a photograph, a thumbprint, and an iris print. Pin numbers could be added and withdrawn for the purpose of obtaining social security payments, state retirement pension, and other government payouts, which would be fraud-proof, from hole-in-the-wall cash dispensers planned for reconstituted ailing Post Offices. Driving licence and other specific numbers such as service ID numbers could also be added. Blood group, donor status, or any other specific information could also be included. Cards would be renewed every five years and could easily be electronically cancelled and replaced if lost, stolen or accidentally destroyed.

The cost of implementation was astronomical but despite that the Conservatives were all for it in principal but the Lib Dems felt that the money would be better spent on providing more policemen and improved border security.

A Lib Dem government would also invest surplus public money in gas, electricity, water, and public transport until they were in a position to take them back into part-public ownership.

Multi-religious centres would be set up in major cities to promote religious understanding and to reduce racial tension. Every Briton would be able to worship who or what God or prophet he or she chose without fear of ridicule or reprisal from single-minded religious fanatics.

Migrants and accepted asylum seekers would be expected to speak English and take an 'Oath of Allegiance' before being accepted into British society after a suitable probation period.

Criminality and incitement of racial and religious hatred would be rewarded with instant deportation and withdrawal of citizenship for first generation immigrants. Second and subsequent generations would automatically be British citizens.

It was a radical program that caught the imagination of the electorate and swept the Liberal Democrats to victory in the November of 1995 with a majority of seats but too few to survive for long in government.

The Conservatives were a close second and, by popular consent, they formed a coalition government with Charlie Kinnear as Prime Minister and the Conservative William Craig as his deputy.

Kinnear appointed the Right Honourable Cedric Parker MP to the post of Defence Secretary who began to work immediately on his Northern Ireland solution. The PM had given him just one month to expand on and refine the ideas that he had put forward prior to the election.

He had needed an excellent secretary after his previous appointment as Defence Spokesman for the party but after reading through the personal files of the secretarial staff he had inherited from his predecessor, had rejected them all. He had then decided to call the Adjutant Generals Corps Records office to enquire into the whereabouts of Corporal Sandra Smethurst, his super-efficient former clerk in Northern Ireland. He had been only half surprised to learn that she had become a Staff Officer and PA to the GOC at Northern Command HQ in York.

Several telephone calls later, using his authority and the old boy network; he had secured the posting of Captain Sandra Smethurst on secondment to his office with immediate effect.

Sandra had been only twenty-two years old when she was Parker's clerk in Northern Ireland. Parker was ten years older and one of the youngest senior officers in the SAS.

He had denied him self the pleasure of female company after his fiancé of four years had gone off with another man after Parker had transferred to the SAS. He also knew of too many marriages that had gone wrong for SAS soldiers and their wives as a result of the work the men were involved in and their frequent absence away from home.

He had developed a professional admiration for Sandra but the thought of succumbing to conduct unbecoming an officer and a gentleman had never crossed his mind. He had remembered the girl as an unattractive skinny shorthaired mousy blonde with boundless energy for the work that she was so good at and great to have around when he needed a coffee.

Her work was exemplary and when she was posted on the disbandment of the Northern Ireland base at Bessbrook, he had given her a glowing report that won her promotion to Sergeant. She had later applied for a commission and was accepted. Prior to her secondment to Parker's department, she had served as PA to several senior officers before being posted to York.

Sandra had been pleasantly surprised to receive the signal ordering her to report for duty at the Lib Dem Defence Spokesman's office at the personal request of

Cedric Parker. She remembered him from Northern Ireland where he had been very kind to her as the only female member of staff and as protective as an elder brother. She had found him quite attractive but never entertained thoughts of a relationship because he was an officer and she was a lowly corporal.

Parker had been pleasantly surprised when he saw Sandra again. She was more mature and slightly rounder in the right places than he remembered. She had taken to high heels when in civilian clothes and looked just that bit taller. Her legs were shapely and her breasts had developed well over the years. She had allowed her hair to grow longer and she obviously took greater care with her appearance. Parker was impressed.

After his meeting with the Bailey twins, they had remarked on the changes in Sandra and he had had the grace to blush when a winking Leo suggested a possible relationship. The thought had crossed his mind several times since but he was still the gentleman and, truth to tell, just a little shy despite the fact that he now found her very attractive.

Chapter 18

The leader of the Northern Ireland Assembly, David Grimble, had read through the Liberal Democrats manifesto before the general election and had given a little shudder when he came to the part about *'curing the problems of Northern Ireland once and for all.'*

He had felt instinctively that they had something radical in mind although no details had been given. There seemed little doubt in his own mind that the Lib Dems would win the election. The other parties had little or nothing to offer but rehashed well-worn remedies, unacceptable rhetoric, and the usual sleaze put about by hacks that specialised in the ruination of public figures.

A fleeting thought that a Lib Dem government might try to dump the province crossed Grimble's mind but was immediately rejected. Such an idea was unthinkable; how could they possibly get away with a stunt like that? Neither the Crown nor the British people would tolerate such a drastic solution but, God knows, there was a limit to what people would put up with. The British public on the mainland had suffered heavy casualties and costly structural damage in the past thirty or so years as well as having to pay for reconstruction both at home and in the province.

The lobby in favour of human rights, formed in the late 60's, had grown stronger since the formation of the European Union. The rest of Europe saw Protestant domination in Northern Ireland as unacceptable. The Catholic community, which numbered about a third of the population, had been politically and socially deprived since partition in 1921. Successive British governments had given Stormont a free hand to sort out its own problems and were loath to interfere when both communities perpetrated atrocities.

The situation came to a head in the mid 1960's when Britain was forced to send in troops to assist the RUC in keeping order against the background of criminal activists who used the Troubles to fuel their own fires.

Grimble's worst fears were realized as he sat in the House and listened to Charlie Kinnear making his maiden speech as Prime Minister.

Among the plans he was announcing was a referendum on the future of Northern Ireland to be held on 1st February next. The entire opposition, especially the representatives from the Unionist camp, and the SDLP, gasped in surprise and began muttering amongst themselves.

Sinn Fein had no voice because Martin McCaffrey and Gerry Eves had again refused to take their seats in the Houses of Parliament, which was seen as an insult to both the crown and the new government by everyone present. The Speaker of the House ordered silence until the PM had finished his speech.

First to his feet when Kinnear sat down, was Ian Pashley. He did not offer his congratulations to the Prime Minister on his accession to office, but demanded in his booming voice. "Will the Prime Minister tell the House why the people of Northern Ireland have been denied the right to vote in a referendum that affects their future existence as British citizens?"

Kinnear replied through the Speaker. "My right honourable friend, of all people, should know the answer to that. Was it not he who opposed the right of every British citizen to vote in the last referendum on Northern Ireland? And now those very same citizens are paying dearly for the failure of the members of the Northern Ireland Assembly to quell the current riots and stop the escalating violence. In fact, it appears that the honourable member and his party positively condone the present situation. The consummate hatred for all things Papal, shown by him and the members of his party, is well known. It does him no credit as a professed Reverend person, nor does it indicate a commitment to the Christian principles of forgiveness and reconciliation by members of his congregation."

Pashley looked as though he would burst with anger. He appealed to the Speaker. "Do I have to put up with this kind of response in the House to a perfectly legitimate question Mr. Speaker?"

The Speaker replied, "I see nothing offensive in the reply by the right honourable gentleman the Prime Minister. If the truth hurts, the fault is not his."

Pashley and the other members of his party left their seats and lined up in front of the Speaker. They bowed and left the chamber without another word. The remainder of the House remained silent for some seconds then, quite spontaneously, they stood up as one and broke into cheering applause. Charlie Kinnear had won the day against the diatribe of the Unionist lexical bully. Even the entire opposition to a man were behind Kinnear at that moment.

The Speaker called for order and business resumed with a question from David Grimble.

"Will the Prime Minister tell the House, that should the English, Scottish, and Welsh electorate decide to *dump*, he used the word deliberately, Northern Ireland and declare it a republic, how soon will it happen and what will be the future involvement of the British and Irish governments."

Kinnear got to his feet once more. "All I can tell my Right Honourable friend is that such a question will have to wait until after the referendum results are known. There is no point in discussing what might be. There are contingency plans of course but they will be implemented at the appropriate time." The Prime Minister was giving nothing away.

The leader of the SDLP, Seamus Miller, arose and asked a question. "Would the Prime Minister inform this House about the expected fate of the Catholic minority in Northern Ireland if the province was indeed *dumped*, as my Right Honourable friend puts it, and the British army was no longer there to protect it?"

The Prime Minister rose again.

"The Right Honourable member knows as well as I do that the Catholic minority, as he puts it, has always failed in the past to resist the dictat of whatever IRA faction, be it Official, Provisional, Real, or indeed any other illegal Republican organisation, nor have they helped to bring any members of these illegal organisations to justice. They know very well who these people are and they know what they have done, at Enniskillen in November 1987 and more recently in Ballykelly for instance, and what they are still capable of doing. And as far as their protection by the British army is concerned, the Catholic community welcomed the troops in August 1969 when they were sent to protect them after an upsurge in sectarian violence by Loyalists. As a direct result, dissenters broke away from the Official IRA for failing to protect those communities and formed their own illegal organisation. Eighteen months later, the soldiers were being shot at and killed by the so-called Provisional IRA representing the very same people the Army were sent to protect. If the British people vote to exclude Northern Ireland from the United Kingdom, the Catholic population will have no one to blame but themselves. But, as I have said before, there are contingency plans which cannot be discussed at this time."

The Conservative party, having achieved a poor second place in the election, sat sullenly as the business of the House continued. There were no congratulations and no 'clever-shit school-boy' questions from their crest-fallen new leader who had been blamed for the poor showing of the Party and was apprehensively awaiting the results of yet another leadership contest.

Gordon Green, for Labour, congratulated the Prime Minister on his successful election campaign and wished him luck for the duration of the parliament.

The next day back in his office at Stormont, Grimble pondered over the possibility of the province becoming a republic. There was no point in waiting for it to happen, there would be all hell let loose as a result. The newspapers had been full of the prospect that morning and just about every phone in the building was busy. There was nothing to tell anyone and his beleaguered members of staff were already showing signs of frustration and stress; and it was only 10 a.m. He had to make contingency plans of his own.

He called his secretary and gave her a list of people to contact; some of them would already be in the building. He arranged an emergency meeting for 8 p.m. that evening over a working supper.

Apologies would not be accepted except in the case of the bed-bound or the dead. No reason was to be given for the meeting; they should all have read the papers by now and should be able to guess for themselves.

Grimble set about preparing a long agenda and wondered if Pashley would attend the meeting. If he didn't, there would be no place for him or his party in any future government.

Miller would be there for the SDLP but he wondered about McCaffrey and Eves and the other Sinn Fein representatives. All of them were committed to the protection of the Catholic minority and the latter two had continuously renounced violence but could they possibly do anything against an upsurge of hostile IRA activity. There was some serious talking to be done and contingency plans to be agreed.

Sir Ronny Finnigan was probably the most important person to have at the meeting. His problems as Police Chief would be enormous if the province was declared a republic. The force had already undergone drastic changes in the past year and had survived beyond anyone's expectations, which was down to Finnigan's dedication to his officers. He could quite easily have resigned when the decision to disband the RUC had been taken, but he hadn't. He'd stayed on and overseen the smooth transition.

Now, however, his officers were hard pressed once again to keep law and order. Without the support of the British army, they would be virtually ineffective. They were no longer armed, except for a few rapid response teams. But arms were still available; they had been withdrawn but not yet disposed of.

Grimble's next consideration was the army. The Ulster Defence Regiment was a regiment of the British army as were the Irish Guards and the Royal Ulster Rifles. Would they come under the jurisdiction of a Northern Ireland Republic should the occasion arise? He had put the hypothetical question to Cedric Parker who told him that there were contingency plans but the final answer lay with the King as supreme military commander.

And what the hell would the rest of Sinn Fein's reaction be. They stood to gain most in the long run from the creation of a republic but their military wing would be forced to fight again if the Catholic minority was seen to be suffering persecution by 'loyalist' thugs. It was important to Grimble as leader of the Assembly that his Protestant Unionist parties and the SDLP and Sinn Fein Catholics, were all seen to be making a go of things in partnership for the good of all the people.

His main worries, however, were the military wings of the UDA and the UDF. Their political wings were already on board the peace initiative but had consistently threatened to dismount when too many concessions were given to Sinn Fein/IRA. He had to convince everyone that it was in the interests of all politicians that they form a broad coalition for the sake of the entire community.

Some renegade members of the paramilitaries were not very keen to disarm and give up the perk of over-lordship within the communities where they were the law. Where they lived off the proceeds of robberies committed in the name of their political organisations. They were every bit as bad as the republican thugs who ruled the roost in their Catholic enclaves. Crime paid for all of them and they would be reluctant to give it up.

The banking and business communities were Grimble's next consideration. He would have to have a separate meeting with heads of these organisations before too many of them decided to quit the province.

He called his secretary a second time and gave her a comprehensive list of significant bankers and businessmen. Notices of an important confidential meeting at 8 p.m. the following evening, once again over a working supper, were to be hand-delivered by couriers that very day. Every effort had to be made to contact everyone on the list by lunchtime the following day at the very latest.

Once again, he felt sure that having digested the news most would realise the importance of the meeting and turn up. He would have to assume that anyone who did not attend had plans to abandon the province whatever the outcome of the referendum. He began to work on what he felt would be one of the most important speeches of his life in politics.

By lunchtime, Joe Bailey, head of Ellis Marine Engineering Belfast, and father of the twin SAS officers, Peter and Leo, received his invitation to David Grimble's confidential meeting the following evening.

He called his junior partner, Liam Casey, into the office and asked him what he thought of the situation.

They had already talked that morning over coffee about the proposed referendum on the future of Northern Ireland and the possibility of it being no longer part of the United Kingdom.

They agreed that Ellis Marine Engineering, a Company born and bred in Belfast, and employing a generous mixture of both Catholics and Protestants, should be unaffected by any constitutional change.

They traded in Europe, America, Canada and the Far East and were essential to the economy of the province. There had been attempts in the past to drive a sectarian wedge between members of the work force but, in one particular case, Joe, when he was a junior manager deputising for the then pregnant personnel officer who was on maternity leave, had been obliged to sack the antagonist. The Ellis workforce had been shaken at the time. They had formed an unbreakable cohesive non-sectarian bond and together, they rejected anyone who ever again attempted to introduce sectarian hatred into the workplace.

Some years later when, unknown to Joe, that same antagonist John McCann, a UDA man, a bomb expert, and criminal lunatic, was the man who had planted the bomb beneath his car while he and his wife were on holiday in Antrim.

Joe rang Grimble's secretary and informed her he would be at the meeting.

Leo Bailey had kept in touch with his brother-in-law Liam Casey who had advanced himself beyond any ones imagination after Leo had saved him from the destructive path he had once chosen as a young member of the IRA.

There was now an affinity between them that was akin to that between Leo and his SAS comrades.

Leo's great uncle, Martin Ellis, had taken Liam into his Marine Engineering Company and had steered him through university. Martin was more like a father to Liam having had no children of his own. Liam's own father had been killed in a car accident when Liam was just a boy.

Liam had discovered that he not only had practical ability, but he also had the brains to go with it. He had wasted too many years being led astray as a teenager. His mentor and great friend Patrick O'Riordan had disappeared after their last encounter in 1995. He had thought about him often and wondered what had become of him.

Leo rang Liam one evening at home and arranged a meeting. He asked him not to let his father know that he was in the province. He would explain when they met. Liam was aware of his brother-in-law's past SAS connection but kept silent.

They met in the bar of a hotel on the shores of Loch Neagh one Friday evening where Leo had booked rooms for them both. They greeted each other more like brothers than brothers-in-law.

It was a full hour before they finished catching up on the past over several pre-dinner drinks.

"I have someone I'd like you to meet," said Leo as they made their way to the restaurant.

The man had his back to them as they approached the table. He turned and looked up at Liam with a grin that almost broke his face in two. It was Patrick O'Riordan and he was wearing the dog collar of a Catholic priest.

"Oh my God!" exclaimed Liam. "Where the f . . . . , sorry Patrick . . . . I mean Father, where in the world did you come from?"

"Hello Liam my old friend, it's good to see you, said Patrick embracing him. "Leo has told me all about your progress since last we met. You've done well for yourself and you look great."

"I'm sorry Patrick. I'm having difficulty taking all this in. What happened to you after you left?"

"I sold up and set off on a cruise for some quiet reflection and a new life in America. While I was on the boat one evening just sitting and staring at the stars, I had a vision and a calling. It's difficult to explain but the whole of my previous rotten existence flashed before me while I sat there alone on the deck in the darkness. The terrible time I had given my parents, the thieving, the lies, the involvement at Ballykelly, and almost losing my life. JC Himself seemed to be speaking to me personally, filling me with a light and an indescribable feeling of peace. When I got to America, I went to see a priest and he put me in touch with the college where I trained as a novice. I was ordained a year ago in New York."

"What are you doing back in Northern Ireland? Why didn't you stay in America?"

"That's the strange thing Liam my friend. I don't really know. Would you believe I hear voices?"

"Do you mean you talk to yourself as well?"

"No, it isn't like that. It's like I am given certain instructions that I feel compelled to obey. They just come to me without warning."

"Were you told to come back here then?"

"I'm here am I not?" Patrick was smiling as he stood up and hugged his friend. "But you are as gullible as you ever were."

"What do you mean?"

"The real reason I'm back in Ireland is because my uncle died, do you remember him from Belfast, the one who handled the sale of my parents' house for me when you and I went to live with your uncle Barney?"

"Yes, I remember him very well, nice guy, just like your da. When was the funeral?"

"Just before Christmas, his next door neighbour found him on the kitchen floor. He'd had a massive heart attack, couldn't have suffered much. The neighbour found my name and telephone number on the pad next to the phone and rang me, I came straight away."

"I'm sorry to hear it Patrick, will you be staying long?"

Patrick looked at Leo while he answered Liam, "I was not planning to but after meeting and talking with Leo here, I will stay for as long as it takes."

"As long as what takes, is there something else I should know?" asked Liam looking puzzled and glancing at Leo.

"I have a little undercover job to do for a good friend who once saved my miserable life, I'll let him tell you about it," said Patrick, also looking at Leo.

David Grimble had only six more months as leader of the Northern Ireland Assembly. He had no idea what the future might hold after the general election planned for after the declaration of the decree nisi. He called a meeting of the entire assembly before whom he would make the most important speech of his entire political career.

"Ladies and gentlemen," he began.

Chapter 17

Larry McArdle sat across the breakfast table from his grandfather who was reading the morning paper. The old man was cursing silently to himself as he read about the Liberal Democrat victory in the general election. Northern Ireland was the only place the Lib Dem's had ever failed to make a decent showing. They had always been looked upon as a wishy-washy outfit with not a lot going for them. He thought that British politicians in general were a bunch of 'fuckin' pricks' anyway.

Larry had already seen the news. He had been up and about since 5.30 a.m. doing his own ablutions and having breakfast before attending to the old man. He was due at work for 8 a.m. The old man started ranting.

"The bastards stole the six counties from the old country in the 17th century and seeded them with bastard Scots and English settlers and that was when the real Troubles began. And now they are planning a fuckin' referendum to cop out of their responsibilities. What a bunch of wankers."

'Why does this stupid old man go on about what happened three hundred bloody years ago?' thought Larry.

The old man banged the table with his clenched fist, "I hate the fuckin' bastards. Mark my words boy there'll be bloodshed as a result of this. Those fuckin' Protestants will want to kill every fuckin' Catholic in the country so that they can have the fuckin' place to themselves. I wish I was younger, I'd show the bastards."

"Just like my da and my uncle Teddy showed them eh granda? Both of them are dead and gone now, all because of you and your stupid beliefs and principles. Your lot and the Protestant butcher boys are every bit as bad as each other. You've lived here all your life on British social security and handouts from the IRA. You've hardly done a days work in your life and you've brought up your sons to hate the prods and the British and to kill their soldiers. You've hardly been within a mile of this shit-hole you call your territory. Grandma was right to bid you goodbye when she did. I only wish I'd met her just to tell her about the pathetic old fart she left behind."

"Don't you be calling me names boy I've served my time for the Cause and so have my sons God rest them. They would still be here today if that bomb they were transporting had been properly fuckin' primed. There were four of them in the car, all young and keen to fight for what they believed in."

"What you brainwashed them into believing you mean. You taught them nothing but hatred and brutality. They were criminals, bank robbers and pushers as well as cold-blooded killers. What way is that to bring up your kids granda, are you proud of that achievement or something?"

"You can't speak to your granda like that, you live under my fuckin' roof and you eat from my fuckin' table."

"And if I didn't granda, who would cook for you and wash for you, and who would bathe you and clean up the ulcers on your legs every night and carry you to bed and dress you and feed you every morning? Who granda, who? Not the bloody IRA, they don't want to know you now. They send round their little gifts of stolen money, fags, and booze now and then but apart from that, they don't give a shit about you or your dead sons."

Larry was twenty-eight years old and a senior nursing officer at the Belfast General Hospital. His mother had deserted his gangster father and taken him off to England when he was quite young. Larry had trained in a London hospital as a nursing officer from the age of sixteen and now considered himself to be more English than northern Irish. There had been only traces of the old accent in his speech when he arrived back in the province but it was all coming back to him now.

He'd come back to Belfast to bury his father and his uncle after their car had been blown-up on a country road where they were planning to plant a bomb meant for a senior RUC officer who travelled that way to work each day.

He'd found his grandfather in an appalling state of health and living in filth. He could quite easily have left the old man there to die but he was all the family he had left. His mother had died in a freak accident two and a half years before his father, his uncle and two other IRA men had been killed.

A mystery surrounded his mother's death which had been blamed on a hit and run driver. But there were no witnesses at 2 am that morning when she was returning home on foot from the bakery, just five hundred yards from her home, where she worked from 8 p.m. four nights a week on the twilight shift making bread. A girlfriend of hers in Belfast had written to tell Larry about his father's funeral. He had been in two minds whether or not to go and now he wished he hadn't.

There was no one else now that the old man could turn to. He'd refused to go into a nursing home 'to die' as he put it. Larry had little option but to stay with him and look after him. The past couple of years had been utter hell but he could not bring himself to desert his now seventy eight year old dependant.

Larry's girlfriend, Sandra, in London wrote to him regularly which kept him from insanity. She was a wonderful girl who understood and sympathised with his predicament and promised to wait for however long it took for the old man be off his hands one way or another. In the meantime, she had a degree to work for without Larry as a distraction although she still missed him terribly. They spoke on the phone once a week for fifteen whole minutes, which was a joy to him. Larry was saving for an engagement ring and a house. Every penny he earned was accounted for. He didn't smoke and he drank very little but he did not pay rent and he did not have to buy all of the food. All he seemed to do was work, sleep, and look after the old man but it kept his mind occupied.

From time to time, a member of the local IRA would visit his grandfather and bring him a few things. Larry always retreated to the kitchen, or to his bedroom, and left the two of them to their whispered conversations. The IRA man never spoke to Larry; he thought that his grandfather might have warned the man off.

It was a different world to Larry's comfortable flat in Woolwich surrounded by nice neighbours who couldn't care less what colour, class, religion or politics you were so long as you kept it to yourself and didn't preach. Back home, people of just about every colour, class and creed in the world surrounded him and nobody bothered another except in neighbourly conversation; Sandra was looking after the place for him.

His only friend, apart from his colleagues at work, was the new hospital padre Father Patrick O'Riordan who had recently arrived from America. He was a wonderful man and a good listener. Larry had told him all about himself and how he had come to be working in Belfast. The padre had told him all about his own sinful life before he had been saved one night on the ship going to America. The Father who was only three years older than him impressed Larry.

The one time Provisional IRA supreme commander, Daniel Doonan, had made the journey from Dublin to see Michael Ahern who was the Provo's West Belfast CO before the cessation of PIRA hostilities three years before. His cell was still active but not militarily. They thieved, pushed drugs, and pimped for a living, and extorted money here and there as well as fraudulently claiming unemployment and social security benefits.

Ahern was pleased to see his old friend from some years before when they were much younger and active Players. They hadn't seen each other since well before the ceasefire.

"It's good to see you Michael, it must be what, eight or nine years, you haven't changed much, how are you?"

"I'm fine thanks Dan but you look like you've been in the wars, what happened to your face?"

"A bit of plastic surgery I'm afraid, I almost got myself killed, along with Colm Neary from Tyrone. We were trying to stop a renegade called Brannigan from embarrassing us. Do you remember Brannigan?"

"Who doesn't, he was a pain in the arse and a thorn in my flesh for long enough in his young days in Belfast, arrogant bastard, always was. What happened?"

"Do you remember that Ballykelly episode in '95 when those poor Catholic school kids were killed?" Ahern nodded.

"Well it was Brannigan and his gang who were behind that. I called him to Dublin and ordered him to stand down but he defied me so me and Colm, along with some of the boys, went after him. We caught up with him just as he was about to blow a batch of bombs planted at a bloody funeral of all places, feckin' psychopath. We attacked him from different directions while he was sat in his car. I was just about to shoot the bastard when the bloody car blew up. Someone else was obviously pissed off with him. Colm was blown in one direction and I was blown in the other and Brannigan was scattered all over the place. We knew nothing more about it until we woke up in hospital.

Ten of the boys were killed that morning along with most of Brannigan's gang when the ammunition dump at his hideout, about ten miles away, exploded. It was a feckin' catastrophe that I will never live down. I took the poor bastards there."

"Fortunes of war as they say Dan, what are you doing here?"

"Have you seen the news?"

"Do you mean about the election results? Yes"

"It looks like the British are all set to pull the plug on the north Michael if their referendum goes the way I think it will, what do you think?"

"I think you are right Dan, it is both good news and bad news at the same time. What do you reckon will happen?"

"Close to all out feckin' civil war is what I reckon Michael. We have to prepare for the worst. That's why I've come out of retirement and that is why I'm here to see you. I'll be doing the rounds of all the old battalions. How many men have you got who would be willing to re-enlist for the struggle?"

"There's only eight of us left now in the inner circle but I can call on at least twenty others who I know would be good for a fight but what will we do about shooters and stuff? We've got a few guns and enough ammunition for our immediate needs but not enough to start a bloody war."

"That might have been a problem if we had declared everything we had to De Chastelaine but we only declared the old and obsolete stuff. The rest is still safely stored and regularly serviced for a rainy day. Some of the stuff is now in the hands of our dissident friends but I'm sure we can bring them back on board. Tommy Hanlon is in charge of the Real IRA here in Belfast, so I have been informed, he's an old friend of mine and I'm sure I can bring him in."

"Sounds good to me, what's the plan now?"

"We need a war council, battalion commanders, quartermasters, CO's, intelligence officers, and soldiers. We need to organise it now, there's no point in waiting until the axe falls on the province, it will be too late to do anything by then; we have to be ready if it comes to fight for survival."

"What about money, Sterling will probably be useless when the Brits pull out. We should start converting our cash assets now and get some Euros behind us."

"One of the reasons I came to see you Michael is because I have always admired your cool headed thinking in all situations. I want you, as my second in command, to organise the logistics in readiness for a meeting of the new army council in a month's time. You can also hold the purse strings when you and your men have persuaded a few banks to give up the contents of their vaults. Are you up for it?"

"I'm up for it alright I would have been upset if you hadn't asked me first. Was Tommy Hanlon your second choice?"

"I think he would have jumped at the chance, he never wanted the ceasefire in the first place but he's a hothead and he hasn't got a brain like yours. He couldn't have handled it Michael, I can't think of anyone else who could."

Ahern produced a bottle of Jameson's and they drank to a successful recruiting campaign.

Doonan asked. "How is old Brendan McArdle these days is he still alive? He and his two boys were three of the best in the old days."

"He's still around but only just. You heard about the boys' own goal didn't you?"

"Yes, it was a sad loss and bloody careless. Are you looking out for the old boy?"

"We keep him in the necessaries if that's what you mean. His grandson is acting as nursemaid since the boys were buried. He came over especially from London for the funeral. I gather one of his mother's friends wrote to him. Brendan would be dead otherwise with those bloody ulcerated legs of his. He can barely stand up any more. The lad does everything for him as well as going to work full time at the General Hospital where he is a staff nurse."

"Where's his mother?"

"Dead"

"Is the boy a potential recruit? He comes from a proud Republican family."

"I don't know we haven't spoken to him. He makes himself scarce when our man goes round. Brendan doesn't say much other than he couldn't manage without the boy."

"I think I'll pay Brendan a visit just for old time's sake and get to meet his grandson," said Doonan. "The boy might listen to me if I lay it on thick enough about the good old days. Do you know what kind of relationship he had with his father?"

"No," said Ahern, "he was just a kid when Mary fucked off to England with him. She was a bit fed up with the beatings she got when Shaun was drunk, and even the poor kid was covered in bruises. I think if Shaun could have gotten hold of her after she left, he would have killed her with his bare hands. He was a vicious bastard by any standards. We took the matter out of his hands. One of my friends across the water traced her to a flat in Fulham Road in London. One of his sleepers did the rest. Shaun was grateful. He would have been up for this fight if he had still been around. His brother wasn't quite so hard but then he was younger and a follower."

Larry McArdle was sitting alone at a table in the corner of the hospital staff room drinking coffee when Patrick O'Riordan came in. The Father poured himself a cup and went over to where Larry was sitting.

"Do you mind if I join you Larry?"

"Please do Father, you're just the person I'd like to talk to."

"Is everything alright at home, is your grandfather OK?"

"He's fine Father, it's his friends I'm worried about."

"Do you want to tell me about it, you know it will go no further?"

"I know it won't Father. You already know that my granda used be a member of the Official IRA and then the Provos after they broke away. Well he told me this evening that he was one of the original rebels who complained to the Official IRA about the lack of protection for the Catholic community where he lived. The Loyalists were murdering people left right and centre. He and his friends decided to break away when the British Army intervened in 1969. He never got over it and he still rants on about it now and again."

"And who are these friends of his that you are so worried about, have you met any of them?"

"Only one, his name is Groddy McGinty but I think the Groddy is a nick name because he leaves an odour wherever he goes. He suffers from chronic hyperhydrosis and halitosis, and it's a fair bet that he doesn't bathe very often. I don't know how my granda puts up with him. I usually go to my room when Groddy visits him; he brings granda stuff from time to time."

"What kind of stuff?"

"Money, cigarettes, cigars, beer, whisky, you name it. They bring him almost anything that he asks for, he used be an important Provo. Don't ask me where they get the stuff; I can only guess that it's stolen.

My father and his younger brother used to be with them as I've told you before. But last night, an old friend from Dublin, a Daniel Doonan, called to see my granda."

Patrick's ears pricked up at the sound of Doonan's name. He had never met the man but he knew all about his involvement after Ballykelly, he must be pushing sixty now.

Larry continued. "He apparently used to be big in the Provos when they were active. His face looked as if he'd had been in some kind of accident, it looked as though he'd had plastic surgery. I once worked in a burns unit and I recognised the type of scarring."

"Did you get to meet the man?"

"Yes, he was quite a charmer. He gave me a history lesson about the Irish Republican movement and an account of my family's involvement. I'm not quite sure what he was after but he said he would call again and have another wee chat."

"How do you feel about that Larry?"

"I got the feeling he was trying to soften me up for some reason but I'm not really interested in violence and religion. I can't wait for the old man to pass on, God forgive me, so that I can get back to London and my Sandra. There's an evil about this place that you can almost taste. There's no love, there's no trust. I hate the place and the people. The only thing I hated before I came back to this God awful country was coffee with no sugar."

"It could get worse Larry. If this referendum thing on first of February results in the province becoming an independent republic, there could be more bloodshed than ever in the fight for control by the two tribes. Have you thought about the implications?"

"I daren't think about it Father, I've never been a violent person but I am beginning to have violent thoughts."

"About what." asked O'Riordan?

"Knocking silly heads together and trying to get these stupid people to see sense. I just cannot understand why they can't live together in peace. What is so wrong with peace that they have to reject it out of hand?" He began to shake with frustration.

"Calm down Larry, you're getting yourself all upset. You have to understand that the hatred has been passed from generation to generation ever since King Billy beat King James in the Battle of the Boyne in 1690. The Catholics have never forgiven the Protestants for that defeat and the Protestants taunt the Catholics with their never ending Orange parades. The hatred is just as strong today as it was over three hundred years ago. The only way to stop it is to take out a complete generation in one go. Cut out the rot before it starts to infect the next generation."

"You mean like a cancer?"

"Exactly, you're a medic, you know what I mean."

"But how could that be achieved Father? God would need an army of surgeons." Larry began to smile at the thought of winged white-clad angels with massive scalpels pursuing little devils and swiping off their heads.

"That would be more effective than knocking a few heads together, don't you think?"

"Yes it would Father. Given the choice, I think I would rather be a surgeon for God than a cancer cell for Satan."

"Well put Larry, I hope you feel better after our little chat but I'm very much afraid that duty calls, I have some last rights to perform on an old lady who has been through many years of the Troubles and has managed to hang on for ninety six of them. Don't let this Doonan fella give you any rot."

"Thanks Father, I'll be on my guard, I'll call and get some holy water from you later."

When he got back to his office, Patrick O'Riordan put in a call to Leo. "I might have a new recruit for your army Leo, his name is Laurence McArdle, better known as Larry, can I bring him to meet you for a chat without giving anything away?"

"You want me to vet him?" asked Leo.

"He's in the right place at the right time, he could be invaluable to us if he's handled properly, he's currently non-violent but he wants to see an end to tribal warfare," said Patrick. "And oh, you should know that our old friend Daniel Doonan is up from Dublin and is planning to see Larry for a second chat. He's already been to see Larry's grandfather who is a retired Provo from the old school. From what Larry has told me, Doonan has been giving him a history lesson, probably to soften him up. Doonan has to be here for a reason and I think we both know what that is."

"Cedric Parker was right, he said they would organise well before the referendum result was known. It looks like it could be very bloody. I wonder what the Prod's are up to at the moment, there's no intelligence from that side yet but I'll bet they are not waiting around either," said Leo. "OK Patrick fix up a meeting, bring him up to Loch Neagh for an evening out and I'll arrange to meet you both by accident."

"I'll do that but is it possible for me to win a couple of tickets for a free meal at the Hotel?" suggested Patrick, "then I will have an excuse to ask him out. I can tell him that he was the only other person I could think of to share my luck with."

"Still as devious as ever eh Patrick you old rascal, why did God choose you for a Sunbeam?" laughed Leo.

"Perhaps he just took a shine to me," retorted Patrick. They both laughed at the pun and rang off.

Larry got home at 8.30 p.m. after a twelve hour shift, it was another shift like yesterday and now he had two days off.

There were no lights on in the house when he arrived and his grandfather was not in his usual armchair and the television was switched off. Larry thought he must be in the bathroom or in his bedroom but it was a bit too early for bed. The old man liked to down a couple of beers with the attendant 'Old Paddy' chasers before he turned in.

Larry called out but got no reply. He went to the bathroom but it was empty. He went to his grandfather's bedroom and found him lying face down on the floor. He checked him for vital signs and was half relieved to find that the old man was breathing.

He turned him over and cradled him in his arms, patted him gently on the cheek and called his name. The old man's eyes opened and he gazed up into his grandson's face and said quietly. "I'm going boy, I know it, you don't have to get me a priest, I'm passed that now but I have something to confess to you before I go. It has preyed on my mind for long enough. I didn't agree with it at the time but I had no more say with the big boys."

"What is it granda, what do you want to tell me?"

"Michael Ahern had your ma killed as a favour to your da. I swear I didn't know anything about it until after it was done. My Shaun couldn't keep his bloody mouth shut; he wanted to tell the world. I was ashamed of him for the first time in my life. It was a bad thing to do. I've wanted to tell you since you got here but I couldn't and when you began to take care of me, it became harder. You would have left me here to die alone and I couldn't have faced that. Forgive me boy, forgive me before I die please."

"I wouldn't have left you granda I would have tried to bring him to justice. Who is this Michael Ahern granda, where can I find him? I can't let him get away with what he and his kind did to my poor ma God bless her."

"He's a very dangerous man Larry, you wouldn't get within a mile of him, he's surrounded by minders and anyone of them would kill you as soon as look at you."

The old man was slurring his words slightly and his breathing was becoming shallower. Larry heard him let out a last rattling breath then felt him relax in his arms; he was dead.

Larry might have cried for his grandfather had it not been for what he had just told him. His tears were instead for his dear unfortunate mother, his curses were for his evil bastard of a father who had beaten her senseless on occasion and for Michael Ahern who had arranged her murder as a gratuitous gesture. What were these people? They were all bloody psychopaths; animals. They should be put to sleep.

He pulled himself together finally and used his mobile to phone his grandfather's doctor; the old man had no phone. Larry then put in a call to the hospital and asked to speak to Father O'Riordan.

"Hello Father, it's me Larry McArdle," said Larry

"Hello Larry, what can I do for you?" asked Patrick.

"Can you come over to my granda's house Father? I need you like I've never needed anyone in my life before, I can't talk right now, I have thoughts of murder in my heart. I'll tell you all about it when you get here. Can you come?" he pleaded.

"Give me the address, I'll come right away. Don't do anything silly," ordered Patrick.

The doctor had been, issued the death certificate, and had gone by the time Patrick O'Riordan arrived. An undertaker, prior to its removal to the mortuary, had prepared the body of Larry's grandfather. It was being carried downstairs preceded by the undertaker who looked at the Father and said. "You're too late for this one Father, he's cold already."

Patrick crossed himself then gave a short blessing over the coffin, which the bearers had lowered to the floor, and then they left.

"You didn't tell me what had happened Larry, when was it?" asked Patrick.

"I found him on the bedroom floor when I got home," replied Larry, "he must have had a heart attack or something, we'll have to wait and see what the post mortem says."

"Was he already dead?" asked Patrick.

"No Father, he died in my arms, he seemed to have clung on to life until I got home. He had something to tell me, something he couldn't take with him to his grave," said Larry. "He must have willed himself to stay alive until I got here."

Patrick put his hand on Larry's shoulder and asked, "what was it Larry, you mentioned something about murder in your heart. Do you want to tell me about it?"

Larry sobbed as he told the Father the whole sordid story.

Patrick understood only too well. He'd known evil people like Ahern and his associates. People who had

299

tried to force him into killing young British soldiers in an ambush but, and he would always thank God, it had all gone wrong and someone else had done the dirty deed. But he had still felt remorse for the victims and shame for his own involvement, he said, "I can understand the way you feel Larry. There is no way that you will ever get close enough to a man like Ahern to take revenge. Your grandfather was right. People like Ahern are almost untouchable but there is a way to bring him to justice if you would be willing to try it."

"Just tell me Father what I have to do?" asked Larry.

"Are you absolutely sure you want to get involved with these people?" asked Patrick.

"What do you mean involved?" asked Larry.

"You're off for the next couple of days are you not?" asked Patrick.

"Yes Father," answered Larry.

Patrick smiled; he now had an excuse to take Larry to meet Leo. "Pack a few things to tide you over I'm taking you to see a friend of mine. You'll have to trust me on this one Larry."

There was a knock on the front door. Larry went to see who it was.

It was the smelly IRA man Groddy McGinty who came now and then to see his grandfather. He asked Larry. "Will you tell Brendan I'm here?"

"I'm sorry he just left ten minutes ago in a coffin. He died this evening just after I got home, a heart attack I guess," said Larry.

"That's tough, what are you going to do?" There was no sign of remorse from McGinty, no 'sorry to hear it.'

Larry looked at the Father and winked before turning to McGinty, "I'm going back to the hospital," he lied, "I have to start nightshift tonight for a couple of nights. I could take the time off but there is no point, as a nurse, I live with this kind of thing all the time and it will do me no good brooding about this place."

The man nodded in understanding. "I'll call back in a couple of days and speak to you about the funeral. I think a guard of honour might be on offer, your granda was an important man so he was."

Larry opened his mouth to protest but the priest pinched his arm and butted in. "Sure now wouldn't that be nice Larry, a guard of honour for a fine man?"

"Eh yes Father, if you say so."

"Well," said Patrick, "I'll be off and let you get ready for work Laurence, I'll see you back at the hospital, and God bless you both." Said Patrick signing the cross then he was gone.

Chapter 18

They were known locally as the Shankill Surgeons because of the neatness of their operations. Any one of the twelve of them could have outshone Jack the Ripper or even a band of cutthroat pirates. They preferred the silence of knives to the bulk and the noise of guns. They met on a monthly basis to discuss business in the anti-room of the local Orange Lodge where their leader, James McKenna, was the paid caretaker.

None of the surgeons was a member of the Orange order. The officials of the lodge turned a blind eye to the extracurricular meetings in return for McKenna's cheap cash-in-hand cleaning service performed under duress by his long suffering wife and two teenage boys.

The meetings of the Surgeons were covert and strictly confidential; no minutes were taken. Each date selected for a robbery or a sectarian killing was committed to the memory of whosoever volunteered to carry out the task. When the job was finished, the loot was shared equally and the incident simply forgotten. It was the most secret of secret societies and totally without conscience.

Twelve grim-faced men sat around the table in the lodge. The Union flag stood in the corner of the room alongside the lodge standard. An emergency meeting had been called as soon as the new British Prime Minister, Charlie Kinnear, had announced the referendum

Every transgression the Surgeons had been responsible for had, they claimed, been committed in the name of a now ungrateful mother country as far as they were concerned. The men had no conception of the evil barbarity of their crimes. They simply saw the Catholic population of Northern Ireland as deadly adversaries of a proud British Protestant nation to which they belonged.

Their fathers and their grandfathers before them had brought them up to revere the great King William of Orange and to continue the persecution of his mortal enemies. They had a duty to carry on the good work by educating succeeding generations of children and filling their hearts and minds with hatred for the 'papist pigs.'

"Why are they doing this to us?" asked their leader, we have dedicated our lives to the British Crown for over three hundred years and now they seem to want to be rid of us, why?" James McKenna was on his feet searching the faces of his colleagues who just stared back at him sullenly.

"You don't seriously believe that the British will vote us out of the Union Jimmy, surely?" asked George Dearden, a dapper little man who had been a fair ballroom dancer and a ladies man in his younger days.

"Why were we not allowed a vote in the referendum this time?" asked Terry Curren, the local barber.

"Christ knows," said McKenna. "We have been loyal to the Cause and we have always done our duty. It's those fuckin' Liberal Democrats, Labour wouldn't have done this to us neither would the Conservatives themselves, they promised us more money and more troops."

"They say that it is costing the taxpayer too much, that's the reason they gave in the newspapers for the Liberal Democrats sharing government," said Bill Patrick, the oldest member of the Surgeons at the age of fifty-nine.

"And whose fault is that? Not ours, there are more Catholics on the fuckin' dole than Protestants. It's them that are costing the country money," said Frankie Chaffey. He had served for three years in the Royal Tank Regiment but had been discharged after almost killing a civvy in a pub fight in 1984.

"Don't talk shite Franky, every one of us here is on the social with all the perks that go with it," said Dearden, "and that goes for most of the Shankill since some of the big businesses have pulled out. The whole fuckin' province seems to be moving that way; the cow is running out of milk."

"It says in the papers that Pashley had a go at the Prime Minister but got nowhere. They say he walked out on the bastards. I should imagine that he and his Presbyterian brothers will be girding their loins for a holy war," said Denis Trimble, the youngest of the gang at the age of thirty-five.

"No doubt about it." Said McKenna, and that's why I have called you here today, if the worst comes to the worst and the rest of the UK votes Northern Ireland out of the Union, we'll be isolated and at the mercy of the IRA. They're bound to close ranks for their own protection and I dare bet they still have a sizeable cache of weapons somewhere. They've always been a devious set of bastards."

"What can a small outfit like ours do Jimmy?" asked Barry Cormack an ex light weight boxer, "if they have guns and bombs and we have nothing to fight them with?"

"We are not the only Loyalist group in the world Barry, there's hundreds, maybe thousands, just like us. We'll have to get together and form an army with a proper chain of command. We have our own paramilitaries who are probably mobilizing as we speak, they'll be looking for people like us. It's just a matter of getting together under one banner and a dedicated leader," answered McKenna. He fancied himself as a high-ranking officer in any new organisation.

Everyone was sitting up and listening now. Eyes were bright and ears were attentive. If adrenaline had a smell, the place would have reeked with excitement.

"What about a provincial government?" asked Dearden, "do you think The Northern Ireland Assembly will do something about it?"

"How else could it survive George? What we have to do is make sure that Sinn Fein doesn't stand a fuckin' chance. The first thing I would do is take-out all of their offices and as many of their politicians as I could before the referendum is even held. Fuck-up the political wing and then the Catholic community and the IRA would be out on a limb."

"And what about the police and the army?" said Curren. "I can't see them standing by while there is a civil war going on around them, can you?"

"If Northern Ireland gets the heave-ho from the union, there'll be no British soldiers to stop us and the police have already had their teeth drawn. It will take forever for them to organise themselves against an army of dedicated

Loyalist volunteers," said McKenna. "The last group standing will be the rulers."

"Loyalist volunteers Jimmy! Loyal to what?" asked Brendan Downes who had been sitting quietly during the meeting. He never raised his voice in argument; he even killed quietly and without feeling. He was a frequent volunteer when a sectarian murder was on the cards.

"A very good question Brendan loyal to what indeed? We will need a new standard to replace the Union flag, but we will retain King Billy as our spiritual leader if I have anything to do with it."

McKenna's wife Maddie and her two boys had been cleaning the lodge when her husband had turned up unexpectedly and interrupted the work. He had told her to take the boys home because he had an important emergency.

There was no love between McKenna and his wife. It had died years ago when she had discovered what kind of person he was. The only thing they had in common was a shock of Celtic red hair. He had looked great when they were young and first married but too much booze and hard living had since taken their toll. His hair was going grey at the temples and his facial skin had the texture of untreated leather.

Maddie's hair was still in good condition and the only facial lines she had were worry lines. She was still quite attractive and only thirty-five years old, eight years younger than McKenna. They'd had two children in the first three years of their marriage, both redheads, and she had known little more than poverty all of her married life. Most of McKenna's ill-gotten gains went on booze, fags, and horses. Maddie got the dole and the family allowance on which to feed and clothe them all. The boys were now thirteen and fifteen and totally cowed by their brutal father. She would have left him years ago had it not been for her precious boys.

Unknown to McKenna, Maddie had another cleaning job for only six hours a week to supplement the meagre pittance that he gave her to keep house. She worked from 9 a.m. until 11 a.m. on the mornings when McKenna regularly attended the betting shop before meeting his mates in a pub. She worked for Mary Bailey, the disabled wife of a businessman who ran a Marine Engineering Company.

Mary was good to Maddie and gave her little perks now and again, a blouse here, a skirt or a dress there, and sweets for the boys. Maddie often poured out her soul to Mary who assured her that a problem shared was better borne but would go no further.

Maddie had been half way home from McKenna's emergency meeting when she'd realised that she had left her reading glasses behind in the kitchen of the lodge. She told the boys to carry on home without her, gave them some money, and told them to call at the fish and chip shop for a bite of supper.

She went back to the lodge and opened the back door into the kitchen as silently as she could so as not to disturb the men. She retrieved her spectacles in the half-light and was just about to leave when she caught a snatch of the conversation in the meeting room that was just beyond the closed serving hatch from the kitchen.

Despite her fear of being discovered, Maddie continued to listen with a sense of horror and growing concern to every word. 'They were little more than savages these men,' she thought. There would now be no future for her and her boys with McKenna if she could help it, she would find somewhere to go; the need had become urgent. She slipped quietly out of the back door and locked it behind her.

When she got home, the boys had not yet returned from the fish and chip shop. Maddie removed her coat and slumped down into a faded armchair. She gazed around the room and wondered why she hadn't taken the boys years ago and left the two-bed roomed terraced dump and her tyrant of a husband. The house now seemed even more oppressive than usual for some reason but where could she go, where could she hide?

The boys returned from the shop and the three of them sat down to supper. When McKenna returned from the bar where he had gone after the meeting, the family were all in bed sleeping as usual. He sat up half the night planning the next move of himself and his gang.

He was still sleeping soundly when Maddie slipped quietly out of bed, dressed, and woke the boys for school. After breakfast, she walked with them as far as their school gate then took the bus to Mary Bailey's house for her thrice-weekly two-hour cleaning session at three pounds per hour.

"Is everything alright Maddie? You look a bit down today," said Mary.

Maddie bit her lip and wondered if she should confide in Mary and tell her all about the meeting of the Shankill Surgeons.

"I need to get away from this place with my boys Mrs Bailey. Belfast is not going to be a very nice place to live if this referendum thing results in the province being no longer a part of the Union. I heard something last night that made my blood run cold and I don't want any part of it with my boys. The trouble is I have no-one to turn to and nowhere to go." Maddie began to weep.

Mary took her into her arms and patted her gently on the head. "Come and sit down and tell me all about it. Calm your self while I put the kettle on, the work can wait." She took Maddie's hand and led her to a sofa then went to make a pot of tea.

When they were settled, Maddie told Mary about the clandestine meeting of the Surgeons. Mary had heard of them vaguely through the odd report in the newspapers but she was surprised to learn that Maddie's husband was their leader. She could understand Maddie's feelings about wanting to run away from it all and asked if she could help.

"It's very kind of you to offer Mrs Bailey but I don't see how you can help. I have no money and I don't have any relatives in this country. They are all in America and Australia. They don't like James McKenna or his politics so they keep a wide berth. They stopped writing to me after I married him; I was only nineteen. They were right but I was young and foolish, and stubborn. Isn't life an education?"

"It surely is Maddie my dear. If I can find a way to help you, would you let me? The last thing in the world I'd want to do is to interfere in your life against your will."

The doorbell rang and Mary went to see who was there. Maddie froze when she heard a little squeal of surprise from Mary and the sound of a man's voice; had McKenna followed her? She was almost cowering when Mary re-entered the room with a man who looked to be in his thirties.

"This is my son Peter," said Mary excitedly. He's paying a flying visit. "Peter, this is Maddie McKenna my home help and newfound friend in need."

"Friend in need indeed mother, you never change," laughed Peter, holding out his hand, "pleased to meet you Mrs McKenna, sorry to intrude upon your conversation but I was over from the mainland seeing dad on business and couldn't wait to come and see mum." Then turning to Mary he said, "I'll be staying for a few days if that's OK mum."

"It's more than OK, it's wonderful."

"Right, well I'll pop my things upstairs and get back to the office. Bye Mrs McKenna, no doubt I'll see you again while I'm here. I'll leave you to your chinwag mum, see you later," then Peter was off again.

"He's a fine looking man Mrs Bailey, you must be very proud," said Maddie.

"I am Maddie, he's one of twins," said Mary. "The other one, Leo, is married to a Belfast girl. They have twin boys as well would you believe it? They live in the north east of England in a little village called Ryhope near a town called Sunderland where we have a branch of the Marine Engineering business. It would have been nice if they all could have come across at the same time. It seems like ages since I've seen my twin baby grandsons and their mother Siobhan, she's a lovely girl."

Maddie was now more composed, she said, "well I'll get on and do some work now, you have made me feel much better. If you can help me in any way without putting yourself out too much I would be very happy but I think I need a miracle."

"The work can wait until tomorrow Maddie, you get yourself away home; you won't lose any money," said Mary.

"I'd rather stay and work if you don't mind, there's nothing to go home to, except McKenna, until the boys get home from school. The less I see of him the better."

"As you wish Maddie and please call me Mary, Mrs Bailey is so formal and it makes me feel old."

"Alright Mrs Bailey, whoops!" They both laughed; Maddie definitely felt much better.

They met for dinner at the hotel on Lough Neagh. Leo, Peter, Liam, Patrick and Larry; all round Introductions were made while they sat in the bar over pre-dinner drinks.

Larry had already been introduced to Liam when he collected him and Patrick from the hospital with the company car. Larry had asked Patrick, in a whisper, who it was that they were going to meet.

"You don't have to whisper Larry, we're all friends here. Liam and I grew up together here in Belfast. We are more like brothers than friends, are we not Liam?" asked Patrick.

Liam half shouted over his shoulder. "We were a couple of right tearaways in those days Larry, you wouldn't have liked us very much then but we were both given a second chance to redeem ourselves. We'd lost touch for a few years until recently. I can't believe that my spiritual brother is now my spiritual Father." Patrick and Larry laughed.

"What will this meeting be about if you don't mind me asking? I'm intrigued," said Larry.

"Intrigue is about the right word Larry. We are meeting a couple of good friends of ours who are on a special mission. You could almost say that it was a holy quest but I could possibly get you to understand better if I put it in clinical terms what with you being a medic and all that," began Patrick. "What happens when the human body is attacked by bacteria or viruses?"

"Are you talking about the immune system?" asked Larry.

"The very same," answered Patrick.

"Well the blood contains a certain kind of white cell which makes antibodies in response to the poison from the attacking bacteria or virus. It then destroys the invader. Cells called phagocytes then take over and devour the debris left by the little tinkers. The antibodies remain in the system forever so that the next time the invaders go calling, the army of antibodies is ready and waiting," explained Larry.

"I couldn't have put it better myself Larry. Now you know as well as I do that there is a terrible sickness in the body we know as Northern Ireland that seems to have been festering forever. And especially after what you learned from your grandfather before he died. Well the people you are going to meet tonight, plus Liam and me, are antibodies for want of a better word. We have all experienced the bacteria at first hand and have come together in an attempt to destroy it once and for all. All we need is a few insiders as antibiotics, if you see what I mean, to stop the spread of the disease. Do you understand?"

"I think so, it's my turn to say well put Father, how on earth did you ever become a priest with such a devious mind?" asked Larry.

"You can call me Patrick," he replied, "I was born with a devious mind as Liam here will testify."

312

When they got to the hotel, Liam introduced Peter and Leo as his brothers-in-law and partners in the family engineering business. There was no mention of their military connection. To all intents and purposes, they were now self-appointed mercenaries employed on a crusade against evil as far as Larry was concerned.

Leo's area of responsibility was the Republican criminal and terror organisations and Peter's was the Loyalist equivalent. Patrick's role was less defined as was Liam's but they would both have important parts to play as intelligence officers.

After dinner, they huddled in a quiet corner of the lounge for a tactical seminar.

"What do you want from me?" asked Larry.

"I gather that you told Patrick that a Daniel Doonan was hinting at you joining the IRA when you first met at your grandfather's house, is that right?" asked Leo.

"Yes I think so, although he didn't come right out with it, I'm sure that's what he was leading up to. But I have no intention of following in the footsteps of my father and his father and God knows how many fathers before that," answered Larry.

"I can understand that. Did you know that Doonan used to be Mr Big in Dublin years ago before the cessation of PIRA violence in '94?" Leo asked.

"I had an idea he was big shot but I didn't realise he was that big. What could I do against a man like that, I'm not an aggressive person, in fact I hate violence," said Larry

"If you went along with him, let him think he's influenced you, you could be invaluable to us as a mole. You wouldn't have to lay a finger on anyone, just keep us informed of their plans then we'd do the rest, what do you say?" asked Leo.

"What happens when I tell you their plans?" asked Larry.

"We pass the information to their enemies through our Loyalist network and then encourage the two sides to do what they do best and that is to kill each other," said Peter.

"Then what?" asked Larry.

"We wipe out the survivors on both sides," said Leo, "it is as simple as that."

"Christ almighty!" Larry exclaimed, "Sorry Father."

Patrick held up his hand. "Call me Patrick please, It's OK Larry, JC will be on our side, I can assure you."

"I was planning on returning to London now that my granda is dead, can I think about it?" asked Larry.

"Five minutes enough?" asked Patrick. They all laughed.

Mary and Joe Bailey were still not aware of their son Leo's presence in the province. Peter had not informed them for reasons of security but it was planned between them that when Leo returned to England, the day after the Lough Neagh meeting, he would ring his parents and ask them if it was convenient to visit with Siobhan and the children for a couple of weeks.

It was late when Peter returned home from the meeting. The others had stayed on in the hotel for the night. His mother and father had not yet gone to bed. Mary had been telling Joe about Maddie McKenna's problems and was asking him if he had any suggestions. Joe sympathised and said he would help if he knew how. He put the problem to Peter and Mary rebuked him for betraying a confidence. After all, she had assured Maddie that what she had told her would go no further and now three people knew about it.

"Don't worry mother, we are family after all, I think I might have a solution. Will it be possible for me to meet Maddie once more?" asked Peter.

"She's here again tomorrow but she might be cross with me for having told you her business," said Mary.

"Just tell her that you asked my advice on behalf of an unnamed friend and that I came up with an answer," said Peter

"Do you have an answer?" asked Mary.

"I may well have, I'll sleep on it," answered Peter, "but I will have to discuss it with Leo and Siobhan before I put it to Maddie. It's too late to ring them now but I'll get through to them first thing tomorrow from the office. What time does Maddie get here?"

"About 9.00 a.m. after she sees the boys to school. We usually have a cup of tea and a chat before she starts work," said Mary.

"You women, you're always chatting. Right I'm off to bed I'll be home about eleven in the morning with Maddie's problems solved hopefully, good night." He kissed his mother fondly on the cheek.

From his room, he rang Leo at Loch Neagh on his mobile and told him about Maddie McKenna and the possibility of a way into the Protestant camp. He explained his plan and asked him at this late hour if he could get Siobhan's approval and let him know first thing in the morning. Leo agreed.

As he lay in bed, Peter quietly congratulated himself on the possibility of recruiting his first mole in the Loyalist camp. She was quite a looker was that Maddie McKenna; he dismissed the thought immediately and crashed out.

Leo rang Peter at the office before he set off for the airport and told him that Siobhan had agreed to go along with his plan but was slightly apprehensive about leaving a stranger in her house while she wasn't there. Peter said he understood and would take full responsibility. If Maddie agreed to the plan, Leo would meet her the following morning in Newcastle then the two women could at least get to look each other over before Leo and his family set of for Northern Ireland.

Peter arrived at his family house just before Maddie was ready to leave. He apologised to her for having eves-dropped on the conversation that his mother had had with his father the previous evening in an attempt to find a solution to Maddie's dilemma.

"I might have a solution to your problem if you will allow me to help you," said Peter.

"Why should you want to help a complete stranger with two children, Peter is it? I'm nothing to you I only work for your mother. I'm of little consequence to anyone but my boys. You don't have to put yourself out on our behalf," said Maddie, looking somewhat offended by his gesture, as though her pride had been severely dented.

"I have to confess an ulterior motive Maddie, I wouldn't intrude upon your business otherwise," said Peter, almost blushing at the sight of her proud handsome features. Her face had turned quite pink and she looked remarkably beautiful beneath the shock of red hair. Peter felt the stirring of an attraction towards her but dismissed the thought as absurd.

"What could you possibly want from me?" asked Maddie.

"Access to your husband's gang," he replied.

"The Shankill Surgeons, what are they to you?" She asked

"Nothing at all Maddie but I have a policeman friend who has been trying to trace this gang for years without success, they are so secretive." All I need is a list of names and addresses if you have any."

"How will that help me and my boys? Asked Maddie.

"I can get you away from this place and away from McKenna if that is what you want." Said Peter, "is that what you really want?"

Maddie was apprehensive at first but realised that Peter's concern for her and her boys was genuine. She agreed to do as he asked; the list would be in his hands by the very next day.

Peter had spoken to Cedric Parker after he had called Leo and told him about his stroke of luck. Cedric authorised him to offer Maddie £20,000 to help her and the boys to resettle anywhere in England, Scotland, or Wales. There would be a wide choice of renovated council housing earmarked at various places throughout the country in which to live.

"When can we leave?" asked Maddie.

"When could I have the list?" asked Peter.

"Tomorrow morning," said Maddie.

"You can leave tomorrow morning," said Peter.

"Oh my goodness," said Maddie, "I can hardly take this in. I was beginning to doubt the existence of God but he has heard my prayers and answered them."

She began to weep again. Peter felt a tug on his heartstrings, which brought a sting of tears to his eyes. He wanted to take her in his arms and comfort her but he turned quickly, excused himself, and left the room. 'Jesus, she even looked good when she was crying, down boy, don't get ideas.'

He returned with a pot of tea and some biscuits.

"What will I do now Peter?" asked Maddie now dry-eyed and composed.

"Drink your tea and listen carefully," answered Peter. "First of all, make out the list of the Surgeons' particulars, their names and as many addresses as you can remember, and put it in your handbag. Then, in the morning, go with the boys to school like you normally do. Tell me where the school is and I will intercept you before you reach it. I will then take you by taxi to RAF Aldergrove where a plane will be waiting for you. You will be flown to Newcastle Airport in England where my twin brother, you can't mistake him, will be waiting for you. He'll take you to his house where you can have a fortnight's holiday together with your boys while you decide where you want to settle. Have you got all that?"

"What about my things" asked Maddie?

"Forget about clothes, you won't need them any more, I'll give you pocket money for your journey and Leo will give you £2,000 in cash when you arrive so that you can have a real good spend-up on new clothes for the three of you. There are some nice shops in Sunderland or you can hop onto the Metro and go to the Gateshead Metro Centre where there are even more shops. The cash is a bonus for your co-operation; a resettlement grant of £20,000 will be put into a bank of your choice. I will give you a phone number to contact when I pick you up tomorrow. You and the boys may have a few personal bits and pieces that you will want to take with you. Just pop them into your pockets or whatever but don't tell your boys what's happening until you are on the plane. I'm sure they will be pleasantly surprised by the secret adventure you have planned as a holiday for them without their father. As far as McKenna is concerned, you will simply have disappeared without trace, he will not have the faintest idea why or to where. The rest will be up to you after the penny has dropped and the boys realise that they are never going back to Northern Ireland. Do you think you can handle all that?" asked Peter.

"I think so and thanks for everything, I think you are all wonderful, especially your ma." She kissed Peter on the cheek and he blushed.

Mary was entering the room as Maddie made to return home. They hugged each other and Mary wished her luck.

McKenna wasn't there when Maddie arrived home. He would be either in the betting shop or at the pub next door to it or alternating between the two.

Maddie busied herself with the list of the Surgeons' names and addresses beginning with her own, she knew them all only too well but so secretive were they that she had not realized that they were members of a notorious gang until that night at the Orange lodge when she had put two and two together.

She smiled to herself at the thought of McKenna being brought to justice along with his murderous gang of thieves. She felt no remorse whatsoever about what she was doing, she was in the process of exchanging a life of hell for a life of Heaven for herself and her boys. God bless Mother Mary Bailey and her saintly son Peter.

That evening, when McKenna went off to his favourite haunt, Maddie suggested a game to the boys. She told them to get out their most treasured possessions and lay them out on the kitchen table. They had precious few, a cheap watch each, a calculator, a yoyo, a couple of foreign coins given to them by more fortunate kids who had been abroad for a holiday, a blunt pocket knife, and a pocket chess set between them.

"We are going to take a trip to the Antrim coast this weekend without your da," she informed them. "While we are there, I'm going to arrange a treasure hunt. The Carnaby's are going along with their two boys and we're all going to have a fine time orienteering and that."

"What is orienteering ma?" asked James, the eldest. He had never heard the word before.

"It's a kind of map reading exercise darlin'. What you do is, you select a course over any distance you like, we will probably do about five miles," she lied. "Then you put in the check points and mark them on a map. At each checkpoint you hide some treasure. The idea is that everyone sets of at ten-minute intervals and map-reads themselves around the course. To make sure that no one is cheating, you have to list all the treasure you find in the order that you find it and then cover it up again. The last person to go collects and brings in the treasure. The person who completes the course in the fastest time is the winner. It's as simple as that. What do you think boys?"

"Brilliant," said young Terrence.

"Sounds fun," said James, unsmiling.

'My poor serious James,' thought Maddie, 'I'm going to make you happy, you'll see'

The two boys ran off to fetch other bits and pieces. 'They really didn't have much,' thought Maddie as she packed them into a small rucksack along with her own pathetic collection. The boys went off to bed excited about the coming weekend, they planned to discuss it with the Carnaby kids at school the next morning; some hope.

The following morning, James McKenna was still abed in his usual alcohol-induced slumber when Maddie dressed in the best clothes that she had. She told the boys to wear their Sunday best so that she could wash their other things before the weekend. She made sure that they had a good breakfast before setting off for the school.

They had been walking for about five minutes when Peter drew-up alongside them in one of Sid Morrell's taxis. He stopped and rolled down the electric window.

"Hello Maddie, nice to see you, would you and the boys like a lift, it looks like it's going to rain."

"Oh hello Mr Bailey," she said in mock surprise, and to the boys, "this is the son of the lady I work for," and to Peter, "these are my two boys James and Terrence."

"Hi men would you like a lift?" asked Peter.

"Oh yes please mister, come on ma, get in," said Terrence, he'd never been in a car in his life, well not one that went.

They all got in and Maddie's new life began at 8.45 a.m. on that cold but cloudless sunny morning. There was no sign of rain but the boys had not even noticed. She slipped the list of Shankill Surgeons to Peter, the touch of her hand sent a pleasant shock wave through him. He could have stopped the car and kissed her. He didn't.

By the time McKenna awoke around midday Maddie and the children were landing in Newcastle. He shouted down the stairs for her to bring him a mug of tea but there was no reply. He got out of bed and stretched, farted loudly, and went to relieve his bladder in the washbasin in the bathroom; the toilet was in the back yard. Wearing only boxer shorts and a vest, he went downstairs to the kitchen and put the kettle on the stove. It wasn't until he sat at the table that he saw the note that Maddie had left, it read.

Jamsey,

By the time you read this letter, the boys and I will be on our way to Australia to live with my sister. I wrote and told her of the unhappy poverty stricken life that you have provided for us here and she sent me the tickets on condition that I did not give you her married name and address. It has taken me three months to obtain the necessary passports without your knowledge. I have been secretly working part time as a cleaner for a lady in the city in order to save enough cash. I cannot say that I will miss you nor will I miss the prison you call home where I have served a sixteen-year sentence of hard labour. The boys believe that we are taking a surprise holiday in Greece. I cannot imagine you missing them much but I can imagine your pride being shattered.

Goodbye and good riddance

Maddie.

PS Australia is a very large country with around 20,000,000 people. You will never find us even if you loved us enough to try, which I doubt. M.

McKenna could not move. He just sat there reading and re-reading the note while the kettle boiled until the whistle blew off and clattered onto the bare stone kitchen floor. His ego was indeed shattered, how could she do this to him of all people? How had he not known that she was unhappy? How had he not known that she had a part-time cleaning job? How did he not see any mail from Australia? How could she do this to him, Jimmy McKenna, leader of the Shankill Surgeons, tough gangster, and feared Loyalist terrorist?

It finally dawned on him. He had not even noticed what was going on around him because he did not care enough for anyone but himself. After he got over his initial anger and he realised that she would not be coming back, he sighed with a kind of relief. He was finally free of the only three people who stood between him and his mistress of six years, Millicent McMannus. He smiled as he screwed up the note and threw it on the floor.

Chapter 19

Barney Meehan, super grass and one-time CO of the Derry Provisional IRA Brigade, sat in his Buncrana home watching TARA on satellite TV. He had been retired from service since the near demise of Daniel Doonan on the day that Brannigan was blown to pieces. It had been fortunate that his part in the fate of Brannigan and his gang had been blamed on the unfortunate Quartermaster Bernard Cluskey who had died of a heart attack while in custody.

The story had been put about by the RUC that Cluskey had been the tout. Meehan had been released without charges from SAS custody as part of the armistice agreement between the PIRA, the UDA, the UDF under the blanket name of the UFF, and the British Government. Doonan had been satisfied and had advised Meehan by letter to retire on the cessation of Provisional IRA activity.

There was a knock on the door and Barney went to answer it. The door had a security chain and there was a spy-hole to see who was outside. He peered through and was shocked to see Daniel Doonan standing there. His face was a bit of a mess, especially when viewed through the spy-hole, but apart from that he hadn't changed much from what Barney remembered of him. He opened the door.

"Dan! What the Hell are you doing in these parts, are you on holiday or something? I haven't heard from you since Brannigan copped his lot, how are you?"

"I'm fine," said Doonan, "aren't you going to invite me in?"

"Oh sure, sorry, you just gave me bit of a shock that's all. You're the last person I expected to see, I thought you were languishing in retirement in Dublin."

"I was Barney but something has come up that I want to talk to you about," said Doonan, wiping his feet on the doormat.

'Jesus, he's found out,' thought Barney.

"Have you seen what the new British Government are up to?" asked Doonan.

Barney relaxed. "I have Dan, it will be interesting to see how their referendum goes, but I can't see them quitting the North, can you?"

"It's a possibility Barney, that's why I'm here, if they do pull out, there will be feckin' hell to pay and we'll all need to be ready. It's their own Loyalist people who are now causing all of their problems and costing them money, I think the Brits want out. We've laid down our arms but those feckin' Protestant bastards are murdering our people again. Tommy Hanlon has been hitting back with his so called Real IRA but he and his crowd are now feckin' outlaws, do you know Hanlon?"

"I know him alright; he used to be one of us before he broke away with a bunch of other fanatics. Sit yourself down Dan and I'll get you something to drink, what do you fancy?"

"Just coffee for me Barney, It's a bit early for the hard stuff. I'll talk while you're making it if you don't mind I'm in bit of a rush." They went to the kitchen together.

"I've seen Hanlon in Belfast," continued Doonan, sitting astride a reversed kitchen chair. "He's joining forces with Michael Ahern and his boys in West Belfast. Ahern has around thirty boys and Hanlon has ten more. That will do for starters as a nucleus of seasoned fighters. There should be no shortage of recruits and we still have enough arms and equipment stashed away to fight a small war."

"Where do I come in Dan? I'm getting a little old for this game don't you think? That last spell in jail didn't do me much good, and Cluskey didn't make it at all, poor bastard, they must have beaten the shit out him to get what they wanted." Barney ventured.

"He deserved what happened to him, he was a feckin' tout. If he hadn't snuffed it with his heart, I would have had him snuffed anyway while he was banged up. I've no time for his sort, he should have died rather than talk, he took the oath. You would have done Barney wouldn't you?" Doonan looked Meehan in the eyes, searching, but Barney held his gaze steadily as he slowly nodded agreement.

"The thought would never have crossed my mind Dan." He lied. Barney no longer had time for the likes of Doonan and his thugs but to express his feelings under present circumstances would probably prove fatal.

Barney handed Doonan his coffee and sat opposite him. He asked again. "What are you here for Dan?"

"The Derry Brigade is without a leader at the present Barney but there are still a number of boys who should be willing to regroup. How would you feel about leading them if it becomes necessary to fight again? You've been a CO and you know the drill. You're not too old for the job yet despite what you say, you're not much older than me," answered Doonan.

Barney wondered how he could refuse without incurring Doonan's wrath. He could stall and say he would think about it or he could agree then get the Hell out after Doonan had departed. He decided on the latter.

"OK Dan, I'll do it but it's been a long time since I was active. How will you get the boys together for briefing and retraining?" He asked.

"I won't, I'll leave that up to you as Brigade Commander. I have a list of names and addresses for you to contact. The Bogside isn't a very big place nor is the Creggan and most of the boys still live there. Have you heard anything of your nephew Liam Casey since he disappeared? Maybe you could recruit him as your 2 I/C, I heard that your niece Siobhan was the victim of a Loyalist car bomb in Belfast. That must have been hard for you both to bear."

Barney knew about the false story from Liam but he said nothing. "Yes I was a bit cut up about it at the time. But I heard that the bomber was also killed along with Dixie Dixon and some social worker boyfriend that Siobhan was keen on. Liam was told the bad news by Brannigan who sent him to Belfast to try to find out what had happened. He didn't get back to the farm before it blew up thank God or he might have been killed along with the others. No doubt you know what happened there."

"I lost ten of my boys as well as Brannigan's lot. I'm still trying to live with it. They were good men," said Doonan sadly. "So where is Liam now?"

"He's working in Belfast as a labourer for some marine engineering company," answered Barney, lying in his teeth. "He drives over now and then to check on me. I'm all he has since his parents and his sister died."

"Do you think you could get him back to the fold? He's young enough to make a difference and he would be a natural successor to you when the old bones have had enough," said Doonan.

Barney had no intention of recruiting Liam or anyone else. As soon as Doonan left, he would be planning a moonlight flit. To Doonan he said, "I'm sure I could get him on board, we talk a lot about when he was my courier in the old days, just leave him to me."

"Right Barney, I must be off, it's been nice seeing you again and I look forward to working with you once more. Here is my mobile number and my home number, the Billy Thompson's are being reactivated as we speak and the Dublin office is back in business. Here is a list of potential soldiers." He handed Barney the paper adding. "Some of them may have passed on by now but do your best and I'll be in touch within the month. I must get back to Belfast, I have to see Brendan McArdle's grandson; he's another potential young recruit. Do you remember Brendan?"

"Yes, how is he?" asked Barney.

"He died a few days ago, massive heart attack apparently," said Doonan.

"I heard his two boys got blown to bits with a bad bomb some while back," said Barney.

"Yes, they were two good boys; the eldest one had a son who has been looking after Brendan, he's the grandson I'm talking about; I'll be seeing him tonight with a bit of luck, I'm sure he'll play. Well good fortune Barney, I'm off."

Doonan's on-loan driver, smelly Groddy McGinty, had stayed with the car throughout the interview. He was pissing on the drive and his toecaps when Doonan went out.

Liam was clearing his desk before the weekend break when the phone rang. It was his Uncle Barney.

"Liam, I need to see you as soon as possible." Barney sounded anxious.

"Why, what's happened?" asked Liam.

"I've just had a visit from Daniel Doonan of all people, that's what. I thought he was on to me but they are still blaming Cluskey for the touting thank God," said Barney.

"What did he want then?" asked Liam.

"He's after recruiting a new rebel army in anticipation of this bloody referendum at the start of next month and he wants me to resurrect and lead the Derry Brigade. He also wants me to drag you along with me as my 2 I/C. Can you put me up for a couple of days if I come over to Belfast? I'm going to quit Ireland and maybe fly to Australia, I have friends there who will take me in until I can find a place of my own. What do you say?" He was almost pleading.

"I say stay right where you are Uncle Barney, I'll be over this evening with a couple of friends of mine and a counter proposition. You have nothing to fear from Doonan, I'll take care of him when the time comes. In the mean time I want you to go along with him; I'll explain it all to you tonight. Can you do that for me?" asked Liam.

Barney was quiet for a few moments before he responded. "There's something you're not telling me Liam, why do you want me to wait?"

"I can't tell you over the telephone, just wait until I get there and I'll tell you then. If you don't want anything to do with it after I have told you, I'll volunteer to take over your roll as Derry Brigade Commander, is that all right? Liam asked.

"I suppose so," said a reluctant Barney, "but if you don't come tonight, I'll be gone by tomorrow, see you later." He put down the phone and wondered what was going on.

Liam called Leo and Patrick and arranged for them to accompany him to his Uncle Barney's house. Meehan was in for a big surprise.

Larry McArdle had been well briefed by Leo about his role as a mole within Ahern's gang. He had been reluctant at first, and scared, but the knowledge of Ahern's involvement in his mother's murder served as the catalyst for his decision to cooperate.

Peter had left the hotel on Loch Neagh. Leo and Patrick had spent half the night with Larry going through the details of Cedric Parker's plan without mentioning the architect's name. Then a tired Leo had set off early for Aldergrove and the hour-long flight to Newcastle.

Larry met Doonan the following evening after the IRA boss had returned from Buncrana and his meeting with Barney Meehan.

"I gave a lot of thought to what you told me the other night about my da and my granda and their involvement in the Struggle. I'm on my own now since my mother died in London, and my granda since, so there's no reason for me to go back to England," he lied to Doonan on this their second meeting. "Just tell me what I have to do."

Doonan could not believe how easy it had been to recruit Larry.

"We'll send you away for a couple of weeks to one of our reopened training camps in the south then you can join the brigade here in West Belfast." He began. "The Commanding Officer is a man called Michael Ahern, he will continue your training and direct you in the field. Welcome to the IRA Larry McArdle, your da and your granda would be proud of you."

Doonan stood up and bade Larry to do the same and to raise his right hand. "Repeat this oath after me and then you're in. Break it and you're dead."

Larry shuddered; he repeated the oath after Doonan but was already harbouring thoughts of killing Ahern. He wasn't himself any more. It was too easy to make killers out of normally docile and decent men.

Before they had left the hotel at Loch Neagh the morning before, Leo had issued him with his kit including an unmarked handgun, which was anathema to him, and a dedicated mobile phone as well as a micro digital camera. He knew nothing about Morse code but Leo had assured him that he would not need it. But just in case, he taught him the SOS signal dot, dot, dot, dash, dash, dash, dot, dot, dot, to be used only in dire emergency via the hash key on his mobile. The satellite receiver in Parker's office would identify the source of the signal and precise location of the SOS using GPS then someone would come to his assistance but he must stay put wherever he was.

Larry was suitably impressed and reassured; he felt a little like James Bond. Ahern was now a marked man and the unsuspecting Doonan was unwittingly clearing the way.

It was close to midnight when Liam, Leo, and Patrick arrived at Barney Meehan's house in Buncrana. Barney was surprised to see Patrick O'Riordan in his new roll as a Catholic priest but greeted him as always, like a son. He remembered Leo from his stay at the SAS HQ where he had grassed on Brannigan et al.

"Will somebody please tell me what's going on for Christ's sake? Sorry Patrick, I'll rephrase that."

"It's alright Barney most of what we're doing is for His sake anyway when you think about it. The devil is his enemy too," said Patrick.

"Tell us all about Daniel Doonan Uncle Barney, and what he has told you to do," asked Liam.

"Like I told you on the phone, he's after resurrecting the brigades in anticipation of the Brits pulling out of Northern Ireland. He says there will be trouble with the Loyalists and that the Republican community will have to be ready for a fight. He has given me a list of people to contact with a view to me leading them as commander of the Derry brigade. He asked about you too Liam, he wanted to know where you were and what you were doing and he asked me to recruit you as my second in command. That's about it in a nutshell really but, as I've told you, I don't want to know, I finished with that kind of nonsense after Ballykelly."

Barney was serious. He'd experienced the futility of conflict. People died for no reason because at the end of it all, when the argument was settled, their lives had been wasted merely on points of principle. Too many innocents, like his little granddaughters, killed by accident in the Ballykelly car bomb incident, got in the way. The memory still haunted him and he often cried himself to sleep at night.

"I don't want to do it anymore Liam it has to stop some time it can't go on forever." Barney's eyes were moist and his lips were quivering.

"Running away won't help Uncle Barney. Intervention is what's required, that's why we are here." Then to Leo, "can I tell him what we are doing or will you?"

Leo was tired after a long night with Larry and the others at Loch Neagh two days before, followed by the flight to Newcastle. The following day, he had travelled back to Newcastle to meet Maddie McKenna and her kids off the plane, taken them to his home in Ryhope, got them settled in, then caught the evening flight back to Aldergrove with Siobhan and the twins.

"I'll explain it," said Leo. "Sit down Barney and listen this could take a little time."

Siobhan and Mary Bailey had spent the evening catching up on family affairs. All that Mary would say about Maddie was that she was married to a brutish man and that the family had helped her to disappear to begin a new life in the UK with her sons. No mention was made of the Surgeons at Peter's request.

Peter had departed for the Company's Sunderland office, shortly after Leo and Siobhan had arrived, to finalise an American contract for marine engines with two executives arriving from Florida the following day.

Liam should have gone but Peter had volunteered to go due to an irresistible urge to see Maddie McKenna again. He could not equate the feeling with that of having fallen in love with the woman because he had never experienced those feelings before. All he knew was that he had to see her again. He did not tell Liam who had been pleased to be still in the office when his uncle Barney had called or God knows what might have happened.

Joe Bailey was entertaining his twin grandsons playing games. They reminded him so much of his sons when they were small, always wanting to win but never cheating.

Leo had been called away by Liam's telephone call, "something about Patrick O'Riordan," he had muttered to his mother and Siobhan who was puzzled. The last she had heard of O'Riordan he had gone to America, could it be that he was back and being a bad influence on her brother again?

Memories of the two of them when they were young tearaways flitted through her mind. She knew, however, that her brother was now an important man in the family business and beyond the reach of the likes of O'Riordan. It had been a few years since they had parted company and Liam was no longer an insecure and gullible kid.

Leo had not told Siobhan about his recent meeting with Father Patrick O'Riordan. She'd had no idea that Leo had been in and out Northern Ireland for the past two weeks, interviewing and organising.

She had been aware of a couple of covert operations in various other theatres with the SAS since his retirement after the Ballykelly incident without knowing the details. She had more recently worried about him and Peter in Afghanistan but they had both come home safe and sound after a couple of weeks.

"What did you think of Maddie McKenna?" asked Mary

"She was nothing like I expected," replied Siobhan. "She is rather a good looking woman beneath that worried countenance, and the two boys are quiet and well mannered. I had no qualms about leaving them there.

I didn't have a lot of time to chat but from what little I gathered, she has had a pretty hard life with her husband. I should think she is well rid of him."

When Leo finished his explanation to Barney Meehan of their mission, it was almost 1 a.m. and Barney sat silent but wide awake. He felt trapped. He had been a man of peace for three years now but his past and his conscience still haunted him.

His previous involvement with first the Official then the Provisional IRA had been a patriotic and spiritual matter rather than a strictly political affair. He had believed that he was fighting for a united Ireland as part of a semi-political agenda peppered with the odd bombing of valuable strategic targets without incurring human casualties. But schizophrenic psychopaths and criminals looking for a legitimate outlet for their psychoses and an excuse for their lawless activities had infiltrated and adulterated the movement.

He had been appalled by the killing of eleven people at a Remembrance Service in Enniskillen in 1987, the eleven army bandsmen killed at the Royal Marines School of Music at Deal in Kent in 1989, the innocent men, women, and children killed by bombs planted in rubbish bins at bus stations and shopping centres on the mainland during the 90's, and the murder of young servicemen going about their duties.

Brannigan and Ballykelly, Hanlon and Omagh, had convinced him of the futility of it all. The accidental killing of seven children at Ballykelly, including his two grandchildren, when their school bus got in the way of a car bomb intended for an army patrol, and the senseless slaughter of innocents at Omagh, had been the last straw.

And now there was this, the probability of more violence and death. There was just no getting away from it no matter how he tried. Even running away would not help. He still had his conscience and the sleepless nights to look forward to for the rest of his life. Maybe Leo's plan would finally put an end to the eon's old problems. Maybe Ireland would be reunited one day.

"I'll do it," said Barney at length, "how long do you think it will take to remove the cancer?"

"It depends on the operation," said Leo, "we have to get all of the cells into one place where they can kill each other off before we take out the survivors. That's why we need insiders to keep us informed about cell movements. Someone they can trust to show them the way to the terminus if you get my meaning. May I have a look at the list that Doonan gave you to see if we know anyone?"

Barney handed over the list of ex Players. There were thirty-six names and addresses on the computer printout. The names would have meant nothing to anyone finding the list lying about because there was no heading to indicate their significance.

Leo scanned the single sheet and recognised the names of a dozen or so previously wanted men. Two of the names leapt out at him from the list, Kevin and Mary Bradley, who he had known as the Kennerleys. They had been Doonan's moles in Brannigan's gang. They had been charged with robbery and credit card fraud in both their cases, and desertion from the army in Kevin Bradley's case. Mary had got off for lack of evidence and Kevin had served two years of a four-year sentence in Shepton Mallet before being dishonourably discharged from the British Army.

Leo was surprised that they had come back to Northern Ireland to live in the house in Lislap that

Cunningham had given them. Mary Bradley must have staked a claim to the property when Bradley went inside or could it be that they were merely squatting? No matter, they were obviously still potential Players otherwise Doonan would not have kept them on his list.

At least three of the people on the list had perished at Brannigan's farm in the firefight with the SAS. Leo knew them from when he had infiltrated the gang with Liam Casey. Both he and Liam would have to be careful not to be seen by the Bradleys, but then, they had left the farm for Lislap before Leo and Liam had joined Peter and his SAS Squadron in the fire fight. They would be blissfully unaware of Leo's SAS role and would believe that he and Liam had only escaped the blood bath at Brannigan's farm because they were at the General's funeral; brilliant.

Chapter 20

Ex SAS soldiers Sid Morrell and Sandy Blewitt, along with preferred ex-serving members of the SAS and SBS, had been requested by Cedric Parker to attend a special briefing session at the Hereford HQ of the SAS. He outlined his plan for the extermination of the verminous terror gangs and criminals in Northern Ireland before inviting those in attendance to volunteer for 'Operation Wipeout,' the name suggested by Peter Bailey.

Living as Sid and Sandy did in the province, for many years, they were ideally situated for covert observation without being seen by the enemy as strangers in their midst. Both men had been involved in intelligence gathering on detachment in the past, Sid for one month each year, as a Territorial Army soldier of 23 SAS (V) in Northumberland, and Sandy as a regular SAS soldier serving in the province.

Sid's taxi business was well established, although he had changed the name from TAVRACABS to SID's TAXIS some years before on the advice of a friendly Catholic rival, Andy Molloy, who ran the fleet of black taxis driven exclusively by Republicans. They met on occasion for a drink and a chat.

It was during one of their boozing sessions that Molloy had asked Sid about the name of his taxi firm, TAVRACABS. Sid truthfully explained to him that he had once been a mental nurse at a hospital in Prudhoe, a small town on the border between County Durham and Northumberland. He lied, however, about being a member of the Royal Army Medical Corps in the Territorial Army stationed with 201 (N) General Hospital (V) at Fenham Barracks in Newcastle upon Tyne. TAVRA, he explained, was the association of Territorial Army members that had given him a loan on his retirement to start his taxi business when he married his Northern Ireland sweetheart, Bridie Burn, and decided to settle in Belfast.

Molloy had accepted the explanation and had obviously passed it on to his Republican superiors because Sid was left to carry on his business in peace after having previously received several veiled threats. Sid was also tolerated because he employed a number of Catholic drivers including his now partner Sandy Blewitt.

Several of Molloy's black cab drivers had been involved in the past with ASU's (active service units) of the IRA, and the likelihood was that they were still on standby for the possible resumption of hostilities, albeit a little older and a lot less fit.

Now in their early forties but still physically fit, Sid and Sandy had no reservations about signing up to Parker's secret task force. They knew at first hand about the trouble simmering beneath the surface in Northern Ireland and they approved of Parker's radical solution.

Sid offered, as Parker had hoped, to put some of his fleet of taxis at the disposal of the task force, employing some of the 'Operation Wipe-out 'volunteers as drivers. It would be an ideal cover and would provide much needed mobility that would assist Leo Bailey in his logistical planning.

Although the majority of Sid's drivers were regulars, others between jobs came and went so it would be no problem fitting people in and getting them established before the referendum took place; the same applied to his partner Sandy. Sid had expanded his business since 1995 and had bought out a company in Derry that was now managed by his friend Sandy Blewitt. Sid ran the Belfast branch with his wife Bridie.

Parker was pleased at the way his plan was coming together. Peter and Leo Bailey had gone through the list of names, provided by Parker from his database, and had selected those in attendance at the briefing. After the briefing, everyone had volunteered for 'Operation Wipe-out'. The next part would not be so easy, the undercover people, from MI5, MI6 and Special Branch, were not so well known to the brothers Bailey. But there was one man that Peter thought could help. He was SAS Captain George Davidson now nearing the end of his military service at the age of thirty-eight. In 1993, when he was a Sergeant, he had been seconded to a team of MI6 operatives minding an important IRA tout in Tyrone. The members of the cell to which the tout belonged were eventually captured while carrying out a bank robbery. The tout was relocated in Canada at the expense of the British taxpayer and the robbers were jailed for ten years also at the expense of the British taxpayer.

George Davidson had befriended one Alan Donaldson, the head of the MI6 minding operation, and had kept in touch with him since. Donaldson had been back in

England since the cessation of IRA hostilities in October 1994 and had retired from MI6 by 1996. Both men were bachelors with a healthy appetite for living. They went on holiday twice a year to chill out on booze and bird-pulling excursions in Spain, Greece, and Turkey, and skiing trips to Italy, Austria, and Switzerland. They were both very fit and active.

Davidson was one of the volunteers for 'Operation Wipe-out'. Peter drew him to one side and explained the difficulty he was having in selecting the necessary MI5, MI6, and Special Branch men on the list of possible candidates given to him by Parker. Davidson agreed to set up a meeting at the Loch Neagh hotel with his pal Alan Donaldson and Peter Bailey. Donaldson, now working as a Head Forester for the National Trust, was sure to know most of the people on the list and would probably advise Peter accordingly.

The meeting took place the following weekend and Donaldson not only volunteered himself, but also agreed to contact everyone on Peter's list of possible candidates that he thought might be suitable.

A further meeting with Cedric Parker would be required for the briefing of whosoever Donaldson managed to recruit. Those on the list he did not know would be known by some of his ex-colleagues who in turn would act as recruiters. Everyone involved was reminded of the obvious need for secrecy and had previously signed up to the appropriate act.

Donaldson raised the thorny subject of training at his meeting with Parker. He had something in mind but he wanted to sound out the boss first.

"'Operation Wipe-out' is essentially a covert operation," said Parker. "Everybody involved is a volunteer.

Bringing them together in one place as a group would cause suspicion, especially in the province, if we had such a place that is, why do you ask?"

"The National Trust has successfully negotiated the acquisition of Ballypatrick Hall and the estate in Londonderry which once belonged to that Colonel who died in '95. George Davidson told me just after the old man's funeral, about the events that led up to the elimination of a bunch of Players near there," explained Donaldson.

"So?" enquired Parker.

"Well it just so happens, that I have applied for the job of Head Forrester cum Head Warden there and it occurred to me that if I got the job, I would need an army of volunteers to help me to sort the place out. The deceased Colonel's only son inherited the estate but he is a geriatric old queen who has been living in London on an allowance since he was thrown out of university for drug addiction in the 60's. He moved into the Hall after his father's funeral but death duties cleaned him out of his inheritance and the place has been allowed to deteriorate while he lived there as a virtual recluse. The National Trust got the place for a song but it will take a lot to restore it before it can be opened for business," said Donaldson. "It is a well known fact that the National Trust has got base camps all over the place to accommodate their volunteers who, would you believe, actually pay for the privilege of taking a working holiday. The presence of a large number of people working on the Ballypatrick estate would not cause suspicion and the place would be ideal as both a training area and as a base camp; what do you think?"

"What about security?" asked Parker?

"I can't see it being much of a problem; I visited the place just last week with half a dozen other job applicants and it is in a very quiet area. The nearest village is about five miles away and seems to be populated by retired people who live in their own little worlds. I think it would be an ideal setup if only I could secure the job," answered Donaldson.

"Leave it with me while I find a few strings to pull; well done Alan," said Parker, shaking Donaldson by the hand.

The following week, Donaldson received confirmation that his application for the post of Head Warden/Forrester had been successful with immediate effect.

Peter Bailey was delighted, as was Cedric Parker, and within a week of taking post, the first of the volunteers began to arrive by taxi at the base camp at Ballypatrick Hall courtesy of Sandy Blewitt. Donaldson had personally vetted the applications so that only those who had volunteered for 'Operation Wipe-out' were selected.

Eamon Finney one time leading member of the East Belfast battalion of the UDF, returned from England on the completion of the motorway he had been working on. He had been offered further employment but the news about the province and the possible result of the referendum had prompted him to return and see what was happening on the ground. He felt instinctively that he would be required for action, there was no way that the UDF would stand by and witness an upsurge in Republican violence in an attempt to dominate affairs.

As he suspected, his battalion had been recalled and was recruiting fresh blood for the new Loyalist cause; there was no shortage of young volunteers. He was welcomed back into the fold with open arms and given charge of a twenty strong group with a brief to brainwash them and bring them up to scratch.

Some small firms were already in the process of moving out of the province and work was going to be difficult to come by. Finney browsed through the jobs in the Job Centre but the only one he felt qualified for, because of the flexible hours and the fact that it was somewhat temporary, was that of relief driver for Sid Morrell's taxi firm. He needed the wheels to get about between fares and for when he was off duty. Recording the mileage after each shift to prevent fiddling did not present a problem; Finney was a dab hand at disconnecting a speedometer. There was an anti-tamper device on the connection behind the dashboard to the actual speedometer but none at the other end attached to the engine. A stupid omission he thought, but very few drivers were as mechanically as minded as he was.

A few weeks into the job at the Ballypatrick estate where Alan Donaldson would be taking on thirty of the volunteers recruited from ex-members of MI5, MI6, Special Branch, Anti-terrorist Squad operatives, and a couple of ex-RUC Flying Squad boys, a training session was planned by Peter Bailey with the express intention of not only testing the fitness of his volunteers for the task ahead, but also to give them the opportunity of familiarising themselves with the identities of their fellow volunteers with whom they would be facing their enemies. There would be no uniforms or other identification aids so it was essential that each man knew who was friend and who was foe. Years of experience in recognising facial and physical features from identity parades to mug shots would be brought to bear before the first one hundred operatives were dispersed and salted throughout the province to wait for the day when they would be required to confront the opposition. The hundred or so reserves would be trained at Hereford but it was hoped that they would not be required.

Peter chose a peak 2240 feet up in the Sperrin Mountains as the rendezvous for the planned fitness test. Each of the hundred volunteers, not yet in position in the province, would be required to participate with the exception of Sid Morrell and Sandy Blewitt. They were both suitably incensed at the inference that they were too old to participate and insisted in being included. Peter backed down with a sly grin on his face; he admired both men enormously.

So as not to draw suspicion, the men would be placed in groups of ten with a serving volunteer SAS or SBS NCO in charge as head-shed. Each group was to report by 10 p.m. on their given day to the ferry terminal at Larne and try to act like members of a private club of hikers setting out on a walking holiday.

The spot height in the Sperrin Mountains was 56 miles from the port and each team was given 18 hours to reach the rendezvous. The first team to arrive would stay for one day after setting up a tented camp with equipment dumped on the site. On day three, the next team would set off on the night march and so on each day until the last team there would strike camp and make the kit ready for collection.

After resting until 10 p.m. that day, the teams would then report, after yet another night march, to the newly acquired National Trust Estate, currently closed for conservation and renovation, near the village of Ballypatrick that lay about ten kilometres from the main Strabane to Londonderry road in the triangle between Strabane, Londonderry and Dungiven.

Geordie Shiells headed the first team consisting of Alan Donaldson, his four initial NT volunteers and four others that he and Geordie were to meet at Larne en route from the mainland to join the others on the estate.

Over the twelve-day exercise period, Alan and his volunteers fed and watered the members of each team as they arrived. Peter and Leo then briefed them, issued them with their kit, and assigned them to their various 'sleeper' locations and jobs to await instructions.

Sid Morrell and Sandy Blewitt, along with eight of their taxi drivers, were in the last team to report. They had delivered their taxis to the Ballypatrick estate on the day that they were to report at Larne, and Sid's wife Bridie had taken them by minibus to the start point.

Those who had been assigned to the taxi firms had reported to their respective offices by the time Sid and Sandy, with Mick Rutherford as the head-shed, arrived at the Ballypatrick estate in record time despite their age. It was a macho thing and they were knackered but very pleased with them selves.

Chapter 21

The referendum on Northern Ireland took place on Sunday 1st December 1997 so that a maximum number of people would have the time off to go to the polls. As promised by the new Liberal Democrat/ Conservative government, the people of Northern Ireland were excluded from the ballot by virtue of the assumption that they had finally rejected the path of peace as a way to settle their differences. There was still no let-up in the violence perpetrated by either side despite the government's threat to sever the UK link.

A secret meeting with the Irish Taoiseach had secured his personal agreement to go along with the British Government's plans, including the acceptance of both Anglican and RC migrants from the north, should the referendum bring about the desired results.

The Taoiseach had not discussed the plan with his ministers. He decided to wait until the outcome of the referendum was known. Considering the prospect of a United Ireland within ten years or so, he foresaw little difficulty in eventually obtaining their approval

The King had also given the idea of a referendum his seal of approval and had indicated his willingness to give the new republic the regiments of The Irish Guards and the Ulster Rifles, minus the 'Royal', and The Irish Rangers, but only after the currently enlisted men had been given the choice of transferring to other British regiments. He had promised to abide by the outcome of the referendum and to comply with the wishes of the majority. He no longer regarded the people of the province of Northern Ireland as his loyal subjects. They had consistently rejected every initiative designed to bring about lasting peace and stability to the region.

Crime in Northern Ireland was again on the increase with the proceeds being used to buy arms and ammunition. The clock had been turned back thirty years to the troublesome late sixties and early seventies when British troops had been sent into the province to protect the Catholic minority from the Protestants.

In February 1971, the first soldier since troops had arrived in the province two years earlier was shot dead. Since then 139 people had been killed including Lord Louis Mountbatten the last Viceroy of India, and the Conservative MP and shadow Northern Ireland Secretary, Airey Neave. Hundreds more had been injured over the next ten years. The wording of the referendum had been straight forward enough.

Since the partition of Ireland in 1922, persistent efforts by the British and Irish Governments to bring about peaceful coexistence between the Protestant and Catholic communities in Northern Ireland, have failed.

Despite government concessions, both sides have broken several cease-fire agreements. Soldiers sent

to assist the RUC in a peacekeeping role have been brutally murdered along with members of the police force.

Foreign visitors and other innocent bystanders, both in the province and on the mainland, have been the victims of indiscriminate bombing which has also destroyed millions of pounds worth of property. The cost to the Province of Northern Ireland alone, in terms of human life, property, and lost business, is incalculable and can no longer be tolerated or sustained by the British taxpayer.

Despite the ministrations of church leaders and the protests of innocents, the barbaric and senseless slaughter goes on regardless. Neither Christian morals nor principles appear to exist among the perpetrators on both sides. These people have bequeathed their souls to Satan for better or for worse.

The people of the United Kingdom, excluding Northern Ireland, are now being asked:

SHOULD THE PROVINCE OF NORTHERN IRELAND BE ALLOWED TO CONTINUE AS PART OF THE UNITED KINGDOM OF GREAT BRITAIN?

YES or NO

The Lib Dem Cons had taken the first faltering steps towards the final solution. Cedric Parker's plan was slowly taking shape. Five teams of twenty of the best volunteers had been successfully assembled in response to his secret appeal. A further hundred specially trained men were being held in reserve.

Peter and Leo Bailey, having been the first to be recruited by the Defence Secretary, had each personally contacted and recruited ten of the most trusted men in as many days after their initial meeting with Cedric Parker. There had been no refusals.

Each of the twenty men helped to recruit a further ten men each and the whole team was assembled, briefed, and located within one month, one hundred of them where in place and working in the province ready for active service, and the other hundred were carrying on with their regular jobs while sleeping in reserve.

Each man was equipped with a dedicated satellite transceiver that was capable of being switched to mobile phone mode with encrypted text and solar recharging facilities, a Morse-sending hash key and a vibrating sensor.

Covert transmissions went directly to Parker's office where messages were deciphered and instructions relayed by either coded text, or, if the recipient was in a position to talk, by direct conversation.

The volunteers were armed with a variety of unmarked lightweight automatic weapons confiscated from convicted UK criminals over the years and held in store for use in covert operations such as Operation Wipe-out.

An ex SAS armourer had invented a carbon fibre sniper rifle with a detachable barrel lined with wafer-thin high tensile steel rifling. It weighed only ten ounces and could be easily concealed about the person. The detachable breach was only ten centimetres long by three centimetres wide and eight centimetres in depth with a retractable trigger and guard. It was lined with a vented high tensile steel shell dampened with springs to counter recoil. A collapsible carbon fibre butt clipped into the breach and was also easy to conceal when folded. The special rounds, in magazines of six, consisted of a thin core of lead covered with carbon fibres that splintered on entering the target causing severe internal damage while the streamlined lead core continued on leaving a tiny exit wound. It was lethally accurate at two hundred metres. The weapon had been tried and tested but was not yet on general issue.

Four men from each team, already living and working in the province, had been delegated the task of infiltrating the ranks of the paramilitary groups in both the loyalist and republican camps two to three months before the referendum was due to be announced.

Parker's idea was that they should have their feet under the enemy's table well in advance of any government announcement. With five to six months to become known and accepted individuals within the ranks of the warring parties, it was hoped that the moles would not come under suspicion if and when the expected hostilities broke out shortly after the birth of the new Northern Ireland Republic which was planned for the beginning of the marching season.

It would be a further three months before the decree would be finally declared absolute so that those people who wished to re-locate on the UK mainland or in the Irish Republic would have time to get out. Those who decided to stay would have to trust in the extant Northern Ireland Assembly to begin the election process for a new Northern Ireland Republic Government.

The overwhelming endorsement by the British people for the expelling of Northern Ireland from the Union surprised the entire world. The people of the province were generally in shock after a 95% vote against their remaining as part of the United Kingdom. Even if the population of

Northern Ireland had been allowed to vote for their own future the result would have been the same but with a smaller percentage calculated at around 65% against. They were in no position to cry 'foul' and to demand another referendum to include them.

The exodus began almost immediately with both Catholics and Protestants, mostly from tenanted accommodation, packing as much as they could carry and leaving to join relatives on the mainland and in the south. Many did not wait to apply for the resettlement grants offered by both governments, most just wanted to get away from what they expected would be an explosive and potentially dangerous situation.

Some young hotheads from both communities had already taken to the streets and were causing disturbances, shouting abuse at each other, and threatening violence. The police stood back and allowed community leaders from both sides to go in and quell their own young people. The war would come soon enough but first of all the battle lines had to be defined. The streets were cleared by paramilitaries as if by magic so strong still was their influence.

What military remained in the province had been confined to barracks since the first announcement that a referendum was to take place. While the provincial police force attempted to cope with sporadic violence the army was packing its equipment in readiness for a possible move back to either the UK or to Germany.

From the 15th of January, small inconspicuous convoys of six to eight vehicles quietly left their barracks to board the ferries that left twice a day from Larne. Others slipped over the border at various crossing points and left the country via Dublin with the connivance of the Irish Government.

By the time the referendum results were announced, most of the army had gone and those that remained were left at the mercy of loyalist protesters who felt betrayed. In armoured vehicles that had been retained for the protection of the rear guard, the soldiers ran a gauntlet of missile throwing youths.

Casualties were mainly on the side of the ill-equipped protesters armed with bottles and stones. Water canon accompanying the armoured vehicles protected the small convoys from possible petrol bombs and also helped to disperse the angry protestors.

Just outside the barracks in Omagh, a small group of youths armed with petrol bombs began throwing them at the armoured cars as they emerged from the gates. A well aimed shot with a plastic-bullet, at a youth who was lighting the bombs and passing them to his colleagues, sent the young man sprawling into the centre of the crates of unlit bombs, saturating those around with petrol and setting alight to their clothes and the young man's funeral pyre.

As the vehicles sped away, several of the crowd were seen running about trying to beat-out the flames and to discard their burning clothes. The area around the crates was a flaming lake; the practice was not repeated by other groups.

Not surprisingly, the Republicans were nowhere to be seen; they thought that they had won the day with the retreat of the remaining British Army. Most were already preparing to go into battle for supremacy over the Protestants in 'The New Republic.

Leo Bailey had been recruiting and interviewing volunteers in Belfast prior to the general election. Sid Morrell had been first choice on Leo's list of possible candidates. He was a Northumbrian married to a local Belfast girl and all of his drivers were either serving or ex Territorial Army men from the province. He had a ready-made team of trusted people and had indicated that he could muster at least a further dozen. Apart from Sandy Blewitt's half dozen or so Catholic close friends his drivers were almost all Protestants but had no affiliations with Loyalist organisations. Their Catholic rivals drove black cabs and mostly had affiliations with Republican organisations but they coexisted peacefully enough. God only knew how long that would last after the results of the referendum were known.

Infiltrating the Protestant camp would not be difficult once the referendum was announced; the Loyalist paramilitaries would also be looking for volunteers.

Catholic volunteers needed to infiltrate the Republican paramilitary groups would be the most difficult to recruit. Sandy Blewitt, Sid's partner and Londonderry branch manager, was a Catholic but his provincial Yorkshire accent was out of place. However, he could still be useful as a sniper and he might even know a couple of anti-terrorist Republicans who would be willing play mole.

Chapter 22

After his final meeting with Daniel Doonan and his subsequent initiation into the IRA, Larry McArdle was taken to meet his potential CO, Michael Ahern. It was hate at first sight.

The man was pushing sixty, half bald and a bit on the heavy side for his height of around 5'7". He looked nothing like Larry had imagined he would and he wondered how this little villain with the cruel piggy eyes and mirthless face could command such respect.

Larry's first and out-of-character instinct was to kill both Ahern and Doonan right there and then. They were alone in Ahern's sumptuous living room furnished lavishly with the proceeds of ill-gotten gains. But Larry had wisely gone unarmed and there were minders in the next room who had frisked him when he arrived. His grandfather had warned him; he would never have made it out alive.

"What do you know about the IRA boy?" asked Ahern without preamble and without even shaking Larry by the hand.

"Only what I have read in the press until Mr. Doonan enlightened me," answered Larry. "I gather that my da, my uncle, and my granda were all in the West Belfast Battalion and very active."

"They were and they'll take a lot of living up to assuming that you pass muster and that I allow you to join up with this battalion." Ahern looked at Doonan who smiled.

"If you don't take him, I have plenty others who will," said Doonan. "Barney Meehan is setting up the Derry Brigade as we speak and he needs as many recruits as he can get. Young Larry here is off to the Drum Hills for ten days from tomorrow, he's taken two weeks leave from the hospital and I'll be taking him down there myself. There's a lot to do at the old training camp. You can make your final decision when he gets back."

"Who's at Drum now Dan?" asked Ahern, "I thought the place had been abandoned."

"It was but we kept the two farms going just in case, they are both under new management by a couple of the boys who retired with me in '95. The place is pretty well isolated and trespassers are discouraged by the old **'DANGEROUS BULL IN THE FIELD'** ploy, it's amazing how it still works. The perimeter fields are holding some valuable stock of bullshit." Doonan laughed at his own little joke but Ahern just snorted.

Doonan's recruiting campaign had produced the required intake of twenty young men for the first training session in the Drum Hills camp. He and Larry had gone via Dublin where Larry was introduced to Doonan's old HQ at Murphy's Bar. It was just a tiny room at the back of the building and it was from there that Daniel Doonan had commanded his army of hundreds of volunteers for several years. The CO's had gone there to report and to take their orders over a pint and a smoke.

Field communications, still in preservation, were simple. Doonan had a large map of Ireland on the wall of his office which was kept securely locked in his absence by his landlord brother Bryan.

Each northern field commander was assigned to a BT pay phone, code named 'Billy Thompson,' in his area. If Doonan wanted to speak to any of his commanders, he would phone them at home and tell them to report to 'Billy Thompson' at an appointed time and he would contact them there to pass on his orders. His own phone was on one of two lines into his brother's pub and ex directory. Only his commanders knew the ex directory number.

The CO's had their own unique phonetic identities known only to each other. For instance, Michael Ahern was known as Mickey Alpha, and Barney Meehan was known as Brave Mickey in the old days, Doonan was known as Delta Dan. All Doonan had to do was to revive the same system.

The numbers scribbled around the map on his wall were all telephone numbers written backwards and prefixed by the phonetic initials of the area CO. It was too simple and Doonan made the mistake of bragging about it to his new initiate Larry McArdle

Larry thought that his family must have had a lot of respect and clout within the ranks of the IRA's for him to be so readily accepted and trusted. But then he had taken the oath of allegiance, which these people obviously took very seriously; or else.

Larry had been supplied by Leo with a state of the art digital camera in the form of a cigarette lighter although he did not smoke and never had. Circumstances forced him to take up the habit that he had got used to in a fortnight. He would only smoke when the occasion arose and on the night that he was shown Doonans office he smoked two cigarettes, one while Doonan was in the office, and a second when Doonan went to the bar for drinks, just to make sure that the wide angle lens took in all of the pictorial information. The number of pixels would have to be high if the details of the telephone locations and numbers on the map were to be highlighted and enlarged successfully. Larry had little doubt about the quality of the technology having got to know the twins.

The ten days training in the Drum Hills consisted mainly of familiarisation with firearms from handguns to automatic weapons and from grenades to rocket launchers. A whole day was spent learning how to conceal and prime bombs in vehicles and public places for maximum effect, detonation by timer and remote control, and the dismantling of them in the event of an aborted mission.

The elderly Provo training staff conducted a certain amount of education and brainwashing in the evenings in a smoky atmosphere over cans of Guinness and nips of poteen that they called 'mountain tea'.

There were lectures in concealment and survival in the field followed by demonstrations and practice in blacking-up and camouflage. There was, however, no bullshit and no marching around like soldiers.

The experience had been interesting and enlightening. Having a natural interest in human psychology, Larry got an insight into the type of people who signed up to terror organisations. He spent as much time as he could with as many of his fellow trainees as possible in the ten days that he was there trying to find out what motivated them.

Few of them showed any real interest in politics, none of them followed the Catholic faith to the letter, and all of them hated Prods and Brits to the extent that they could kill without conscience. The one thing they all had in common was a certain look in the eyes that varied from one person to another. Larry had noticed that same shifty look in the eyes of schizophrenics that he had encountered during courses in mental nursing. He wondered about mankind.

To avoid suspicion, on his return to the north, Larry reported to Patrick O'Riordan via the confessional in the hospital chapel. He handed over the camera for onward conveyance to Leo and arranged to visit him at his firm's offices the following evening.

"The pics have come out great Larry, the detail is astounding, bloody well done," said Leo, spreading the images around the table in the conference room of Ellis Marine Engineering. "It's amazing how such a tiny camera can produce such resolution I'll bet you feel like James Bond after what you have achieved. Were you afraid at any time?"

"Most of the time really," replied Larry, "but not for my own life. These people have no conscience about killing in cold blood, if innocents get in the way, tough. I tried my best to find out what motivated them to commit such acts but couldn't find any answers. Politics and religion seem to be more like excuses than reasons for murder and the only people I can think of that need excuses to kill are psychos. Real soldiers in civilised countries need good reason and officially sanctioned orders before they put a bullet up the spout. My mother always taught me to try to live my life in accordance with the Ten Commandments but it's bloody difficult when you are up against terrorists, thugs, and gangsters intent on death and destruction. Why did you lot drag me into this?" asked Larry.

"You kind of wandered in by divine intervention I think Larry, perhaps your mother had something to do with it from up there," said Leo, pointing to the ceiling.

"Do you believe in that kind of thing Leo?" asked Larry.

Leo looked thoughtful for a few moments before he answered.

"I once went to a spiritualist meeting with one of mine and Peter's friends in Newcastle, a guy called Alec Shiells. His wife Kitty had died having their second kid and he was pretty cut up as you can imagine but the baby girl survived. About six months later, I got a phone call from him asking me to accompany him to Durham to see a clairaudient at work. She had been recommended to Alec by a friend who had lost his brother in a car bomb blast while on patrol with a squad of Fusiliers in Ballykelly in Northern Ireland in 1995. We were all serving in the province at that time. Geordie, sorry, Alec, had gone to school with the lad. However, the Fusilier's brother went to see the clairvoyant in action and was surprised to be contacted by his kid brother who apparently said he had come face to face with his murderer on the other side and that all had been forgiven."

"Did the medium know the Fusilier's brother?" asked Larry.

"How could she?" replied Leo, she lives somewhere in Yorkshire. Never mind, Geordie was of the same opinion but wanted to see for himself so he booked two tickets to see the medium when she was next in Durham. He armed himself with a photograph of Kitty and we met in the city as arranged so that I could witness the proceedings." continued Leo.

"What happened?" asked Larry, the hairs on the back of his neck beginning to stand up.

"It was weird," said Leo. "We were sitting in the middle of the auditorium when the medium came on stage. After a short introduction and preamble, he suddenly took on a weird stance and pointed straight at Geordie and said, 'you have brought Kitty's picture with you and she is with me now. Who is Kitty?'"

"What did Geordie do?" asked Larry, his eyes almost popping out of his head.

"He looked like he had been struck by lightning. Tears welled up in his eyes and he said, 'she was my wife.' I thought he was going to break down but he kept his cool."

"She still is your wife," Holborne said, "and she sends her love to you then he paused as if listening to someone and asked, 'who are Peter and Laura?'"

"Our kids," answered Geordie with a smile of relief on his face.

"The medium then said to Geordie, 'she says Laura was a lovely name to call your new daughter. She sends you all her love.' And that was that, she went on to someone else.

The tears were streaming down Larry's face now at the thought that his own mother might still exist in the spirit world but he could not speak for fear of breaking down altogether.

"Let the tears go Larry, I did I can tell you. Geordie and I could not believe what we had just witnessed and there was no way in this world that the medium could have known anything about Geordie's life. There is obviously more to this existence than meets the eye but I am still keeping an open mind," said Leo.

He left the room to answer a distant phone and Larry gave way to his feelings as he thought about his mother and how it would be if he could contact her like Alec Shiells had contacted his Kitty.

Ahern had received a good report on Larry's progress at the Drum Hills training camp. He sent a message round to the house with the man who used to deliver Larry's grandfather's comfits, smelly Groddy McGinty, for Larry to report to him ASAP

When Larry arrived, Ahern took him straight outside and pushed him into the driving seat of a BMW and told him to drive where he was told. They headed for Dungannon at high speed on the MI motorway and found a place to park on arrival. Larry had never been there before he confessed but Ahern said it was no matter.

They walked around the town to familiarise Larry with the layout in preparation for a bank robbery the following week when Larry would be driving a stolen getaway car. Ahern and three of his seasoned gangsters would carry out the robbery while the remainder of Ahern's and Tommy Hanlon's men would be carrying out robberies at nine other locations at exactly the same time in order to confuse and stretch the resources of, and cause as much chaos as possible for, the police. The other towns included Ballymena, Magherafelt, Randalstown, Lurgan, Portadown, Moy, Lisburn, Armagh, and Comber.

Ahern had been appointed Paymaster General by Doonan in preparation for the expected conflict. The Stirling haul from the robberies was to be laundered in the south and converted to Euros in readiness.

Robbing all ten banks at the same time was Ahern's idea and he lost no time in bragging about it to Larry just to show him why he had been given the job of Doonan's right hand man. He was very excited about getting back into the terrorism business and the adrenalin was boosting his ego and stimulating a bout of verbal diarrhoea. Larry's father had been one of his best men and he now obviously trusted the son also; unbelievable.

"Your da and your uncle would have been well impressed with the plan and they would have been involved if they had still been around" Ahern said.

"I'm well impressed myself Mr Mickey Alpha, I can see why Delta Dan chose you for the job." replied Larry.

"Where the Hell did you learn those bloody code names?" asked Ahern, with a hint of alarm and suspicion, they're supposed to be confidential.

"Doonan explained them to me at Murphy's, he said that he was going to give me my own command after I had been with you for a while and if I kept my nose clean. Don't tell him I told you for Christ's sake, he asked me not to put it about but you are my boss now and I think you have the right to know," answered Larry.

"Too bloody right I have a right to know, but if that is Dan's wish, I'll see to it that you are properly trained, just take your time from me and note how I work." Said Ahern

They made their way back to Belfast at a slower speed while the hitherto quiet Mr Ahern just kept on feeding Larry with valuable information.

Geordie Shiells was on leave in Newcastle seeing the kids for a week before taking up his undercover post in Northern Ireland. The night before he was due to return to duty, he'd been for a drink or three at a nightclub down town and was returning on foot to his house in Westerhope. It was about five miles from the city centre and very good up and down hill training after a few bevies. He planned to jog lightly along the West Road, and then turn right into Chapel House Drive.

Just past Newcastle General Hospital, at about 1 a.m., Geordie passed an opening between two buildings shaded from the lights of the main street. Three skinheads were confronting a young coloured man and were about to close for an attack when Geordie intervened and put himself between the man and the skinheads.

"Come on lads, what's going on here?" asked Geordie.

"We've got this fuckin' pakkie here, the al Qaeda bastard," said the biggest skinhead wielding a knife. "We're going to do him for what they did in Afghanistan and for what they are still doing in Iraq."

He asked the coloured man, "Where are you from bonny lad?"

"Fenham," answered the man, with a slight Geordie accent.

"There you are lads, he's English and a Geordie the same as us, now come on, get yourselves away home and don't be so daft."

"Fuckin' nigger lover," shouted the knife wielder as he made a lunge at Geordie.

Geordie parried the man's knife arm, grabbed the wrist and flicked the man over onto his back with a sickening thud. The thug was quite fit and back on his feet in a flash, attacking Geordie once more. Geordie parried the knife arm again but retained his grip on the wrist forcing it down and sideways. The razor sharp blade of the knife sliced into the man's right buttock and he screamed in pain, dropping the knife and writhing on the road in agony.

"Now you know what it feels like to be stuck mate," said Geordie, kicking the knife to one side and then booting the man's leg just below the wound causing him to yelp with pain. "It's not very nice is it?"

One of the gang grabbed the knife and rushed at the coloured man who copied Geordies actions almost to the letter and sent the skinhead flying through the air towards a signpost with **'No Entry'** written on it. The man turned his face away to avoid having it smashed against the post and took the full weight of his airborne body on his collarbone that fractured with a loud crack.

At that moment, a policeman on foot patrol rounded the corner from the dark back street and took in the scene at a glance. The third skinhead was standing with body bent and arms outstretched as if ready to charge.

"Don't move, any of you," shouted the policeman, baton in one hand and radio in the other requesting backup and an ambulance.

"I can't move," said the skinhead, "I've shit myself."

Geordie turned to the coloured man and asked. "Are you all right mate? Where the hell did you learn to defend yourself like that?"

"The back streets, the school yard, St James Park, 29 Commando and Hereford." said the man grinning and showing off his perfect white teeth.

"F 'kin'ell, I might have guessed it y'bugger, I'm Geordie Shiells Delta troop." He said, offering his hand.

"Bloody hell! Geordie Shiells. You and Delta are bloody legend Geordie mate; I'm honoured to meet you," said the man, almost shaking Geordie's hand from his wrist. "I met one of your old mates, Peter Bailey, at Hereford just after I finished Selection; he's a Makam isn't he?"

"Right," said Geordie, in mock disgust, "he retired but he's back in again, I suppose you're one of the Toon lads eh?"

"Not bloody likely, Man United's my team," answered the man.

"Bloody Hell," said Geordie, in real disgust this time. "What's your name mate?"

I'm Hari Baskaran, Echo troop E Squadron, I'm from Wingrove Road just round the corner, my grandfather emigrated here from India forty odd years ago and my dad was born here, he's a surgeon at the General. We're Indian Hindus not Pakistani Muslims; some people don't even know the difference." They shook hands again and chatted about Selection while they waited for the ambulance and the police to arrive.

"When did you join the mob?" asked Geordie.

"After medical school, my dad wanted me to be a doctor but my heart wasn't in it so I took up pharmacy instead. I joined the RAMC after I qualified and got a taste for the army life. After a couple of boring years at Catterick Military Hospital, I resigned my commission, went on a commando course, joined 29 Commando as a medical assistant then a year later, I applied for Selection to the SAS and here I am," explained Hari.

"F'kin'ell, I thought you were just a bairn when I first saw you, how old are you for Christ's sake?" asked Geordie.

"Twenty six yesterday, I was having a double celebration all by myself after having passed Selection last Friday. Then I was followed and attacked by those three clowns."

The ambulance had arrived and the two wounded skinheads were patched up by the paramedics and taken off to the nearby hospital accompanied by a police officer. Geordie and Hari were obliged to share the back seat of the police van with the stinking third skinhead. After producing their IDs and giving their statements, they were released before parting as mates promising to keep in touch.

The next day, they bumped into each other again at Newcastle Airport en route to Aldergrove. Hari had volunteered for 'Operation Wipe-out' before leaving Hereford and was on his way to report to a Father Patrick O'Riordan at Belfast General Hospital where he was to front as a hospital dispenser to be held in reserve as a 'sleeper'. He and Geordie became instant friends.

Chapter 23

Before opening the door on hearing the doorbell, Kevin Bradley, alias John Kennerley, peered through the spy hole at the familiar face of Liam Casey. He was astonished to see him again; the word was that he had quit the country after Ballypatrick along with Leo Bailey. He opened the door.

"Liam, what a pleasant surprise, I thought you were in the UK, how long have you been back?" asked Bradley, shaking Liam by the hand and patting him on the shoulder. "You look really great, what are you doing back here?"

"Hello John, nice to see you again, aren't you going to invite me in?" asked Liam.

"It's Kevin actually, I'm not John Kennerley anymore, that was an alias when I was on the run from the British Army, Kevin Bradley is my real name," said Bradley in his familiar Liverpudlian accent, standing aside and ushering Liam in.

Mary Bradley appeared in the hall at the sound of their voices. She was wearing a revealing pink negligee and almost transparent white lace underwear. Liam eyed her with appreciation; she was looking good.

"Hi Mary, you look as beautiful as ever, how are you?" He took her outstretched hands and kissed her on the cheek.

"Liam Casey! Look at you, you haven't changed a bit since we last met, how long ago is it now?" said Mary, still holding his hands. "You look wonderfully fit and well, and as handsome as ever, doesn't he Kev?"

Bradley said, "It was only three years ago come May if my memory serves me right, I got out of nick in June '97 after serving two years of a four year sentence. Come and sit down Liam and tell us all about yourself. Mary love, can we have some coffee, or perhaps Liam would like something a little stronger?" He said, with a querying glance at Liam.

"Coffee will be fine thanks," answered Liam, "it's a bit too early for the hard stuff, I've got a lot of calls to make today and I'll have to stay alert,"

As Mary swung round to go to the kitchen her negligee swung open below the waist to reveal a pair of beautiful limbs. She was gently tanned for the time of year.

"Have you been abroad?" asked Liam, his eyes following Mary as she disappeared into the kitchen.

Kevin Bradley was amused at Liam's attraction to Mary, his wife's frequent but brief periods of infidelity always turned him on; they still had an understanding.

"No, we have all mod cons here, we have a stand-and-tan thing upstairs in one of the bedrooms, and so we have instant sunshine 365 days of the year," explained Bradley who also sported a slight tan. "So what have you been doing with yourself for the past few years Liam?"

"I'm working for a marine engineering company in Belfast, just a labouring job you understand, but it's better than nothing," said Liam, "what are you doing these days?"

"Do you remember Sean Cunningham?" asked Bradley.

"Will I ever forget him?" said Liam. "I believe he copped his lot back at the farm when they accidentally blew up Brannigan's ammo dump. I gather from Doonan that you and Mary got out before the SAS got there."

Bradley flinched at the sound of Doonan's name and the smile disappeared from his face. "Do you know Doonan?" he asked.

"He sent me to see you," answered Liam, amused at the Bradley's reaction, "he needs your services again."

Bradley relaxed. "I heard he had been badly injured, I've never heard from him in years. What could he want with me now?"

Mary wheeled in a trolley laden with coffee, toast, butter, and a selection of jams and marmalade. She sat opposite Liam deliberately and allowed the negligee to part, revealing her shapely tanned legs that she crossed demurely.

"Help yourself please Liam, we don't stand on ceremony here," she said. "Did I hear you mention Dan Doonan's name just now?"

Liam helped himself to coffee and toast; he had started out very early that morning for the trip to Lislap and had not eaten since the previous night. He had intended to stop on the way for breakfast but then decided to push on instead. The sight and smell of the food stimulated pangs of hunger but he ate only two slices of buttered toast.

He had difficulty in averting his eyes from Mary. She kept crossing and uncrossing her legs as she bent to and fro to reach from the trolley revealing the cleavage between her perfect breasts that were scantily covered by the see-through bra. Both Mary and her husband were enjoying themselves at Liam's expense. He was less than comfortable with the situation.

"You mentioned Cunningham Kev what were you going to say before the subject of Doonan came up?" asked Liam. He needed a diversion.

"Oh, just that he gave this place to Mary and me. He was going off to America if you remember and he wanted us to look after the business over here. It was Doonan who advised us to leave the farm the night it went up. We took Cunningham's car and came over here otherwise we would have copped it along with the others."

"I gather from Doonan that you were touting for him, is that right?" asked Liam.

"Yeh, Brannigan was a pain in the arse to Doonan, he asked us to keep an eye on him and report anything that might embarrass the Provos' that's all, they just wanted to keep the peace for a while and Brannigan was in danger of sparking off the conflict again," explained Bradley. "We felt a bit guilty about Sean but I suppose he never felt a thing along with the other poor sods. Mary managed to hold on to the whorehouses while I was doing time but the rest of the business folded when the police rounded up the UK operatives. They should all be out now courtesy of the peace initiative."

"Doonan sends his best regards," began Liam, getting back to the reason for his visit. "He's resurrecting the Derry Brigade in response to the Brit referendum which you no doubt know about. He expects big trouble with the Prods and has appointed my uncle Barney and me as recruiting officers as well as CO and 2 I/C."

"What does he want from me?" asked Bradley.

"We need a Quartermaster among other things and I need your help with the recruiting, there isn't much time before the Brits pull out altogether and we need to have a force in place before the trouble begins," said Liam. "I have a list of thirty six names including yours. I need to contact all of them and your help would be much appreciated."

He handed the list to Bradley who nodded as he recognised most of the ex Players of the old Derry Brigade. He glanced at Mary and she nodded her approval.

"Thirty six is not many, is that the best Doonan can come up with?" asked Bradley.

"He expects each of the experienced respondents to recruit as many young bloods as possible there are still plenty hot heads in the Bogside as you probably know. He's opened the Drum Hills camp for training and retraining. He wants at least twenty people every fortnight to train for ten days. Belfast is already sending new people and the word is out in the other counties. We need a whole army in the next three months," said Liam.

Bradley folded the paper along line eighteen of the list of names and tore it into two. He handed Liam the list with his own name on it and said, "That's one name on your half and I will visit this lot. Where can I contact you when I need you?"

"Right, your code name is now Kilo Brad instead of the planned Junky Ken OK? I am known as Lima Case, your 'Billy Thompson' is number 028 620333. The box is situated on the main road about a mile south of Limavady. Doonan would like you to contact him from there, you know the Dublin ex-directory number I gather," said Liam. "I'm on the move most of the time but you can leave messages with Barney Meehan my uncle in Buncrana, he's known as Bravo Mickey. He handed Bradley the number."

"The Dublin number is indelibly printed on my memory is he still using that old security System?" asked Bradley, "I'm surprised the Brits haven't cracked it by now. He must have used it these past twenty years or more, it's incredible."

"The simpler things are, the harder they are to crack," said Liam. "Knowing the Brits, they'll be looking for something much more sophisticated. They must have been searching for non-existent radio waves forever. That's Doonan's secret, he knows his enemy better than they know him."

Liam stood to leave. "Thanks for the refreshment Mary, I'll have to get on and contact the rest of these people before I get back to Belfast, I've taken the day off work to come here and I'll have to be back by tomorrow."

"I was hoping you might stay a while," said Mary, sidling over to him and linking arms with him. She snuggled close to him and he could smell her perfume which was not over strong but powerfully attractive. She kissed him on the cheek and led him to the door. "Come and see us again soon and stay the night, we'll have a party," she said as she opened the door. "By the way, what ever happened to that pal of yours, Leo Bailey?"

"He got me away from Ballypatrick in all the confusion when Brannigan's car was blown up. We got to England but the Military Police nabbed him and banged him up for a couple of years in some place called Colchester." Liam knew that Bradley had served his time at Shepton Mallet. "He's back in Belfast now I hear but I don't know where, he hasn't been in touch. Doonan wants a word with him if I can find him. You remember, he was one of that tout Cluskey's protégé's, he would have made a good Quartermaster but you've got his job now Kev."

"So it was Cluskey who touted on Brannigan after Ballykelly!" exclaimed Bradley in some surprise. "It figures I suppose, but I hate to say it Liam, your uncle Barney was suspected by Brannigan and the others for a while, I overheard them talking one night at the farm." said Bradley.

Liam smiled to himself. He said in parting, "right then, Kevin, Mary, great to see you again, thanks for everything and good luck with the recruiting drive."

Peter Bailey was having no luck in his attempts to infiltrate the Loyalist paramilitary groups. Leo, Liam Casey, Patrick O'Riordan, and Larry McArdle were having all the luck at the moment.

Michael Ahern and Tommy Hanlon had finally joined forces in West Belfast according to Larry who had allowed himself to be recruited by Doonan. Great progress for them but Peter was getting nowhere. The trips back and forward to the Sunderland office were not helping either but someone had to take care of the business that was doing very well. He was director of the export side and Leo looked after the home trade. They both had excellent managers who could cover for them but the American contract demanded a lot of his personal attention hence the toing and froing to Sunderland.

He wished he could find time to see Maddie McKenna. He'd popped in a couple of times to see if she and the boys were OK at Leo's house but now she had found a place of her own at last and was moving on.

Chapter 24

The planning stage of Operation Wipeout was now complete and all of the operatives were in place awaiting orders to proceed. An elated Cedric Parker presented his situation report to Charlie Kinnear who studied it with interest while Parker slowly drank his scotch.

"I'm amazed at the speed with which you've got everything in place Cedric, you don't appear to have had many setbacks," said the PM.

"I chose two of the best people I knew to implement the plan. They volunteered without hesitation and recruited most of the two hundred undercover men needed to carry the operation through to completion. I have worked with both of them for many years and know their capabilities. It would be better, however, if you didn't know who my people are in case there's any cockup in the operation. I wouldn't wish to compromise you or the government in any way. The buck stops with me Charlie, it was my idea, and I am prepared to carry the can if anything goes wrong," said Parker.

"Thank you Cedric, I appreciate that. We are getting enough flack about the results of the referendum as it is. The admission of a covert operation on top of that would finish us before we even got a started, I have not confided in my Conservative deputy for obvious reasons.

Kinnear put the secret document into the safe behind the picture of Lloyd George that hung on the wall behind his desk. He refilled his glass and held out the bottle to Parker who waved it away with a shake of his head.

The PM continued. "Stormont is in turmoil at the moment with only three months to go before the province is declared a republic. And to think that it could all have been avoided with a modicum of mutual tolerance. Self-interest motivates most people at the end of the day though I suppose, overriding both religious and political considerations. Then there is the criminal element of course; they never miss an opportunity to exploit these conflicts for their own ends no matter what country it happens to be.

Nevertheless, I have recruited and sent in a team of retired top civil servants to advise Grimble and his emergency cabinet and to help them get their act together. The existing civil servants will stay on to train new people who will eventually replace them but to protect them, I've ordered that they all be given CD status. The elders will stay there for as long as they are required working with a similar team from the south provided by the Dublin government. With a bit of luck, they should have bureaucratic stability within the year providing your cleansing operation is successful. If the finale goes as well as the overture, there should not be too much of a problem. We don't want to be clashing head on with the police," said the PM.

Parker said with some assurance. "As you have seen from the report Charlie, we already have intelligence on two Republican outfits and one Loyalist gang. One of the republican gangs, from West Belfast, has joined forces with the Real IRA and has been infiltrated by an unlikely new recruit. The other mob in Londonderry is in the process of being infiltrated during the reformation of the Provisional IRA's Derry Brigade. I am led to believe that the entire PIRA is planning to regroup under the leadership of our old adversary Daniel Doonan who was once its top man operating from his Dublin HQ until 1995. He has apparently come out of retirement and is recruiting new blood as we speak. The loyalist paramilitaries are a little trickier to tap into but we'll get there I'm sure."

The four-man executive team, of Peter and Leo Bailey, Liam Casey, and Father Patrick O'Riordan, met in the conference room of Ellis Engineering to discuss Larry McArdle's intelligence report with Larry in attendance.

"You've done a really fantastic job Larry," said Peter Bailey, shaking Larry by the hand. "We are well impressed with all the information you have obtained in the short space of a couple of weeks, your talents are wasted on the nursing profession."

"Thanks," said Larry, "but I now have a special interest in the demise of Mr. Michael Ahern otherwise I would never have been a part of this set-up. I would just have returned to London and my Sarah when my granda died if he hadn't told me about Ahern and how he'd had my mother killed. I will not rest until he pays for his sins one-way or the other I owe my ma that much God rest her soul.

"Your grandfather has undone some of his evil past by doing us a favour Larry, he has signed Ahern's death warrant along with the rest of his thugs. It's a bit of poetic justice in a way. Would you like to be his executioner when the time comes?" asked Peter.

Larry hung his head and thought about it for a while before answering.

"No, I don't think so; such a thought would never have entered my head before I learned what Ahern and my father had done. I felt like killing Ahern when I first met him but I've calmed down now, evil begets evil it seems. And of course, 'vengeance is mine' sayeth the Lord so how could I take the law into my own hands and just walk away with a clear conscience? I must admit again though that my first reaction was to contemplate killing the evil bastard but I think I am going to have to leave it to the professionals. I have no qualms at all about leading that particular lamb to the slaughter, I'll be content with driving the car that we use for the robbery, the rest will be up to your people," answered Larry.

Leo said. "Not our people Larry, we are giving Ahern's and Hanlon's gangs to the loyalists to play with, they will love it. Our people will do a hit and run on the survivors then disappear into thin air. That has been the plan from the beginning of this operation, terrorise the terrorists; neither side will know who's hit them. We can give you a licence to kill if it would help to salve your conscience."

Patrick O'Riordan said. "You don't have to do it if you don't want to Larry, I understand your feelings if the rest of us don't, I've been there, but Ahern has to go and we just thought that you would like to avenge your mother that's all. I'm sure God would forgive you under the circumstances, Ahern has a whole list of sins to atone for."

They got down to the business of the forthcoming bank robberies.

"Our people, Alec Shiells and Hari Baskaran, will take out Ahern and his gang when they enter the bank," said Leo. "We can't take a chance on leaving them to the loyalists when you are sitting outside the bank in the getaway car Larry. The loyalists are welcome to take out the rest of the gang at the other nine banks before our people take care of them. You just stay put in the car or, better still, drive away when the shooting starts, it's up to you what you do after that. We just wanted to give you the chance to get even that's all."

"Thanks again all of you, but I don't think I'm up to it," said Larry finally.

He left the others to their conference and went off to his night shift at the infirmary. In his pocket was a letter inviting him to an interview for the post of Industrial Nurse at Ellis Marine Engineering just in case he had been followed by any of Ahern's men; he wasn't.

Ahern's planned robberies were only six days away and Leo was in a quandary as to how to get a Loyalist gang in place for the planned ambushes. He might well have to revert to his own active men and some of his sleepers to carry out the job; he had already used the sleeper Hari Baskaran on Geordie Shiells' advice. He desperately needed someone in the loyalist camp but Peter had been unsuccessful in planting one of his Protestant men up to now.

Maddie McKenna had supplied a list of around twenty-five loyalist player/gangsters to Peter but how to get amongst them and use them without arousing suspicion was beyond him. Leo put the problem to Peter and the others and asked them to sleep on it to see if any of them could come up with any ideas.

There was not much time left before the robberies were due to take place and Leo would need at least two days to organise his own men. He didn't really want to use all of his sleepers at this early stage in the game, it was not supposed to work that way, and there could be casualties amongst his volunteers, that would be bad risk management.

The very mention of Maddie's name set Peter's mind thinking about her and wondering how she was getting along in England. He had seen her briefly a couple of times before she had completed her two-weeks holiday at Leo and Siobhan's house in Ryhope. But his trips back and forth to the Sunderland office had been done in a day on both of those occasions due to pressure of work and the current covert operation. Out on the first flight from Aldergrove and back the same evening on the last flight of the day followed by meetings with the 'Operation Wipe-out' executive late into the night was not easy to sustain.

Maddie had been so pleased to see him but their meetings had been all too brief. He desperately needed to get to know her properly, he had fallen in love with her and he had to know how she felt about him. An evening out to dinner would have been nice but there was no time.

She had found a council house that she liked in the tiny village of Tanfield near Stanley in Co. Durham. The houses had been refurbished to a high standard, which she thought was quite posh compared with the terraced hovel she had been accustomed to in Belfast.

The semi-detached house with its own garden stood in a cluster of about fifty other houses and was surrounded by fields and hedgerows. Tanfield Hall, the one-time family home of Judi Bowker of Black Beauty fame, stood nearby. The old coalmining town of Stanley overlooked the flat plain from the hill about a mile to the southwest.

Her new neighbours had welcomed her and the boys unconditionally, which touched her almost to the point of tears. The locals spoke with a strange accent of their own and never tired of listening to her and the boys with their distinctive Northern Irish twang.

She thought about Peter often but dared not entertain the possibility of a relationship with him considering his high position as a company director and an obviously quite well off one at that. What would a man like him want with an insignificant nobody like her and a married nobody at that?

She had fallen in love with him at their first meeting but had denied herself the pleasure of such a thought immediately it sprung to mind. But it was becoming harder to suppress the feelings that she had for him especially when she was alone in the evenings when the boys had gone to bed. She read a lot to keep her mind off him without much success and the television did nothing to distract her.

The boys had settled well in school and had made lots of new friends. They never asked about their father, as far as they were concerned, he no longer existed.

Thinking about Maddie, Peter hit on an idea. He phoned Sid Morrell and asked him if he could come to the office for a chat. When Sid arrived, they sat down with a beer and Peter explained his problem in the knowledge that the information was safe with Sid who was trying to forge links with the loyalist paramilitary community in East Belfast where he lived.

As it happened, Sid had been attempting to wheedle his way into the confidence of one Andrew McClelland, a UDA man and member of a local social club, who had used Sid's taxi on a regular basis. They had become quite good friends and had even been for a drink together on a couple of occasions.

The man was a political activist and had no connection with any criminal element as far as Sid knew but from some things that he had let drop during their conversations, he obviously knew a few dodgy characters. He had told Sid in confidence, after they had put away a good drink one night, that the loyalist paramilitary boys were secretly recruiting as a result of the Brit referendum and that he was afraid that the fragile peace was not going to hold for long. He'd said that there would be no shortage of volunteers but there would be a shortage of cash for weapons.

"Do you think he would pass on the information about the planned bank robberies if he was given it?" asked Peter.

"It depends on whether or not I could tell him where it came from, I don't want him to think that I have a foot in the republican camp or he might clam up on me altogether," replied Sid.

"Does he know that you employ some Catholic drivers?" asked Peter.

"Yes, he does not appear to take sides. I've been honest with him about that, he doesn't seem to mind as long as they are not activists," answered Sid.

"Right, do you think you could fool him into believing that one of your Catholic drivers has been asked to use his taxi as a getaway car in one of the robberies and that he has come to you for advice rather than get involved?" asked Peter.

"He might swallow it if I can convince him that the driver has done a runner rather than get tied up with criminals. As it happens, one of my Catholic drivers has taken up the government's offer and has relocated with relatives in Aberdeen he went two days ago with his wife and six kids so he's out of the way if there are questions asked. I'll give it a go," said Sid, "how many days did you say we had?"

"Six," said Peter, "best of luck Sid, keep me posted."

Sid phoned Peter at home at almost midnight with good news. McClelland had swallowed the story and had taken down the details of the banks' locations and the time of the robberies with the exception of Dungannon, which Sid had purposely neglected to mention. It only remained to be seen whether or not his friend's paramilitary contact would swallow the bait and organise a reception committee for the gangs of Ahern and Hanlon.

Peter called Leo, who was now staying with Siobhan and the twins at Liam's house, and arranged a meeting in the Ellis conference suite at 7 a.m. the next morning before the staff arrived.

Leo was relieved by the turn of events but, erring on the side of caution, he intended to have armed observers in fast cars at each location as well as the two-man teams on motorcycles who had been selected to take out the stolen getaway cars en-route to the car park of an out-of-town supermarket where a coach would be waiting to transport the villains to safety. The police would be looking for speeding getaway cars rather than a slow coach full of innocent shoppers.

Contenting himself that his brother had everything in hand, Peter made some excuse about an urgent export contract that had to be completed on time at the Sunderland yard. He told Leo that he was leaving early the next day to take care of business and would be returning in three days time to help oversee the final arrangements for their first encounter with the enemy. Leo assured him that all would be well at this end until he got back.

James McKenna was at his usual place on a stool at the end of the bar when Eamon Finney walked into The Masons Arms and made straight for him.

"Hello Jamesy, how's it goin'?" asked Finney, "how are Maddie and the boys? Givvus a pint John," he called to the barman before McKenna could answer.

"She's fucked off to Australia, haven't you heard? Or are you taking the piss? Just about everybody else has." Replied McKenna sullenly.

"No, I hadn't heard, I'm sorry Jamesy, I've been away for a while working on a motorway on the mainland," said Finney, "can I get you a drink?"

"I'll have a pint of bitter thanks, what are you doing at this end of town?" asked McKenna.

"I've come to see you, I have a proposition for you and some of your boys, what are you up to right now?" enquired Finney.

"There's nothing much going on at the moment," said McKenna, "we are waiting to see what happens when the bloody English pull out. There hasn't been much talk of a rising like we expected, at least not in this area but it's a fair bet that the republicans are preparing for a fight."

"I can tell you that they definitely are, get your drink and let's find somewhere quiet while I tell you what I know," said Finney, in a low conspiratorial tone.

They found a lone table in a corner of the half empty lounge and Finney told McKenna what he had learned on the grapevine about Ahern's planned robberies. Four pints and three whiskies later, they had agreed to combine forces and set up an ambush for Ahern's robbers by posing as customers at the various banks. One man would be left outside each of the banks to take care of the getaway drivers then steal the stolen cars.

The following evening, forty-five men met at the Orange lodge where McKenna still had the cleaning contract.

Peter's heart was beating just a little too fast when Maddie answered the doorbell. She flushed when she saw him and before they knew it, they were in each others arms and kissing like long parted lovers. He gently lifted her off her feet and shuffled her into the hallway still kissing her as he nudged the door shut behind them. They kissed for what seemed like an eternity until they had to stop for breath.

"I love you." They said in unison and they both began to laugh as they hugged each other.

"I'm mad about you Maddie McKenna I haven't been able to get you out of my mind since I first saw you," said Peter.

"Oh God Peter, I didn't think it was possible, I've thought of nothing else since the night your mother introduced us but I have had to suppress my feelings. I love you, I love you, and I love you, what's to become of us?" said Maddie, her eyes suddenly filling with tears. "Hold me tightly and tell me this isn't a dream."

"It's no dream Maddie, it's a dream come true," said Peter. He held her at arms length and gazed into her greyish green eyes. "God you are more beautiful than ever, this new life must be agreeing with you, you look bloody marvellous."

"I have you and your ma to thank for all this," she said, "I've never been so happy in my whole life. McKenna would kill me if he knew where I was right now but he believes we are in Australia with my sister."

"It will take two years for you to get a divorce Maddie but I will wait that long now that I know you love me too. I take it the boys are at school, do they like it here, do they miss their father?" asked Peter.

"If you knew how he used to treat them, you would understand why they never give him a moments thought now that we are free of him. They will be home at around four, we have about three hours to spare." She led Peter towards the stairs. "I've never committed adultery before," she said, smiling, "shall we?"

Barney Meehan had been busy checking out the people on the list that Doonan had given him and that Liam and Bradley had located. Four of the thirty-six people listed had died of natural causes and two had been killed in a car accident. Four others were too old and were rejected out of hand although they were keen to fight again. Of the remaining twenty-six, Kevin Bradley was the youngest.

Barney phoned Doonan at Murphy's Bar to report on the success of his mission. He was told by Doonan's brother Bryan to go to his 'Billy Thompson' in two hours time and wait. His brother Daniel was in West Belfast but he would get a message to him to ring Meehan at the appointed time.

SAS Warrant Officer, Mick Rutherford, ex Royal Signals, had tapped into several of the phone boxes used by Doonan's CO's north of the border with the help of the map that Larry McArdle had photographed in Doonan's office. All 'Billy Thompson' calls would now be relayed to a listening post set up by Mick in a disused van parked in Sid Morrell's taxi compound where they would be filtered and the relevant calls recorded. The van was manned twenty four hours a day and all messages prefixed by an IRA field commander's code were filtered out and relayed by encrypted satellite transmission direct to Parker's office in London. Mick was tapping into the twenty-four known 'Billy Thompson's' at the rate of four a day; just six more to go.

Doonan was in touch within the hour. "It's about what I expected," he said, when Barney gave him the recruiting numbers. "We've had more luck with the other battalions, we have a small army of almost two hundred and the training camp at Drum is very busy, we've extended the intakes to thirty. Did you manage to get young Liam on board like I asked you Barney?"

"Not only is he my 2 I/C," answered Barney, "but he has done most of the running around, good lad that he is. Do you remember the fella that was with him when he escaped from the RUC while they were transferring them and Flynn from the police station at Limavady to Belfast and when Flynn was killed in the escape before the boys made it to Danny's Bar?"

"I had heard," said Doonan, Bradley had told him, "what about him?"

"Well they kept in touch and he has joined Liam along with the Bogside and Creggan boys. He was one of Cluskey's men if you remember, one that Cluskey neglected to mention, secretive bugger that he was. He'll make a good replacement for Dixie Dixon God rest his soul," said Barney with as much reverence for the deceased Dixie as he could muster. "Bailey is also a good bomb maker."

"His bombs didn't go off at that funeral, did they Barney? Brannigan was blown to pieces and I got badly singed if you recall. There's something funny about that episode Barney, I don't think I trust the man, do you?" asked Doonan.

"I questioned him about that and he thinks that somebody who had it in for Brannigan planted the bomb under his car then tampered with the signal on the remote control," lied Barney.

Doonan was less than satisfied with Barney's explanation but said nothing, he would find out in his own way when he met this Leo Bailey the supposed British Army deserter. Doonan neglected to tell Barney about the robberies planned by Ahern and company.

After a long pause in the conversation, Doonan said, "Barney, I want to meet this Bailey fella, there's a few questions I need answered. I can be with you in three hours, make sure that Bailey is there.

It was 3.45 p.m. when Maddie finally opened her eyes and looked at the bedside clock. She shot out of bed and shook Peter wildly; the boys were due home just after four. They dressed quickly and went downstairs; they were the happiest couple in the entire world at that moment. Their lovemaking had been urgent, passionate but short-lived before they had fallen blissfully asleep in each other's arms.

"Just give the boys a snack when they get home Maddie, an old friend of mine has a pub not too far from here and I'd like to take you all out to dinner tonight if that's OK with you," said Peter.

"It will be a rare treat for them as well as for me. The only eating out we do is on a Saturday morning when we go shopping at ASDA in Stanley and have an all-day breakfast. I'm sure they will love it. Who's your friend?" asked Maddie.

"Keith Conroy, we met in Dubai in '92 when I was in the Army fighting Saddam Hussein's lot. He was an engineer for some American oil outfit. An old army colleague and, mutual friend, introduced us when were on R & R. I promised to look him up if he ever got the pub he dreamed of and I heard from my friend Brian that he did, Brian called it 'The Gallowa's Byuts,' whatever that means, The Three Horseshoes, or something like that as far as I can remember. It's located at some place called Maiden Law, but I have the address and the map reference, I booked a table for us before I left the office." explained Peter.

Not only did Peter take them all to dinner that night, but the following day they were chauffeur driven to the Stadium of Light in Sunderland to watch the home team play Leeds United. The boys were thrilled and Peter was their instant hero.

Two days later, Peter returned to Belfast a happy and contented man. He had left Maddie with instructions to start looking for another house. He arranged for driving lessons for her and gave her the contact number for one of the Company drivers whenever she and the boys needed transport. Maddie could not believe the change in their fortunes.

Doonan, accompanied by Groddy McGinty and another of Ahern's gang, arrived at Barney Meehan's house just minutes after Leo and Liam who had also dashed from Belfast at Barney's urgent request.

Doonan's two minders stayed with the car and made a show of openly carrying Russian made machine pistols. Doonan was taking no chances and Leo's plan to take him out on sight was mentally shelved. He did not want a blood bath at Barney's place.

"So Mr. Leo Bailey," began Doonan, "we meet at last, I've heard things about you that just don't quite feckin' add up. I gather you were one of Bernard Cluskey's men, is that right?"

"Right," said Leo, "I take it he didn't always keep you informed."

"He kept too much to himself, he was well known for it. That is why I find it difficult to believe that he touted on Brannigan and Barney here. What do you think?"

Leo thought quickly, he could be in serious trouble if he didn't come up with a feasible story.

"OK Mr. Doonan, I'll come clean with you, it was Brannigan who had Cluskey banged up," he lied, "I overheard him telling Monaghan at Danny's Bar the night that Liam and I escaped from custody."

"Why would Brannigan do that?" asked Doonan.

"Cluskey had an arms cache moved to a new location and he refused to tell Brannigan where it was. He told me that they had argued and that he had told Brannigan that the stuff belonged to the IRA and not to Brannigan," answered Leo, expanding the lie.

"The bastard was getting back at me through Bernard the evil shit that he was." Doonan said, as though he was thinking out loud. He asked Leo a searching question. "Do you know where the cache was moved to?"

"Eh Yes," said Leo, "would you like me to show you where it is?" Peter had told him about the cache that had been interfered with by Geordie Shiells and Jock Shand the day that the psychopath, Eamon Flynn, had been taken out and his body left spread-eagled on top of the plastic protective sheeting.

Liam and Barney kept quiet throughout the conversation. They were both worried about the questions that Doonan was asking Leo but Leo seemed to be coping quite well. He hadn't mentioned any arms cache to them.

"Where is the stuff?" asked Doonan.

"Not far from Danny's Bar at Ballyshiel, a few miles up the road and about a mile from the border at the edge of a wood, I helped to move it," he lied.

"Could you take us there? We could use those weapons in the near future," said Doonan.

"We could be there within the hour, it's just off the main road between Strabane and Derry," answered Leo, truthfully this time.

"OK," said Doonan, "you stay here Barney, and you Liam, come with us.

It was late in the afternoon and the light was fading. They put torches and shovels in the boot of the car. Leo drove and Liam sat in the front passenger seat while Doonan and the other minder sat in the back. Smelly Groddy McGinty was left behind with Barney; Doonan was not looking forward to the return journey to Belfast with the man.

They reached the area where the cache was buried within the hour and Leo took some time to locate it having only his brother Peter's information about the movement of the spiked weapons cache and the map reference from all those years previous. Luck was on his side.

The cache had been covered with corrugated iron sheets laid on top of wooden spars. Bales of straw, which were disintegrating with age, had then concealed the sheets. Exposure to a couple of years of wind and rain revealed rusting patches of corrugated iron. When they finally uncovered the dump, they discovered the skeleton of Eamon Flynn spread-eagled on top of the polythene wrapping that protected the wrapped boxes of arms and explosives beneath. Wisps of red hair blew around in circles in the light breeze. It was an eerie sight in the torchlight. The site had obviously remained undisturbed all those years.

"Jesus Christ!" Exclaimed Doonan, "who the feck have we here?"

"One of Brannigan's men we thought, we caught him spying on us when he disturbed a pheasant just after we had finished putting the stuff down," lied Leo. He hoped that Doonan was swallowing it all.

Doonan got down into the pit and inspected the skull of the unfortunate Flynn.

"He was shot in the head from behind! Who did it?" asked Doonan.

"I did," lied Leo, "we couldn't take any chances, if he wasn't one of Brannigan's men, he could have been working undercover for the security forces, or he could just have been an innocent bystander in the wrong place, either way, he had to go."

"Evil bastard aren't you Mr. Bailey, a man after my own heart. Now while we are here, will you please explain to me why the bombs you planted at that funeral where Brannigan's car was blown to pieces, failed to go off?" asked Doonan.

"Because they had no detonators, I couldn't go along with the murder of hundreds of innocent people at a funeral just to please the man who touted on my boss now could I?" said Leo.

"Who planted the bomb under Brannigan's car?" asked Doonan.

"I did," replied Leo truthfully, "he had it coming."

"Why am I now so pleased that you are on our side?" said Doonan. "Barney said that you were lethal and I believe him. Get this lot covered up and let's get to feck out of here, I'll have the stuff moved to the training camp at Drum within the week."

"How will you manage that without being seen?" asked Leo.

"Like we used to do in the old days Leo m'boy," said Doonan with his hand on Leo's shoulder. He had obviously believed everything Leo had told him; he was actually relaxed and smiling.

"The stuff will be loaded onto a farm trailer, covered with shit, and taken in relays down to the farm in the Drum Hills. We have a need for it and more. Now let's get back to Barney's place, I've asked Kevin and Mary Bradley to meet us there, it will be nice to see them again.

Kevin Bradley put down the phone after speaking to Doonan; he was not too enthusiastic about working for the man again. He and Mary had discussed the implications before setting out for Buncrana and Barney Meehan's house. The prospect of violent confrontation with loyalists was unbearable to Bradley and Mary was not too happy at the prospect either. It was not because he was a coward, after all he was a trained soldier; he just hated brutality.

They decided to go along with whatever Doonan said then act accordingly. It would be a shame to give up the house at Lislap but they wanted no part in any violence. They might be pimps but they were reformed petty thieves not psycho's like that Leo Bailey and his pal Liam Casey. They decided that they would return to England at the earliest opportunity once they were rid of Doonan's unsavoury entourage'.

After their reunion at Meehan's house, Doonan took Bradley by the arm and gently led him into the garden out of earshot of the others.

"Tell me about Leo Bailey Kevin, how well do you know him?" asked Doonan.

"I met him and Liam Casey just a couple of days before General Patrick's funeral at Ballypatrick in '95," began Bradley. "Brannigan put him in charge of the operation because of his organisational and planning ability, he was very good. He had some of us dress up in the uniforms of British military policemen pretending to search the area around the church for evidence of terrorist activity while at the same time planting bombs under the boulders lining the driveway."

"What happened after that?" asked Doonan.

"We hijacked an armoured personnel carrier belonging to a troop of cavalrymen on patrol in the area. Leo lured them into a clearing and he and Liam shot the poor bastards in cold blood after herding them into a ruined farmhouse about half a mile from the road. They made them strip first and then they shot them with an SMG and threw grenades into the building afterwards just to make sure that there were no survivors, it was gruesome. Two of us saw them backing away from the building, firing as they came, before they threw in the grenades." said Bradley with just the hint of a shudder.

"The Brits kept that one quiet for obvious face-saving reasons," said Doonan, "but I was in hospital for a good while afterwards, maybe I missed the news."

"There was no mention of it anywhere," said Bradley.

"Strange," said Doonan stroking his chin thoughtfully. They went back inside.

Doonan gathered everyone around and gave them the details of Ahern's plan to rob ten banks at the same time on the same day in order to confound the police and fund the coming battle for supremacy in the province.

"Barney, you're off the hook, you are hereby relieved of command of the Derry Brigade," said Doonan, "I'm leaving Leo Bailey in charge with Liam remaining as 2 I/C." Turning to Bradley, he said, "Kevin, you are now the Brigade Quartermaster, Leo will show you where there is an arms cache, decide between the two of you what you need here and organise for the rest of it to be shipped to the training area at the Drum Hills farm in the South, do you know where it is?"

"No I don't," answered Bradley, he was not a happy man.

"No problem," said Doonan, "I'll show you on the map but you don't have to go with it, I'll send along a friendly farmer to see you and he will take it from there. He will be the first link in the relay chain."

"What do you think of the bank robbery idea Leo?" asked Doonan.

"Brilliant," said Leo, "I can imagine the police running around like blue-arsed flies with ten robberies being carried out simultaneously."

"How about twenty robberies," said Doonan?

"Sorry, I thought you just said ten," interjected Liam. "You did say ten didn't you?"

"I did," said Doonan, "but now I would like you both to organise another ten robberies for the same time on the same day, that will confuse things even more and get us all the funds we need. Can you do it?"

Leo looked at Liam and smiled, Doonan was unwittingly playing into their hands. "What do you think Liam, could we do it?"

"We will need more getaway cars but stealing them at such short notice is going to be difficult. Does anyone in the Brigade know how to go about the business of car theft?" enquired Liam of the assembled group. Nobody ventured an answer.

"What about taxis" said Groddy McGinty, an expert car thief? It would not be the first time that we've commandeered taxis, we used to do it lot in the old days."

"There's a Catholic outfit in Derry run by an Englishman, some of his boys have just been recalled to the Brigade. Maybe we could borrow his cars," said Liam.

"What about drivers?" asked Doonan.

"The Brigade will supply them," said Leo, "I'll put the order out."

Doonan was satisfied that everything was in order and departed with his chauffeur. Leo waved them off then excused himself to go to the bathroom. He took out his mobile and sent a text message to Sid Morrell's HQ for onward transmission to Sandy Blewitt in Derry, Parker in London, and all other field operatives for information. It read:

> **GTS** (*go to secure*), **POA** (*plan of action*), **CODE3** (*read letter plus 3*). **PHVVDJH UHDGV** (*message reads*), **VDQGB** (*Sandy*), **GR ORW UHVLVW HQHPB UHTXHVW IRU WDALV. SDUNHU ZLOO FRPSHQVDWH. ZLOO FRQWDFW ODWHU LQ FOADU. OHR** (*do not resist enemy request for taxis. Parker will compensate. Will make contact later in clear, Leo*).

At the earliest opportunity, Leo rang Peter and updated him on the play so far. Peter rang Sid Morrell and passed on the information. Sid received a copy of Leo's message and called on Andrew McClelland to take him to his UDA club and to which he drove in silence.

Chapter 25

Sid Morrell uttered not a word to his passenger and new friend Andrew McClelland as they drove to the social club.

"What's up Sid?" asked McClelland. "You are very quiet tonight, what's on your mind?"

"I'll tell you when we get to the club Andy, it has been one of those days and I could use a drink right now," said Sid. "The IRA have been at my boys again but up in Derry this time. My partner, Sandy Blewitt, has just rung me with disturbing news."

They reached the club and Sid parked the taxi. He wasn't planning to work any more that evening, he had important news to impart to his unwitting messenger boy.

Andy bought the first round of drinks and they found a quiet corner in which to chat.

"What's happened then?" asked Andy.

"Do you remember me telling you about those bank robberies planned by that republican gang from West Belfast?" said Sid in a low conspiratorial tone.

"Yes," said Andy, eyes darting and mimicking Sid's tone. "What's happening in Derry then?"

"The Derry Brigade of the IRA has been resurrected, that's what," said Sid.

"Where does your partner come in?" asked Andy.

"They are going to carry out a series of bank robberies at the same time as the Belfast gang as far as I can gather, at another ten more banks including Coleraine, Ballymoney, Gravagh, Dungiven, Maghera, Strabane, Newtonstewart, Omagh, Ballykelly, and Limavady. They are looking for getaway drivers according to Sandy, two of his best men have signed up to it under duress so he tells me and he's worried. The word is that they are going to commandeer his fleet for the getaway. I'm worried too I can tell you do you think I should inform the police Andy? They are going to have a hell of a job coping with twenty bank jobs at the same time," said Sid.

"If I were you Sid, I would tell your partner to do nothing. You know what the IRA is capable of and if you blow the whistle on them, they'll blow your friend away. They will know that somebody has touted if the police get in their way, they are not kind to touts," said Andy. "You haven't told anyone about the Belfast job have you?"

"Only you Andy, I know I can trust you," said Sid.

The day after his meeting with Leo Bailey, Daniel Doonan arranged to meet the resurrected Derry Brigade veterans and new recruits in the barn of his friendly farmer's holding on the Derry side of the Donegal border, just off the road to Newtown Cunningham.

He introduced Leo as their new Commanding Officer and Liam Casey as his second-in-command. Kevin Bradley was to be their Quartermaster and he required volunteers immediately after the meeting to load the retrieved arms cache onto the friendly farmer's trailer. He told them about the planned bank robberies and handed over the meeting to Leo who outlined the strategy that he had worked out the night before.

He listed the locations of, and designated the teams to, the individual banks with strict instructions regarding the modus operandi. Eight men volunteered to supplement Sandy's two co-opted drivers to drive the getaway vehicles, which would be picked up the night before the robberies.

There were enough men to form teams of five, which should be enough to ward off any trouble. Trouble, however, was not expected considering the size of the towns and the ease of entry and exit and the relative lack of security since the beginning of the ceasefire. The current disturbances were confined to Belfast and Derry and had not yet spilled over to the outlying small towns.

Doonan produced a selection of weapons for those who had not retained theirs from previous active service. They had been well greased and wrapped before being stashed. After wishing the men good luck, he set off back to Belfast to inform Ahern and Hanlon of his clever addition to Ahern's plan.

Sandy Blewitt, having survived the Sperrin Mountain escapade although he was the oldest one in the team, had kept himself fit over the years and still had lots of stamina. Having been invited by Leo to attend, he had stayed in the background at Doonan's recent meeting with the Derry Brigade having recognised him from his time with the Det in the late seventies. He had been following a senior IRA Player for weeks without getting too close for fear of being 'pinged'.

One day in the Ardoyne he spotted Doonan who he did not know at the time as the PIRA chief of staff who seldom left the Dublin base where his minions normally reported to him. He had made one of his rare visits to the North to attend an important strategic meeting of cell leaders in the company of the Player being followed by Sandy.

Sandy tailed them to the meeting house and waited in his car for them to re-emerge. On that occasion, he got too close to his subject and was almost taken out by a gunman who was monitoring his movements. Fortunately for Sandy, the man approached him gun-in-hand from behind but Sandy clocked him in his side mirror and shot away from the curb just in time. It was not until weeks later that Sandy had recognised Doonan from an updated list of wanted Players.

After the recent Sperrin Mountain exercise, Leo had gathered the incoming teams into a circle and briefed them on the impending bank raids. He now had to organise another team for the additional raids but fortunately, he now had sufficient trained men to cope.

As a contingency, he sent signals to all of the reserves and put them on standby for a possible airlift from Breize Norton at a moments notice in the hope that they may not be required. Although they would have the element of surprise, they would still be outnumbered two to one by the two opposing gangs initially. It would be essential to let one side take out as many of the other side as possible before finishing off the survivors. Gung-ho heroism was not the order of the day; stealth and professionalism would be more appropriate.

He had instructed them on the role of the motorcycle teams who were volunteers, selected from among those present, who would be riding on country roads as opposed to the motorway route to a hypermarket car park as planned by the Belfast gangs.

In the less busy wintry countryside, it would simply be a matter of hanging back from the robbers' getaway cars until a suitable opportunity arose to overtake them and take out the occupants.

A rendezvous had been arranged at a 'Singing Pub' on the Donegal side of the border for the opposing Derry Brigade gang but Leo did not expect any of them to make it if the motorcycle teams did their job efficiently.

George Davidson, Alan Donaldson, Dave Affleck, Alan Barclay, Billy Stewart, Jimmy Frazer, Pat Deathers, Denis Cross, Eddy Graham, and Louis Hughes, all SAS and SBS with the exception of ex MI6 agent Alan Donaldson, were advised to wear Kevlar vests and pose as customers at each of the additional ten banks. If no loyalist gangs turned out to thwart the IRA gangsters, they were to take out as many of the robbers as possible with the help of the motorcyclists who would be waiting outside near the bank ready to act on the sound of gunfire from within. Each had been issued with the new lightweight sniper rifle and twenty-four rounds of ammunition. It was hoped, however, that Sid Morrell's meeting with McClelland would produce the expected results. The scene was now set and the players were ready.

Andrew McClelland lost no time in informing Eamon Finney about the new developments in Derry. Finney did not know many people there but one of his East Belfast associates and a casual workmate on the highways, Sam

Keeley, was from Derry originally and had a criminal record. Perhaps he could muster a few villains to ambush the Derry Brigade and steal the stolen loot.

It turned out not to be a problem, Sam Keeley knew several members of a gang who were always on the lookout for easy pickings and the promise of stolen riches was too big to turn down. Keeley had been persona non grata for several years with the Derry loyalists for cheating his confederates in the past but was now accepted back into the fold having approached them with this new project.

A tactical meeting was arranged between James McKenna representing the Shankill Surgeons, Eamon Finney representing a gang in East Belfast, and Sam Keeley accompanied by gang boss Stuart McBride representing the Derry loyalists.

They met at McKenna's house where they studied the locations of the banks and the various escape options. They would now need two getaway coaches, one at the hypermarket and one at the 'Singing Pub.' They all laughed at the idea of the loyalist gang's hijacking of the republican gang's coaches and escaping via the motorway with police cars chasing up and down looking for speeding getaway cars.

Kevin Bradley was not the happiest of men. He felt trapped by this unexpected development when Doonan had announced his role as Quartermaster of the Derry Brigade. He and Mary had planned to disappear at the earliest opportunity but now it was impossible. Doonan would find them and punish them as only he knew how. Where could they go, where could they hide?

The ringing of the doorbell brought the pair to their feet. Kevin answered the door, it was Leo Bailey and Liam Casey; shit.

"Hello Kev, can we have a word?" asked Leo.

"Come inside," said Kevin, "would you like a drink?"

"No thanks," said Liam, "we are here on business to discuss the movement of the arms, has anyone contacted you yet, I mean the farmer?"

"Not yet, I'm expecting him this evening, is there anything wrong?"

"We need to arm the rest of the Brigade, Doonan gave us what he had but it wasn't enough. Do you mind if Leo and I go up to the trailer and take out what we need before the farmer moves it? It's your decision, you are the Quartermaster and you have a say."

Kevin was a little taken aback he had never held a position above Corporal cook in the British Army before he had deserted.

"Take what you need by all means, you don't need my permission Leo, you are the CO, you give me the orders and I obey," said Kevin sulkily.

"You don't seem too happy with your new role Kev, are you up to the job I wonder?" said Leo.

Mary interjected acidly. "He doesn't want the bloody job and Doonan had no right to palm it off on him when he has had no experience. He isn't even violent, not like you two bastards, he wouldn't harm a fly and he's being dragged into God knows what."

Kevin glared at her and pleaded with his eyes for her to shut up but she was in full flight.

"My Kevin is no angel but he's no killer either and you lot are going to turn him into a monster against his will. What kind of bloody people are you anyway?" She was weeping now and hanging on to Kevin's arm. He eyed the other two with a mixture of fear and despair after Mary's outburst.

"Take no notice of her, I'll handle it." He said at length.

Leo felt pity for the man; he remembered how shocked Bradley had been when he and Liam had faked the killing of Mick Rutherford and his troopers at the derelict farm near Ballypatrick.

"Do you wish to resign your commission?" asked Leo.

"Don't be funny, you know Doonan wouldn't allow that, he'd have me shot first," said Kevin in a resigned tone.

"Only if he knew," said Liam, smiling, "and we won't tell him will we Leo?"

"You were Doonan's tout in Brannigan's gang I believe, is that right?" asked Leo.

"Reluctantly yes," admitted Bradley, "Donnan is a difficult man to refuse and we took the easy way out. I sometimes wish I'd stayed in the army instead of doing a runner. If you have to punish me on Doonan's behalf, I would ask you to leave Mary out of this," said Kevin, drawing Mary closer to him.

"Relax," said Leo, "nobody is going to hurt anybody; we don't like Doonan any more than you do, but he is the boss and we are under orders. As far as he is concerned, you are still Quartermaster but in name only, Liam and I will handle the arms cache and see it on its way once we have extracted what we need. Now how about that drink?

Leo had let Bradley gently off the hook and the relief showed. He was not, however, about to disclose his or Liam's real identities. The robberies were to take place the day after tomorrow and he needed the spiked guns for the unsuspecting Players without delay. Mary's attitude changed to one of smiling acquiescence as she busied herself attending to the men. Her beloved Kevin was safe for the moment.

An hour later, they met the farmer who was organising the movement of the weapons. They would be transferred overnight to the Drum Hills on Doonan's orders instead of the planned three-day relay. They were urgently required to arm the newly trained recruits before they left the training camps.

Leo and Liam selected thirty Armalite rifles and the ammunition to go with them. They delivered them to one of the cell leaders for redistribution to the hitherto unarmed members of the Derry Brigade. They then went to Sandy Blewitt's house and briefed him on events for onward transmission to the others in his group.

Geordie Shiells accompanied them back to Belfast and bunked at Liam's house for the night.

Siobhan and the twins departed for Sunderland the following morning and that evening, the final briefing before the robberies was held at Liam's house.

Chapter 26

On the eve of the planned bank robberies, McKenna and Finney had split their men into teams of four. Three men would pose as customers and enter each of the allotted banks at about 9.55 a.m., just five minutes before the robberies were timed to take place. One man would remain outside and deal with the driver of each getaway car within two minutes of the others entering the bank. The republican robbers would then be shot after the stolen monies had been handed over and bagged when they were expected to be slightly off guard having succeeded in their task.

En Route to the out-of-town rendezvous, they would transfer the cash to shopping bags collected previously, from the hypermarket, and casually carry them from the parked-up getaway cars to the republican gang's waiting coach which would have been commandeered earlier and the driver disposed of.

On the morning of the robberies, Larry McArdle was presented with a Range Rover stolen from Donegal by

Groddy McGinty the night before. The interior of the vehicle still smelled of the man even after it had stood overnight in a lock-up.

McGinty and two of his fellow gangsters sat in the back seats of the Range Rover and Ahern sat in the front passenger seat. The weather was not very nice although there was no fog, snow or ice to hinder the gang's progress, which was unusual for the month of February. But it was still cold and damp and they had all been obliged to wear extra layers of clothing. That combined with the efficient heater in the cab of the vehicle tended to overheat them and McGinty smelled even worse than usual.

"Open that fuckin' window Groddy, when was the last time you had fuckin' bath you evil smelling bastard?" asked Ahern, in some good humour. The other two were holding their noses and making 'pooh' sounds and laughing at the unfortunate McGinty.

"I had a bath just last month," objected McGinty, opening the window a little while showing a pet lip.

They parked in a lay-by and Ahern tuned into the police band on the short-wave radio that he had brought with him. All was going to plan and there was little police activity to worry them according to the clipped routine messages.

It would take only ten minutes to get to the bank and at precisely 9.50 a.m. they set of for the centre of Dungannon and the Bank of Ulster. Larry parked in the 'Disabled Parking Only' bay outside the bank and waited while the others casually got out of the Range Rover and strolled into the building.

Inside the bank, two old ladies were at the counter and a third was discussing an account with a young woman at a desk near the far wall. Two men, one of them obviously

Asian, were sitting at another desk apparently filling out paying-in slips or something when Ahern pulled a machine pistol and shouted for everyone to lie on the floor face down and not to look up for fear of being shot.

Whether the people were too used to that kind of incident or they had been primed to obey, no one panicked. They quietly lay face downward and waited while Ahern gave orders for the tellers to back away from the counters.

One of his men held a pistol to the head of the young woman who had been at the desk with the old lady and promised to shoot her if anyone touched the under-counter alarm buttons.

The elderly bank manager opened the vault without hesitation and Ahern and Groddy McGinty filled the sacks with money within two minutes. The third villain who had the bank staff face down on the floor away from the counters, shuffled impatiently while the other two filled the sacks.

When they had taken all the money they could carry, the four of them began to back slowly towards the door. Ahern saw the gun come up from beneath Geordie Shiells, one of the men on the floor. Ahern fired instinctively as the man rolled away behind a desk firing as he did so. McGinty died in a hail of fire as Ahern ducked behind him for cover firing wildly as he did so and hitting one of his own men in the back, killing him instantly, and wounding one of the old ladies on the floor. The Asian man, Hari Baskaran, took out the last of Ahern's men with a well-aimed shot to the head. Ahern, still firing blindly, made it to the door and ran for the Range Rover, while Larry was in the process of starting the vehicle.

"It was a fuckin' ambush you bastard McArdle, you set us up, you were the only one who knew about this." He shouted as he ran towards the vehicle pointing the machine pistol at Larry. He fired just as Larry ducked below the dashboard. The windscreen and side windows shattered showering Larry with beads of toughened glass. He thought he was about to die when shots passed over his head and then there was silence.

Leo Bailey ran around the vehicle and stood above the body of Ahern. He pumped two more shots into his head to make sure that he was quite dead. Larry shuddered.

Using her own silk scarf, Hari Baskaran hurriedly put a tourniquet on the elderly woman's leg to arrest the bleeding then instructed one of the bank clerks to administer first aid and another to call an ambulance for the lady whose life had been saved when Ahern's man got in the way but she had been shot in the leg by a stray bullet and was bleeding profusely. "You'll be alright pet," shouted Geordie Shiells as they ran for the door, "I should know he's a doctor."

Leo and Larry were waiting for them in their fast car when they emerged from the bank and the four of them sped off in the direction of the hypermarket.

Tommy Hanlon had the misfortune to choose the bank in Lurgan for his part in the robberies. He was the first of his team to die from a well-aimed commando knife thrown by the leader of the Shankill Surgeons, James McKenna. Hanlon was running for the door of the bank while being covered by one of his men. The man went down with a bullet in the back and as Hanlon half turned to return fire McKenna's knife hit him in the side of his neck and went clean through to the other side almost severing his spine.

Every single one of the gangs of Ahern and Hanlon perished along with five of Finney's men, and three of McKenna's Shankill Surgeons. The surviving raiders were heading for certain retribution.

One of the favourite tricks of terrorists from both tribes in bygone days was to employ motorcyclists, especially in towns, to fire into the vehicles of their intended victims before lobbing in a grenade and speeding off. They were about to get a taste of their own medicine.

A biker and his passenger who were in turn followed by a backup car containing two more of Leo's men followed each vehicle involved in the robberies. The idea was to take out the robbers before they got to the hypermarket and the getaway coach and to leave them and the stolen money for the police to deal with.

Great care had to be taken not to involve other motorists in accidents as a result of the action. Two of Leo's cars would effectively ride abreast of each other blocking both lanes and slow the traffic behind them sufficiently for the getaway cars to speed ahead followed closely by the bikers who would pull alongside the getaway car and take out the driver before lobbing their grenades and speeding away.

They succeeded in taking out six of the nine getaway cars but the three cars that made it to the coach park had an unpleasant surprise waiting for them.

One pair of bikers crashed when the pillion passenger with the gun and grenades was shot in the back just before the grenade went off in the car, which then careered into the crash barrier and exploded.

Every other pair of seats on the getaway coach was occupied by what McKenna thought were his and Finney's men, all strangers to McKenna, congratulating each other on a job well done but who were in fact SAS men in disguise. When McKenna's men took their seats, the SAS people behind them took their lives. Ironically, McKenna's throat was cut and he died the way he had killed on numerous occasions. Not knowing the blacked-up McKenna by sight, Peter Bailey was blissfully unaware that he had just made his future wife a widow.

By the time the police got their act together, Leo and his mercenaries were long gone and celebrating their first encounter with the enemy with the unfortunate loss of only two of his men. Some of the stolen money was destroyed when the getaway cars exploded, but most of the haul was recovered by the police who were left scratching their heads and wondering what was going down.

The authorities decided that it was the gang warfare that had been predicted as a result of the referendum, war in which, on this occasion, there had been few if any winners.

The two motorcyclists who died were an SBS volunteer and pillion passenger Dave Affleck of the SAS.

The Derry Brigade faired little better, Sam Keeley and his loyalist confederates simply waited outside each of the banks for the robbers to emerge with the money bags then shot them in the street. The getaway drivers were hauled out of the vehicles and executed before their cars were driven away at high speed.

Six out of the ten cars didn't make it more than a mile outside the towns; they were taken out by the bikers who then sped off to their hides. The other four cars got no further than having their engines started before hooded mercenaries stepped out of the shadows and executed the occupants with a withering hail of machine gun fire before disappearing back into the shadows and making off.

The coach driver at the 'Singing Pub' was one of Sandy Blewitt's drivers enjoying a good book while he waited for the signal to go home with an empty bus.

The previously supportive families of the all of the gangsters that had perished in one day were themselves terrorised by the events. They had been given a dose of the foul medicine that the relatives of the victims of their respective republican and loyalist grandfathers, fathers, husbands, brothers, and boyfriends had been forced to suffer in the past and they did not like the potion.

The resultant funerals were well covered by the press, radio, and television reporters who rubbed salt into the wounds of the bereaved. Years of suffering at the hands of the dead terrorists and gangsters had been avenged at last and there was more to come. Personal profiles of the known criminals were aired in the media without fear of reprisal for a change. One hundred and eighty-four of them had perished on that fateful day and they were going to be difficult if impossible to replace.

Daniel Doonan was stunned into disbelief that such a thing could happen in his lifetime. He resolved to take revenge on whoever had perpetrated what he had the temerity to call 'an evil crime.' He would redouble his efforts to recruit an army with sufficient clout to instil fear as he had done in his younger days.

He called six of his remaining dozen Brigade Commanders and gave them specific times to ring him back from their respective 'Billy Thompson's' to receive strict instructions for a renewed recruiting campaign. He would call the remainder of his CO's the following day.

The calls were intercepted and by the time the Commanders arrived at their respective phone boxes, a

413

mercenary marksman was in position to take them out, but only after they had received their instructions from Doonan which were relayed direct to Sid's yard and finally to Parker's office. The exceptions were Barney Meehan and Liam Casey.

Each mercenary marksman was contacted on his mobile when a CO was called to his 'Billy Thompson' to ensure that no innocent person using the public phone would be killed by accident.

Doonan had no way of knowing that his instructions would never be carried out and it would be days before he realised that something was seriously wrong. Each of his CO's bodies was taken away and dumped unceremoniously in an unmarked grave on waste ground as was the custom of both republican and loyalist terror gangs in the past.

Terror was beginning to grip the remaining terrorists and their supportive families and friends throughout the country as word got around about the disappearance of their leaders at the hands of a third and unknown force that was intent on their total destruction.

Wives, mothers, girl friends, and other members of their families beseeched their men to give up the struggle and call it a day.

Some of the sensible politically motivated Players, seeing the writing on the wall, did give up but there were still a number of criminally motivated hard men left who felt they had too much to lose by quitting their chosen way of life. They were the extortionists, blackmailers, drug dealers, petty thieves, and assassins who lived off the proceeds of crime in the name of their respective republican and loyalist organisations without actually belonging to them or adhering to their political principles. However, Judgment day was at hand.

Chapter 27

Daniel Doonan had been staying at his old friend's house in Fulham for ten days before he received a plain envelope containing a photograph of Cedric Parker and another of an unknown man with a goatee beard. There was also an unsealed plastic holder containing an ID card with the name of the man typed on it. Doonan now vaguely remembered but could not quite equate the name with the picture. There was also an unsigned explanatory note from McCaffrey.

The next day Doonan went to a fashionable hairdressing salon in the city and had his hair cut and styled like the man with the beard; he looked well groomed. A false goatee beard and moustache helped to cover the scars around the lower part of his face and he looked passably like the person in the photograph named on McCaffrey's unsigned note. Doonan had then gone out and acquired a passport photograph of himself from the machine in a Woolworth's store and attached it to the ID card. The likeness to the bearded stranger was uncanny.

Scouring the more up market charity shops, he found himself a quality pinstriped suit, a white shirt with close blue stripes, and an Irish Guards tie. He looked smarter than at any time in his life and would have passed almost anywhere for a city gent. The highly polished shoes and the bowler hat accompanied by a rolled umbrella completed the image of the character he was trying to portray.

He spent the following two weeks wandering around the corridors of power at Whitehall and Westminster sporting his ID tag and generally getting himself noticed by the security people who appeared to recognise him by virtue of nod and wink.

Doonan had borrowed the name of ex Irish Guards officer and SDLP MP, Major James Kennedy, whose stature he resembled slightly and whom he knew from McCaffrey's note, was on extended post-operative sick leave in the Bahamas for several weeks and was not due back in the foreseeable future.

Doonan made it his business to be seen by Cedric Parker on a number of occasions and doffed his bowler hat in respect as they passed each other in the street or in the corridors of the House of Commons. Parker acknowledged the gesture with a slight nod of his head. He had a vague idea that he knew the man but could not recall from where, there was something about the eyes.

On the Friday before lunch when Doonan watched Parker leave Whitehall in a chauffeur driven car, he went to the Defence Minister's office and asked Parker's secretary, Sandra, for an appointment with the minister to discuss security matters on behalf of his Catholic constituents. It transpired that Parker was an extremely busy man with a full diary for at least a month ahead. However, one of his appointments had been cancelled for the following

Monday morning and Doonan was pencilled in for 9.30 a.m. sharp.

After he left Sandra's office, she looked up his name in the register of MP's on her PC database and satisfied herself that James Kennedy, the SDLP member for County Fermanagh actually existed and resembled the black and white low pixel picture alongside the name. He was not a frequent visitor to the Commons and there was no indication that he was currently out of the country.

Cedric Parker and Charlie Kinnear had finished a private lunch at No. 10 and had returned to the office for coffee.

"It would appear Charles that 'Operation Wipeout' has been a complete success," said Parker to the PM. "There has not been a single terrorist or sectarian incident for two weeks now. The streets of Belfast and Derry are relatively quiet and criminal activity has been reduced to the odd petty theft and a couple of muggings, well within the capabilities of the police to deal with.

The other counties are also reported to be quiet with people going about their normal business in a relaxed and friendly atmosphere. According to our people on the ground, there should now be no need to mobilise the reserves. The majority of the hard men are dead and those who have managed to avoid the chop have either done a runner or are keeping a very low profile.

Daniel Doonan has disappeared without trace and is thought to have suffered the same fate as some of his brigade commanders but at the hands of his previous masters and not one of our men."

"Well done Cedric," said Kinnear, "and achieved well in advance of the province going solo. It is amazing how only a comparatively small number of antagonists have been responsible for the problems in Northern Ireland over the past thirty years or so. They must represent about 0.0001% of the entire population when you think about it".

"It doesn't take many people to cause chaos when they are bent to the task. Look at the predecessors of the present SAS during the Second World War; a handful of dedicated men in the Long Range Desert Group caused more problems for the Germans than a whole armoured brigade. They instilled terror into the enemy before disappearing into the desert. That's what gave me the initial idea for the present operation and the more I thought about it, the more feasible it became but I could do nothing about it while I was still in the service, too many politicians to tie the hands if you know what I mean," smiled Parker. "Couldn't see old Warbacker going along with the plan, could you?"

"What plan would that be Cedric?" asked Kinnear grinning broadly and signalling the end of the meeting.

The coarse fishing season had just begun and Parker had taken his first full weekend break since he had taken up his ministerial post. After leaving the PM, he had dashed to his London bachelor flat, changed clothes, packed a weekend valise, picked up his recently delivered Hardy six-piece fly-fishing rod complete with two reels and a selection of flies, all neatly packed in a leather-trimmed canvas case little bigger than a briefcase, and caught the 5.15 p.m. train to Newcastle upon Tyne then on to Alnmouth in Northumberland.

The Duke of Northumberland's land agent was an old army pal of his and had fixed him up with a permit to fish the river Coquet near his home in Warkworth where Parker would be staying as a guest until Sunday afternoon.

The Saturday morning weather was fine although it was still a little chilly, at least five degrees colder than London he expected. His friend Ben Turvey had been called to the estate office to sort out a problem and had excused himself from the fishing session hoping to join Parker later.

Parker stood alone in the shallows of the river with the cold water half way up his waist high waders. He had time to reflect on the past several months while he cast his line repeatedly down stream.

He was satisfied with the outcome of his assault on the hard line political and criminal remnants of both the republican and loyalist organisations. At least the Stormont assembly would now be in a better position to concentrate on elections in preparation for the final departure of the British diplomatic corps advisors.

David Grimble had successfully convinced the other parties at Stormont of the consequences of failure to bring the two communities together as one nation regardless of religious and self-interest.

There was no such thing as 'British' any more as far the people of the province were concerned they would soon be Europeans as well as Northern Ireland Republicans with the equality that went with it.

The people of the province had been the architects of their own fate and could do nothing but accept the consequences if civil war was to be avoided. Grimble had eventually won the day and even the voluble Ian Pashley had reluctantly seen the sense of his argument and was on the election campaign trail under the Christian Democrat label.

After a weekend during which he had bagged two large salmon and a sea trout with a borrowed rod, and six brown trout with his new Hardy rod, a contented and rested Cedric Parker returned to his office on the following Monday morning oblivious of the appointment with Daniel Doonan arranged for him by his super efficient secretary Sandra Smethurst.

He opened his diary and recognised the name of retired Major James Kennedy and even put a face to the name recalling subconsciously that there was something about the eyes.

At precisely 9.30 a.m., Sandra ushered Doonan into Parker's office and returned to her desk. She switched on the intercom and donned her headphones as per standing instructions and began to record the conversation between her boss and his visitor.

"Take a seat Kennedy." Said Parker, without the formality of shaking hands, "what can I do for you."

Doonan remained standing with his hands behind his back like a soldier standing at ease.

"Several of my friends and colleagues have been mysteriously killed recently Mr. Parker and I am led believe that you are possibly responsible for it, you are an ex SAS Colonel are you not?" said Doonan, backing away from the desk and producing a gun from the rear waistband of his trousers.

Parker suddenly realised the significance of the eyes, one green and the other blue. Doonan's colour photograph from the 'most wanted' list on his database flashed into his memory.

"Well I'll be damned, Daniel Doonan of all people, we meet at last. We thought you had been executed by the Official IRA, your former employers," said Parker, calmly and without any sign of fear. "What makes you think that my department has anything to do with what goes on in your country right now, the army has been gone for quite some time and I retired, as a Major incidentally, two years ago? Your loyalist enemies are surely the ones to blame for what has been happening. Give it up man, the security people will be here at any minute."

"I have nothing more to lose now Parker, I was a dead man before I came here but I have promised myself that before I go I will have justice for my men. Everything that has happened in the North during the past few months has happened since the Liberal Democrats came to power. Your leader said in the manifesto that your Party had a solution to the Northern Ireland problem. All I had to do was put two and two together and yours is the name I came up with. Your position as Defence Secretary, your SAS background, and your access to undercover contacts puts you firmly in the frame; it is now pay-back time," threatened Doonan raising the gun and aiming it at Parker's chest.

Sandra Smethurst had heard it all from her office and had pushed the panic button on her desk to alert the security staff. She casually walked into Parker's office and said. "Would you gentlemen like coffee?" and then, "oh my goodness what are you doing Major?" she shrieked, and insinuated herself between Parker and Doonan with her back to the desk.

Doonan took two steps forward and grabbed her by the arm to push her to one side; he would not kill the young woman. He had the gun in his left hand and used his right hand to move her out of his way when suddenly he felt a sharp sting under his chin, which exploded into a violent pain in his head. He staggered back dropping the gun and clutching his neck as his body went rigid with shock before he fell backwards, dead.

The jewelled-handle of the solid silver replica commando-knife letter opener, presented to Parker by his fellow officers on his retirement from the SAS, protruded from just between Doonan's chin and the front of his Adam's apple where Sandra had thrust it upwards with such force, after reaching for it behind her on Parker's desk, that the tip of the blade stuck out a half inch through the top of Doonan's skull.

"Good Lord Sandra, where in God's name did you learn that," asked Parker, springing from behind his desk and staring down at Doonan's prostrate body.

"Back at Bessbrook," said Sandra. "There wasn't a great deal for an off-duty female to do among all those blokes so in return for a little cooking, washing, ironing, and sewing, I got the lads to teach me a few survival tricks on the side. Alec Shiells taught me that one in return for a cheese and ham soufflé. He said it was standard procedure when being interrogated by an enemy but he demonstrated it with a pencil. He said anything with a sharp point would do."

Parker gazed at her with admiration.

"Will you marry me Miss Smethurst?" he asked, taking Sandra in his arms and kissing her full on the lips.

"I thought you'd never ask," she gasped, as two security guards dashed into the room.

Epilogue

Doonan's demise was kept an official secret and his body disposed of at a crematorium for military animals. The rumour was put about that he had been assassinated by persons unknown and buried in a secret grave somewhere in Northern Ireland.

The peace appeared to be holding in the new Republic of Northern Ireland while the remaining member countries of the UK looked forward to a prosperous future and a strengthened security force relieved of duty in that once sad province.

Alec Shiells, Mick Rutherford, George Davidson and Mal Spencer all retired together from the SAS and formed a partnership in the business of the close protection of those who could afford to hire them.

Peter Bailey and Maddie McKenna along with Cedric Parker and Sandra Smethurst were married by Father Patrick O'Riordan in the Regimental Chapel at Hereford attended by friends, family, and comrades.

Posthumous gallantry medals were awarded to the only two servicemen killed during the secret war against the IRA dinosaurs and criminals opposing the will of the British people.

About the Author

Brian Walker Denton aka Thomas Brian Denton

B rian was born in January 1935 at his grandfather's colliery house in South Moor, Stanley, County Durham. The eldest of eight children, he and four of his brothers were secondary school educated and earmarked for the coal mines; the mother's of many sons could look forward to a comfortable life until their boys became men and were married off or otherwise left home.

Brian's father, Joseph Walker Denton, served in WW2 until 1945 then stayed on as a commando in Palestine until 1947. Brian escaped service in the mines when he became a regular soldier in the Royal Army Medical Corps at the age of 17 after serving for 3 years in the Army Cadet Force. He served for 15 years during which he was army educated to 'O' level standard, then on to night school prior to qualifying as a Pharmacy Technician. Having attained the rank of WO2, he resigned in 1967 after a medical downgrade ruled out further promotion. In civvy street, he became a self-employed commission sales agent.

However, in 1969 still army barmy, after his medical condition became treatable with newly discovered medication, he joined the Territorial Army and was awarded a commission, Army Number 500000, in May 1975, resigning on the advice of his GP in 1981, after suffering a mild cardiac infarction.

He had spent time working for half a dozen companies until starting his own business in 1982 in the wrong place at the wrong time which led to bankruptcy in 1986 losing his business, the family home and just about everything he had worked for in the previous 20 years.

Starting again from virtual scratch, he and his supportive wife Audrey applied for the post of joint residential caretakers of a National Trust historic house in Northumberland. It was the worst paid job with longest hours but the most spiritually rewarding job they'd ever had. As Caretaker cum House Steward cum House Manager and Audrey as assistant Housekeeper cum senior Conservation Housekeeper, Brian retired after 9 years on medical grounds, resulting in open heart surgery and a quadruple by-pass, while Audrey stayed on for 7 more years during which Brian began to write poetry, short stories, a novelette and a thriller.

Hobbies: First tenor in male voice choir, guitarist, fiddler, harmonica, banjo player and with choir pal and keyboard player Arthur Walker, entertaining fellow senior citizens in care homes and sheltered accommodation complexes.

Lessons learned from life: Life is a terminal condition; treasure and enjoy it for as long as possible.

Every morsel we ingest is potentially poisonous depending on the dose; eat drink and be merry in moderation. Non-genetic illness is mostly self-inflicted and down to over indulgence in alcohol, tobacco, and drugs.

Life is a serious business not to be taken seriously; a sense of humour is essential.

Non-religious but tolerant of the piety of others.

Causes of conflict: Greed for possession, lust for power, religious intolerance and xenophobia.

Lightning Source UK Ltd.
Milton Keynes UK
UKOW042218110613

212115UK00001B/5/P